VENTURE IN THE EAST

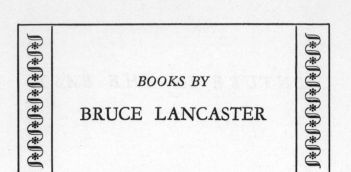

BOOKS BY

BRUCE LANCASTER

THE WIDE SLEEVE OF KWANNON

GUNS OF BURGOYNE

BRIDE OF A THOUSAND CEDARS
(*In collaboration with Lowell Brentano*)

FOR US, THE LIVING

BRIGHT TO THE WANDERER

TRUMPET TO ARMS

THE SCARLET PATCH

NO BUGLES TONIGHT

PHANTOM FORTRESS

VENTURE IN THE EAST

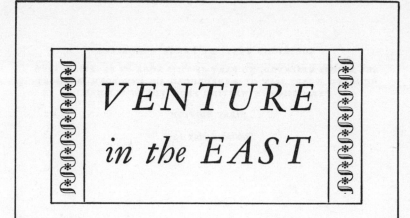

VENTURE
in the EAST

BY BRUCE LANCASTER

AN ATLANTIC MONTHLY PRESS BOOK

LITTLE, BROWN AND COMPANY · BOSTON

1951

ATLANTIC–LITTLE, BROWN BOOKS
ARE PUBLISHED BY
LITTLE, BROWN AND COMPANY
IN ASSOCIATION WITH
THE ATLANTIC MONTHLY PRESS

Published simultaneously
in Canada by McClelland and Stewart Limited

PRINTED IN THE UNITED STATES OF AMERICA

FOR MY WIFE
Jessie Payne Lancaster

FOREWORD

BUT for the Shimabara Rebellion of 1637, the setting of this book, Japan might have assimilated and contributed to the great discoveries of the Western World that followed the Dark Ages. There might have been a Japanese Columbus or Magellan. A Harvey, a Galileo, might have appeared in Kyoto or a Descartes on Mt. Koya. And world history could have been very different.

When the Portuguese stumbled on Japan in 1542, the islanders welcomed the material symbols of the West. As more Portuguese ships, followed by Spanish, British and Dutch, wore up the long corridor of the China Sea, Western ideas were an invisible cargo along with tangible trade goods. The Japanese, mentally and physically acquisitive, saw a vast new window sliding open.

Their desire to step through this window and out of their own world, which had known little change for a thousand years, was tempered by fear. Knowing of Mexico and Peru, they dreaded a new Cortez or Pizarro. Japan was pulled two ways — on toward the new and back into the old.

In general, the first urge prevailed and foreign traders came and went much as they wished. Catholic missionaries, notably Saint Francis Xavier, made converts by the thousands. Later, the zeal of these new Christians spurred them to attack the native cults with a violence that led to persecution and then to total proscription. There was no objection to Christianity, but the government feared for the peace of the land. Many, too, viewed these converts as a possible Fifth Column in the event of a Spanish or Portuguese invasion.

But trade went on. That window on the outer world remained open and might have stayed open but for the Shimabara Rebellion which slammed it shut. Only the Dutch were allowed to stay. As virtual prisoners, they kept an uneasy foothold which they maintained from 1640 until Perry's treaty in 1854. This rigid restriction

vii

of foreign trade and ideas was important in world history. More important were the checks placed on the Japanese themselves. New laws closed minds as well as ports. Only carefully chosen officials were allowed contact with the Dutch. Foreign books were forbidden. No Japanese could leave the Empire under pain of death, and the size of Japanese ships was so limited that even China or Korea seemed as remote as Peru or Java. So Western progress, physical, mental and spiritual, rolled on unheeded and Japan sank back into the virtual sixth-century culture which it had known before the arrival of the Komo, the Westerner.

It stayed in that century until well after Perry's treaty. Then in a rush it tried to assimilate what the West had evolved over hundreds of years. In our own time, sixth-century Japanese minds have grappled with the nineteenth and twentieth centuries, largely because of Shimabara.

Most readers are familiar with the Japanese organization, which has survived in substance into our own time. At the top, in theory, was the Heaven-born Emperor. Actually, the throne had been powerless for nearly a thousand years at the opening of our story, and its occupant, as in 1941, a voiceless puppet. The nation was run by the Shogun, a dictator who pretended to act in the name of the Divine Emperor. Thus, speaking for a God, the Shogun shone in reflected divinity. Actually, the Shogun was a warlord, powerful enough to enforce his claims that he represented a near-celestial being. He governed through docile lords known as Daimyos, each in charge of a given district. Sometimes the Shogun sent out a personal representative to act in his name, like the Daikwan at Nagasaki in this story. To translate all this into modern experience, read "War Department" for "Shogun," and "Prefectural Governor" (appointed, not elected) for "Daimyo." In substance, our arbitrarily chosen sixth century flourished until V–J Day.

Details about the ghastly days of the ruined Castle of Hara are hazy and contradictory. Several dates are given for the outbreak. There is no agreement as to who the leader was, nor — perhaps more important — what he was, whether starving peasant, dispossessed samurai or ardent Christian. Most Japanese treat the Rebellion as an entirely Christian uprising, thus justifying the closing of the Empire as a matter of internal safety. It seems more likely

viii

that the causes were economic and political, occurring in a region where there happened to be many Christians. The main facts, however, are clear enough. *There was a rising at Shimabara and, as a result, Japan slammed the door.*

This story of the closing of Japan sets forth what could logically have happened to some members, real and imaginary, of the Dutch East India Company stationed there in those days. Where so much detail is blurred, I have made adjustments in time and people to suit the story. François Caron is shown at Shimabara at a time when he may have been en route from Batavia. The slaughter of the Portuguese mission took place rather later than in these pages. The fate of the Dutch was probably not known as early as shown here.

Of actual characters, François Caron alone is well documented and there seems to be no question as to his stature. His plan for the Dutch-Japanese invasion of Manila and Macao is a matter of record. Had it been mounted, there probably would have been no Shimabara Rebellion and Japan would have plunged into the world of the 1630's. Caron later became Governor General at Batavia, eventually left the Dutch service to take over French India for Louis XIV. He died at sea on his way to his new post, or Indian history, too, might have been different.

To suit the modern reader and the story, I have shortened the name of the Dutch Director at Hirado and altered what little is known of his character. The Daimyo of Hirado, actually Matsuura, appears here for simplicity as Matsura. To avoid confusion with the Daimyo, I refer to a known rebel leader by his first name of Tokisada, rather than as Masuda. Modern place names — Tokyo for Yedo and so on — have been used for clarity. "Factory" in its old sense designated a trading post (the name is still used, I believe, on Hudson Bay), and is so employed here.

The pronunciation of Japanese words and place names is simple, being largely phonetic. Thus "sake" (Japanese rice wine) becomes "sa-keh," "ume" (plum) is "oo-meh." The letter *g* is always hard, as in the English verb "get." Syllables are seldom accented, and "Shimabara" could be written as "Sheema-bara," the *a*'s being broad as in "bar."

B. L.

BEVERLY, MASSACHUSETTS
December 1, 1950

CONTENTS

Foreword		vii
I	The Hollanders	3
II	Trudi Van Os	19
III	Manila Venture	31
IV	Gathering Storm	49
V	Ruined Castle	65
VI	Calm Waters	84
VII	The War Barges	99
VIII	Reconnaissance	115
IX	The Tower	133
X	The Storm Breaks	150
XI	City of Huts	167
XII	To Shimabara	187
XIII	Fra Hilario	197
XIV	The Mortar	213
XV	The Tunnel	230

XVI   Deep Peril   255

XVII   Escape   269

XVIII   The Daikwan Speaks   288

XIX   West to the New World   309

VENTURE IN THE EAST

I

The Hollanders

THE careful Dutch had built a fragment of Holland on the north arm of Hirado Bay. The powder magazine at the end of the point, whose gray sides bore the date 1615, ran up in stepped gables as steep as any in Leyden. Inland, stone godowns crowded along the twisting sea wall and behind them a cluster of burghers' houses clung to the swift-rising hill. The largest of these, the Director's, was still masked with bamboo scaffolds among which breech-clouted Japanese clambered, fixing a tall, iron 7 in line with the *1, 6* and *3* already set in the broad chimney side. Higher up the slope, apart from its Dutch neighbors, the roof tiles of a Japanese house shone silver among wind-bent pines and silky bamboos.

From the inland end of the sea wall, the bay cut west into encircling hills, spreading a great horseshoe of beach whose apex was broken by the tile roofs of the village of Hirado. Along the southern arm, the abandoned English factory stood, desolate and gap-windowed, among clusters of fishermen's huts that straggled on toward the white walls of the fort on the far point. Dominating bay and village and anchored craft, the palace of the Daimyo, the lord of the province, spread its eaves in a high, inland glade.

The sea and the hills slept under a heavy noon glare. The bamboos drooped as motionless as the blue and white banner of the Dutch East India Company on its pole by the main building of the factory. Heavy-winged carrion birds high above the island tilted lazily. The workmen climbed down from the scaffold and were lost under cool pines. Save for the wheeling birds, all creation seemed to have crept away into some shade-soaked hollow — the birds and one broad-hatted man who leaned on the sea wall and stared east across the narrow straits to the cliffs of Kyushu.

Oblivious to the heat, Nicolas Becker, Director of the factory, muttered irritably in his beard and hitched at his baggy knee

3

breeches. The night before, a Company ship, weeks out of Batavia, had dropped anchor in the little roadstead at Kawachi down the coast from the forts, and hours ago a Company barge had been sent to meet it.

A door in the main building opened and a fat, gray-haired man stepped into the sunshine. "No word from Kawachi yet, Heer Directeur?" he asked pleasantly.

Becker looked sourly at his chief accountant. "No! Damn it, Van Os, what's the matter? They could have made the trip four times over."

Van Os answered easily, as though weighing tolerantly his thirty years in Japan against Becker's scant two. "The Japanese officials wouldn't have boarded the *Roode Hert* till this morning. And they always check the crew as well as the cargo. Besides, they've been getting much stricter about our Batavia ships."

"Stricter! Yes, and why? Because until I came here you'd been letting them dictate to you. I'm sick of it. The Portuguese down at Nagasaki do what they please. *They* don't truckle. It took me a while to find my feet here, but I'm beginning to know my way around. We've wasted too much time on that verdomd Daimyo and his laws. Do you think that he'd close us out and lose his profit from our trade? Of course he wouldn't!"

Van Os observed placidly, "I have been here since 1607, thirty good years, and I do not agree with you, Heer Directeur. Nor would Heer Caron. Why, just last year when the new laws came through, he —"

"I'm sick of hearing about Caron," interrupted Becker. "He's the worst truckler of the lot. I've got my opinion of a European who'll lower himself to make friends with the Japanese. You know what *he* wants? He wants to be Director in my place. He's plotting with the Japanese, hoping they'll close us out, cut our throats, maybe. Damn him, he isn't even a Hollander, except by birth. He's a Frenchman."

"He's been very valuable to the Company," said Van Os.

"Valuable to himself! And he's training up Jongh to truckle, to talk Japanese. That pair will sell out our rights." His face flushed. "Do you know what I'm going to do, Van Os? I'm going to write to —" He faced the bay quickly as a faint hail sounded across the

4

light drift of the waves. The Company barge, wet oar blades glinting in the sun, appeared off the white walls of the forts, worked on past anchored sampans, under the stern of a Ningpo junk and finally brought up smartly by the low wharf under the sea wall. A squat Dutchman sprang from the stern sheets and ran panting up the slimy steps.

Becker took a swift stride forward. "Pieters! What the devil took you so long? Where's the master of the *Roode Hert?*"

Pieters made a helpless gesture. "I don't know where he is. The Japanese took him ashore and —"

Becker clenched his fist. "What do you mean by saying you don't know?"

"Because I *don't,* Heer Directeur," said Pieters sullenly. "No one knows, but —" his voice rose suddenly — "but I *do* know this! There's a Dutch girl on board."

Becker went white and even Van Os was shaken. Among the countless rules and regulations by which the Japanese grudgingly permitted Dutch trade and residence in the Empire, none carried greater penalties — or more permanent ones — than that which forbade the presence of European women in the Empire. In the past, it had been winked at once or twice, but in recent years the Japanese had stressed it more and more, indicating unpleasantly what would happen in the event of its violation.

Becker stammered, "The Japanese mustn't see her. Go back to the ship. Have her kept below. Dress her as a sailor. The Daimyo will —"

"They've seen her," said Pieters. "They took her ashore at Kawachi."

Van Os spoke quietly. "Batavia knows the laws as well as we do, Pieters. How did she get on board in the first place?"

"The ship's got a new master. She bribed him, the mate told me. The master got his money. That's all he cares about."

"Who is she?" asked Van Os, still outwardly calm.

"I wondered when you'd ask that," said Pieters dryly. "She's your niece."

Van Os's eyes went blank as though he hadn't understood, but his hands gripped the coping of the sea wall behind him. His niece, Gertrude Van Os! Little Trudi! But his brother Syvert had taken

5

her and her mother to Batavia at the time of Syvert's transfer there over ten years ago. When the fevers of the tropical port had carried off mother and father, the daughter had stayed on, a ward of the Governor. It couldn't be Syvert's daughter. How could she be on a ship bound for forbidden Japan? He glanced at Pieters, but there was no doubt that the latter was speaking the truth. For reasons which the uncle couldn't fathom, the niece had come to Japan, the only other home she had known, a land that held for her memories of her mother, the only Dutchwoman ever to set foot in the Empire. It had been an odd business, the presence against all laws, of his brother Syvert's wife. But she had been slim and dark and, dressed in the native kimono, could almost pass for Japanese. It had pleased Matsura, the Daimyo of Hirado, to assume officially that she was Japanese, so she had stayed on and on until Syvert's transfer to Batavia. The daughter Trudi was dark like her mother and Matsura had treated her too as a Japanese, even calling her Sayo-ko, or Night, because of her coloring.

Becker was speaking in an icy, level voice. "What do you say to all this, Van Os? It's no concern of mine, you know. She's your niece and *I* had nothing to do with her coming here. Just what are you going to tell the Daimyo?"

Van Os's tone was low but steady. "This can be very bad for all of us — and the Company, Heer Directeur. If only Caron were here! We've got to play for time until he comes home. *He'll* know what to do."

"No! We can't wait. The Daimyo might — and anyway, we'll manage without that damned brabbling Frenchman. I'll send our head interpreter to see the Daimyo. No. That won't do. The interpreters are all Japanese. Can't trust them. Hell roast this language." He broke off and shouted toward the main building, "Jongh! Come here, as soon as you've finished that entry."

Inside the high-ceiled office, four men looked up from the Company ledgers. The one nearest the door stood out in contrast to his fellows, with their placid Dutch faces and long, straw-colored hair. His brown hair was cut close to a well-shaped head and his gray eyes under level brows held glints of light that suggested humor and a controlled temper. Becker had called him Jongh, and so his name was written on the rolls of the Company — Dirk Jongh. But

6

in the Bible of his family, he stood as Dirk Young, born in Holland in the year 1612 of English parents, Lincolnshire folk who had been part of that migration which flowed out of England to Leyden in Holland and thence, in large part, to Plymouth on Massachusetts Bay. Dirk's father had gone to the New World on one of the earlier ships, planning to set up a homestead there to which his wife and only child would come in the following year. The New England winter had proved too much for the Lincolnshire man and now a stone marked his grave on Burial Hill overlooking Plymouth harbor. Before the news of his death had reached the remains of the English colony at Leyden, the mother had been carried off by one of the fevers so common to the Low Countries, leaving Dirk to be brought up by relatives. When it was known that Dirk was an orphan, his guardians had planned that when he was older he should join the Winslows, the Carvers, Bradfords, Allertons, Aldens, Places and Youngs at Plymouth, where many blood ties would assure his welcome.

Becker called again and Dirk pushed back from his ledger. As he put on his short brown jacket and smoothed the broad linen collar of his shirt over it, he wondered what his lot would have been had he gone to the New World instead of taking service with the Dutch East India Company. For seven years he had toiled at the Hirado factory, working slowly but surely through the Company hierarchy from apprentice to clerk, his eyes fixed, in the earlier years, on finally reaching the rank of koopman or merchant, at which time he would leave the Company and with his savings circle the globe and set himself among his own blood and kin at Plymouth. He knew, by the regular letters from his Cousin Japhet Place of Plymouth, a heavily conscientious family correspondent, that those savings would be imposing along cash-short Massachusetts Bay. But for the last three or four years, the New World had faded into the back corners of his mind. François Caron, the gifted Huguenot who was second in command to Becker, had noticed Dirk, had taken a growing interest in him. Under the Frenchman's guidance, Dirk had come to see that the Company reached far beyond the walls of the Hirado factory, that there was much to be studied beyond the ledgers under Van Os's meticulous care. Despite the gibes of his fellow clerks and the disapproval of Becker, he had set himself doggedly to learn the

7

Japanese language, to try to fathom the minds of those who spoke it, to know their manners, customs, prejudices, beliefs and to adapt himself to them, to use them for the benefit of the Company. It had been hard work, for languages did not come to him as they did to Caron, who seemed to learn by intuition.

As he settled his jacket about his broad shoulders, one of his fellows snapped, "Do you expect us to do your work while you look for tea-house girls for Becker?"

Dirk disregarded the remark and stepped out into the sun. "The Heer Directeur called me?" he asked politely.

Becker eyed him with a distaste that was tempered by the current emergency. "You talk Japanese? Can you get along without an interpreter?"

"Haven't used one in three years."

"Have you ever seen the Daimyo?"

"Matsura-san?" Jongh looked surprised. "Yes. Very often. Heer Caron took me to call there once. Since then, the Daimyo's sent for me from time to time."

"*Sent* for you? What did you talk to him about?"

Van Os laid a hand on Becker's broad cuff. "Better explain our situation to him."

"All right," said Becker gruffly. "There's trouble about the *Roode Hert.*"

Jongh looked surprised. "Kuwada, the chief interpreter, usually settles things like that with the Daimyo's steward."

"You say you can see the Daimyo," snapped Becker. "Then go up to the palace. Now! Do exactly what I tell you. No gossiping with any of your friends. Understand?"

Politely, but with still less enthusiasm, Jongh said, "I'd understand better if I knew what you wanted me to tell him."

"You just tell him exactly what *I* tell you. Report to me exactly his answers." He looked sourly at Van Os. "Tell him about your niece. After all, I've got nothing to do with this."

Jongh nodded from time to time, saying, "I see," in a low tone, as Van Os spoke on.

Becker broke in. "Now that's all you need to know. See the Daimyo. Make him see I had no hand in the matter. Tell him he can't hold *me* responsible."

Jongh said slowly, "He won't be interested in *who* was responsible. All he'll see is that a foreign woman came to Japan on a foreign ship, against the laws that govern us."

"But you've got to make him see," spluttered Becker. "He can do what he likes."

Jongh looked curiously at him. "He's bound by what the Daikwan at Nagasaki says, and the Daikwan's bound by what the Shogun at Tokyo says. No lord will risk displeasing the Shogun. The Shogun's the law. He *is* Japan."

"Pah!" Railing at a subordinate seemed to increase Becker's courage. "You talk up to the Daimyo and this trouble'll be over."

"Did you hear what happened to the Chief of Customs who let the Portuguese, da Silva, smuggle out camphorwood from Nagasaki?" asked Jongh gravely. "Do you know *why* young Yamada vanished from Hiroshima?"

"I don't even know where those places are. What's more I don't want to. See the Daimyo. Cut through all that infernal bowing and hissing and tell him what happened and how." Returning fear swept all bluster from him. "Hurry! This could mean our heads."

Dirk started to speak, then bowed and went into an inner office where the Dutch clerks wrote languidly in thick ledgers. On a platform behind them, two Japanese knelt, clicking away on an abacus and writing on soft paper with brushes that deftly swept into being the graceful characters of their land. Disregarding the questioning looks of the clerks Dirk opened an oak closet, slipped into a fresh white shirt, put on a silver-buttoned blue jacket. His face was grave and his eyes half closed in deep thought. Then he reached deeper into the closet and drew out a long, narrow wooden box, tucking it under his arm.

One of the clerks called querulously, "What's that?"

"Something I'm taking to the village," said Dirk shortly as he buckled on a light dress sword and gold-hilted dagger. He adjusted his broad-brimmed hat and stepped through a side door, ignoring the stream of questions that followed him.

Box under his arm, he went along the sandy track that led on to Hirado. A law of the land had been broken and the Japanese were capable of any sort of punishment. The Daimyo, Matsura, might be forced by Tokyo to curtail or even completely abolish the privi-

9

leges under which the Dutch East India Company operated. Over a decade ago, the Spaniards had been abruptly banished from Nagasaki, leaving the field clear to the Dutch and the Portuguese. It was conceivable that the next day, the next week, the next month might see the Dutch following the Spaniards, leaving the Portuguese to enjoy a complete monopoly.

What then? He recalled Caron's teachings. The infant and struggling Dutch Republic survived in Europe largely because of the profits of the Dutch East India Company, of which Hirado was the northernmost outpost. Were the Hirado operations to cease, the flood of wealth that rolled south to the headquarters at Batavia would cease with them, bringing repercussions that might wreck the whole Eastern Empire that the Dutch had built. Then what would happen to Holland and the stone cities by the canals?

He felt a tingling across his cheeks as though the blood were draining from them. The whole matter was in his hands. He would have to deal with an alien lord in a bewildering tongue. Could he comply in all ways with kenson, that elaborate ritual that must at all costs be observed by him on such a visit? The least slip might mortally offend the frail, smiling Daimyo before the object of the visit could be discussed. And if he did sail successfully through the shoals of delicate meanings, gestures, attitudes, there was the problem of how to present the Company's case. Caron had told him over and over, "We are here by sufferance only. Our trade is based solely on privileges granted, not on any inherent rights."

He groaned inwardly. There was no use wishing that Caron, who had time and again soothed the Shogun himself, were on Hirado. The tall Frenchman, absent on one of his mysterious trips, might be pitching in a sampan to the south of Okinawa or drinking brandy with the Daikwan at Nagasaki or even matching Japanese verses with Tokyo palace officials.

The tile roofs and high board fences of the village lay ahead of him, beyond the bamboo grove. It would be well to note the attitude of the villagers, most of whom he knew well, as the least frown from the Daimyo's palace would be reflected on all faces from the head of the fishers' guild to the crone at the door of the baths.

An ox cart creaked toward him and the teamster, naked save for a breechclout and a cloth about his head, bobbed and grinned, calling, "Ii o-tenki des' né, Yang-san?"

Dirk returned the greeting: "Ii o-tenki des' na, Noda-san."

The spokeless wheels ground on and Dirk felt a little easier. This simple passage about the excellence of the weather seemed, for the moment, a favorable omen. He reined in his optimism. Noda, passing through the village, could easily have missed the tempo of the people. At this moment, men and women in the baths, fishermen in the sake shops, might be calmly speculating on the peculiar tortures awaiting the offending Komo, the foreigner.

Japanese torture, he knew from Caron, had reached the dignity of an art, further refined by exquisite Chinese importations. In the days of the persecutions of the Christians, foreign and Japanese alike, men had lived suspended for days over a cunningly tended fire. He told himself that he was growing worse than Becker in his imaginings.

The day was like any other in Hirado, where low sloping roofs peeped over the fences. People called to him from the wide doors of shops, answered his greeting pleasantly as they wrapped slices of fish in thin bark or blinked in the sun at their open gates. Dirk wondered what Caron would have read in the smile of the flower woman, hobbling by under her great basket, in the glances of the fishermen who were hauling up a sampan to the rhythmic chant of "Ya-en-sa! Ya-en-sa!" From far fewer signs he had seen the Frenchman, with a single cool glance, state accurately what had happened, what was happening and what was about to happen.

The friendly atmosphere of the village eased Dirk's anxiety a little. But perhaps it was too soon for the temper of the palace to show in the village. At a broad street he turned west and followed it until he reached the tiled gates and high fence of the palace. Settling hat and sword, he walked boldly to the sloping roof of the main gate where a soldier in vizored helmet and lacquered cuirass leaned on a long halberd.

The guard looked keenly at him, then reversed the blade of his weapon and stepped aside. Dirk drew a deep breath. At least the Daimyo's laissez-passer had not been revoked. He inclined his head, then looked at the guard who stood impassively waiting for him to enter. "The health of the first-born continues to improve, Nishi-san?" asked Dirk, the Japanese flowing easily from his tongue.

Nishi bowed deeply and a broad grin shattered his military sternness. Ah, it was magnificent of Yang-san to concern himself with so humble an object. Yes, the fever had broken and had not returned, as Caron-san had predicted. And when might Nishi's eyes be brightened by the sight of Caron-san? All was quiet at the palace, where Yang-san would be ever welcome.

Dirk passed on under the heavy roof and walked slowly up a long slope where flat stones were cunningly set in the turf to form a winding path to the palace. Right and left the ground had been elaborately landscaped with grassy hummocks and gray rocks forming miniature mountain ranges. Silvery brooks appeared like rivers spanned by red-lacquered bridges. Unconsciously, Dirk interpreted the meticulous conventions that governed the placing of each stone, each stunted tree or graveled slope.

The guards at the palace entrance passed him without question into the ground level vestibule, fragrant with hinoki wood. Other guards knelt on the high matted step that led to the mysterious sliding panels of the inner entrance, watching the officer of the day who frowned at bolts of dark red cloth. Dirk took off his hat ceremoniously as the officer looked up, scowling, and Dirk felt a sense of disappointment. He had hoped that it would be Gentaro Mori's day on guard instead of the thickset, surly and xenophobic Toda. With much formality, he requested that word be sent of his presence to the Daimyo's steward.

Toda grunted an order and a guard slipped through the panels, closing them carefully after him. Toda continued his grumbling survey of the cloth. Dirk said pleasantly, "No doubt Toda-san chooses cloth for the daughter of the Doi family who is to be honored by becoming his bride."

Toda shook his head. "I choose for Matsura-san, who wishes new clothes for Ohta-san."

Dirk felt a chill run over him. Ohta-san was the Daimyo's executioner. He stammered, "New clothes?"

Toda nodded curtly. "He wants a color that won't show bloodstains. The responsibility is mine." He fingered a thick fold. "How can *I* tell?" His scowl deepened, then he growled, "Where's that Korean?"

A guard sprang from the platform and dragged out of a corner a man in white trousers, with a varnished gauze hat perched on his head. Pinning his arms behind him, the guard bent him backward until the skin of his naked torso was taut. A second soldier snatched up the cloth and held it close while Toda drew a short knife and slashed it across the Korean's ribs. There was a yelp of pain and blood spurted onto the red cloth.

Toda said, "That's enough. Put it out to dry." The Korean was flung into his corner where he lay whimpering. Dirk bit his lips and turned away. For all his seven years in this country, he could not accustom himself to Japanese callousness to pain or death.

His name was called and the panels slid back, showing Suzuki, the steward, kneeling on the mats beyond, his forehead touching the floor. Dirk rallied himself to play his role. He slipped off his buckled shoes, then unslung his sword and laid it on the platform, the hilt pointing ostentatiously toward the guards. With assumed carelessness, for he knew that all eyes were watching for some error in etiquette, he started to lay his dagger beside the sword, then fastened it more securely to his waist.

Suzuki rose to a kneeling position and the approving glint of his eyes showed that so far nothing had been forgotten. He apologized elaborately that so humble a person as himself dared to offer his services as usher to so distinguished a Komo. Dirk answered in profound self-abasement and followed him down a corridor whose walls were sliding panels covered with rich paper, gold and silver flecked. A deep silence filled the palace, but Dirk was sure that people moved, unseen and unheard, behind the thick paper.

Suzuki dropped to his knees by a pair of wide, sliding doors whose clear wooden panels were bare save at a lower corner where a red-crested heron, superbly painted, swooped toward a suggestion of snow-covered pines. The steward tapped, then rose and glided away. One of the doors slid back and Dirk, kneeling, bowed low to the gnomelike, gentle-faced man who knelt just inside the little room.

Matsura, Daimyo of Hirado, murmured a graceful welcome and Dirk's whole consciousness was centered on the age-old ritual. The Daimyo rose and glided toward a wide niche that ran from floor to ceiling where a long scroll painting of mountains, feathery trees

13

and swift water hung above an ancient bronze incense burner. There he knelt again.

Dirk, bowing, seated himself just inside the door. The Daimyo stretched out an ivory-yellow hand, silently indicating Dirk's dagger, which the latter placed carefully on the mats to his left, far from his sword hand, as token that he had no fear under Matsura's roof. The Daimyo smiled and urged Dirk to seat himself nearer the niche, a more honorable position. Dirk at once protested that he was not worthy of such consideration. The play went on, the Daimyo insisting, his guest declining, stressing again and again his humble station. At last, convention satisfied, Dirk found himself kneeling at the right of the niche, the most honored spot in the room.

His mind tense with the real object of his call, Dirk fought his way on through the mazes of kenson, not daring to hurry, fearful of omitting the smallest step. As though another person were speaking, he heard himself say, "Go busata itashimashita," the formal apology for having neglected to call on his host, a phrase which he would have had to use if he had left the Daimyo a half hour before.

Matsura answered in his old, gentle voice and Dirk drew a deep breath. The worst of the ceremony was over and he diffidently laid his long wooden box on the teak table before the Daimyo, saying that it was a gift of no account but one which he hoped his host would deign to receive.

Matsura lifted the lid of the box and drew forth a roll of thick papers which he carefully spread out, his thin, shrunken fingers rustling the sheets. Then he gave a cry of pleasure. "Ma! Kaisen-e," he exclaimed, bending his shaven head over a collection of engravings of long-forgotten naval battles between English and Dutch, Dutch and French, French and English.

Dirk closed his eyes in relief as Matsura leafed through the sheets, exclaiming from time to time. Months ago, François Caron had told Dirk that Japanese, high and low, for reasons best known to themselves had suddenly been seized with a craze for such pictures, would pay fabulous sums for them. Sons fought over their fathers' copies. High officials were bribed with them. To be permitted to see the Shogun's collection was a dizzying honor. "Don't ask me why," Caron had laughed. "It's just a Japanese custom, like the rage for

Portuguese caps that swept from Hokkaido clear down to the Goto Islands five years ago."

Dirk glanced at Matsura. There was no doubt that his gift had been well chosen, for the old man was chuckling like a child. "And this one, Yang-san," he crooned, holding up a sheet. "It is the finest I have seen. I doubt if even the Shogun Iyemitsu owns a copy. Ah! But in my pleasure, I forget that I am host."

He turned to another low table by his elbow and began preparing tea, his delicate hands busy with earthenware, brass and lacquer of a fineness that drew admiration from Dirk. The Daimyo carefully tested the temperature of the water, ground tea leaves to a powder between his frail fingers. The brew completed, he handed Dirk a cup of fragile Imari ware, his wide sleeves sweeping the mats. That the Daimyo should prepare the tea with his own hands was a very great honor, and Dirk bowed in profound acknowledgment.

Matsura sipped contentedly. "So. Now we sit here, two good friends, with no care save the enjoyment of this tea, which the Shogun deigned to send me from his own reserves at Uji." He sipped again, murmuring, "Ah, the world is good."

Freed, at least partially, from the tension of etiquette, Dirk felt his deep anxiety return in full force. He knew that it was not yet time to bring up the matter of Gertrude Van Os. Yet at any moment Matsura might courteously intimate that the visit was over. With equal courtesy he was quite capable of sending a messenger to the factory announcing the immediate banishment of the Dutch. Nor was it impossible that at that very moment Toda and the guards waited in the corridor to arrest him.

He forced himself to exclaim over the tea, which seemed flat and bitter on his tongue. He admired the rear gardens that stretched west from the open end of the room in smooth turf, silvery gravel, stone lanterns on their granite bases, pines grouped about a fish pool. Matsura complimented him gracefully on his knowledge of the technique of Japanese gardens, then clapped his hands twice.

"Ah, but you have yet to see my newest treasure." The panels slid back and a servant crept in, placed an elaborate lacquer cage by the Daimyo's elbow, retired. Matsura's calm old face was aglow. "See, Yang-san. The new cricket, and the sweetest singer in the Empire. Rejoice with me that I find such a tone to console my fading years."

15

Dirk bent over the shiny-winged creature in its home of black and gold lacquer. "I dare not hope that he may sing for me, Matsura-san, but I am honored by the sight of him. And the cage? Surely, that was made by Komai."

The old man chuckled delightedly. "By Komai? You do not mean Yamamoto?"

Dirk shook his head. "Yamamoto can't produce such a depth of glaze."

"Yes, yes. It is Komai," smiled Matsura. "You have a fine eye, for many of our experts would be deceived." He picked up a ripe persimmon from a cloisonné bowl, cut out a morsel of the soft flesh and gently pushed it through the bars. "Come, my little friend, eat and then sing for our foreign guest who knows so well our ways."

The cricket stirred, crept forward toward the fruit. Someone scratched softly at the door and a guard entered, kneeling, a bolt of red cloth held humbly above his head. Matsura took the cloth absently, dismissing the soldier with a nod. With one hand he unrolled the bolt, talking cajolingly to the cricket.

Dirk caught his breath as he recognized the cloth that Toda had tested so grimly in the genkan. Matsura merely glanced at the red fabric, then tossed it into a corner. "Yes, that will have to do. You know, Yang-san, Ohta is in many ways without peer as an executioner, but — " he shook his head sadly — "he *does* spatter when he takes off a head. Now the man who filled that role for my father — Ah!" he held up his hand. The cricket stirred, rustled its wings and trilled out a long series of clear notes. Matsura closed his eyes in ecstasy, his shaven head inclined toward the cage.

Dirk covertly dried his moist palms on his breeches. How long would this go on? He repressed a wild impulse to tip over the cage and shout, "Let's talk about the *Roode Hert* business!"

The cricket's song ceased and Dirk managed to frame a sentence of thanks and wonder, trailing it out in the hope that his host would be led on to new subjects, that the visit might not terminate with the song. The Daimyo sighed deeply. "Today, I have had much pleasure. My little friend here has sung for us. You have done me the courtesy of taking thought of an old man's loneliness." He smiled at Dirk. "You know the tale of the great island to the north of Formosa, the island that the gods sank under the waves on account of the wickedness of its people?"

The sunken island had excelled in pottery and the ancient kilns still lay far under the sea. Skilled divers plunged to the far bottom and sometimes managed to bring up specimens made by the dead potters, deeply encrusted with coral and other marine growths. Most pieces were shattered in the process of removing the matrix, but the few samples that survived were cherished as being beyond price by Japanese experts.

Matsura slid open a cupboard and brought out a lacquer box, on whose top a Daimyo's train worked in gold and silver wound across a river, over a plain, to vanish within the gates of a castle. The box was a treasure. The old man explained, "This belonged to the father of my father's father, Yang-san. His spirit will be pleased to know that it passes into the possession of a man of deep courtesy and good heart."

Dirk unconsciously drew back his hand. When Coelho, the Portuguese, had been turned over to the executioner by the Daikwan at Nagasaki, he had been loaded with presents. Now — he steadied himself by plunging into a mist of words that stressed his own unworthiness of such a gift.

Matsura smiled. "The box is a trifle, a mere receptacle for what it holds. Open it, my friend."

With uncertain fingers Dirk freed the lock which was fashioned in the shape of a bat, raised the lid. Within, resting on a bed of plum-colored silk, was a tea caddy, its swelling lines lightly streaked with green on a surface of deep cream. There was no mistaking the glaze, the superb workmanship. The caddy had been brought up from that lost island. He said with difficulty, "This has come a long way, Matsura-san."

The Daimyo raised a delicate hand. "Like yourself. And, like you, its travels come to an end on my island of Hirado." Dirk felt a drumming in his ears and his mouth was dry. Little by little, the Daimyo was pronouncing a sentence from which there was no appeal. The thin old voice went on. "I have learned, too, of other journeys' ends. Yes, yes. A countrywoman of my own, so my agents tell me, arrived at Kawachi on your *Roode Hert,* after a long absence. My father esteemed both her father, a Komo, and her mother." He laughed softly. "Eh-to! I remember the little traveler well. A courteous child who did honor to us. She used to play about your foundry, running after the old Englishman, Martin Trelawney, who casts cannon and mortars for the Shogun. Now she returns to her birthplace. For my father's sake, I wish you to bring her to call on me, although it is unusual for a woman to be so honored."

Relief, almost shocking in its intensity, swept over Dirk. He could only stammer out his thanks at being chosen to present Juffrouw Van Os to the Daimyo.

Matsura went calmly on, "You must come more often, Yang-san. One day, my firm friend, Caron-san, after being made Director here, will move to greater honors. Who but you may hope to succeed him? Then, through the years, you and my son, when he returns from the Shogun's court, will walk together the same road of friendship that time has laid out between my palace and your factory."

"The Company," thought Dirk. "The Company will live on!" The recollection of personal peril was forgotten in that knowledge. In the past, Matsura had maintained the polite fiction that Gertrude's dark mother had been a Japanese. Now he showed that he was still willing to extend that fiction to cover the daughter and hence no law was violated.

I I

Trudi Van Os

THE two months' voyage up from Batavia had been far more trying than Gertrude Van Os had expected, but she had buoyed herself up by the thought that once the *Roode Hert* had dropped anchor she would be taken at once to her uncle's house, that sure haven which she had so trustingly visualized to herself as she fled from the Javanese city and the wishes of the Governor General of the Company there. Now, slim and dark-haired, she knelt in the hutlike building at Kawachi, desperately weary and discouraged as the Japanese officials began their third hour of questioning. One was round-faced and smiling, the other a bony man with eyes like bits of black glass. Struggling against impatience and exasperation, she faced them bravely and courteously. "I tell you I come here because it is my home," she cried in Portuguese, the lingua franca of the Orient. "I was born here."

The round-faced man hissed through his teeth. "Ah, so! And you talk to priests before you leave?"

Little gold flecks showed in her brown eyes and a flush mounted under her clear skin. "I tell you again, there *are* no priests there."

The bony man nodded. "Ah, so. No priests." He leaned forward. "What they tell you?"

She tried to smile at him. "Listen! No — priests — in — Batavia!"

The round-faced man bobbed his head with a short, sucking laugh. "No priests. Yes. Now you tell what priests say to you in Batavia. Then you go on board *Roode Hert*. If not tell, perhaps we send you to Maruyama."

The flush deepened on the girl's smooth cheeks and her eyes snapped. "Maruyama! But that's where the bad women are!"

Her questioner giggled. "Not bad. Some very, very good. Yes."

The bony man cut in. "*Why* you leave Batavia?"

She answered firmly, "I've explained that. I was a ward of the Governor General. He wanted me to marry a factor's son. I didn't

19

want to so I ran away and boarded the *Roode Hert*. That's all there is to it. Now, please may I go to Hirado?"

The smiling man beamed harder. "Ah, so! Governor General. He is priest?"

"No, no, no! He is — well, like a Daimyo of all Java," cried Gertrude. "He insisted that I marry. So I came away."

The men exchanged glances. One of them said in Japanese, "She disobeyed a high official!" The other repeated the words, obviously shocked and disapproving. Then the two rose from the mats and, with a "You wait here," scurried out, sliding the door shut behind them.

She drew a deep breath and leaned against the wall. They would return shortly to shower her with the identical questions with which they had begun, hours ago, aboard ship. Through parted screens she looked out onto the roadstead. On the shore, coolies idled and gossiped by the beached sampans that were supposed to have taken the *Roode Hert's* cargo on to Hirado. The ship itself rocked gently on the tide a couple of hundred yards out and the crew, a weird mixture of Europeans, Malaysians and Chinese, leaned on the rail looking dully shoreward.

A deepening fear crept over her. Mechanically she smoothed out the folds of her blue dress as though seeking reassurance in the touch of the familiar fabric. Her eyes roved about the matted room, fell on a shallow, oval bowl where camellia stalks rose from water that gave back the reflection clear and unbroken. As though confronted by a stranger, she stared at the smooth-piled black hair, the troubled brown eyes, the firm young lips and chin. Slowly the reflected eyes became calmer, and the lips tightened. Under her breath she murmured to herself, "You came of your own will, Trudi. Don't weaken now!"

She turned her head quickly as other voices joined those of her examiners outside. The door rustled open and she stared with what she hoped was cool dignity at the bony man who entered alone. "Well?" she asked.

He bowed deeply, the gray sleeves of his haori coat swinging far behind him. "The Daimyo, Matsura-san, sends word that he will be honored if you will permit his barge to take you to your friends at Hirado."

20

Her lips parted in surprise. Then she rose with a dazzling smile. "Dom' arigato gozaimas'!" The Japanese phrase of thanks flowed easily. Her head high, she sailed past him in triumph into the summer sunset.

By a low wharf to the left, the Daimyo's barge waited, a buck-toothed official beckoning to Trudi. Her eyes filled with pleasure as she noted the high, carved prow, the silken canopy and the piles of soft cushions under it. On the broad stern a short, powerful man leaned on his oar, ready to set the barge sculling up the coast to Hirado and the Dutch factory.

She bowed to the official, whose kimono was embroidered with the Matsura crest, and sprang nimbly under the canopy where she knelt among the cushions. The barge pushed out and she closed her eyes with a contented smile. In the end it had all been so easy! And the language of the land, which she had learned almost before she could speak Dutch, had come back to her as though she had never left the mountain empire.

More at ease, she watched the shore slip past her and suddenly felt that she was truly coming home. She looked out at a golden beach where fishermen hauled in their nets to a rhythmic chant. Beyond the sands, pines hung above thatched huts and in a deep grove a red temple shone. A group of white-clad pilgrims plodded along a north-twisting road and Trudi could just hear the steady beat of their hand drums — *clock, clock-clock; clock, clock-clock*. She had not thought of pilgrims in years but from this glimpse she could guess their probable destination, where they would spend the night, how they would cross to Kyushu and thence to the main island of Honshu.

She looked east to the Kyushu coast. There was the hill at Tebira where the Dutch used to go on picnics, Trudi trotting along with her Japanese nurse. An old nursery rhyme ran through her head:

> Nen neko-yo, nen neko-yo
> Nen nen ko-yama-no ko-usagi wa
> Dosh'té o-mimi-ga o-nagai na —

Soon she would be sighting Hirado and her journey would be over. She sat up suddenly. It had been all very easy to assume, on her hurried departure from Batavia, that Uncle Van Os would take her unheralded coming as a matter of course. But would he? He might have married some Japanese woman since his last letter to her, more than a year ago. He might not welcome this sudden descent of a niece whom he had not seen in ten years! "Gunst!" she thought. "What ever should I do?"

She had been looking landward and had not seen the battered sampan sweep up to starboard. She started as a voice called, "Welcome to Hirado, Juffrouw Van Os!" A tall European with strong, dark features sprang aboard, wide hat in one hand and his black hair flying in the wind. He made his way aft to her, saying, "I am François Caron, of the Company. At your service."

Caron! She vaguely remembered him from Hirado days. In Batavia she had heard amazing tales of him. He was the man who, singlehanded, had saved the Company in that terrible affair of Pieter Nuyts in Formosa. She looked up at him, noting the high-bridged nose and the determined lines about the mouth. "Please be seated, Heer Caron. It is good of you to come from Hirado to meet me."

The Frenchman knelt on the cushions, Japanese-fashion, and returned her smile. "You have grown quite as pretty as your mother, Juffrouw. Ah, I wish I might accept your thanks, but I did not come from Hirado. I've been away from the factory for some time — in Tokyo, in Osaka and Nagasaki, not to mention the isles to the southwest."

"You haven't come from Hirado? Then — then how did you know about me?"

Caron waved airily. "But it is quite simple. Yesterday morning, your ship was becalmed off the Goto Islands. You were hailed by a sampan. You remember?"

"The calm, yes. I heard shouting, but I was in my cabin."

"And I," said Caron, "was in the sampan. I hailed ver Stratten, who told me of passenger and cargo. I had hoped — in fact I tried very hard — to be at Kawachi when you anchored. But there were delays." Caron glanced at her. "I gather, from your being on this barge, that you had no trouble landing."

"Oh, no. They asked a lot of questions and I just told them my story. Then I waited until the Daimyo's barge came for me. There was no difficulty."

"None indeed," said Caron blandly. A faint line showed between his keen gray eyes. He thought, "Peste! In that case I needn't have hurried so to catch up with her. And yet — the law — no! Someone — someone from the factory must have managed to get to Matsura. A look of deep gratification crept over his face. He cried out, "Dirk!"

"What?" asked Trudi puzzled.

Caron smiled. "Your pardon. A mere exclamation, caused by the pleasure I feel at the way in which you must have answered the Japanese to be on your way so soon. They love meaningless delay."

She settled herself afresh on her cushions. "Oh, I tried to be patient," she said, pleased at his praise. The offshore breeze freshened and she had to hold the brim of her blue hat with both hands. From its shelter she looked at him. "Did you go to Tokyo and all those other places in that little sampan that just left us?"

"Not at all. That one I rented from Ono of the Shishi-shima boatmen's guild to take me to the Gotos. I came to Shishi from Kagoshima with a boatload of pilgrims bound for the Ise shrines."

She looked at him in growing wonder. "Do you just roam about the Empire as you please?"

"Oh, I go here and go there," he answered negligently. "There are always things to be learned, things to be discovered, and often they may be turned to the profit of the Company. For that reason the Director humors me, gives me a free hand."

She looked speculatively at him. "Heer Caron, could you explain one thing to me? The men who questioned me at Kawachi couldn't seem to talk about anything except priests, priests, priests. Why was that?"

Caron was suddenly grave. "That's a long story. When men like the great Saint Francis Xavier brought Christianity here, they converted people by the tens of thousands, nobles as well as peasants. But some of the converts were, let us say, a little extreme, and went about burning each other's churches and burning Shinto and Buddhist temples. Many people were killed. So, to put an end to this sort of warfare, most of it right over there on Kyushu, the Shogun banned Christianity. That is, they banned Catholicism, the only kind that they knew, because neither we, nor the English in their time, brought predikants here to preach."

"But the Daimyo's men certainly didn't think that I'd come here to burn their temples!"

Caron shook his head. "There's more to it than that. The Japanese didn't object to Catholicism, nor to the priests, most of whom were very well liked. But, you see, they know what happened to Mexico and Peru. Once a Spanish captain bragged at the Shogun's court that the priests and the merchants were only preparing the way for a Spanish army and galleons. Spain, he said, would soon rule Japan. The Japanese have never forgotten that boast, and the Spanish were closed out entirely. The Portuguese are very strictly watched."

"If priests are barred, then why did the Daimyo's men question me about them?" she persisted.

"Because, from time to time, priests do manage to get ashore and try to take up their old work of preaching," said Caron. "They are always caught and I can assure you that their fate is not a pleasant one. But none of this is anything for you to bother about. You'll find life on Hirado pleasant. The country is quiet, the Daimyo's a good friend of ours and our trade and our life flow along gently, but never dully."

"I remember Hirado very well, Heer Caron," she said softly.

"My dear Juffrouw, I am not trying to reassure you, for I know you are a young lady with spirit and courage enough to bribe one of the Company's captains and sail off to a far country merely to avoid a distasteful marriage. I only point out to you that you will be most comfortably lodged with your uncle. You will find agreeable people among both the Dutch and the Japanese. My own house, at the top of the hill, will always be open to you. I'll be grateful if you'll make it a habit of taking tea with Madame Caron. She'll be so glad of your company."

"Of course!" cried Trudi. "Madame Caron! My mother's close friend. She's Japanese and used to wear the prettiest kimonos."

Caron smiled. "And still does."

"Oh, so much is coming back to me now. She made me a kimono for my sixth birthday. Oh! We're almost there. Look — the Daimyo's forts on the point! And the old English factory! It's all tumbling down. There's the village and the Company foundry!"

The barge worked on into the harbor. On skiff and sampan, men stopped work, peered at the Daimyo's craft and cried out in joyous recognition, "Anoné! Caron-san, Caron-san!" The Frenchman waved in reply, calling out in fluent, slangy Japanese. Trudi saw a

24

young officer of the Daimyo's court, a beggar in a leaky boat, a sleek merchant join in the welcome. One and all, they also took note of the girl, and a feeling of gratitude spread over her. Her position, so far as the Japanese were concerned, was settled, since she rode into the harbor under the aegis of François Caron.

Dirk Jongh leaned on the sea wall beside Van Os, squinting through the lavender dusk that was settling over the harbor. Nicolas Becker rocked back and forth on his heels. Van Os wiped his face with a square of purple silk, muttering to Dirk, "I'm getting worried. You're sure that the Daimyo meant that my niece could land?"

Dirk answered with growing uneasiness. "Matsura's word's always been good. He said — Hey! What's that? Out there beyond Noguchi's ship? It's the Daimyo's barge, heading this way." Had something gone wrong? He leaned forward, his concern deepening.

Becker strode to the wall. "You're sure? Now remember, Jongh, I had nothing to do with this. If there's bad news, you and Van Os are responsible. Who is in it? Can you see?"

The craft swung deftly by the little landing and the Company boatmen, reverently awaiting the barge of the lord of the island, suddenly began to shout. Dirk swung astride the sea wall, ready to drop to the wharf. Becker caught his shoulder. "You stay right here. It may be the Daimyo himself."

Dirk shook off the hand, gave a great laugh. "Daimyo nothing. It's Caron."

Stumbling as he landed, Dirk caught himself, then ran to the barge. A small white hand reached out from under the crimson canopy, caught his, and he found himself looking down in amazement into a pair of bright eyes set in a smooth oval face. A pretty voice thanked him as he mechanically helped her out. Van Os's niece! A slim girl in her blue silk of European cut and a wide blue hat. In the turmoil that had followed the news of her arrival at Kawachi, he had never tried to visualize her. She had been a problem requiring a swift, urgent solution, not a living person. Now she stood before him while he unconsciously stared at her. Then he recovered himself, sweeping off his hat with a low bow. "Dirk Jongh, of the Company, Juffrouw, and at your service."

She smiled. "You are very kind, Heer Jongh," she said, and his cheeks tingled at the sound of her voice, the first European woman's voice that he had heard in years. She asked, "And my uncle?"

"Right by the sea wall," said Dirk eagerly. "Here. This way, up the stone steps. Better take my arm. They're slippery."

He crooked an elbow, but the girl, gathering her full skirts, skimmed lightly up the steps, calling, "Uncle Van Os!"

Dirk followed in her wake, keenly aware of the trim ankles under the hem of her skirt, thrilling again at the sound of her voice. A hand fell on his shoulder from behind and a lazy voice said, "No hurry, Dirk. She's not apt to leave for a long time."

From the top step Dirk glanced down at Caron, then toward the promenade by the sea wall where gay paper lanterns were beginning to gleam and bob. Trudi was clinging to her uncle, while Becker stood close by, rubbing his hands and bowing, waiting to be presented. In the main doorway, the clerks de Groot, Hofmeyr and Meynders gaped unabashed as they settled their collars and smoothed their rumpled hair.

Dirk, catching an amused glint in Caron's eye, grinned at him. "Now tell me how *you* managed to ride up here with her — and in Matsura's own barge?"

The Frenchman swung himself easily on the wall and sat dangling his long legs over the gravel. "Oh, by the merest chance — and not an important one," he said.

"I see," said Dirk. "The barge just happened to go by and you jumped into it because it would get you home quicker. And what a surprise it must have been to find that Juffrouw Van Os was its passenger."

"Let us say what a deep pleasure — particularly as there was no doubt in my mind about *who* was responsible for her being there. Fine work, Dirk."

Dirk flushed with pleasure, stammering, "Oh — well — I'm not sure I really did anything. It seemed to me that Matsura was going to let her land anyway."

"No," said Caron gravely. "If you'd made the least mistake, he would have decided not to run the risk of winking at the law. In that case, with that gentle smile of his, he'd have abolished our trade and very likely us along with it. You must have been skillful. I'm proud of you."

"I wish I felt sure that I accomplished anything," said Dirk uneasily.

"Don't stew over it too much," laughed Caron. "In combing the past you can miss the present — as you're missing at the very moment the fact that a pretty and most courageous young lady is calling to you from her uncle's arm."

Dirk forgot Daimyos and laws as he left the sea wall, broad hat under his arm. Becker scowled at him while de Groot and Hofmeyr stared enviously. Trudi, head atilt, smiled at Dirk. "Heer Jongh, I'm so worried about my boxes. Couldn't you —"

Becker moved closer to her, booming heartily, "That's just what I told you, Juffrouw. Just tell me what you want and I'll get it done. The sampans from Kawachi are coming in now." He motioned roughly to Dirk. "You, Jongh! Get down to the wharf and help the coolies with those boxes."

Dirk's jaw tightened and his eyes snapped. Then Trudi glided between him and Becker. "I'd be so glad if you'd help, Heer Jongh. Won't you come to the house with Uncle and me? You can see where the boxes can stay until they're unpacked." She slipped her arm through her uncle's. "Could we start now?"

"At your service, Juffrouw," said Dirk, with a warm glow of pleasure.

As Trudi and Van Os started up the hill, Becker crowded in past Dirk. Then a lazy voice sounded from the sea wall. "A word with you, Heer Directeur! The matter is important, or I wouldn't intrude."

With a muttered "Verdomd!" Becker strode angrily to the sea wall where Caron lounged. Dirk soon overtook Trudi and her uncle. "I was just telling Uncle Van Os how frightened I was once we were at sea," she said. "I didn't know if I should have come, or whether he would like to have me here. I left such a long time ago."

Van Os rumbled, "Don't worry, my dear. Seeing you down by the sea wall was like seeing spring in the cold countries. I'm happy to have you with me. All Hirado's yours, as it was your mother's."

As they walked on, the evening air brought the scent of fresh-cut hinoki wood from the Director's new house, brought the thin smell of fish frying, the clean reek of charcoal fires. Far up the hill in the gloom came the clack of cloglike wooden geta as their wearer hurried on some mysterious errand. Off by the Daimyo's palace a temple bell boomed out in prolonged vibrations. "It's all coming back to me," Trudi said happily. "I'm really home! Oh — there's Father's old house and yours just beyond it, Uncle Van Os. There's a light in the window. Why, it's as if I were expected."

The two halves of the Dutch door swung open to a chorus of "Irasshai, ojo-san!" as the servants, already notified in some weird Oriental fashion, greeted the new mistress of the house, their foreheads touching the floor. Trudi flew in among them like a swift blue bird, her uncle and Dirk following. Dirk heard her going from room to room, heard her questioning the servants, who trailed after her. Her Japanese became more fluent with each word. Footsteps and voices died away. Van Os tramped off to the inner parts of the house and Dirk was left in the hall, hat in hand.

Then a door by his elbow opened unexpectedly and Trudi's head popped out. "You are so kind to help, Heer Jongh. Shall we put the biggest boxes right here? The little ones they can take to the room just above."

Looking down at her from his six feet, Dirk smiled. She seemed absurdly small and young. And yet — he knew she had risked the long voyage to Japan alone. Also, she had effectively resented Becker's rudeness to him down by the offices. He stepped to the door, calling to the Japanese clerk who had unobtrusively followed them from the sea wall. When Dirk had given the necessary instructions and sent the clerk to hurry the coolies by the wharf, he joined Trudi. The room had apparently been used as a catchall since the death of Van Os's Japanese wife more than ten years ago, and neglected by the servants. Unopened packing cases dug their edges into a thick Chinese rug. Rare bits of unglazed pottery from Hizen lay carelessly about. Trudi sat in a huge carved chair that had come out from Holland. Over its back a gorgeous crimson and gold priest robe from Kyoto dangled negligently, one fold hidden by a tattered cotton coat. She crossed her hands in her lap, her feet swinging clear of the floor. "Will the coolies be here soon?" she asked.

"I told Murao to hurry them," said Dirk. "Ah — I hope your voyage was pleasant, Juffrouw."

"Thank you, Heer Jongh. It was agreeable," she said politely.

Then her eyes began to dance. "Oh, so many things happened. I caught a dolphin off Manila. We ran into a terrible typhoon but I wasn't a bit sick. And off Formosa, Chinese pirates chased us for three days and the sailors ran out the guns and I sewed up pieces of silk for powderbags. Yes, and our rudder broke, south of Okinawa." Her expression grew graver. "But that wasn't the worst. It suddenly occurred to me that perhaps I might be a trouble to Uncle Van Os — you heard me tell him so on the way up, didn't you? I can't tell you how I worried about it. I kept thinking that he hadn't seen me in ten years and that he might find it a real embarrassment when I suddenly appeared here. Why, he might have remarried since his last letter to me. He might have been sharing a house with other Company men. I couldn't bear to think that I might be a burden to him and I knew that I ought to have thought of all that before I left Batavia."

Dirk settled himself comfortably on a packing case, watching the play of expression on Trudi's face. Directing the coolies when they came up with the boxes could be strung out most pleasurably.

He jumped to his feet as a Japanese voice called from the path outside, "Gomen kudasai! Gomen kudasai!"

"That'll be Murao, back from the wharf. Please excuse me while I speak to him."

In the night outside, Murao bowed deeply. Becker-san required the presence of Yang-san at once. Caron-san said that the matter was urgent. Dirk swore under his breath. If the call had come from Becker alone, he would have prolonged his talk with the girl. But François Caron never abused the word "urgent." He would have to go at once.

He took reluctant leave of Trudi, then swung downhill at a brisk trot, passing the first of the coolies who were toiling up with the boxes. As he ran, he saw with surprise that the main Company building was aglow with lamplight. What could the emergency be? He quickened his pace. Could Matsura have suddenly changed his mind about Juffrouw Van Os?

An hour later, in a big, square room that looked down across tiled roofs to the harbor, Trudi was darting from box to box, jingling keys and snapping open clumsy locks. A fat amah, swathed from chin to toes in a puffy-sleeved apron, padded obediently after her with an expression that changed bewilderingly from moon-faced stupidity to a knowing leer as a recurrent tic caught up one eye and one corner of her perpetually open mouth. "There," she said, flinging back the last lid. "Fold those blue dresses and put them in the kas, Nobu-san. And those two green ones with them."

Muttering "Maa!" and "Ara!" as the strange foreign garments were piled in her arms, Nobu stowed them deftly in the great carved cupboard. Trudi plunged deeper into the box. "Now these. Pile them on the bed. What a huge bed! And feathers in it! And those heavy chairs! I wonder if — Nobu-san, please go downstairs and ask my uncle if he can come here."

Nobu stared at her over a heap of clothes, leering as though the two shared some deliciously scandalous secret. Then her face relapsed into normal vacuity. Didn't the ojo-san know that danna-san had been sent for from the factory?

"He's gone to the factory? Well never mind. I'll ask him later." She wondered what the meaning of all this was. First, that very handsome Heer Jongh had gone. Now her uncle. At least the latter would return soon, for she could smell nachtmaal cooking. She went on with her unpacking, hunting for a carefully wrapped portrait of her mother which a drunken German had painted in Batavia. When she found it, she uncovered it with gentle fingers and placed it on the heavy dresser between the windows. "You loved Hirado, little mother," she whispered. "Now I've brought you home to it."

With a last glance at the delicate face on the canvas, she crossed to the south window, opened the casement wider and leaned out. A soft breeze from the bay touched her cheeks, sent a tendril of black hair weaving. As though her mother were beside her she murmured to herself, "It's as you remembered it? The Director's house is new, but the rest — listen! There's the temple bell again, off by the palace. It's in that grove where you used to take me to look for jushimatsu nests. And hear the pilgrims' drums? *Clock, clock-clock.* They're late. Where do you think they'll spend the night? There's the old powder house on the point. I can just make it out. And all those lights down in the main building! Burning so late, too. What do you suppose is happening down there?"

30

III

Manila Venture

AT the long table in the Director's office, Dirk watched Becker paw through a sheaf of papers. At his right, Caron lounged in a big chair, idly examining his strong hands and humming to himself. At the foot, Van Os studied more papers, checking and rechecking the columns of figures that showed on the last sheet. Dirk was puzzled and yet was greatly relieved that the summons had nothing to do with Trudi. The matter of the Besshi copper that Caron had explained was of great importance to the Company, but why did it call for a special conference, including his own presence which Becker obviously resented?

As Becker read on, his heavy face lightened, took on an almost amiable expression. At last he shuffled the papers and turned to Caron with an excited laugh. "Why, our profits will double, treble!"

Caron smiled. "I'm a poor hand at such matters." He looked at Van Os. "What does our man of figures say?"

Van Os frowned judicially. "I'm prepared to say that —" He burst out into boyish laughter, his fat face shaking. "Why — why they'll more than treble and besides it'll open more China ports to us and other exports will benefit. We'll do five, seven times the business we used to do."

"I might suggest," observed Caron, "that the opportunity for private trade, in addition to the Company cargoes, will be a pleasant prospect for each of us here."

Van Os said mechanically, "Trading on their own behalf by agents of the Company is strictly forbidden." Then he beamed. "But of course no one pays attention to that anywhere. No one ever has. Ja. Our pockets will bulge."

Becker cleared his throat importantly. "Of course, I've been thinking about this Besshi copper for a long time myself, and while this isn't quite the way I'd have done it, I'm glad to be saved the

31

trouble. This will do." His face seamed over in a tight grin and his eyes shone with cupidity. "Goede Gunst! The profits!" He shoved back his chair noisily and got to his feet.

Dirk looked quickly at Caron, who remained seated. He was calm and unruffled as ever, but something new had come over him, a keenness of expression, an inner tensing. Then the Frenchman spoke evenly. "One instant, Heer Directeur," and reached for a square, flattish package that Dirk had noticed on a side table. With a bow, Caron handed it to Becker, who took it, reseating himself grumbling.

Becker broke the red seal and a cascade of tightly folded papers poured out onto the table. "Open the first one, there under your hand," said Caron. His voice was smooth, but Dirk saw that his dark eyes were alight.

The Director's thick fingers fumbled open a sheet that spread out, square by square. Then he went white and sprang back from the table, jaw sagging. "Get — get that out of here! Burn it!" His hands moved in clumsy, ineffectual gestures. The sheet was a detailed, carefully drawn map of Japan. By strict Shogunal order it was death for any foreigner to see such a map, let alone own one. Dirk felt sweat creeping over his forehead, knew that his hands were trembling. The Frenchman was watching Becker carefully, a smile playing over his firm mouth. The Director lunged at the map, panting, "I'll burn it! I'll swear I've never seen it. You — you — I'll ruin you for this!"

Caron caught up the map with a quick movement. "Your pardon, Heer Directeur," he said pleasantly. "I'd forgotten that the cares of office have never given you time to read Japanese." He passed the map to Dirk. "Since you'd probably like to have someone else verify the writing down in this corner, I'll ask Heer Jongh to translate."

Still shaken, Dirk took the wide sheet. The margin by his right hand was covered with red-ink seals, with vertical columns of characters that had been obviously set down by a master of calligraphy. Astonished, he felt his way through the sweeping curves and arabesques, until sentences and names began to take form. It was unheard of, incredible. And yet —

Becker's unsteady voice broke in. "Well?"

Dirk passed his hand over his forehead and looked at Caron, who

32

seemed absorbed in the set of a bit of lace on his cuff. Then he drew a deep breath. "Heer Directeur, there's no mistake about this. The biggest seal is the Shogun Iyemitsu's. Then — I'll just give you the gist of the writing here. It says that the map is given with the Shogun's consent to François Caron; that no Shogunal officer may question his possession of it; that he need surrender it only at the order of the Shogun. Then down here is the seal of Heizo, the Daikwan — that is, the Shogun's agent at Nagasaki, verifying what's above it."

"That's a good summary, Dirk," said Caron. "You see, Heer Directeur, there's no danger in our having the map."

Still pale, Becker sat down. "Just the same, I'd like another eye on that. Van Os, can you read this damned trash?"

Van Os shook his head. "You know I can't. I'm responsible for the Company's ledgers and nothing else."

"Then get in the chief interpreter!" ordered Becker.

Caron raised his hand quietly. "I think not. Dirk, there's another endorsement — there, on that corner. Read it, please."

Dirk turned the sheet. "Yes — I have it. The Shogun's own signature, not his seal." He looked at Becker. "This map, and the other papers, are to be shown to no Japanese other than those listed — and Heizo's is the only name."

Caron leaned his elbows on the table. "Heer Directeur, you must rely on our translation."

Becker flushed. "Very well. We are allowed to have the map. What are we going to do with it? Frame it?"

"I'll give you the answer," said Caron amiably. "I guarantee that you'll find it far more interesting than the matter of the copper." He placed his finger tips together and leaned back in his chair. "I'll review the past a little."

Van Os yawned while Becker growled, "Get on with it."

Caron inclined his head pleasantly. "We all know that Japan had had nearly a thousand years of civil war, largely because no man who pretended to act in the name of the long chain of powerless and unconsulted emperors was strong enough to pass on the power to a chosen successor. Once a strong man died, call him Shogun or whatever you like, there was usually a war to seize that power. Is that clear?"

33

"Yes, Heer Schoolmaster," Becker said grimly. "It is also clear that my dinner is waiting."

"I promise you a relish better than the finest shoyu sauce," answered Caron. "Now in the middle of the last century, the pattern began to change. One strong man appeared, was able to pass on his power to a chosen successor and that successor to still another. The process lasted until well into this century. The civil wars stopped, and the line of Shoguns has become hereditary, to all intents and purposes. The holders swear that it shall remain so."

Becker eyed him suspiciously. "What's all that got to do with me?"

Caron shrugged. "A good deal. To make sure that no one challenges the Shogun's power, many steps have been taken. Some of them deal with us and our trade. Tokyo wants no chance of foreign interference, of a European power backing some rebellious lord and putting him on the Shogunal throne. That's why our trade and the way we live are so strictly regulated. That's why the Spanish were driven out at Nagasaki."

"Faugh!" said Becker. "We should talk up to them. They'd knuckle under quick enough."

Caron smiled at Dirk. "That's one way. But we must remember their measures touch other people than ourselves. To make sure that no Daimyo will ever be powerful enough to challenge the present family, the Tokugawas, the lords in all the provinces have been forced to disband their private armies."

Becker flung up his hands. "What's this all leading to? Roll up your map and end your lecture. I'm hungry."

"Remember my promise, Heer Directeur," said Caron equably. "These disbanded armies *do* affect us and very directly." He began to speak more quickly. "The men who made up these armies of the Daimyos have been brought up to nothing but war. To them it's the only honorable calling. Where are they now? Some of them have been taken into the Imperial army. The rest, starving, masterless men, are thrown into idleness. Many of them, especially those who fought in Korea, are Kyushu men. Others have joined them until you can count disbanded soldiers in Kyushu by the thousands and tens of thousands. Across the straits there, they're being ground down mercilessly by the local Daimyos. Remember — these aren't

34

ordinary peasants. They're trained fighting men. There *could* be a rebellion. A rebellion could be very dangerous for us, Heer Directeur."

"Pah!" said Becker, though Dirk could see that he was growing uneasy. "We'd weather it. We'd gain by it, if we'd only — "

Caron cut in quickly. "Wait! Most of these disbanded soldiers, especially the Kyushu men, are Christians, or come from converted families. If they revolt, they'll be crushed by the whole force of the Empire." He rose abruptly, fists on the table. "Only — they won't be crushed as mere rebels, they'll be crushed as *Christian* rebels. Can you tell me, Heer Directeur, what *our* position will be then?"

Becker started. "Those people over there are Catholic Christians. We aren't. We'd be all right."

Caron sat down, shaking his head. "There's a very strong anti-foreign clique at Tokyo. They want *all* foreigners banished forever. If this revolt came about, they wouldn't bother to distinguish between one brand of Christianity and another — just as we might not see the distinction between the Shingon and Monto or Nichiren Buddhists."

Becker gnawed at a broken thumbnail, looking over the knuckle at Caron. "But you know the Daimyo here. Couldn't you make him see what he'd lose if we sailed out of Hirado?"

"We wouldn't sail," said Caron.

"Of course we wouldn't."

"We would never sail — anywhere. You haven't seen, as I have, lines of Christian men, women and children, all roped together and pushed over the cliffs of the Papenberg in Nagasaki harbor. That was fifteen years ago. Worse could happen today."

Dirk felt his stomach contract as the full implications of Caron's words sank deeper in his mind. Van Os said quietly, "You've been in Kyushu a lot, Heer Jongh. What do you think?"

Dirk moistened his lips. "I know what conditions are over there. Frankly, I hadn't thought of a revolt. But it could happen."

Becker's voice was a dry rustle. "Wha — what are we going to do?"

Hope came alive in Dirk's mind as he saw Caron pick up the map and the other papers with a steady hand. "We shall do this," said Caron firmly. He spread out the map and Dirk noticed for the

35

first time that its seaways were marked with spidery red lines that ran up the Inland Sea, touched at Osaka, went on to Nagoya, to Tokyo Bay itself. Others wove into Shikoku ports, on to Kagoshima and Nagasaki. Another section of the map fell open, showing that the lines merged, ran south past Okinawa, past Formosa, then separated to swing sharply to Macao on the China coast and to Manila.

Caron began in a level, easy voice. "I've worked on this plan for a long time. I completed it on this last trip of mine. When I first explained it to the Shogun Iyemitsu, he was shocked. Later, he became enthusiastic."

Suspicion momentarily hid fear in Becker's eyes. "This is something you've brewed up with the Japanese? Without my knowing?"

Caron inclined his head courteously. "Until now I had nothing to report. Of course, I acted on the written authority which you gave me to treat in your name and in the name of the Company."

"That is in order," said Van Os to Becker. "My books show the grant of power."

"Get on with it," said Becker.

"With your permission, Heer Directeur," said Caron. "This plan insures the continuance, the strengthening of the Company trade. It insures it in two ways. Just look at this map while I explain." His finger touched Nagasaki. "We used to share the trade with the Spanish and the Portuguese, who based down here. The Spaniards were driven out, and we divided affairs with the Portuguese." He lowered his voice. "The Portuguese will be driven out next. That will happen soon."

Becker rallied a little. "Then we'll have *all* the Japan trade?"

"Who else is there to share it, except the Chinese who don't compete with us?" said Caron patiently.

Van Os looked at Caron respectfully. "And you arranged this, with the Shogun?"

"In return for certain obligations which we assume."

Becker threw himself back in his chair. "I knew there'd be some hole in it. What did you promise?"

Caron swept his hand far south on the map. "I'll come to that in a moment. When the Portuguese are banished, they'll go to their Chinese colony at Macao. They will not be in a pleasant frame of mind. Now look to the northeast of Macao, across this rather narrow channel. There is Spanish Manila." He looked at Dirk. "You've heard something about their feeling, haven't you?"

Dirk nodded. "From the Portuguese Remedios at Nagasaki. The Dons don't like us anyway and they still are furious that we're here and they aren't. There is talk of interfering with us."

Caron turned to Becker and Van Os. "You see? With Company ships sailing north from Batavia, they'd eventually be preyed on by hostile raiders from both Macao and Manila. They could ruin our trade, even end the Company."

"End us too," agreed Becker.

"We don't count," said Caron tersely. "It's the Company, and what it means to Holland, that counts." He rose suddenly and Dirk felt a change come over the room. No longer was Caron the lazily respectful subordinate, hoping for approval of his plans. He dominated both Becker and Van Os. The Frenchman's fist struck on the maps with a crackling sound. "Our trade will not die. Look at the red lines that run south from here to Macao and Manila. This I have promised the Shogun, in the name of the Company. In the spring, we shall send up from Batavia four large ships, none under seventeen guns. With them will be two yachts of eight guns each. They'll hit first Macao, then Manila, seizing both ports in the joint name of the Company and the Shogun. We'll change the whole map of the Orient. Spain and Portugal are both rotten. We could do it with half the force. But I never heard of a venture failing by being too strong."

Dirk pored over the map, still uncomprehending. Why did the lines run north straight to Japan, and then south to Manila and Macao? Why not —

As Becker rose, his chair overturned with a crash. "No!" roared the Director. "I'll put my name to nothing like that! Suppose we lost a ship? I'd be responsible! Verdomd! I see it now. You're selling the Company to the Japanese. We take the risk. They take all profits."

"Please hear me out, Heer Directeur," said Caron politely. "It would not surprise me to find that the Governor General van Diemen will approve of our plan. He has plenty of ships at his disposal."

"Oh, he has, has he?" shouted Becker. "And he'll have one ready to send you back to Amsterdam."

Van Os interposed. "One moment, Heer Directeur. I think that my books show that we tried such a venture some years ago. Yes. I'm sure of it. It was against Macao alone. We lost ships and a great many men. The Portuguese tortured the prisoners. Trelawney, the Englishman at our foundry, was there. He lost a son in the fight."

Becker whirled on Caron. "And you want to try it again! Macao! And now you want to add Manila to that!"

As though Becker had not spoken, Caron went on. "This plan will succeed. Van Os is right about Macao, but that plan was improvised and bungled. This will *not* be! Then look at our position! Alone in our trade here. A safe passage to Batavia. A fine share in the Manila and Macao trade and the Shogun under deep obligations to us."

"To you, you mean," Becker put in.

"To the Company," answered Caron. "That is the first insurance for our continuance of which I spoke. The second — " he turned to Dirk — "can you guess what *that* is?"

Light began to dawn in Dirk's mind. His head spun as the magnitude of Caron's plan struck him. He looked at Van Os and Becker. The former was watching Caron quietly. The latter was red with fear and anger. Dirk nodded, a vast sense of relief sweeping over him. "I think so. You have not told us what the Shogun and Heizo undertake for *their* part."

Caron nodded in approval. "Heer Directeur, you seemed concerned about the composition of our force. Then reassure yourself. The only Hollanders on board will be the crew and the gunners. But — see how the lines running north touch at Japanese ports? Our ships will be packed alow and aloft with equipped, trained Japanese fighting men, the best swordsmen and archers in the world. Our ships will take thousands of those same starving ex-soldiers of whom I told you earlier, men who fought in Korea and at the siege of Osaka. *They* will be the ones to land under cover of the Company's guns."

"A rabble," scowled Becker.

"Not a rabble, Heer Directeur. And more than that, I've ar-

ranged that they'll be commanded by — he dropped his voice —
"the great Shimadzu himself!"

The name obviously meant nothing to Becker or Van Os, but
Dirk, carried away by the Frenchman's words, slapped his hands on
the arm of his chair. Caron looked confidently at him. "You were
going to add something, Dirk?"

"Not I!" cried Dirk. "Shimadzu! About the most famous military
man in the Empire! That's all. I just — wait a minute. Now I see
your second insurance for the Company. You'll fill those ships with
the very men who might touch off trouble around the Gulf of
Shimabara, over there in Kyushu!"

"Exactly," said Caron. "We could recruit the whole force right
there in that area."

Becker sat dazed. "All that — and the Japanese do the work, except
for our crews and gunners, who will stay on board?"

Caron's lazy smile returned. "With two exceptions, Heer Directeur. I shall be on the Macao flagship. With your permission, Heer
Jongh will sail with the Manila force."

Van Os stared. "But that means — why we and the Japanese will
control the Orient! The office here might even become deputy to
Batavia!"

Becker muttered, "And this is done in my name!" His expression
suddenly became that of a man who sees great visions. "Why —
that'll mean — "

Caron broke in, "It will mean that you will follow van Diemen
as Governor General at Batavia. It will probably take you on to
Amsterdam as a Director of the Board of the Company."

"Yes!" cried Becker. "Yes!" He banged his fist on the table.
"We can't fail. To be sure, there are several items of the undertaking
that I'd have arranged differently, but since you seem to have got
them well enough together with the Shogun, we'll let things
stand."

"Your knowledge will be indispensable in all this, Heer Directeur," said Caron.

Becker got up. "Any time! Any time!" he said. "Now come and
sup with me, Van Os. We'll talk over the trade end of all of this.
Good night to you, Heer Caron. Good night, Jongh."

He clumped out of the room, Van Os after him. Dirk glanced at

39

Caron, who was calmly polishing the blade of his dress sword, humming to himself. "Well?" said Dirk.

"Well, my friend?" said Caron without looking up.

"How the devil did you do it?" Dirk burst out.

Caron shrugged. "There wasn't so much to it, once I had the pieces in my hand." He talked on, in humorous self-deprecation. There was an old noble whose house overlooked the Gulf of Shimabara who had told him this and that. In the heart of ancient Yamato, Caron had talked with an abbot. A court official of the shadow-Emperor in Kyoto had remarked on this and the remark had been confirmed by the head of the fishermen's guild in the little village of Kobe. "It is odd," concluded Caron, "how interested they all were when I reminded them of the Spanish boast of galleons and soldiers following the priests and the traders. Not that they needed much reminding. They were interested, too, when I commented, in passing, how the Portuguese, of the same faith, had made Macao in China and Goa in India their own." He smiled indulgently. "It's odd too, isn't it, how one idea leads to another?"

Dirk drew a deep breath. "You happened to meet this man, you talked to that one and at once we're all of us ready to take Macao and Manila. Will you ever give me the details of it all?"

"Surely," said Caron, sheathing his sword. "After you've given me the full story of your call on Matsura. But both matters can wait for the moment. In the meantime, Dirk, what we've got to do is hurry the months until spring. We must keep a close watch, you and I, of events across there in Kyushu, especially around the Gulf of Omura and Shimabara, clear up to the Unzen hot springs." His fingers drummed on the table. "I'm afraid that's my Achilles' heel. The three men on whom I used to depend for news over there are dead. Do you know anyone? You've been there often enough."

Dirk got up and went into the main office where an old coat of his was hanging. He fumbled in a pocket, returned with a piece of dark brown silk in his hand. "This may help," he said. "I had to spend a night over by Shimabara not long ago. I thought it might be worth while to have a look at the old ruined castle there. You know the one. They call it the Castle of Hara or the Castle of Arima. I heard, by chance, that the malcontents meet there, from time to time."

40

A quick glint came into Caron's eyes. "In the castle? Dirk, that's worth knowing."

"I thought so. And while climbing around the ruins, I picked up this." He tossed the silk onto the table.

Caron caught it up eagerly and spread it out. The cloth was old and worn, but of good quality. Woven into the center was a simple design of two arcs which interlocked at their upper ends, a family crest that he recognized. "So," Caron said, his finger tracing out the arcs. "Gentaro Mori. You know him?"

"Yes," said Dirk.

"What do you think of him?"

"He's proud as the devil and not easy to know. But I think he's come to look on me as a friend. I'd call him about the finest Japanese I've ever met."

Caron nodded. "Yes. I knew his father before he was shaved a priest and retired to that temple near Tebira. I think the son might be pleased if you called on him tomorrow at bath time. Unless he's officer of the day at the palace."

"No. Toda's on duty today and tomorrow. Monogi follows Toda, so I've got plenty of time to see our friend."

Caron looked pleased at Dirk's knowledge of the inner workings of the palace. "That's good. See him tomorrow. For my part — h'm — there's a silversmith down on Amakusa I ought to see. There's the head groom of that new lord near Arima, and he'll know — yes. That'll be all right." He stretched himself, catlike. "We're going to be busy, you and I, and we'll be working alone. Becker knows nothing of the country and won't learn. Van Os is a good man, but his interest and knowledge end with his ledgers."

Side by side they climbed the flagged path that led up the hill, Caron waving a casual good night as Dirk stopped at the little stone house that he shared with de Groot and Hofmeyr. Hand on the latch, Dirk hesitated, then turned and went swiftly up until he came to Van Os's house. He swore, in English and in Dutch, as he saw that all the windows were dark. "I ought to have left the offices earlier," he said to himself. "I wonder if Murao had the boxes stowed where she wanted them?"

* * *

41

Next morning the sun climbed slowly over the edge of the great island of Kyushu which Hirado folk called the mainland. Slanting rays picked out the tops of the sharp green hills, fell between the worn red pillars of a temple, lighted up the sails of a sampan that was scudding north through a jade-green sea and finally spanned the narrow straits and struck full on the sea wall and the cluster of Dutch houses.

Snug in her vast bed, Trudi stirred in her sleep. Outside, a breeze rustled the fronds of tall bamboos and whispered through swaying pine boughs. In a clump of bushes near the house, brown and white finches bubbled and chirped over their rich harvest of silver-winged flies. The ringing *clock-clock* of wooden geta sounded clear from the sea wall; a flower woman, bright basket strapped to her back, chanted endlessly, "Hana! Hana!" as she pushed up past the Dutch doors. Away by the Daimyo's palace a bronze bell throbbed and muttered. A fish peddler called melodiously, his voice running easily over four high-pitched notes. Close by, a windlass groaned and protested as someone drew a heavy bucket of water from the deep, cool well.

She woke as the orchestration of the waking island flowed into the room. This was not her cool room in Batavia, nor was it the narrow cabin of the *Roode Hert*. Recollection came to her. Hirado, and the house of her uncle! She must get up at once and begin her duties in this new home to which her uncle had welcomed her as though she had been his own daughter. She swung her feet to the floor, slipping on a pair of sandal-like zori. Nobu's dull voice sounded beyond the door. Trudi's bath was ready. Probably Nobu had been kneeling beyond the closed door for some time, waiting for the first sound of life from within the room.

The routine of a Hirado household came instantly to her mind. The bath, then breakfast, then a solemn conference with the servants about the problems of the day. Should eels be served that night? Or wildfowl from the marshes beyond the Daimyo's forts? And would this be an auspicious day for the servants to unstitch their kimonos and sun the strips of cloth on bamboo frames? Now as mistress of the house, she would have to meet all these grave questions and solve them.

She called to Nobu and slipped on a brown and blue dressing

gown of oddly patterned Javanese cloth, then stepped to the window and breathed in the clear air pungent with smoke from the bath fires. Up the hill toiled a pair of oxen towing a long cart on which was lashed a heavy stone lantern, destined for someone's garden beyond the crest of the hill. Close by the Dutch door, a tiny Japanese girl in a red and white kimono bearing a graceful bamboo pattern hopped up and down for the sheer joy of nothing at all. She clapped her hands and her little voice floated up to Trudi:

> Tsuki-sama ikutsu?
> Ju-san nanatsu!

She marked each syllable with a higher hop. Trudi laughed down at her, joining in:

> How old is my lady moon?
> Thirteen and seven!

The bright-clad mite looked up startled, then pattered away, her wide sleeves flying.

After a long soak in a round, deep tub of aromatic wood, Trudi dressed herself carefully in a silver-gray dress, slashed with blue, and ran out to the side garden to find her uncle.

He was sipping tea under a spreading magnolia, looking drawn and worried. When he caught sight of her, his face lighted up. "Ah, my dear Trudi! You look like one of the great ladies I used to see as a boy in 's Gravenhage! A pretty dress and so much more sensible than these kimonos that look like nightgowns! Take this chair. Here are persimmons and Formosa oranges. Ship's biscuit from the *Roode Hert* and a sight better it is than the bread the Japanese bake for us. And here's tea from the Kyoto fields."

Trudi poured pale, mellow tea from a pot of Satsuma ware into a thin, handleless cup. As she daintily peeled a persimmon she sighed, "This is so nice, Uncle Van Os. Like the breakfasts I used to have here with my mother."

"I hope you'll be happy here," said Van Os. "Allemachtig! I should have sent for you long ago. Batavia's a roistering, drunken port and no place for a girl. Life's quiet here, but the folk are good. Down at the factory de Groot and Hofmeyr and Zell are sound Dutch stock, even if they are only clerks. They'll rise, though. They'll be good company for you."

43

She looked at him over the edge of her cup. "And Heer Jongh was most obliging."

Van Os glanced quickly at her. It had been agreed at the office the night before that she be kept in ignorance, so far as possible, of the grave danger she had run in coming to Hirado. Could a hint have reached her? He was relieved by her expression. Obviously she knew nothing. "Ah, yes. Jongh," he said. "A good boy, although like Caron he won't pay proper attention to the ledgers. Always running across to Kyushu or up to Hiroshima and Osaka. Can't think why the Director allows it. But he's a bright lad and well mannered."

"I know I'll be happy here with you, Uncle Van Os. And I can never forget your welcome of me." She smiled at him.

His face clouded over as he looked across the straits to the cliffs of Kyushu and the green, sunny mountains that rose beyond them. Then he shook his head as though driving away uneasy thoughts. "Yes, yes. We'll try to make you happy here. Ah — there are several things I want to talk over with you. In the first place, I suppose you know that, for the times, you're a wealthy young lady. In Batavia you lived on the income of your father's savings, which were considerable. The principal by law is yours."

"Mine? But the Governor General will never let me have it, after my disobeying his orders and coming up here!"

"The law is mightier than van Diemen. When you're twenty-one he'll have to turn it over to you," announced Van Os firmly. "And another thing — you're my only relative, and I — well, I've made my little economies over the years."

With a quick gesture she laid her hand over his. "I'm going to stay here and keep house for you year after year."

Gratified, he chuckled. "Bless you for the thought. But here's another thing. I've served the Company for a long time. I've made application for retirement. I've my savings. I'll have a good pension. I'll buy property near Zandaam and spend the rest of my days watching the windmills along the Zuider Zee. I hope you'll come with me — to the real home of your father and your mother. I've connections there, good connections, and we'll find some Dutch boy for you to marry."

44

She looked at him in astonishment. "*Another* voyage? And soon!"

"Next spring perhaps, or fall. We'll ship to Batavia and then on south and south again. We'll see Madagascar and Mozambique channel. We'll see the great mountain back of the Cape of Good Hope. Or we could sail for Basra on the Persian Gulf and go home overland. They say it's an easy journey these days." He looked wistfully at her. "But by land or by sea, it would be a sad journey to make alone and with an empty heart, Trudi."

Spring or fall — an infinity of months before she need even think of sailing again, of leaving Japan for an unknown home in faraway Europe. She said impulsively, "Of course we go together — and whenever you decide!"

He beamed on her. "Then that's settled. Only — " His content-ment faded as he looked east again. "Maybe I should have applied sooner," he muttered, as though to himself. "The world's uncertain. If I'd sent in my papers last year, we might be sailing out on the *Roode Hert*. Still — Caron is sure that nothing — " He rallied him-self. "And we'll have busy days that will delight you, and very soon. At this moment, merchants are coming from all over Japan, head-ing for Hirado and the great sale of the *Roode Hert's* cargo. And the things they'll bring with them! We'll look them over, you and I. We'll pick up some silks and lacquer ware and ivories to brighten up our home in Zandaam. Now I'm for my ledgers. Don't give a thought to the house for a few days. Naka-san'll see to things until you get your land legs."

When he had gone, Trudi sat under the magnolia, pleasantly aware of the solidity of land beneath her. As she sipped her tea she found that she was thinking with more and more pleasure of Holland. Of course, the prospect shimmered vaguely across the immeasurable span of months. There would be so many new things to see during the long voyage. Names that her uncle had mentioned rang pleasantly in her ears. Madagascar, Mozambique, the Cape of Good Hope. She wondered if they would sail past those almost mythical cities whose names she had heard — Paris and London and Madrid, or Leipzig or Vienna.

In the meantime there was the country of her childhood to dis-

45

cover all over again. It was nice, too, to know that there were the young clerks of the factory — like Heer Jongh.

Nobu appeared by the side door, alternately leering and gaping stupidly. Madame Caron, she told her, had sent word that she would be honored if Sayo-ko would call on her that morning. Trudi, pleased by the sound of her Japanese name, jumped to her feet. "Yes, Nobu-san. Say that I'll start right away." She ran up to her room, plunged into a deep box for a hat, gave a swift pat to her hair, a tug to her skirts. Madame Caron had been a great friend of her mother's and now was showing that she had not forgotten old ties by this prompt invitation.

Out in the sun, Trudi started up the steep hill toward the big Japanese house at the crest, its silvery tiles showing above the plain board fence that girdled it. To her right, the land fell away swiftly to the straits that shrank to a mere quarter mile at the northern end. On the Kyushu shore she could see a narrow dirt road lined with high cedar trees. The train of some great Daimyo must be passing along it, for she saw the glitter of fine lacquer as a palanquin was borne high on men's shoulders. Bright in the morning air, great vertical banners fluttered at the head of the procession, others brought up the rear. A leisured peace hung over sea and islands, deep and unshakable.

The wide doors of curiously grained, unpainted wood swung back and it seemed to Trudi that she stepped past the kneeling servants and into her childhood. This was the same garden where she had played, the same strips of turf, the same sheets of water crossed by miniature bridges. The stone lantern at the south side of the house was unfamiliar, but beyond wound the gravel path that led on to the fish pond, the dwarf pine trees and the little thatched house for the solemn tea ceremony, the cha-no-yu. How many times had she run among the azalea bushes while the Carons' tawny cat, Akachan, raced madly after blowing leaves or scraps of straw! Here she had swung a gaily lacquered battledore while her mother sipped tea with Madame Caron under the low eaves. Inside the house, she slipped off her shoes, whose high heels would have cut the thick straw matting that paved each room. Silver-flecked panels slid back with a soft hissing and a voice breathed, "Sayo-ko-san!"

Madame Caron stood in the opening exactly as Trudi remem-

46

bered her, her unlined face serenely beautiful under smooth-piled black hair that gleamed like lacquer. Her ivory hands were folded across the broad lavender obi that bound in her dove-gray kimono. The hands moved toward Trudi, caught hers. In swift Japanese Madame Caron said, "I thought to welcome the daughter. My happiness is greater in that the mother's memory walks with the daughter. You are so like her."

Trudi said huskily, "She was your friend, Caron-fujin. May it be given me to take her place."

Madame Caron's hands tightened on hers. "The daughter has the mother's pretty manners, even remembering to call me after the fashion of my own people. But I am known as Madame Caron after the fashion of my husband's people, as is proper." She guided Trudi into a little, matted room that looked west across the garden to the high ridges beyond. "How well you remember your Japanese. So. We sit here and speak of your mother while I make tea for you."

It was cool in the little room with its rare bronzes and lacquers, its silk scroll of mountains and waterfalls. Outside the sun climbed and the long shadows in the garden shrank, became dark pools at the foot of pine and stone lantern. Preparing the second infusion of tea, which surely must have come from Uji, Madame Caron said, "And have you found any of your old playmates with whom you used to romp through this garden and along the ridge trail?"

Trudi shook her head. "They've all gone. There was Haru-ko Van Santen. Yes, and Tsuta-ko Schmidt, but the Company has moved their fathers to other posts, Uncle Van Os tells me."

"Of course. Van Santen-san married a Yoshida and Schmidt-san a Mikawa. What a pity my Petronella and Maria are little girls. And our son, Tobias — " she smiled with quiet pride — "did you know that he is nearly as tall as his father and stands for the Company in far-off Amboina in the Moluccas? Ah, this talk of the old days! Sayo-ko-san, would you please your mother's old friend by sometimes dressing like her? You remember that she always wore the kimono."

"Of course!" said Trudi eagerly. "I'll find some silk and have Nobu make me some. This dress of mine — " she tucked the hem hastily about her knees — "it's impossible to kneel, Japanese fashion, in it."

Madame Caron slid back the door of a lacquer cupboard built into the wall and drew out a long wooden box. "Then perhaps you will allow me to spare you the time of waiting, at least for one costume."

Trudi cried out in delight as the lid was thrown back. The kimono was of blue silk with a heavily embroidered pattern of chrysanthemums that trailed their long petals down the back, reappeared on sleeve, on hem. The wide obi, or sash, repeated the pattern in miniature against a cherry-colored silk that matched the vivid lining of the garment. There was a short red kirtle to be worn next the skin, a thin muslin vest, white glovelike tabi for the feet and thick zori covered with silk-fine straw.

"A little early in the year for the chrysanthemum pattern," said Madame Caron apologetically. "But it's so becoming to you. Come. I'll help you into it and then we'll call Maria and Petronella to bow before their new Japanese friend."

I V

Gathering Storm

THAT same afternoon Dirk walked swiftly along the soft dirt of Hirado's main street. A wind from the hills stirred the gay, vertically slashed curtains that hung before the open-fronted shops and sake booths. Water gurgling down the stone-lined drains told him that baths were being emptied. The smell of frying fish and bean curd and boiling seaweed blended pleasantly with the tang of charcoal fires. At the edge of sake booths, men knelt by checkered *go* boards, frowningly moving the black and white pieces from square to square. A pipe cleaner, trundling his cart with its brazier and shrill-whistling kettle of boiling water, stopped by a bamboo shop, took a clogged tobacco pipe from its owner, clapped it over the spout of his kettle and blew it clear, bowing as he received a worn copper for his services. An umbrella mender went chanting along the beach road, hoping for one more customer before sunset brought an end to his work.

Pipe cleaner, fish peddler, *go* player alike called to Dirk, who waved and passed on, pleased with the knowledge that Yang-san could have stopped to chat with any one of them and been welcome. He cleared the curved south end of the town, walked along a narrow path that ran between rich rice fields, mounted a long gentle slope that led inland. The land was poorer here, the fields thin and starved looking. By a dry plot he took a path that led deeper inland, finally halting before a single-story house whose roof was barely visible over the board fence that sagged with age despite the neat patches that showed here and there.

Under the tiled gate, he rapped on weather-gnawed wood, so thin that it seemed to bend to his touch. The door swung open and a gray old man bowed low before him. He wore a peaked-top farmer's hat of straw, but the old brown haori coat, neatly patched and mended like the fence, was that of a feudal retainer of a bygone day. As the old man bowed again, Dirk could just make out the house crest below the collar, a simple design of two arcs whose upper ends crossed. Dirk acknowledged his greeting, then asked, "Mori-san-wa irasshaimas'ka, Kema-san?"

Kema bowed lower. Mori-san was indeed at home and would be glad to welcome Yang-san, if the latter would deign to enter so poor a house. The flags of the walk were worn and chipped, but swept spotlessly clean. The paper that covered the latticelike shoji was patched, mended and patched again. Inside the house the straw floor mats, the tatami, showed countless trimmings and rebindings. Everything spoke of a taut proud poverty.

In a rear room that looked out over a bare garden, Dirk bowed carefully to his host. Gentaro Mori, in his early twenties, was tall for a Japanese, with broad, well-set shoulders. His thin, high-bridged nose and square chin suggested a Southern European, but the unmistakable fold of his eyelids marked him as full-blooded Japanese.

When the last flowery and long-drawn-out compliments had been exchanged, Mori smiled. "An end to formalities. I only go through with them because old Kema would be shocked if I omitted a step. He served my father, who was most exacting." He settled his gray haori about his shoulders, a haori as neatly patched as his servant's, but marked with a larger crest. "You find me, Yang-san, rejoicing, and I hope that you will rejoice with me. I have been working in my rice fields all day and the new crop promises well. We shall share a jar of sake." He clapped his hands and Kema crept into the room bearing on a lacquered tray a bottle of pale-green glaze and two tiny matching cups.

While Mori poured ceremoniously, Dirk looked about the room. In startling contrast to their surroundings, two magnificent swords, one long and one short, lay on a rack. A bronze incense burner, centuries old, stood in the deep niche. In a recess in the wall a long case gleamed, its lid showing in gold and silver a scene from some old clan war. Mori, handing Dirk a cup of steaming sake, nodded to the case. "An arquebus, presented to my father by the great Konishi himself, for valor at the taking of Ping Yan in Korea." He raised his own cup and drank Dirk's health with a formal phrase.

Kneeling on the worn mats and answering the toast, Dirk wondered, as he had wondered before, at the contrasts that Mori presented. A "two-sworded" man of ancient family, attached to Matsura's household; yet he actually worked a small rice field with his own hands. Owner of swords that many Japanese would have killed to own, not to mention the unseen arquebus in its superb case, a gift from the almost legendary Konishi; yet the house in which he lived could have been called a hovel, except for its scrupulous neatness and cleanliness.

Dirk murmured something conventional, wishing increasing yield in the Mori fields. As though reading his guest's unspoken questions, Gentaro Mori set down his cup. "I thank you. The yield needs to be great — if greatness can come from so small a holding. Ah, you and your friends of the Company have always dealt fairly with me. It is only right that you know why I toil like a peasant over a few tsubo of land."

"Surely a two-sworded man may please himself in such matters," said Dirk quickly.

Mori shook his head. "It is not a question of pleasing, Yang-san. You may know that in the old days my father became Christian."

"So Heer Caron told me," said Dirk.

"Then he must also have told you that he renounced the faith, became Buddhist again and was shaved a priest."

"That, too, I have heard," said Dirk, wondering how all this was connected with the present Mori poverty.

"So, you see," Mori went on, "it is all very simple."

"Simple!" echoed Dirk.

"Naturally," said Mori. "The lands of all Japanese Christians were confiscated some years ago, to be returned only on formal renunciation of Christianity. Many privileges went, as well."

Dirk was bewildered. "But your father made the renunciation," he said.

"Ah," said Mori. "That is not the point. He became a Buddhist, hence his lands and privileges reverted to me."

"But you were never Christian," protested Dirk.

"No. But my father, as head of the house, was; therefore, on the koseki-tohon, the family was. It is perfectly simple. All the Mori holdings would come to me were I to go before our Daimyo, who allows me to serve him, and make formal denunciation. That, of course, is impossible because by doing that I criticize the action of my father in becoming Christian in the first place. That would be unthinkable. Matsura-san understands very well why I cannot do that, although he wishes that I would. Hence it is only by special dispensation that I keep my post in his household guard and my little rice patch and retain this roof over me."

The course of Japanese reasoning was clear to Dirk. Mori would rather live on the verge of starvation than commit an act which might be held unfilial. The train of thought was like so many other Japanese twists that he had met before, logical to a Japanese mind, maddening to a European who tried to follow them. Mori went on, "There is another matter, too, that affects the present course of my life. Not long ago I sent my second retainer, Goto, across to Kyushu. No doubt he was mistaken, but he thinks that he saw you leaving Isahaya in the direction of the Gulf of Shimabara."

Dirk thought quickly, deciding to do away with circumlocution. "Goto was not mistaken, Mori-san. I was there. In confidence, I tell you that some of us of the Company are worried about events over yonder."

Mori's expression did not change, but Dirk felt somehow that he was relieved. "Worried?" he repeated. "About your trade?"

"That's only part of it," answered Dirk.

Mori began to speak rapidly. The story he told followed closely that which Caron had outlined at the factory only the night before.

But there were more details. Not long before, a new Daimyo, on orders from Tokyo, took up a fief in the district. Normally, he would have left his own suite of officers, retainers and what soldiers he was allowed at his former estate, ready to serve the new incumbent. But this man had brought a vastly swollen train with him, displacing the retainers of the former Daimyo, who were thus thrown, without resources, onto the land. Then the Daimyo, accustomed to living most luxuriously in a rich fief, saw no reason to cut down his lush and rather riotous scale of living. His taxes picked the bare bones of the countryside. His tax collectors swooped mercilessly on any delinquent, recommended increased taxes, swooped again.

52

"They are merciless," concluded Mori.

Dirk eyed him somberly. "This can't go on. Something will happen."

"It cannot go on," said Mori. He was silent for a moment, then said, "But it must."

"It must?" echoed Dirk. "How in the name of — well, there will come a breaking point, one way or the other."

"It must not come," repeated Mori. He dropped his voice. "I tell you this, Yang-san, that you may understand — you and Caron-san. It must not go beyond you, for the knowledge is dangerous and confined to very few — perhaps to no others on Hirado than my own retainers. The poor folk over yonder — some simple peasants, others ruined samurai who served under my father — look to me for guidance. From time to time, I slip over to the Gulf of Shimabara to advise them."

"They plan a rising?" asked Dirk quickly.

Mori's hand slapped on the thick matting. "No. That *must* not happen. For one thing, the Imperial armies would sweep down across Kyushu. You, who have learned so much of my country, do not need to be told what would happen to those unlucky rebels who lived — but who would not live much longer. But more important than that — they would be rising, not against the local lords in Kyushu, but against the Shogun in whose name the lords act. And in whose name does the Shogun act?" His voice sank to a whisper. "In that of O Tenshi-sama, of the Emperor. To rise would be to strike at the Divine Presence."

"They realize that?"

"I try to keep it in their minds. Some hotheads are shouting that the lords and the Shogun are twisting the Emperor's wishes. They say if they rise, it is to protect him. Some are secretly bringing out the old Christian banners. They would make it a holy war instead of a revolt."

"And you work alone to keep them calm?" asked Dirk.

"Luckily, no. I have friends over there — working all the time," answered Mori.

"Will you be able to keep the sparks away from the powder?"

"I think so. But it will be difficult. There is much trouble with the older men who've spent most of their lives as soldiers. They know only the sword and the arrow. Many served with my father, as I told you, which gives them a hold over me. It is not fitting to dispute with one's elders. I think — yes — that we may keep the peace across there, though."

Dirk eyed Mori with a new respect. There was no questioning his devotion to the people of Arima and Shimabara. His scanty leisure and slender means alike must all go in his efforts to find a better remedy than armed revolt. And if he failed in his attempt, his very association, regardless of motive, with the malcontents would surely mean a painful and lingering end for the last of the house of Mori. "The Empire is lucky to have such a subject as you — and the men of Arima such a friend," observed Dirk.

"What other course could I follow? It is only my duty," said Mori simply, looking surprised.

"It is hard to think of adding more cares to you, but would it be possible to let us at the factory know the pulse of Shimabara from time to time?"

"That was already in my mind. I'll get word to you or to Caron-san, whom my father esteemed. Yes, I'll gladly do that. And there is something more. Would you care to come with me, to take the pulse along the gulf with your own fingers?"

"I?" exclaimed Dirk.

"Why not? You must have reasoned that, in the event of a rising, many would be eager to show it to be fomented by Christians — and you at the factory are Christians. It all may involve you, and you'll be better guided if you see with your own eyes."

Dirk's hands tightened in excitement. What he might see and hear in Mori's company would be invaluable. Out of it, he and Caron could shape a fairly sure forecast of a part of the future. Then doubt struck. "Will your people over there accept me — a Komo?"

"A Komo who accompanies me will not be questioned," said Mori quietly. "I do not know just when I shall go, but I'll send word to you by Goto. The call may come unexpectedly, so be ready at any time."

The sun was still bright when Dirk walked back through Hirado village. He thought over what he had learned from Gentaro Mori. In some ways, the picture was even worse than Caron had painted. Of course Mori knew nothing — and Dirk knew better than to tell him in view of Caron's warning — of the great plan that would siphon off the bulk of those men and their fellows and send them south against Manila and Macao. If Mori could manage to keep the peace over there until recruiting actually started, all would be well.

Dirk followed the harbor road that led on past the Company foundry to the sea wall and the Dutch houses. The wide doors of the great shed were open and he caught a glimpse of a white-headed man in European clothes. Martin Trelawney, the Company's Master-at-Arms, must have returned from the hot springs of Beppu where the Daimyo had sent him for a cure for his rheumatism. Then the sun, about to drop behind the western ridges, struck full on a Japanese girl who was talking with old Trelawney. She was tall for a Japanese and the sky-blue kimono and cherry-colored obi set off her slim figure to its fullest advantage. "Who the devil!" muttered Dirk. "She's never from Hirado. I've seen girls that tall around Sendai and in the north of Mutsu — "

The girl, her back toward him, turned, her wide sleeve making a graceful flutter as she pointed toward the Daimyo's palace. Before Dirk could rid his eyes of the sun's dazzle, she called out, "Good afternoon, Heer Jongh!"

Dirk snatched off his steeple-crowned hat. "Trudi — I mean Juffrouw Van Os. My apologies. I didn't recognize you — "

Trelawney, with his clean-shaven bishop's face and mane of white hair, broke in. "But I recognized her. The instant I saw her, for all I thought she was still in Batavia. I'd no more than landed from the sampan and unlocked my doors when there she stood, just as she used to in the old days." He smiled at Trudi. "Always at my heels, you were, clapping your hands when we poured out the molten metal."

"And getting into your tool boxes until you'd have to stop work and take me walking along the cliffs, watching for a school of fish coming down the straits," she laughed. "Martin, I'm afraid I plagued you badly."

"You did not!" said Trelawney emphatically. "You were sunshine in our dark shed. Eh, what a lady you've grown into — you're your mother's own self again and I'm proud I had a hand in raising you, for help I surely did!"

55

"You see, Heer Jongh, some people do recognize me — even in Japanese clothes," said Trudi.

Dirk recovered himself. "My compliments on a most becoming kimono."

She swung her foot a little so the cherry lining flashed bright over white tabi. "It's a gift from Madame Caron. You know, I'm sure that Heer Caron told her about my coming last night, and then she and her servants must have sat up until dawn sewing on it for me." She turned gracefully to show the chrysanthemum pattern that splashed over the back. "I think I'll wear Japanese clothes all the time."

That would be wise, Dirk thought. A girl going about Hirado in foreign clothes would attract every curious eye in the Daimyate. Word would spread, innocently perhaps, to Kyushu and farther. Awkward questions might be asked the Daimyo — who would be forced to answer them. But the anonymity of the kimono — Dirk nodded. "I hope you will. You agree, Heer Trelawney?"

"Let her dress like a mandarin, so long as she stays among us," said the old man. Then he caught a look in Dirk's eye that told him there was a story which, in far-off Beppu, he had missed. "Yes, yes. The kimono, by all means. Ha! That makes me think! I've snippets and tags of brocades laid away in my house. You must choose from among them, Trudi." His face grew somber. "They were bought for the girl my son was to marry."

"I remember, Martin," Trudi said gently.

As though to himself he went on, "I was the last to see him, when we tried to take Macao from the Portuguese. In a gun flash I saw him, fencing with three bearded men and singing in English and Japanese. Then no one saw him — ever." He shook himself. "No good comes of white man warring with white man in these parts."

Dirk felt an ominous chill at the mention of the Macao disaster, years ago. But *this* venture would be different.

Trelawney turned quickly from old memories. "You were asking, Trudi, to see the foundry again. It's not much changed."

Together they entered the gloomy shed, Dirk following close by Trudi, who pointed to a remembered bench, a scarred tool chest, the heavy frames that held the molds. Trelawney pointed out completed work, ready for shipment — squat, thick-trunnioned mortars, blunt-nosed carronades. "My work," he murmured. "All my own work." His hand rested on the breech of a mortar and Dirk read the words wrought into the metal, "Cast at Hirado in the month of August, 1637, for the Shogun Iyemitsu, by Martin Trelawney, Master-at-Arms."

"What things the old man has seen!" thought Dirk. Nearly forty years before, he had been wrecked off the Kyushu coast, gunner to Will Adams, the mysterious English pilot who nearly made himself Shogun. Trelawney had known those days, for he had been set to work casting guns and mortars for the Shogun, a feat beyond Japanese skill. An odd life, it seemed to Dirk, year after year casting these weapons for the Shogun alone —

Trudi called from a corner where light streamed through a paper-covered window. "Heer Jongh, do come and see this."

She and Trelawney were bent over a table where a thatched cottage stood, complete to its miniature windows. The old man touched the thatch. "Next spring I sail for England and this is a model of the cottage I'll build me in Kent."

"Next spring!" cried Trudi. "Martin, we might sail on the same ship."

"Next spring!" said Dirk quickly. "You're not — but you've only just come!"

"Didn't you know? Uncle Van Os is retiring and I'll go with him."

Dirk was surprised by an odd feeling of disappointment at her words. What difference did it make to him if she went in the spring or the fall? Anyway, in the spring he himself would be sailing south, on the deck of an eighteen-gun ship, bearing toward Manila and the crumbling Spanish Empire.

Trelawney talked on. "Yes, and here's the very bench where I'll sit in the sun and look out to sea. There I'll sit in Gillingham, not far from Chatham where the King's ships do lie. Ah, the Kentish hop fields. I last saw them in — let me see — in 1596, more than half a lifetime gone. Yet — I wonder. England calls to me, but there in Kent will my ears hear English sounds — or will they be reminding me of the boom of the great bell in the temple up there? Will I hear an English surf, or will I be listening for the break of the waves against our old sea wall?" The corners of his mouth drooped and his worn eyes were haunted.

Dirk said sympathetically, "You'll have your memories and you'll have England too, Heer Trelawney."

Trelawney touched Dirk's shoulder. "That's kindly said. I hope I'll have them both." He straightened his jacket. "Now it's time to lock up. It's a good sleep I'll have tonight, Trudi, knowing that you're on our island again. Mind you see her right to her door, Heer Jongh."

Trudi and Dirk took the road back to the factory through a soft sunset that filled the bay with a golden light. She looked up at him. "Why were you cross, all of a sudden, when Martin was showing us the cottage?"

Dirk felt pleased that she had noticed his impatience. "That must have been when I remembered going back to your house after we were through at the office," he said.

"And why should that have made you cross?"

"Because, Juffrouw, the house was dark. I had hoped I could help you with the boxes — at least with the last of them."

"You came back? I wish I'd known. I really shouldn't have bothered you about my things, but — well, you were the first person I saw when I landed. You were right there as though you had expected me."

"Yes," said Dirk dryly. "I was lucky." He shaded his eyes and looked toward a cluster of fishermen's huts on the shore side of the road. Four men in official robes, marked with the Matsura crest, were facing a respectful semicircle of villagers.

"What are they doing?" asked Trudi, following his eyes.

Before he could answer, one of the officials opened a flat leather case and drew out a brass plate that winked in the sun. A woman held up a naked baby, dangled it over the metal so its little feet touched the plate.

Dirk muttered, "I haven't seen that for years. It's the image trampling, the e-fumi, they call it. It's the old test to detect Christians. There's a crucifix or a Madonna and Child embossed on that plate and everyone from the head of the house down to the youngest baby is supposed to trample on it. See? The mother's holding up that littlest one now."

58

"You're not serious! What could that show?" asked Trudi incredulously.

"I am serious. The theory is that if there are any real Christians in a family, they'll refuse to step on the image. Then — " he paused — "they disappear rather suddenly. But *why* have they started it up again? Mori didn't say anything about it. Look — now they're moving on to the Widow Kishioka's house."

One of the officers intoned from a thick scroll. "House of Kishioka. Head of the house, Takeo Kishioka, aged two years. Other inhabitants, Mitsuo, his mother, Haru-ko and Hana-ko, his sisters."

The Widow Kishioka held her son deftly up, then slowly lowered him until his naked feet touched the brass surface. The child suddenly began to struggle, then cried piercingly, perhaps because the metal was hot in the sun, perhaps out of fright at seeing the strange officers about him.

The leading officer looked grim. "Kusaka-san! Note on the records that the head of the house of Kishioka evinced grief at the act of e-fumi." The widow caught the child to her, then wailed and pressed her forehead to the ground. Dirk caught broken words. Her son was glad to trample on the image. His tears came from awe at being presented to such high officers of the great Daimyo's court. Mother and child wept on together under the stony gaze of the officers, one of whom wrote busily on the rolls.

Trudi was indignant. "Of all the silly — why, that baby didn't know what he was doing! They can't do that! Go tell them, Heer Jongh!"

Dirk shook his head silently.

"You won't? But it's really serious. Look — I'm going to speak to the officers!" She took a quick step toward the group, was brought up abruptly by a strong hand that caught the collar of her kimono. "Let go! Do you think I'm going to stand by and see — "

Dirk's face was pale. "Don't you know you'd be picked up at once for lèse-majesté for the least protest? Those men are under the Daimyo's orders and he's under the Daikwan's and he's under the Shogun's, who pretends to carry out the Emperor's wishes. You can't do it, you, of all people." He let go her collar.

She faced him. "You have no right to stop me. And just *why* is it any worse for me than anyone else?"

He said quickly, "Because you're foreign."

"So are you!"

"Yes, but they know all about me. Don't you see, it's different in your case. You've been away a long time," he went on rapidly. "For all they *know*, you might have been sent up here to stir up the Christians."

Her dark eyes snapped. "They know I wasn't. Why, they asked me a lot of questions about priests when I landed and then sent me along in the Daimyo's own barge. It seems to me, Heer Jongh, that you take too much onto yourself. Please don't bother to come any farther with me. I can find my own way home." She walked off rapidly toward the factory.

Dirk started after her, then slowed down. "What's the use?" he said to himself.

The officials had now moved on to another family, leaving the Widow Kishioka weeping and white-faced in her doorway. Dirk wished that he dared go to her and console her. In all probability the report would be filed away in Nagasaki and forgotten, but the fear of incurring displeasure would leave a deep scar in the widow's mind.

Hands in the pockets of his baggy breeches, he walked on, lost in thought. If only the Manila-Macao coup could be set in operation at once! In that plan lay the answer to most of the questions which gnawed at him.

A new week had begun and the esplanade along the sea wall glowed like the tulip beds of Holland. Merchants from Yamaguchi, from Hiroshima, Osaka, Nagoya, and even from the lost peninsula of Noto had set up their booths in front of the factory. Long strips of green or red or blue bunting, marked with the merchant's name in white characters, fluttered and danced in the wind from the light wood frames. The bunting blew back to show deep-hued bolts of silk, rolls of brocade on which white phoenixes rose from beds of golden flame against a pale blue ground. Narrow shelves held carved ivories, painted fans, incrusted lacquer boxes, more silk. Toward the inland end of the esplanade, plainer booths gave out a reek of salt fish, of tangy packs of seaweed, the sharp smell of daikon or the scent of shoyu sauce in squat earthenware jars.

Dirk went from booth to booth with Van Os and Becker, bargaining, joking, chaffing while Van Os took careful note of each transaction and Becker fumed over each long exchange of compliments, each pause while they took tea with a merchant. His elbow was always in Dirk's ribs as the latter chatted on with seeming aimlessness, scrupulously observing the countless formulae that led up to the clinching of a deal.

Dirk, intent on his work, found it difficult to maintain a semblance of politeness to his superior. Besides, he was uncomfortably aware of Trudi, lovely in a dark red kimono marked with the flying cloud pattern, standing by a lacquer booth. At her elbow, bowing and laughing, was handsome young Souza from the Portuguese factory at Nagasaki, his skullcap gay with a scarlet tassel and his light full cape glinting with heavy clasps of Chinese silver.

Since the day of the image trampling, Dirk had had no real chance to talk to her. On their rare meetings she had been distantly polite. He had offered to go with her and her uncle when she called on the Daimyo, at the latter's command, but she had said, pleasantly enough, that she could manage quite well alone. That very morning he had sent her a note, offering to guide her through the booths and help her choose the things that she was buying to take to Holland. She had declined, saying that she couldn't think of taking him from his duties.

The crowd thickened. A few officers from the palace strode haughtily about. Painted girls, their hair lacquered and bows of their obis knotted in front in sign of their calling, walked daintily with lowered eyes, each attended by a watchful old woman with shaven head. A juggler danced lightly along the combing of the sea wall, shouting as he kept a whirl of glittering knives in the air. A blind beggar stood by the booth of rich Ozawa and beat his head against a tambourine-like tray, crying, "Dozo — dozo, please — please."

Emerging from a booth where a complicated deal had been arranged involving several bales of seaweed to be exchanged for coral goods from the island of Tomie just to the south of Hirado, Dirk glanced out at the harbor. A string of lighters was pushing away from the sea wall. Beyond them heavy sampans worked south to the Kawachi anchorage and the *Roode Hert,* their decks piled high with smooth wooden boxes all bearing the mark of the Besshi copper mines. The sale was going well, and the temper of the people reassured Dirk a little. If only Caron were there! He had vanished in his usual mysterious fashion the day that Dirk had called on Mori. Madame Caron could give him no hint of where he had gone or when he would return. She had left him sunning himself lazily in a wicker chair in the garden. A few moments later she had come to look for him. The chair was empty, but down in the harbor a sampan was pushing out and she could easily make out his tall figure in the bow.

Becker was leaning over the sea wall calling to lame Aoki, the head boatman. Knowing that the Director would be busy for some time, Dirk stopped by an oden-ya and bought three little roasted birds, neatly skewered. He finished the first one, and just as he began the second, he heard a familiar laugh ring out from behind the curtain at the rear of the booth, and Caron appeared, an empty skewer in each hand and two cooks following him, nudging each other. Caron waved a skewer. "Dirk! I've just found an old friend here! This is Tanaka-san and his eldest son. They've come all the way from Korai-bashi in Osaka to sell their oden at our bazaar."

Dirk forgot his remaining birds. "Let's find a quiet corner if we can. I've been busy since you left."

"Where is our revered Director?" asked Caron, laying down his skewers.

"Blasting at poor old Aoki. Luckily, he won't be able to understand what Becker's saying, but he'll have to wait until he's through," said Dirk. "Let's slip out behind the buildings."

Caron strolled carelessly after him, wiping his fingers on a bit of soft paper. In the rear of the main offices, Dirk turned. "I saw Mori."

"I know, I heard that over in Kyushu. Mori has sent word to his friends there that you're a man to trust. That's going to be valuable, Dirk. What did you get from Mori?"

Briefly Dirk gave the gist of his conversation, Caron listening gravely and nodding from time to time. When Dirk had finished, Caron said, "Yes. You've filled in several gaps I didn't know about.

So Mori wants to keep people quiet over there. Good. So do others. I think they can do it."

"We can hope, at least," said Dirk. "But there's one other thing." He told of the image trampling and Caron looked very grave.

"Dirk, I'm afraid I came back too soon. I'm sure it hadn't started over there, up to last night anyway. I don't like it. You're perfectly right in thinking that it's by no order of Matsura. It comes from the Daikwan or the Shogun. I think I better get to Kyushu again. Perhaps I'll go today."

"But suppose a call comes from Mori?" said Dirk. "I'll have to go at once. Do you want both of us in Kyushu at the same time? Lord knows what might be happening here and neither of us on the spot."

"We'll have to risk it. I think it'll be safe, though. I met a rather remarkable man over near Arima on the Gulf of Shimabara. From what he told me, I think you'll have no immediate call."

"Who was he?"

Caron shrugged negligently. "A man I met partly through arranging ferry passage for a dozen oxen in Isahaya, and partly through identifying the maker of a very fine sword which the owner wanted to sell. Yes, the meeting was most interesting. He's a gentle old soul who looks very much like our good friend Matsura. His name —" Caron paused, flicked a bit of dust from his laced cuff — "his name is Fra Hilario."

Dirk stared. "A priest?"

"A friar. He got himself smuggled ashore somehow from Macao. He found, he tells me, plenty of Christians to shelter him. He's going to help us a lot, Dirk. He's preaching nonviolence and the people seem to be listening to him."

Dirk whistled. "Verdomd! If he's caught —"

Caron sighed. "I know. So does he. I think that Mori better hear about him. Would I find him at his house now?"

"No. He's at the palace, but he'll be off duty until three."

"Good," said Caron. "I'll go up there now. Meet me at my house at noon and we'll see what more we can fit together." He waved and swung away toward the village at a brisk pace.

Dirk returned to the esplanade, wondering if Becker had noticed his absence. He was relieved to see the bearded man speaking Dutch very loud and holding up seven fingers to one of the shaven old women, whose pretty charge waited patiently a few feet off.

There was a light touch on Dirk's elbow and he turned, looking down in surprise at Trudi. Her eyes were troubled. She said gently, "I'm sorry, Heer Jongh. I didn't know, you see."

"Sorry?" echoed Dirk.

"Yes. I was angry with you when I should have thanked you. But I only just heard what you did for me when I landed. Then I understood why you had to move so quickly at the image trampling."

"I didn't do anything when you came here, except to go through the usual formalities at the palace," said Dirk.

She looked gravely at him. "I heard the whole story from an officer at the palace. His name's Toda and he looks like a skull. Of course, he didn't tell *me*—a mere woman. But he did tell Heer Souza while I was with him. I feel very badly that I treated you as I did, Heer Jongh."

"Toda was exaggerating," said Dirk, mentally cursing the xenophobic officer of the palace. "He hates all foreigners. He just said that to make you feel uncomfortable. Why, look at your call on the Daimyo. I heard that he gave you a nest of lacquered boxes, and let you hear his cricket sing."

"Heer Jongh, it's better, really, that I know. You see, Heer Souza had learned the whole story over at Nagasaki. It seems everyone was talking about it. But I do thank you for what you did, and thank you for trying to keep me believing that I just sailed in here without any trouble."

"Well, it's all over now," said Dirk.

"Yes, it's all over, but I don't forget. Now I can stay here happily until the time comes to sail. There'll be no more trouble." She smiled up at him suddenly. "Are you very busy now, Heer Jongh? I do so want to get one of those ivory Dutch trumpeters for my uncle. I've been from one booth to another and no one seems to have them."

All care and worry left Dirk. "A trumpeter? We'll find a whole regiment of them. This way—Anoné! Yamamoto-san! Genzan Yamamoto-san! Bring out those boxes that you've been keeping against a higher price. Juffrouw Van Os wants a trumpeter."

V

Ruined Castle

OCTOBER was ten days gone — October, the godless month, when all the deities of the Japanese Empire fly from their shrines to the ancient temple of Idzumo on the Japan Sea, leaving the land to the sole care of fat Ebisu, god of wealth and commerce. Now the gods had all streamed back to their eager devotees. Every temple in the Empire was swept and garnished. Gold lacquer and red gleamed in dim recesses where gorgeous-robed Buddhist priests intoned. Clean and bare were the simple shrines where white-robed Shinto ministrants chanted. In temple courtyards, in city and village streets, booths crowded thick, hangings and banners blowing in the wind. Along the canals of Osaka and Kyoto sampan and barge drifted, lantern-hung. Thick-voiced gongs throbbed and boomed in pine groves about Nagasaki and Hiroshima. Along the path from the temple behind the Daimyo's palace on Hirado a long procession moved, white-robed men towing huge painted floats a-dance with banners. Ahead and behind, groups of bikuni, half nun, half beggar, walked in gay parade, the hill winds plucking at their ceremonial kimonos and quivering to the steady beat of hand drums and the blare of conches.

The din of the cortege rolled on toward the horseshoe bay, carried by the glass-clear air to the sea wall where Dirk watched impatiently while a sampan was prepared for him. At last lame Aoki shouted, "Dekimash'ta! All ready!" Dirk was about to spring aboard when he caught sight of Caron, motioning to him from the door of the office. Dirk joined him and the Frenchman said in a low tone, "Where are you going to meet Mori?"

"I'm to go straight to the old castle at Hara. He'll be there."

"Then good luck. Don't forget to look in on those people I told you about if you get a chance."

"Trust me," said Dirk over his shoulder as he strode across the esplanade and down the steps to the sampan.

Dirk shouted "Cast off!" and the sampan edged away from the float. From the esplanade came a cry, "Oh, Heer Jongh! Wait for me!" Trudi appeared with Nobu puffing behind her under the weight of a straw trunk.

Aoki backed water and brought the sampan to the wharf. Dirk struggled between pleasure at seeing Trudi and the urgency of his mission. "I'm afraid — " he began.

She glided down the steps. "If you could take me with you —"

"I wish I could, but I've got to get off right away, Juffrouw. We're making straight for Isahaya on the Gulf of Omura," said Dirk.

"But that is perfect — if you could just make room for me. You see, the Widow Niwa, a friend of my mother's, has asked me to visit her and I wrote and said I'd come today. I heard the servants say that you were leaving, so I came right down." She sighed. "Of course, I could wait for the afternoon sampan, but then I'll get there so late — about sunrise tomorrow."

"Where is the Niwa house?" asked Dirk.

"Not far beyond Isahaya, by the foot of Mount Unzen, Madame Niwa says."

Dirk held out his hand. "Get in, Juffrouw. I'll be able to see you most of the way there. When we land, I'll get you a palanquin, and you'll have an easy trip."

"Oh, thanks so much, Heer Jongh," said Trudi as she stepped into the stern. "Nobu can take my trunk up forward." She settled herself on the cushions of the stern with a grateful smile at Dirk.

Dirk was relieved. He would have her company on the run down the straits and deep into the Gulf of Omura, where he could see her well on her way without deviating from his course. The Kyushu shore came closer and Trudi recognized places where she had rambled as a child. The sampan headed south and she watched the steep cliffs slide past. The sea rushed into mysterious caves and crannies, burst in a grumbling roar and poured hissing into the straits again. Now and then gusts of silver spray glinted in the sun among the treetops as some sea surge battered its way through a rock tunnel to hang between green and blue and then die in a rustle of vanishing drops. Red lacquer and black shone among the trees where a high torii, like a doorless and wall-less wooden gate,

66

straddled a path to show that a Buddhist temple lay somewhere beyond.

Trudi was content to watch quietly, absorbing the beauty of the island-dotted waters. Dirk sat just below her, pleased by her presence while his mind was busy with speculations on what he might see and hear on his trip deep into the fistlike peninsula of Shimabara. With sail set, the sampan plowed on past beach and village, sharp hill and narrow valley, while the mountains of inner Kyushu rose sharper and sharper to the east. When the sun was high eels and rice and raw red fish with pickles were served, neatly packed in black boxes. One of Aoki's men brought tea. Trudi, her chopsticks poised, looked at Dirk's box. "You've got the same things I have!"

"Of course. You know how the Japanese are. One sort of meal for a short sea voyage, another kind when you're going over the mountains to see a sick uncle and a third if you're going to an officer's funeral."

She finished her box, mechanically stirring the last of her rice into her tea, which she drank to the last drop. Dirk grinned at her. "So you remember the ceremony of the last grains?"

"I ought to. My nurse used to stand over me at each meal to be sure I used them with my tea. And I remember this, too." She snapped her wooden chopsticks in two, tossed them overboard. Now no inferior would be unduly honored by using the same chopsticks, and no superior offended, even though unknowingly. She beckoned to Nobu to take the empty cups and boxes, then sighed with deep satisfaction. "I've enjoyed this all so much, Heer Jongh. It was good of you to let me come."

"It's been a pleasure for me, Juffrouw. Besides, you brought us good winds and a good tide. You must be in the graces of Kompira, the god of travelers. Look there."

Off the port bow, and still well ahead, a white castle shimmered in the sun, its outsloping walls standing like a cliff against a green background and its many slant-roofed turrets lifting their silver tiles to the sky. "Beautiful!" cried Trudi. "What is it?"

"The castle of the Omura family. It's pretty, but your friend Trelawney's guns and howitzers have ended its usefulness. We're going to land at the town below the castle."

"At Omura?" she said, startled. "But I want to go beyond Isa-haya."

"That's where we were heading, but this is right on your road inland and I can get you better transportation here."

"You changed your course for me? That's very thoughtful of you, Heer Jongh."

"Not at all. As a matter of fact, we'll really save time that way," said Dirk, watching the thatch and tile of Omura town drawing nearer.

The sampan swung shoreward, grated against a low wharf. Dirk sprang out, held out his hand to Trudi, who balanced herself on the broad thwart. "Steady," he said encouragingly. "There's another wave coming in. Wait for it and then take your step." It was a very small wave but at least it was an excuse for her soft hand to lie in his an instant longer.

She gave a skip, her geta clacking on the stones of the wharf. "Oh, I thought I was going to go right into the water. I —" Then her face went pale and she looked past Dirk. "Who is that?"

At the end of the wharf a man in official robes marked with the Matsura crest came toward them. Trudi whispered, "Isn't that the man who blamed the baby for crying over the e-fumi, the image trampling?"

Dirk wondered what one of Matsura's officials could be doing at Omura and what he wanted with them. Could someone have learned the real reason for his presence here? He tried to sound reassuring as he said, "Oh, that's only Oda."

Then to his surprise, Oda halted, bowed, came on, bowed again. It was his first chance, he said hissing and bobbing, to speak to the daughter of an old friend. Yes, Van Os-san was a Komo who really thought like a samurai. When he had left for Batavia he had presented Oda with a dwarf pine tree over two hundred years old. If the daughter would call at Oda's house, during his absence, one of the women — his wife or daughters — would be honored to show her the pine which still flourished. Yes. Oda-san was now a powerful official, but in his junior days, Van Os-san had shown him many kindnesses.

Trudi could hardly believe her ears. Other Japanese men on Hirado had spoken of her father in such terms — but Oda! She

68

recalled the glacial impersonality of his face at the image trampling in stern disapproval of the child's cries. Now he seemed almost pathetic to her, humbling himself to speak to a mere girl because she was the daughter of a Komo who had befriended him. She took refuge in etiquette, inquired about his health, that of all the male members of his family. Oda acknowledged her courtesy with a compliment. As for himself, he had come to Omura the day before to celebrate a feast for his brother's eldest son, a fine young gentleman of seven. Happening to be near the waterfront, he had seen the Company crest on the sampan's sail and had at once hurried to the wharf to see if he could be of service to his friends, the Komos.

When he had bowed himself away, Trudi turned to Dirk. "I can't believe that's the same man."

"It is. You saw him at work the other time. Now he's at leisure. It makes a big difference with the Japanese. Do you mind waiting here with Nobu? I'll see about horses and a norimono for you." He strode off toward the buildings at the end of the wharf, calling. Trudi saw three or four Japanese pop out of a shed with a long stable built on to it. They began to stamp their feet, hailing Dirk as "Wakai-san," a direct translation of the English form of his name. Dirk answered addressing one of them, obviously the leader, as "Tochimenya" or "Acorn-face." The group vanished into the shed. It was remarkable how easily Dirk moved among those stable people whose nicknames he knew and who had a special name for him. She had heard that he was equally at home in Matsura's palace. Her uncle had said that perhaps some day men would speak of Dirk as they now spoke of Caron or of Willem Janz of an earlier time.

Dirk emerged from the shed and a swarm of little men with trussed-up robes scurried about. Trudi watched while they slung a palanquin, fore and aft, between two shaggy, ponylike horses that were shod with woven straw. By the head of each animal trotted a man with a bag of fresh horseshoes for the hoof coverings would have to be renewed every few miles.

Trudi flung back the curtains of the palanquin and slipped inside where she could stretch out at full length. Nobu tumbled into a plainer conveyance behind her as Dirk called, "All ready?" He waved to her from a sad-faced horse whose saddle was a high, box-like affair from which his long legs dangled on either side of the beast's neck. The attendants shouted and the little procession clopped off along the soft dirt road that ran inland along the gulf. The motion of the palanquin was pleasant and she settled herself to watch the waterside huts give way to cool bamboo groves, the bamboos to shimmery rice fields. Such a beautiful land and so friendly. She looked forward to her visit at the Niwa house with increasing pleasure.

From his horse Dirk called down to her, asking if she were quite comfortable. "This is better than the sampan," she said. "Are you going to ride along beside me?"

"In a few moments. I want to talk to the betto, the head groom, and then ride on a little. I'm looking for a hermit's hut in a pine grove somewhere along here." He shook his bridle and cantered off, his shoe bearer trotting nimbly beside him.

From the palanquin Trudi looked right and left onto level plains that led up to climbing ridges. The gulf was no longer in sight and the life about her had changed abruptly from maritime to agricultural. Vague brown roads wound over the levels, joined in knots about village or hamlet, wandered on. At her right, a score of houses clustered about a crossroads that formed a sort of square or market place. It was full of people and she could hear their shouts, thin and clear. The village must be having some kind of festival, she thought, for while the streets were crowded, the open square was empty. A man capered out into the open, going through all sorts of antics. The village clown, of course. And despite the fine weather he wore one of the shaggy, porcupine-like minos of woven straw, the raincoat of the peasant. He darted this way and that, as though trying to run down one of the crowded streets, but at each turn men shoved at him with the butts of long poles. There would probably be a flask of sake as prize if the clown managed to turn the laugh onto the men with the poles. She was sure that he would, for he jumped so comically and dodged with such nimble steps. Now he would —

Chalk-white, she stiffened, and her fingers hooked over nothing. Then she cried, "Dirk!"

There was a clop of hoofs and a strong hand pulled down the

curtains between her and the village. She cried again, "Dirk!" heard someone drop to the ground and dart between her lead horse and the end of the palanquin. Dirk, bent nearly double, appeared on the open side, tense and grim-faced. He said hastily, "One of those village festivals. Harmless enough, though they usually go far beyond what we think is decent. I hope you saw nothing offensive." His quick, stilted words came vaguely to her.

"But that man's hands were tied behind him and his straw coat was burning! The others had spears and pikes!" Face in her hands, she rocked back and forth.

"Oh — that." His voice sounded thin and uncertain. "That's part of one of the village games. The straw's all wet, you see. Just makes a lot of smoke and —"

She cried, "No! I saw it, I tell you." With a quick motion she ripped away the right-hand curtain and the whole plain was before her. The spearmen were at the east end of the village, leaning on their weapons. Across the open fields a man ran desperately. A pool of yellow smoke hung over him and red-gold flames licked up through his straw coat. Head down, he raced on, smoke and flames growing thicker. Suddenly he vanished over the edge of a deep ravine, rock-studded, that cut the plain beyond the fields.

There were fresh shouts from the village. She tried to cover her eyes, but her hands fell to her lap. More spearmen were dragging a naked girl into the square. Other struggling, nude bodies appeared, long hair afloat, as they were driven on toward wide bamboo frames where men stood with coiled ropes.

Dimly she heard Dirk's strained voice. "Keep your curtains drawn. It's just the new Daimyo Nagato's men trying to enforce more taxes. You're perfectly safe. There's no danger for you. We'll have you at the Niwa house very soon. That family's beyond Nagato's reach."

"No! No! Take me home, home to Hirado!"

Standing by the palanquin, Dirk looked down at her. Then he glanced over the top toward the village. The spearmen were shouting, passing flasks from hand to hand. Others were carrying the frames, each with a naked girl strapped to it, into a wide house. One by one the captors trooped in after the laden frames.

He said abruptly, "I'll send the betto and the rest along with you. You ought to find Aoki still at Omura. If he's gone, send word to Oda — but *don't* tell him why you're changing your plans!"

Her mouth quivered as she said, "I'm to go to Omura with these people? I'm afraid. I can't help it. Do come with me."

"I'm sorry. I can't."

"But how do we know what's happening between here and Omura now? Suppose other men like those down there should stop our horses?"

He shook his head. "I have to go on."

She started to protest, then saw the expression on his face. She rallied herself as best she could. "I think I understand, Dirk. It's for the Company. I'll go to Omura. Oh, if I could only forget what I've seen!"

He bent from his clumsy saddle. "Just remember, none of this touches you. And believe me, if I possibly could I'd see you aboard the sampan."

"I know you would. Now don't worry about me. I'll be all right."

Dirk signaled to the leading hostler and the little cortege turned, started back toward Omura and the gulf. He watched the palanquin swaying along the road. "I wish that I could go with her. Gunst, how she pulled herself together after a sight like that! And she called me Dirk. She's never done that before."

Light was fading as Dirk struck the neck of land that divided the Gulf of Isahaya from that of Tachibana to the south. He saw no more parties of Nagato's men, but much of their handiwork. There were gutted cottages, a charred body or two in a dooryard. On the edge of a ditch a severed head lay, a rude crucifix jammed into the bloody jaws. By a signpost a girl crouched, huddling a few rags about her and staring out of cold, vacant eyes.

Dirk tried to force all emotion from his mind, to fall back on sheer reason. What lay behind Nagato's swift, vicious raids? He was known to be violently anti-Christian, but that would account only for chance manifestations such as the crucifix and the severed head. What did the mass looting and killing mean? The most likely answer was that Nagato, utterly ignorant and careless of his new fief, had arbitrarily set tax rates and then farmed out the collection of them to his bailiffs, who would turn over to him a fixed amount and pocket any surplus by way of fee. Why should people submit to such treatment, rather than rise?

His road now swung inland, onto the Shimabara peninsula proper. The Gulf of Isahaya was behind to his left and the Bay of Ariake shimmered to the north. Later his horse was halted for a second relay of shoes, then cantered on, following the track that wound through a thick growth of shiny-leaved pomegranates which gave way to heavy-trunked cedars.

Suddenly, something thin and taut struck him across the chest, catapulted him to the ground. He rolled to his feet, snatching at the two-handed Japanese sword that hung by his saddle. An unseen form clamped onto him from behind and he dropped a shoulder, threw out a leg in a writhing twist. The judo trick was successful and he saw a ragged man land heavily among some roots. But there were more hands, more clutching arms, a harsh rope that pinioned him.

It was quite dark among the trees where his captors dragged him, but he could see fairly well. That there were several of them was apparent from heavy breathing in different keys behind him. Directly in front of him a man in a trussed-up kimono and flat lacquer helmet leaned on a sword and seemed to be eying him keenly. Then a level voice asked, "What brings a Komo to the shores of Ariake-umi?"

Dirk, secretly testing his bonds, answered, "Business of the Dutch East India Company, under a treaty executed by the Shogun Iyeyasu and renewed by the Shogun Iyemitsu."

The man stepped closer. "What commerce can there be now on the peninsula?"

"That is what I came to see, being a trader," said Dirk evenly.

"Your people have bought up treasures like dirty straw from men who had to sell or starve. Nothing is left. You know that. Once more, why are you here?"

"For many reasons, as any trader knows. One reason might be something like this." With the toe of his buckled shoe he hastily scratched in the dirt, where faint light still shone, two simple arcs that crossed at their upper ends.

Metal winked dully and Dirk's bonds dropped in coils about his

73

ankles. The man bowed deeply. "That reason is enough. Are you expected?"

"I was told I might meet friends, whose names I was given. Not having the honor to be informed of yours — " Dirk left the sentence unfinished.

"And one name perhaps was Suzuki?"

"The name I have heard, but not in connection with the peninsula," said Dirk.

"Another might have been Tokisada?"

"All things are possible," said Dirk. "Still another might have been Shiro Nirado-san."

"That is enough. I am Nirado-san. I did not know of your coming or we would have let you pass."

"You didn't know?"

Nirado shook his head. "I've just come up from Amakusa, where matters are very bad. You were to meet Gentaro Mori-san?"

"Either him or Tokisada-san, who had been told about me."

Nirado straightened his basinlike helmet, eyes on the ground. Then he called to his men, telling them to stay by the ambush that had trapped Dirk. He turned to the latter. "I'll take you on to Tokisada-san — or at least, I'll take you where he's apt to be. There's your horse. Don't worry about the rope that knocked you out of your saddle. It's only pulled taut when someone's coming who looks suspicious to us. Your name? Ah — Yang-san. I believe that I have heard it mentioned with that of Caron-san. I regret your fall as much as I admire your judo. You threw Taniguchi most skillfully."

Dirk mounted the clumsy saddle, strapped on his sword again and followed Nirado through the swift-falling dusk. The Japanese left the road and wound across country, climbing rough spurs and dropping into deep ravines. Sometimes Dirk rode along a knife-edge crest, high in thin cool air while many hundred feet below him waterfalls gurgled and muttered. At other times, his mount floundered down the bed of a stream or moved breast-deep through a heather-like growth. By a fantastic mass of boulders where acrid steam welled up from a hot spring he reined in as he heard a plaintive bleat behind him. From the darkness, his shoe bearer, whose very existence he had forgotten, panted up beside him, knelt, re-

74

placed the worn straw shoes, then smacked the horse on the rump and resumed his own easy trot.

It was hard to keep Nirado's squat, broad-shouldered figure in sight, as the broken ground vied with the night in creating fresh difficulties. There were other things that bothered Dirk as well. He could see nothing, hear nothing definite, but he had the impression, deepening with each mile, that others were moving in the same direction, unseen and unheard. Yet each open space, vaguely lit by a young moon, showed empty save for the two horsemen and their respective shoe bearers. Dirk was sure that he heard running feet, hushed voices in a bamboo grove, but when he entered, the long cathedral-like lines between the slim trunks were vacant. Feet splashed in a rice field, but when the riders mounted the dikes that marked holding from holding, the surface of the water was unbroken. All at once Nirado threw up his hand and Dirk halted. The ground before him was open and sloped gently to the east, ending at sharp-edged cliffs whose bases, far below, must be washed by the waters of the Gulf of Shimabara. Dead ahead, outlined against a rising moon, roofless towers loomed, jutting from crumbling, outsloping walls and chaotic heaps of masonry.

Thickets rustled close by and then Dirk heard a voice call, "Ma! Yang-san! Welcome to the Castle of Hara."

Dirk and Nirado swung to the ground while their shoe bearers bowed and hissed in awed respect. Gentaro Mori, tall and broadshouldered, emerged from the darkness, a shorter slimmer man at his elbow, whom he introduced as Tokisada. Mori took off his helmet. "You had no trouble finding us, Yang-san?"

"It was your men who found me," Dirk replied. Then he told Mori what he and Trudi had witnessed on the road from Omura.

Mori sighed wearily. "How can it end?" he muttered.

"End?" said Dirk. "It can end by Nagato's men killing off all the people who pay taxes. What can they expect to gain?"

Tokisada said somberly, "By killing the head of a delinquent house, the bailiffs gain title to the land. They do not think beyond that, nor do they realize that they themselves assume the tax burden. As for their violence, they claim that all these people have hidden wealth and they hope to make them disgorge by torture or death. It has happened."

75

"They need only look at those people to see they've got nothing," Dirk said solemnly.

"There are always daughters to sell," muttered Nirado. "Or so the bailiffs claim."

Dirk turned to Mori. "Has no one told the Shogun how this fief is being run? Just as a matter of keeping the peace of the land, he ought to put an end to such conditions."

Nirado said sharply, "You take it on yourself to say what the Shogun *ought* to do?"

Mori interposed soothingly, "Yang-san translates his thoughts from his own tongue, which has meanings hard to put into Japanese. No, Yang-san, no word from us has reached the Shogun. You see, he himself appointed Nagato and to criticize or complain would be to question the judgment of the Shogun, who speaks for the Emperor. It would only make matters worse. Of course, if Nagato himself offended the Shogun, that would be different."

Dirk felt the futility of trying to force reason through a maze of centuries-old usage and convention. "What will you say to your people tonight, Mori-san?" he asked.

Mori ran his hand along the two up-sweeping horns that framed the dragon on his helmet. "First I must judge their temper. Come. It's time to start."

The four men crossed the plain toward the gaping walls of Hara. Dirk saw moonlight sifting in broad bands through the breaches, saw solid stretches, more gaps in the outer wall that shut in nearly a square mile of broken ground. He followed Mori and the others over a cascade of stone and found the main building of Hara before him, its shattered towers throwing weird shadows over the ground.

Except for the shafts of light that broadened slowly as the moon rose, the base of the castle keep reared itself from the ink-black night. Then Dirk saw that there was life within the blackness that seemed to ripple to the movement of many men, to give out the vague humming of uncounted voices. From the shadow of the outer walls, men crept in threes and tens and twenties to the intense zone of black at the base of the keep, as the unseen people of whom he had been aware on his ride flowed from the countryside into the old ruin.

Mori made his way surely past heaps of dressed stone, stepped over fallen beams. Dirk followed as best he could, ducking from time to time to keep the fantastic outline of the helmet between him and the sky. A hand on his chest brought him up short. "Here we wait," said Mori, while Nirado and Tokisada ranged themselves beside him.

The observation point was well chosen, being formed by the angle of a wall of the keep which, to judge by random shafts of moonlight coming in through the torn walls above, dominated a wide, bowl-like space. "Aren't you afraid of spies?" asked Dirk.

"No," said Mori. "Each man will speak to his neighbor. If the reply is suspicious — it will be his last. Besides, we have the roads blocked, as you found out, and all Nagato's men are working over towards Omura. We may — Saa!" He held up his hand.

The moon, climbing higher, topped the outer walls and its light fell in a silver flood on a vast block of masonry whose far end trailed away into infinite blackness. Then, with startling suddenness an old man in farmer's clothes bounded onto the fallen stones. A murmur rippled through the night. The old man raised his hand and his voice piped out, reedy but clear.

"You know me! I am Asakawa of Arima. I led my own men through the Korean wars nearly fifty years ago. I bear wounds from Sang-ju and Syen-san. With my own hands I broke down the temple gates of Tong-nai and our troops stormed in behind me. This was in the service of the Emperor, as Asakawas have always served. For that service, we have held our lands, father to son, since the beginning of time. Now!" His arm shot out and his voice cracked. "Now, the new lord Nagato has come to this district. He — "

From the darkness came angry mutterings as men pressed closer about the great stones.

Asakawa went on. "Nagato would not have our swords. He brought with him armed strangers, unused to our ways. He brought his swarms of wenches, stewards. And for all this we others paid. Samurai like myself went into the fields with the peasants. Two-sworded men plodded behind oxen that they might live. Our women toiled with us. And all this was not enough. Taxes and more taxes. You know well the fate of those who could not pay. Time and again we have met here in the old Castle of Hara. We

77

curse, we weep. And we do — *nothing!*" His tattered sleeve fluttered as his arm swept down.

Someone near Dirk muttered, "It is true!"

The old man clenched his fists. "With all our wailing, do times mend? No! Listen to me. Yesterday the bailiffs came for Morita-san, a true samurai with whom I marched in the Korean wars. His little fields, all that he has left, could not in five years pay what Nagato demanded in six months. I found him — my old war comrade. The bailiffs had amused themselves with the dance of the raincoat. There he lay before his cottage, his charred body wrapped in charred straw."

Dirk remembered the agonized man racing over the fields beyond Arima and shuddered.

Asakawa's voice ripped on. "This very day, in my absence they came to my house — to the house of Asakawa, servant of the Emperor. They killed my daughter. My granddaughter was exposed naked in the market place, where she will be allowed to earn a little to apply against the debts assessed by Nagato's men. I do not say this because it all happened to me. It has happened over and over again." His fist shot into the air. "Pikes, I say! Pikes and swords and arrows until the last man of Arima is dead or Nagato lies in his own blood!" The old man's knees gave way. Two tall youths sprang onto the block, carried him off into the shadows through an angry buzzing.

Dirk wiped cold sweat from his forehead, and found that his hand was trembling. Old Asakawa was right, a hundred times right. And yet — if these people rose, what about the Company? He touched Mori's elbow. "Aren't you going to answer him?"

Mori shook his head and held up a hand as a clumsy, thickset man lumbered onto the stone block. "Asakawa-san speaks for the samurai," he began haltingly, as though unused to talking. "What about the peasant — the *Christian* peasant?" His voice strengthened, grew in assurance. "Like us, the samurai has toil and labor, the rain and the winds in the fields. But he also has the shelter of his noble name. What have we? Nothing but the new faith that was brought to us from over the sea. For that, we have burned, have gone to the pit and to the cross. We have seen our teachers die with us, have seen them banished. Now Nagato, with fire and cross and spear, tries to stamp out the last of that faith which we so dearly acquired. Like the noble Asakawa, I say take up our pikes in the name of the True Cross."

Dirk could see hands reaching up toward the peasant, straining out of the blackness below the block. Suddenly, he knew panic. The tide was running and nothing could stop it. He had a wild notion of slipping away from the corner of the wall, making all speed back to Hirado to warn Caron.

Out by the block, men were shouting, full-throated for the first time. They were calling Mori's name, the sound swelling and swelling until it seemed to shake the walls of Hara. There was quick motion by the block and Dirk saw Mori leap nimbly into the moonlight.

Then came a dead hush. Mori's voice rang out: "Have you gone mad, to listen to treason? Our law is the law of the gods who first settled this land for us, ages ago. We bow to those gods and to their word. And whence does that word come? From the Emperor, their heir, at his palace at Kyoto. And how do we receive it? From the lips of the Shogun at Tokyo to whom all Imperial power is delegated, whose word *is* the word of the Emperor and of the gods. Obedience to that law and that word is our life blood. We are a small nation. If we do not follow our ancient way, as a nation we die — or live as slaves to another nation, which is worse."

From the depths a man called hoarsely, "How is such slavery different from our lives today?"

Mori whirled toward the voice. "Discipline! That is our life. We live only for the Empire, which owns that life. You strike at Nagato? Then you strike at the Shogun, and through him at the Emperor and the gods. You talk about the pride of the samurai, the virtues of the samurai! From the dimmest dawn of our land, the pride and virtue and strength of the samurai have lain in the samurai's devotion to the lord above him, who holds power from the gods themselves."

A short man, bent and twisted from torture, crept into the moonlight. "What virtue is there in obedience to a lord who throws his people into slow fires — and laughs?"

Mori pointed to the twin sword hilts that showed above the man's obi. "The samurai always has his sword, which the law allows him

79

to bear. That sword is his life and his honor. He may not turn it against his lord who holds power through that same divine law, for that is dishonor. But a samurai may turn his own sword against himself in all honor."

Dirk watched the sway and shift of the crowd. So far, Mori had spoken only of the samurai and, by implication, of his dependent peasants. There was a third group. Dirk began to wonder if Mori underestimated its importance. As though his thought had reached Mori, the latter looked out into the darkness, then beckoned. On the other side of the block, the crowd parted and Mori reached a hand down. A robed friar, probably the same of whom Caron had spoken, stood beside Mori. His cowl was thrown back and the moon struck on his shaven head and on his face that was at once firm and gentle. He held up a crucifix and Dirk caught a long, steady rustle as men knelt, crossing themselves.

The friar began to speak in a low, carrying voice, marked by a strong Iberian accent. Dirk caught the words "Yaso Kuris'to . . . Seirei, the Holy Ghost . . . Roma Kyokwai . . ." He was not pleading with the people. His words flowed on as though merely restating old truths that were changeless. His flock had a surer shelter than the pride of the samurai and that was their faith. Let them cling to that. Suffering and death meant nothing, so long as the faith was maintained.

Easily he turned to practical matters. They must give Nagato no chance to start a general Christian-hunt. They must get rid of any sacred objects, for what was in the heart far outweighed picture or image. Let them do as the Christians of Rome had done in the old days. Let their houses and cottages serve as catacombs until a fuller light was abroad in the land. He absolved them in advance for any act or speech that they might be forced to do or utter in seeming blasphemy. There must be no violence.

There was a quick flutter of a robe and Mori stood alone on the block. Dirk listened tensely to the murmur of the people, trying to gauge its meaning. Certainly Mori and the friar had produced a profound impression on samurai and peasant. But was it enough? Let all these people drift away from the personal influence of the two speakers and the fires could easily flare up anew.

Mori's voice rang out again. "There is one other thing that I do not need to point out — the strongest reason of all. If you rise, others will rise. We'll have endless wars again from Hokkaido south to Kagoshima. Some men will rise in all justice, others will merely make use of them for their own purposes. Again and again that has happened."

A man struggled to the edge of the block, shouting, "Yes! But the Empire went on!"

Mori swung toward him. "It went on because in the old days, we had no one but ourselves to fear. But today!" His arm shot out. "Today, things are different. Let the old clan wars break out and you will see this. You will see the Spanish returning here from Manila. You'll see Portuguese galleons and soldiers off Nagasaki. You will see one powerful Daimyo dickering for Spanish aid to push him forward. Another will turn to the Portuguese. And then? We are in a far corner of the world, but we know what happened in Mexico and in Peru. Do you want to see a Spanish viceroy in Tokyo? Or a Portuguese governor in Nagasaki? If you do, then I tell you that you'll see viceroy and governor not through the eyes of samurai, peasant, Christian or Buddhist, but as beasts of burden — the same way the Incas and the Aztecs see them."

Dirk nodded in approval. He whispered to Tokisada, "Now he's carrying them with him. Listen!"

Mori's voice soared in peroration. "So I do not speak to you as samurai or peasant, Christian or Buddhist. I speak to you as Japanese, who know the story of Mexico and Peru, who know of the Spanish captain's boast of conquest. Strike one blow against the peace of the land and you lay a plank in the bridge over which Spanish troops will march onto our islands."

Old Asakawa dragged himself onto the block and bowed deeply before Mori. "You have recalled us to our duty. We do not count. It is all for the Empire which our gods built for us."

A thick mutter came from the crowd. "We hear. We follow the way of the gods." With that mutter Dirk knew that, unless things grew much worse, peace was assured for a time. And in that time, word would come from the Shogun that would send these men marching to the transports anchored off Nagasaki, would send them south against Manila and Macao. The Company could look forward to endless years of untold prosperity.

81

Dirk turned to Tokisada. "Surely you will have little trouble with your people now."

"I think very little. The hold of the Mori name is strong over here and he has strengthened it still more. I'll go back to the island of Amakusa and watch things there. Only — " he frowned, twisting his fingers about the hilt of his short sword — "our people down there are very restive. A spark from the island *could* reach up here. I keep Mori-san posted as best I can, but suppose that there is urgent word and my messengers do not find him."

"Let them come to me," said Dirk quickly.

"That is what I hoped you would say," said Tokisada. "Since he vouches for you as his friend, there could be no objection."

"I'll help in any way that I can," Dirk assured him. "I'll do my best to find Mori-san. If I can't — well, I'll arrange with him so that I can get in touch with the proper people over here and tell them what he wants."

Mori was making his way toward them through the crowd. Asakawa and the twisted man walked with him. There was no sign of the friar who was probably being spirited away by a group of Christians. Tokisada stepped out to meet Mori, who said, "You must let me know the least thing that happens in Amakusa, Tokisada-san."

Tokisada told him quickly of the plan he had made with Dirk. Mori glanced at the latter. "You'll do this — for us?"

"Of course," said Dirk.

"It could mean trouble for you, trouble that might reach to Tokyo itself."

"There's little danger, as I see it," Dirk said. "In any event it's a risk I'll have to take. This is about as important to us as it is to you."

Unexpectedly, Mori held out his hand, European fashion. Dirk took it as Mori said, "My people are in your debt for your offer. Now let's get our horses and make for the gulf."

As they rode side by side, Dirk said, "I was worried about your speech, until the very end."

Mori sighed. "I know my people. I had first to appeal to the samurai's code." He lowered his voice. "We hold it sacred — and yet I sometimes wonder if it fits modern times. Blind obedience to

82

your superior just because he *is* your superior. Demanding blind obedience from the man below you, just because he *is* below you. In the old days it might have been necessary, but now — "

He fell silent and Dirk knew better than to comment on Mori's thought which ran counter to every phase of Japanese life. Times would change, however, and thought and custom would change with them. With the Manila coup, Japan would step out of its centuries of seclusion and adapt itself to a larger world. Ingrowing thought and belief that had hardly changed in a thousand years would be reshaped. He felt his eyes closing as he rode on through the night, the soft pad-pad of horse and shoe bearer in his ears. He wondered how long it would take to reach the Gulf of Omura and how quickly he could find a sampan to take him the thirty-odd miles to Hirado.

He sat up abruptly. For hours Trudi had been utterly out of his mind, and yet in a way he was responsible for her. Had she found Aoki waiting? Had Oda used his powers to see that she got passage in the event that Aoki had gone?

The sun was well up when he alighted stiffly at the Omura wharf. He was relieved to learn from the head boatman that Trudi had arrived just as Aoki was pushing off, and had sailed with him. He found a sampan with little trouble and climbed into it. Farther along the shore he waved to Mori, who was getting into his own patched craft. It would never have done for the two to sail into Hirado together in broad daylight. Dirk stretched out in the stern and sleepily ran over the events of the night in his mind. What a budget of news he would have for Caron.

V I

Calm Waters

SEVERAL days after Dirk's return from Hara, Becker, at Caron's urging, threw open his new house for inspection by Japanese officials and merchants, a matter of courtesy whose omission would have been resented by high and low. Invitations, from a list carefully drawn up by Dirk and Caron, had been eagerly accepted and now Dirk stood at the second-floor landing. An open letter in his hand, he looked down into the cavernous room where the guests swarmed about trestle tables where platters of European and Japanese food stood among clusters of bottles. Heavy tapers in wrought-iron holders shone down on richly figured kimonos of black, gold-brown or gray, on shaven heads, on topknots drawn tightly from nape to crown. Becker, glass in hand, stood at the far end of the room, his bearded face alight with alcoholic amiability that would slowly darken in sullen dislike of his guests and their country. By the deep fireplace softly ablaze with driftwood against the December night, Caron carefully guarded his full-skirted azure coat against flying sparks as he explained the workings of the chimney to Matsura, whose "Maa!" and "Mezurashii-na!" of amazement could be heard above the high-pitched buzz from about the tables.

Caron had asked Dirk to stand by the head of the stairs to explain the second-floor wonders to the guests when they had finally become satiated with the ground level. No Japanese, of course, would move until the Daimyo had mounted the stairs and the old man seemed endlessly absorbed by his first real fireplace. Dirk turned to his letter again. It was over two years old and had just been delivered to him from the *Berg-op-Zoom,* weeks late on its voyage up from Java. It had come from "Ye Colonie of New Plimouth" to Amsterdam and thence to the north arm of Hirado Bay.

He held the letter close to a taper that jutted from a writhing dragon of black iron. Japhet Place, his cousin and, in old Leyden

84

days, his chief playmate, wrote a scholar's hand, but good ink and paper must have been scarce along Plymouth Bay. Also Japhet's references and allusions to people and events half a world away were hard to follow. As nearly as Dirk could make out, the settlers of Plymouth, over the years, had pushed west into a place that Japhet called sometimes "Conightcute" and sometimes "coneticott" and had set up a trading post on a river. There had been a threat of trouble when "Holanders to the number of seventy, full armed," had marched against the post from a place called New Amsterdam. Dirk was puzzled. Hollanders, marching against Japhet, himself born in Leyden! What a topsy-turvy place the New World must be. "But as we had done ye Dutch no wrong," wrote Japhet, "they parleyed and straightway marched home."

Dirk turned a page. More trouble. People from Boston had come to settle close to the post and not far from a Dutch place called Fort Goed Hoop. Jonathan Brewster, in charge of the Plymouth men, was worried, "not knowing what trouble & charge he shall be further at, for they come in dayly." Boston? But that was in Lincolnshire, in England. Jonathan Brewster? Did he mean Elder Brewster?

Completely at sea, he skimmed ahead but only floundered deeper. References to old days and people called Massassoit and Hobomok. The name Standish he vaguely recalled from earlier letters and memories. Here was Brewster again, and Bradford, but was Matianuck a person or a settlement? What was this reference to the Piscataqua? He began to feel very sorry for Cousin Japhet and all those who had gone to the Plymouth Plantation. Indians were dangerous. The country was a wilderness. Who would ever be able to cope with names like Naumkeag and Wampanoag and Aptuxcet, let alone the language from which they sprang? He turned to an earlier line. "The Pequots strive Mightily against us and menace with warre. But with God's blessing —"

He tucked the letter away as he heard shuffling steps at the foot of the stairs. Hand on the thick railing, Matsura's white-tabied feet had begun the ascent, Caron at his elbow. Dirk looked down at the pair and caught a quick glance from Caron. The Frenchman, though somewhat relieved by the account of the meeting at the ruined castle, had been unusually silent and thoughtful. Now his face showed growing relief. Dirk wondered what his superior had heard. Then he bowed to Matsura, murmuring the usual apology for remissness.

The Daimyo's wise old face brightened and he held out his hand. "In a foreign house, foreign customs, as you and Caron-san shape yourselves to our usages when you call on me. In your case, a call has been so long delayed that you deserve a rebuke." The old ivory cheeks wrinkled in a smile.

"I can only rely on the well-known mercy of the Daimyo of Hirado," answered Dirk.

"The rebuke will not be harsh," murmured Matsura. His voice dropped still lower. "By no means as harsh as the one which the Shogun has just administered to my neighbor, Nagato-san, over on Kyushu." Then in a more natural tone, "Now, Caron-san, you said that you would indulge an old man's curiosity by showing me the rest of this strange house. Maa! So many marvels I see!"

The two moved off down the corridor and Dirk found himself face to face with a swarm of elderly Japanese who had followed the Daimyo as closely as they dared. There were merchants from Hiroshima, from Nagasaki and Kumamoto and Isahaya, ship-owners from Omura and pottery men from Satsuma and Hizen. There was nothing that he could do for them. They trailed on after Caron and the Daimyo, keeping a respectful distance, stopping when their lord stopped, bowing and hissing if his head turned even slightly toward them. They opened the same closets that he did, exclaimed over everything that had drawn comment from him.

Dirk realized that he had grown very hungry and went quickly down the polished stairs into the buzz and clack of the less distinguished Japanese who either had not dared to go up so soon after their superiors or who found the trestle tables with their platters and bottles too strong an attraction. He greeted a lacquer-guild head whom he knew, exchanged compliments with the owner of a vast number of draught cattle up Karatsu way and helped himself to a slice of Westphalia ham, a cold pheasant leg and a bowl of Japanese custard wherein shredded chicken and vegetables were artfully mixed. One by one, the guests edged and sidled toward the stairs, leaving him alone. By the fireplace Becker, still amiable, laughed and rumbled with Zell and Hofmeyr, both of whom were ill at ease in the face of their superior's joviality and bored by the guests of whose tongue they barely knew a dozen words.

Setting down his plate, Dirk filled a brandy glass and drank appreciatively, one eye on the top of the stairs in case his help should be needed. Confidence as well as brandy warmed and relaxed him. The dangers yonder in Shimabara shrank and shrank as he considered them. There were Mori and the old friar. Now Matsura had told him that Nagato's excesses had at last drawn a rebuke from the Shogun. Times would be hard over there, of course. But the peace ought to hold until the Dutch ships had sailed in, ready for their freight of Japanese fighting men.

As he refilled his glass, his mind went back to his journey beyond Omura with Trudi. Since his return, her manner toward him had undergone a change, slight, it was true, but still enough to set him apart from the rest of the clerks. At the same time, there was no hint of intimacy. He sipped from his glass. She was a fine girl, no doubt about that, and a very pretty one. But in the spring, now not many months away, she would sail out of Hirado and out of his life.

His thoughts turned toward Nagasaki and the broad hints of the Portuguese Remedios that Dirk marry his daughter, whose mother was an Obama from the Satsuma country. He had never seen the girl, who lived now with her Japanese mother, but Remedios was wealthy, the Obama family prominent. Of course if he made such an alliance, with the wedding consisting of an exchange of sake cups, he might be able to bring to the Company a whole untapped field of fine pottery for which there was a good market down the China coast. Just the same—

Some of the Japanese whom timidity had prevented from going far beyond the head of the stairs now came padding back to the tables. Dirk poured sake and brandy for them, watching anxiously as a few of them mixed the two alien beverages in equal proportions in big glasses. Their voices rose higher and higher, and they began playing the scissors-stone-paper game, which involved much shouting, brandishing of fists, followed by a quick showing of two extended fingers, an open palm or a clenched hand. They bawled, "Ichi—ni—san!" as their arms shot out. They bawled again as the loser was forced to drain his glass or cup at one gulp. Dirk joined in the game, winning as his fingers, extended in the scissors-sign, met his opponent's open palm signifying paper — since scissors will cut paper — and losing when his repeated scissors met the stone of the clenched fist, since stone will blunt scissors. He was raising his fist for the third and deciding round, gambling on the hope that his adversary would not expect the scissors three times in a row. His hand started down, then hung in mid-air.

The lower half of the broad Dutch door had swung open and Trudi stood on the sill, lovely in a kimono of dense black on which were embroidered snow-laden pine boughs in sharp greens and whites and browns. Perfectly self-possessed, she surveyed the growing tumult, her hands folded across her crimson obi. Behind her, Dirk saw the big, smooth face of her uncle.

Dirk went quickly to her, an uneasy eye on the guests about the tables. Why had her uncle allowed her to come to such a gathering where the guests expected only a highly specialized addition of femininity? She smiled at him as he bowed to her. "Oh, Dirk! Doesn't the house look pretty? I'm — why I'm sure that those dragon candlesticks came from the Carons! And Uncle! That Persian rug that I found in the kura! Surely that's it, hanging from the stairs."

Dirk raised his eyebrows in understanding. The servants, he knew, had scurried from house to house in search of ornaments for the party. Thus they increased their employer's prestige and, consequently, their own, in the eyes of other Japanese.

Van Os lumbered into the room. "Do you mind looking after my niece, Jongh? Old Matsura especially asked that she come, so I brought her for a few minutes. I'll pay respects to our host for the whole family. By his looks, he's been very busy with the brandy and that always puts him in his frolics for a while at least."

Dirk offered Trudi his arm and led her to a side table away from the Japanese. He said in a low voice, "They've been as busy as Becker, most of them. We'll stay over here, out of earshot."

She colored a little. "Thank you, Dirk. But I couldn't hear anything worse than I used to hear in Batavia. You've no idea what a — well, thank you anyway. Oh, really, I couldn't eat a thing. Uncle and I dined at home and — oh, just that sliver of Westphalia ham, then. And *is* that Heer Caron's Uji tea? Yes, I'd like a cup of that."

Dirk added a chicken custard to her plate, pushed forward a heavy chair for her and tried to talk above the clack and whine of Japanese voices. As a further safeguard, he sat on the arm of her chair, a vast piece that could nearly have held the two of them. Between dainty bites she smiled up at him. Then she looked past him, calling, "Why, Raas de Groot! I was wondering where you were."

Dirk thought, "*I* wasn't!" as de Groot joined them. Almost oxlike in his stolidity in the office, de Groot now chatted easily with Trudi, saying just the right things in a perfectly natural manner. Zell and Hofmeyr soon made their appearance, but Dirk was still perched on the arm of her chair and she addressed quite as many remarks to him as to the others.

More Japanese had pattered down the stairs, heading for the tables. Their voices rose higher and higher. Someone started a song with an idiotic, meaningless refrain:

Yori-ya, aikori-yo, aikori-yo!

Trudi slid her plate and cup onto the table. "What dreadful screaming! And it just doesn't mean anything, does it, Dirk?"

Dirk signaled to his fellow clerks to make as much noise as they could. "No, Trudi. Just about an Osaka fair and then that zany chorus. It doesn't mean anything." He added mentally, "Yet!" knowing well the full-flavored verses that followed.

"Yori-ya, aikori-yo, aikori-yo!" bawled the guests, while Dirk looked about, wondering how he could gracefully and plausibly move the girl into another part of the house.

A sudden hush fell over the room and Dirk jumped to his feet. Arm in arm the Daimyo and Caron were coming down the stairs and all the Japanese faced toward them, bowing. Matsura's calm voice reached Dirk — "Ah, but you forget, Caron-san, that my father-in-law was once a Christian, even taking a Christian name. Don Bartolomeu Sumitada — " he made heavy weather of the unfamiliar *l* of the name — "and my own relative, down in the Gotos, to this day signs himself Don Antonio Matsura. Thus, as I tell you — "

89

He saw Trudi, then stopped at the foot of the stairs, smiling at her. Dirk touched her elbow. "He'll expect you to go to him and bow. I'll take you, if you like."

She was on her feet in a graceful sweep of cherry-lined kimono. "Don't worry, Dirk. Madame Caron's been drilling me in kenson."

Just as she began a low bow, Matsura held up his hand. "Gishiki wo sh'te kudasai — no ceremony, please," he said. "Thus I often met your father and your mother in the old days. Caron, my old friend, we must find her a husband among *your* people. That was how her mother married — Hollander and Japanese." The Daimyo passed on to say good night to his host, having shrewdly endorsed again for all listening Japanese, who would take his fiction far into the Empire, that Trudi had been born of a Japanese mother.

Dirk stepped out into the night to warn the Daimyo's escort of his departure. Just within range of the house lights, pike points and halberds glittered as the troops sprang to attention. From the darkness beyond, bearers shouldered the black and gold norimono, the old man's ceremonial sedan chair. In the vague light he saw the cold-eyed Toda aligning the halberdiers. Someone snapped an order to the pikemen and Dirk stared. It was not Mori's turn for duty, yet he could not mistake those wide shoulders, that tall figure, nor the old helmet crowned with a dragon. The pikemen dressed, then stood at ease, leaning on their weapons. Dirk called, "Mori-san!" and the tall Japanese in his antique armor and bear-paw shoes raised his hand in salute. "I thought you didn't go on till tomorrow," said Dirk.

Mori adjusted the two swords in his obi. "Hamada-san is sick, so I took his place, Yang-san."

"Then why didn't you come in and join us? Better have some brandy. The Daimyo'll be some time getting away from Becker."

Mori shook his head. "It is not permitted to officers on duty."

"A pity," said Dirk. Then he lowered his voice. "I heard good news about Nagato."

"Very good," said Mori. "I had the word from Tokisada-san. He writes that the effect on the people is excellent. Just the same — "

"Don't be pessimistic," said Dirk. "A slap from the Shogun is nothing for Nagato to treat lightly."

"If the slap, as you say, were really meant. I have also heard that Nagato is bringing into his fief a hundred or more roughs from Osaka."

"From Osaka?" exclaimed Dirk. "I know what they're like — the worst in the Empire. But he'll never dare use them."

"So we may hope," said Mori slowly. "Eh-to! I must go to Shimabara often. We must watch and watch and watch, Tokisada-san and I. It is difficult."

"I don't see why. You've got your sampan. No one cares what you do when you're off duty."

"It is very difficult," said Mori again. "Yes, I have my sampan. But it is an old one. I have been keeping it in a little cove near the old English factory where few people see it. The bottom is bad there and the planks have begun to start."

"Anchor at our landing. There's plenty of room. I'll speak to Aoki about it in the morning."

"You are very kind," said Mori. "But — there are people who seem too much interested in when I go out of the harbor. They must not know where. My colleague yonder, Toda-san, in particular, is far too curious. I must find a hidden cove with deep calm water. And it must be close by. But there isn't such. I know every inch of Hirado from Tsubo-saki to Shishiki-saki."

Yes, Dirk thought, if Mori's sampan went to pieces, matters on Kyushu would be complicated. Probably even the simplest repairs would be beyond Mori's means, but Dirk knew that the young samurai's pride would be mortally wounded at any offer of assistance. Again the Japanese mind, he thought. Mori invited him to witness things on Shimabara the very knowledge of which could be dangerous. Yet he would coldly refuse planks and oakum to the value of a guilder or two.

"There must be a good anchorage for you somewhere nearby, Mori-san," said Dirk. "I'll keep a discreet eye out."

Mori bowed. "I am your debtor. But there is no such place." He drew himself up. "Ah — Matsura-san comes!"

Dirk stepped aside as Caron and the Daimyo appeared in the doorway. The pikemen were filing forward while the halberdiers gave way toward Dirk. As they drew near, Dirk heard a junior officer ask Toda, "What's to be done?"

Toda ground out a few words, then called his men to attention. What had Toda said? Dirk was sure he caught the words "Ran wo bibo ni — " The meaning was clear. To crush a revolt before it started. Or was he sure? If only he had caught the verb! And even if he had interpreted correctly, might Toda not have been referring to some unrest in his own command? Doings on Shimabara could mean nothing to Toda.

The Daimyo climbed into his sedan chair as Dirk and Caron bowed to him. Then the slatted panels slid shut and the bearers heaved at the poles. Dirk nudged Caron. "Have you spoken to Mori?"

"No."

"Then you can do it inconspicuously. I've been talking to him and people would notice if I stopped him again. Tell him this." He whispered Toda's words to Caron. "They may not mean anything. But they might."

Caron frowned. "Yes. They might indeed." Then he raised his voice a little. "Well, there they go, Dirk. Ventre de dieu! Isn't that young Gentaro Mori with the pikemen? Excuse me a moment. I must at least compliment him on the smartness of his men." He strode easily across the short grass toward Mori, who brought up the rear of his little column.

Dirk entered the house, craning his neck as his eyes hunted for Trudi. He found her close by the stairs, talking gravely with a white-haired Fukuoka merchant who remembered her father. "Does every Japanese in the Empire remember him?" thought Dirk. "I wish I'd known him. I'd like to think that when I finally leave here people will speak of me a quarter as pleasantly as they do of him." The merchant backed away, bowing. Before Dirk could join her, Raas de Groot's sleek brown coat came between them and Dirk heard her say, "Oh, Raas. Have you seen my uncle? Really I think it's time that I went home. I only came for a minute, you know."

De Groot moved off through the crowd resignedly and Dirk bore down on her triumph. "A little more Uji tea? Or do you want some of that yokan, that Kyoto bean paste?"

"Oh, thank you, but Claes Hofmeyr brought me some while you were outside." Just then Becker's voice filled the room. "Does he

92

have to shout like that?" she said impatiently. "And where's my uncle? Really, I must go."

Becker was facing his guests, perfectly steady on his feet but with a flush that showed through his thick beard. "Here, you! Caron! Jongh! Tell 'em what's going to happen. I'll make 'em open their slant eyes!" A servant shoved a heavy chair into the middle of the room, slid smaller ones beside it. Becker bawled again. "Come on. Don't squat on the floor. Ga zitten! In a chair." He seized the nearest Japanese, lifted him clear of the floor and thumped him into a small chair. "There! Stay by me and I'll have you acting like white men — maybe."

Trudi whispered, "How awful! Can't someone stop him?"

Dirk moved swiftly across the floor, muttering an apology to the Japanese whom he passed. Becker slapped him on the shoulder. "That's it. Grab that one and — "

Dirk nodded, then said quickly, "Heer Directeur, they'll take to chairs quick enough, but — you know the Japanese. If you let them sit up in a chair the way you do, they'll think they're your equals."

Becker scowled, then laughed. "Right, jongen. Ha! Jongh de jongen. Smart, you are. Lie down with women but don't sit up with the men! Tell 'em to squat, then, but not to blame me if they get splinters in their rumps!"

Becker seated himself facing a broad, curtained door. Dirk nodded to the Japanese, who sank gratefully to their knees. Trudi looked at him uneasily as he rejoined her. "How *can* he say such things, even if they don't understand Dutch? And where are Raas and my uncle?"

Dirk heard footsteps above him and saw Van Os talking to one of his own servants, lent to Becker for the occasion. De Groot fidgeted by his elbow, glancing nervously down at Trudi. Dirk started to call to Van Os, but a louder shout from Becker made him turn. The curtains were drawn back, revealing another candle-lit room. Somewhere out of sight a hand drum mingled with the sharp *plank-plank* of a zitherlike koto.

"Oh! A dance!" Trudi exclaimed. "How pretty! Mother and I used to watch them in the temples at festival times. Look! Here they come!"

Feet stamped softly from right and left of the door and two thin, haggard women in cheap, gaudy kimonos appeared, their white-shod feet thumping on the floor and their arms moving in stiff gestures. They advanced toward each other, retreated, turned, came on again. Trudi laid her hand on Dirk's cuff. "Let's get closer. I want to see."

The women, faces expressionless, danced on in slow ritual. "I want to see better," urged Trudi.

Dirk turned quickly. "No you don't! Is Nobu waiting for you outside? Then she better take you up the hill if your uncle isn't ready." He made himself as broad as he could trying to shut off the inner room from her.

"Dirk Jongh!" she protested. "I know these dances. They're pretty — "

There was a clatter as Van Os started quickly down the stairs. Dirk called to him. "Heer Van Os, Juffrouw Trudi is ready to go home."

Trudi stared in sudden dismay. The dancers' gestures and poses were appallingly explicit. As the pair revolved slowly back to back, arms rose and fell in slow precision. They faced each other again, their obis dropping to the floor and their kimonos floating wide and showing stunted breasts, hip to knee kirtles of sleazy red cloth.

Dirk reached out and caught Trudi's arm. "Here's your uncle now," he said quickly, turning her toward the door as the kimonos followed the obis and the kirtles the kimonos. Trudi, face burning, hurried toward the door, her uncle following anxiously. Out in the clean air of early winter, she looked up at Dirk, who still held her arm. She said in a very small voice, "Well — at any rate, you warned me, Dirk. You tried to get me out of the house. Dirk, when you tell me things, remind me to listen to you."

Reluctantly he let go of her arm.

"And you took so much thought for me all through the evening, you and Raas and Claes," she went on.

"Obliged to you, greatly obliged," rumbled Van Os. "Now, my niece, home we go. If I'd known what Becker — ha, hum! — yes, home we go."

Dirk watched them from the stoep, caught a flutter of a white

94

hand as Trudi waved to him. Then he turned and went into the house, oddly depressed.

The dancers had gone and most of the Japanese were bidding a rather cold good night to Becker, whose asperities Caron was carefully mistranslating into suave Japanese. Dirk shook his head as he watched the faces of the guests. There was no doubt that Becker had lost whatever stature he had ever possessed in the eyes of the Japanese. That was not important. But the Company would lose too, since Becker was its head. Why hadn't the Director consulted Caron or himself about the entertainment? They could have told him that the Japanese would be mortally offended, not by the brazen indecency of the so-called dance, but that it was performed by two of the lowest-grade inmates of the Maruyama brothels, maintained solely for the diversion of the crews of the Company ships down by Kawachi. And the dance itself was not Japanese, having been brought up from rowdier ports for the delectation of common sailors. Thank God that Matsura had left before it started.

When the last guest had gone, Dirk stood on the stoep, filling his lungs with the crisp air. He had had to drink more brandy with Becker before the latter had stamped off toward the sea wall, yelling for a boat to take him to Maruyama. Thanks to a good head he felt comfortably mellow and no more, but not inclined for sleep. Then he caught a glint of light from the offices by the sea wall and strolled down to see who might be stirring there.

The door of the main office was locked, but when he rapped it opened quickly and Caron waved him in. The big table was covered with the Shogun's maps that dealt with the Manila venture and other sheets nearby showed the Frenchman's neat script. "Lock the door, Dirk, and look at some of these with me," said Caron. "We'll pick up most of our troops right down here at Nagasaki, of course. But I think we'd gain by showing our flag — and also our guns — up here at Shimonoseki. Another ship ought to sail up Osaka Bay. We can pick up the Settsu troops there."

Dirk bent over the map, his finger following the red lines that Caron had drawn to the Honshu ports. "Yes," he said. "Then — I wonder — " He touched Tokyo Bay. "Here's where our flagship ought to anchor."

95

Caron's strong-featured face showed surprise. "Tokyo Bay? In sight of the Shogun's palace? Not even Japanese ships, except the Shogun's own, can do that."

"I know. But think of this. Our finest ship *must* show itself there and dip its colors. If we don't, then all that antiforeign pack at the palace will be shouting that we've slighted Iyemitsu."

Caron shook his head. "If the venture wins, we shan't need to worry about them, although — " he rubbed his high-bridged nose — "although — yes! Parbleu! You're right, Dirk. I'll make the offer through the Daikwan. If he says no, at least we've made the attempt. If he agrees — well, I'll see to it that he and the Shogun know who made the suggestion." He dipped a quill into a carved iron inkpot that must have been fashioned in far-off Tibet and drew a neat red line up to Tokyo Bay. "You know, we ought to hear from van Diemen by the next ship or two. It's getting close."

Dirk pushed back from the table. "Yes. Just the same, now that things are fairly quiet in Shimabara, I wish the venture could be put off till 1639."

"Till 1639!" exclaimed Caron. "No! This must happen at once."

"One more year would be better," said Dirk stubbornly. "Look here. There are hints about that Becker may be sent down to Amboina next year. That would leave you in full charge. As it is, Becker's the one who'll benefit by any success we have, not you. He'll succeed van Diemen as Governor General. He'll go on to Amsterdam. Becker. Not you. Wait one year. Then — well, there's hardly a man in the Company who wouldn't fight to see you in Batavia and then in Holland. Becker'll be lost in both places. But have you ever thought of what you could do in van Diemen's place? How would you like to sit as a member of the Board of the Company in Amsterdam and, with your knowledge, help shape the whole Eastern world?"

Caron shook back his black hair and his firm mouth set. "Of course I've thought of that."

"Then arrange a postponement. You can handle Iyemitsu and Heizo. Van Diemen will follow your advice," urged Dirk.

"All true," said Caron, eyes on the ceiling. "I've dreamed of sitting in van Diemen's place, building our power. I've dreamed of facing the Directors in Amsterdam, of telling them of the blunders they've made, not through stupidity but through lack of knowledge. I could show them how all these islands from Hokkaido clear around to Sumatra blanket the Asia coast. I could show them what those islands could mean in Dutch hands."

"This is your chance," said Dirk.

Caron got up, paced up and down the room. Then he shook his head. "Dirk, I can gamble with my own future and my own life. But this would be gambling with the Company's. In a year's time, our venture might be too late. The Spanish and the Portuguese might get wind of it, probably would. It could easily happen that van Diemen would wake some morning and see both those flags in Batavia roadstead and his own ships sunk."

Dirk made an impatient gesture. "No! You know how slowly those people move!"

"It's bad strategy, Dirk, to gamble on your opponent's doing the wrong thing. We go south this spring, not next. And when Becker is translated to higher spheres, let us give thanks that the Company can easily absorb him and his shortcomings and go on to enjoy what the venture will bring it. Never forget — the Company comes first."

"I know, I know," said Dirk, as Caron carefully locked away the maps and his notes. "By the way, you haven't a good chart of the Hirado coast line have you?"

Caron shook his head. "These maps from the Shogun are the first I've ever held in my hand. You know how the Japanese are about such things."

"I ought to," said Dirk ruefully. "One of Heizo's officers found a little sketch I'd made of the road from the shore on to Isahaya and I thought he'd send me to the pit. I wonder they don't blindfold the birds that fly up the coast."

"I find it hard to blame them," said Caron tolerantly. "They've always been afraid of invasion ever since Kublai Khan tried to land his Chinese troops here four-hundred-odd years ago. So if anyone ever tries it again, the Shogun wants to make sure that there'll be no maps to help him. What do you want one of Hirado for?"

"I want one to see if I can find a safe, hidden cove for Mori, a deep water one where he can slip across to Kyushu without every blind masseur on the island knowing about it."

Caron looked inquiringly at Dirk. "His present anchorage is unsafe? Well, if Mori doesn't know of a better cove, I doubt if any map, even one drawn by the goddess Amaterasu, who created Japan, would help. Turn out the lamp on your side of the room and we'll close up. Ugh! I had to drink sake on top of brandy and I'll probably dream that Becker has gone to call on the Shogun, taking his slightly gamy dancers with him as a present."

VII

The War Barges

THE next morning, fresh from a bath that was heated nearly to the boiling point, Dirk shaved carefully before a round bronze mirror fastened to the wall of his room. The mirror, a rare piece, had been the gift of an old samurai in Northern Kyushu, who, in addition to being pleased by Dirk's interest in Japan and things Japanese, had found a fancied resemblance between the young Anglo-Hollander and his own eldest son, killed at Sekigahara in the dawn of the century. The mirror and Matsura's tea caddy from the sunken island were his most treasured possessions. This morning, however, his thoughts were far away. He was trying to recall some chance-seen bit of coastline that would answer Mori's need. Mechanically, he washed his face, made sure that the knots at the base of his knee breeches were properly tied and went down into the dark room where he and his fellow clerks ate. The others had already finished breakfast, so he sat alone eating persimmons and drinking tea while the bent old amah fussed about the table.

As he refilled his cup, he wondered why Caron had not taken the matter more seriously. If things *should* grow tense along the Gulf of Shimabara, every person crossing the narrow Specx Strait to Kyushu or heading down toward the Gulf of Omura would be carefully watched. With Mori confined to Hirado, the Company would not know about events over there. The whole area might erupt with no warning — and then it would be too late.

The amah set before him a fist-size red octopus that seemed to look up at him in mournful reproach through pulpy gray eyes. He disliked the dish at any time, but to see it the morning after Becker's celebration was too much. He waved it away, steadying himself with more tea. Then his thoughts returned to the hypothetical cove, the cove that must exist, had to exist.

It was barely three miles, if that, from the sea wall to the narrow north tip of the island, but there must be stretches where people rarely went. Who could tell him of those cliffs and the coast? He set down his cup. Children went everywhere. They scaled cliffs, romped on beaches, played in the dusty crumbling rooms of the old English factory where no one else had gone since the abandonment in 1623.

He pushed back from the table, put on a coat of sober brown, taking care to settle the broad white shirt collar smoothly outside the neck. A few minutes later he rapped on Van Os's door only to be told that the ojo-san had gone up the hill to Caron's house. Beyond Caron's gate he caught a trace of color far along the ridge trail that ran east beyond the sloping tiled roof. Bamboo grass, nodding over the little used path, slashed at his ribbed stockings, rasped his hands, as he swung along. He topped a low, steep rise and saw Trudi, a black haori over a deep red kimono, sitting under a twisted pine tree with little Petronella Caron. A few feet away Nobu squatted, her round face twitching. When Nobu saw Dirk, she muttered "Ara!" and shrank away against a clump of azalea bushes.

Dirk raised his hat, and called out a greeting.

Trudi rose, a hand on Petronella's shoulder. "Can you answer him?" she asked.

The scarlet-clad mite looked gravely at him. "Merci, monsieur. Et vous?"

Dirk bowed to her, Japanese fashion, murmuring, "Arigato. And I didn't mean to omit Nobu-san —" He glanced over his shoulder. The aproned maid had not only burrowed deep among the azaleas, but had turned her back, her hand over her eyes. "What's the matter with her?" he asked.

Trudi looked baffled. "I'm afraid she thinks you're a tanuki."

"I? A tanuki?" exclaimed Dirk. Many Japanese, high and low, firmly believed that the harmless, badgerlike little animal was capable of assuming any form it wished and, thus disguised, played tricks that might range from the mischievous to the tragic. Nobu undoubtedly believed that the real Dirk Jongh was bent over company ledgers at the very moment, while the tanuki-Jongh had appeared to sprinkle sand in their bean paste, make their obis unknot mysteriously or lead them all over a cliff.

Petronella sidled up to Dirk and put her hand in his. "*I* don't think you're a tanuki, Heer Jongh."

Dirk patted her black head.

"But Uncle Van Os will, if you don't get to the office, Dirk," said Trudi.

"Actually, I'm working now more than if I were elbowing Raas over the ledgers. I came up here to ask if you'd help me."

"Help you? How?"

"It won't be hard," Dirk said reassuringly. "I just want you to try to remember something. When you were a little girl, you rambled all over the island, didn't you?"

She looked puzzled. "You mean, around this part?"

Dirk hesitated. "Ye-es — say from the north point down to Kawachi."

"Oh, of course I did. Martin Trelawney used to take me looking for shells and birds' nests and flowers. Mother and I went everywhere, too, and my amah, Fumi-san. But what's all that got to do with helping you?"

"Just this," said Dirk. "I want you to try and think of the shore line — the east shore of Hirado."

"Oh, that's easy! Why, I've walked clear around the point from here to Usuku-wan on the west."

"Try to remember what it all looked like," urged Dirk. "Then see if you recall any gap in the cliffs, any deep fault running inland. It ought to be easy to remember, if there is one, because you would have had to leave the beach and climb the cliffs again."

She gathered her kimono and sat down on a jutting root, her chin in her hand. Dirk sat on a nearby stone, watching her. Sunlight caught hidden lights in her hair, so much finer and softer than Japanese hair.

She shook her head at last. "I'm sure there's nothing like that, Dirk. The cliffs get lower and lower as you go toward Tsubo-saki. I can see the whole stretch so clearly. I was walking along the beach with Martin — no, it was with Fumi-san. Sea on our right and the cliffs on our left —" She stopped, then rose, eyes closed and hands lifting slowly. "Wait! Yes. A little cove that goes right into the cliffs, twisting and twisting. There's a scrap of beach along one side and you can walk in and in. The water's very deep. I remember that because Fumi-san held me by the obi to keep me from falling in. Isn't that odd? I hadn't thought of that cove for years."

Dirk sprang to his feet. "The cove goes into the cliffs? Are there rocks offshore?"

"No. It's a place where the beach stops, then goes on again. There used to be an old trail down the cliff face to this one spot."

"This may do it!" cried Dirk.

She looked surprised. "What's important about a little cove?"

"I'm afraid I can't tell you. But it is important. Very, and to all of us. Could you show me how to get to it?"

"Yes, I think I could. Let me see, tomorrow I'm going to drink tea with the Hashimotos and the next day Madame Caron is taking me to call on the Takawas and then —"

"I mean now."

"Now?" she echoed. "But I was going to —"

Dirk smiled. "Last night you told me always to remind you to listen to me."

"Yes," she said slowly. "I did, but — you say this is really important. I'll show you. But it may not be easy. That was a long time ago and while I remember the strip of beach, I've got to guess how to get there." She picked up Petronella and kissed her. "Nobu-san will take you home. Now run along."

Nobu, leering and staring, muttered a warning, "Eh, ojo-san. Abunai-yo!"

"It's all right, Nobu-san," said Trudi. "I'm a tanuki myself. Take Petronella home."

Nobu reluctantly edged away, Petronella skipping and hopping ahead of her. "I think it's this way, Dirk. Follow me," Trudi called, starting along the trail.

The path dipped and rose and dipped, now masked by heavy banks of rhododendron and pine, now opening to show the Kyushu shore with its bamboo towers where men watched the surface of the straits for a telltale ripple heralding a heavy run of fish. The sun beat down pleasantly and a sea-scented wind drove slow masses of puffy white clouds down the deep bowl of the sky. Dirk, a few paces behind Trudi, watched her as she walked surely along, her white-clad feet twinkling against the brown of the trail as the breeze plucked at her hem. He felt a strange pleasure as she smiled encouragingly over her shoulder at him.

Suddenly she stopped. Before her, the trail ended in a sheer drop of thirty feet with a sharp current whirling about black rocks below. She shook her head. "I was sure this was the way. Where did we turn? I remember coming along here. Fumi-san used to stop by a stone pillar, a very old one. Then we went north from it, not toward the straits. But where's the pillar?"

Dirk, his mind on the cove, began to thrash through the undergrowth with a stick, then worked back inland, moving slowly and carefully. Suddenly he shouted, "Is this it?" parting branches and brambles to show a lichened stone upright. "Look! There's something carved on it." He scraped at the lichens with his stick. The gray-green flakes fell away, showing the upper part of the pine radical, the Matsu character.

Trudi cried, "That must be it! Fumi-san showed it to me and told me that it was a boundary post, put there by the very first Matsura. But there ought to be a path running in from it."

Dirk plunged waist deep among the tough bushes, casting to the right and then to the left. The expanse of dusty-looking leaves seemed limitless. His ankle turned and he staggered, felt smooth ground under his feet. He forced ahead one step, two steps, following a shallow trough. He shouted to Trudi, "I've found it! Look!" He ripped up a dead shrub and pointed to an old, hollowed path that was green with moss. No one had passed that way for many years. Dirk held a thick azalea branch aside as Trudi stepped past the pillar. "Keep going, Dirk. I'll be right behind you," she said.

He thrust his way ahead like a wader and a gentle tug at the skirt of his coat told him that she had caught hold of it. The path twisted among low pines and stunted bamboo, the undergrowth becoming sparser with each yard of advance. Suddenly there were no trees in front of Dirk. He stood on the edge of a steep cliff, looking glumly down the slope. Fifty feet below, the tides swished and bubbled. A bare quarter mile away, the Kyushu shore loomed. Across the water, a road paralleled the channel and he could see a peasant dully prodding a pair of oxen along its soft length.

"This is the path," Trudi said, "but there must have been a landslide. The slope used to be very easy." Still clinging to Dirk's coat, she leaned cautiously over the edge. "That's the beach. And the cove is only a little way north. But you'd need ropes to get down there now."

Dirk threw himself flat on the ground, studying the face of the cliff. He rolled a stone downward, watching its course. Then he jabbed at the soil with a sharp stick.

Trudi, kneeling beside him, said, "I'm sorry, Dirk. Perhaps there's another path."

He swung his legs over the edge. "I'm going this way. It's easier than it looks if I keep sloping to the left, and the dirt's good and firm. I won't even have to hold on to anything. You say I just keep north along the beach to find the cove?" He dropped a few feet lower.

"Dirk! I want to come with you! After all, it's my cove, isn't it?" She sat down, swung her feet over the edge. "Of course I'm coming with you."

Dirk dug his shoes into the dirt and joined her. "All right," he said reluctantly. "But be careful." He held out his hand and she steadied herself on it, began the descent. He slid in front of her and she rested one hand on his shoulder. "All right?" he called.

"Of course. Why, this is easy, and it looked impossible from above."

Dirk worked his way carefully downward, edging past a jutting rock, taking advantage of a stretch that ran nearly level for a few yards. At his right the voice of the straits sounded louder and louder. He could hear waves slap against boulders, could make out the mournful dying sound as the tide slid back from some hidden gully. All at once he was close to the bottom. He held up his hand. "There's a straight drop here," he called in warning, "but it's only about three feet." He bent, jumped to the firm sand of the beach, then turned, holding out his hands to her.

She shook her head. "Don't bother. This is just as easy as the rest of it." She caught an outcropping root, gave a little hop and then a squeak of alarm. The dry ground had crumbled under her feet, too close to the edge, and she pitched forward.

Dirk took a quick step and caught her before she had gathered momentum. For an instant she lay lightly in his arms, one hand clutching his shoulder. Then she wriggled free. "Thank you, Dirk," she said rather breathlessly. "I — I was clumsy, I'm afraid. Oh — look at my tabi." The white socks had split during the descent and she quickly stripped them off, standing barefoot on the white sand. "It doesn't matter. I left my geta at the top. I can wear them home. Now —" Hand to her lips, she looked about her. "It must be — yes! There it is, just ahead on the left. You don't really see it until you're right there!" She ran on, her haori fluttering. Dirk followed her.

Trudi was standing, waving to him, beside an inlet that seemed to end at the foot of the cliffs. All at once she vanished, but he could hear her calling to him, her voice muffled. When he reached the inlet, he found that it ran on past what looked like a mere jog in the cliffs, to twist in and in. The channel was wide enough for two sampans and seemed about ten feet deep with a bottom of clean white sand. Along the side where Dirk stood, a broad spread of sand paralleled the channel like a towpath. He looked upward and saw light sifting in through mysterious faults, but the enclosing walls seemed to reach on and on, to the very top of the cliffs. He called, "Trudi! Where are you?" then saw her standing in a stream of soft light that slanted down from the right, across the channel from him.

"Isn't this what I said it would be like, Dirk?" she said in triumph.

"Better. A paper boat could float here for years. And it's out of sight, a real secret anchorage."

She flipped white pebbles into the silky water, watched them sink in slow spirals. "Dirk, now that I have found it for you, don't you think you ought to tell me why you were hunting for it?"

Dirk walked slowly along the path, looking in vain for signs of rough water in the past. He circled the deep pool at the far end, explored the shore where Trudi stood. "Don't you?" she repeated.

"It's not my story."

She looked at him suspiciously. "Has it got anything to do with a girl?"

Dirk, standing in shadow, eyed her sharply. Then he said slowly, "It concerns a good many people."

"You mean, a good many people, but not me?" She began to move toward the entrance.

"You? No—yes, perhaps it does, or may. I suppose you've a right to know, since you found this place. But I can't tell you unless I've your word that what you hear will go no further."

"Dirk, I can see that you're serious about it. So am I."

"You remember what you saw beyond Omura?"

"Yes," she said, and passed her hand over her eyes.

Briefly he told her of conditions on Kyushu, of how they might develop and how disastrous such development might be to the Company and its people. He sketched Mori's part in trying to prevent an outbreak, of the secrecy involved that led to the need for safe, hidden anchorage for his sampan.

At last Trudi said in a voice that was almost a whisper, "They'd never dare move against us, against free Hollanders."

Dirk looked grim. "Ask Caron about what he saw in the early days, when he first came here. Or rather—don't ask him. He might tell you."

She looked pale in the odd light. "But Uncle Van Os has never hinted at anything like that."

Dirk coughed. "Your uncle is one of the most valuable men in the Company. A good deal of our prosperity is due to the fact that he's really outstanding at figures. To be as good as he is, he's had to devote himself entirely to Hirado matters. He's rarely left the island, so far as I know. He told me he'd never been farther than Nagasaki. And he doesn't speak Japanese, let alone read it. Caron and I told him a good deal about the danger, but I don't think that he realizes quite how bad it could be."

"Uncle Van Os doesn't realize?" asked Trudi, surprised. "Why, he's been here longer than Heer Caron, even, and much longer than you."

"But he simply hasn't had the time to get about the country as Caron has."

"And you?"

He nodded. "And I. When I first came here, in '30, Caron found me asking questions of one of the interpreters about the language. I seemed to be the only person at the factory who was interested, so he took me in hand, trained me, taught me to speak, to read and to write. It wasn't easy. Things like that come naturally to him, but I had to grind out every syllable, every character. You see, I felt that every new thing that I learned gave me that much more to offer the Company."

"Yes," Trudi said, "I've heard you talking to Japanese, to all kinds of Japanese. Does the Company mean so much to you?"

"Holland gave me a home," he answered. "The Company pretty well keeps Holland alive. Also, it gave me a livelihood when times were hard. Yes, in every light, I owe the Company a lot."

"Anyway, I'm glad my cove will be a little help."

He looked at her as she stood, silhouetted against the entrance to the cove, her face serious and her dark eyes on the slow ripple of the tide. He said abruptly, "Trudi!"

She turned as he stepped into the full light and her eyes widened. He said hurriedly, "Do you really have to go back to Holland this spring?"

"Go back?" she echoed. "Why, Uncle Van Os is retiring. Of course I must go with him."

Dirk lowered his head. He scraped little ridges in the sand with his shoe, trying to think of something that would set their conversation in a different channel. He found himself almost blurting, "But why go with him? Trudi, I'm rated a clerk now, but as soon as Becker goes, I'll be made full koopman. Caron will push me ahead as fast as he can."

She said quickly, "Dirk! Don't."

"You know what I'm trying to say. We wouldn't be on Hirado forever. The whole Orient's open to us — or will be. If you don't like that, we could always leave the Company and join my people on Massachusetts Bay in the New World. We could grow up with it. You wouldn't find them strange, Trudi. A lot of them were born in Leyden and most of them have lived there. We can grow with the Company or grow with the New World."

"Please, Dirk! I *am* going home in the spring. I like you very much, even if you do make me angry by being right so often. But it's only a matter of a few months, a few weeks really. In another few weeks you and the others will have forgotten I was ever on the island."

"No," he said stubbornly. "You know that's not true. Will you have forgotten me by the time your ship clears the Gotos?"

"I'll remember you, Dirk, a good comrade who always took

107

thought for me." Her eyes, full of friendly concern, were on his. Then she colored and looked at the ground.

He caught her hand and it lay soft in his. "Your lips are saying one thing and your eyes another. Your eyes are saying that you don't want to sail away, and I believe them." There was a sharp gasp of protest, the silk of her haori was warm and smooth under his hand and her black hair was against his shoulder. She pushed her arms against his chest crying, "No, Dirk, no!" Then her hands tightened about his neck and she breathed, "Oh, Dirk!"

"Now what do you say about Holland?" he asked in a low voice.

She straightened, pulled herself free and stood in the entrance, her back toward him. Without looking around she said, "I sail in the spring. And Dirk — think of this. I'm the first girl of your own people whom you've seen for I don't know how long and — "

"That doesn't matter."

"It does matter. I've everything on my side here on Hirado, because I am the only one. But supposing you went to Batavia. There are more and more Dutch girls there each year. Then how would I seem to you?"

"Just as you seem now." He took a quick step toward her, then halted, one hand held up. "What's that?"

"What's what?"

"Listen. That throbbing! Can't you hear it? It seems to be coming right out of the surface of the water."

"Throbbing?" She listened. "I don't hear — yes! Like something vibrating. It's getting stronger. How odd! It's like — why Dirk — what's the matter?"

He stood frozen for an instant. Then he said, "Drums! Heavy war drums and cymbals. Somewhere outside. We're just getting the echo in here."

Trudi stepped out into the sunlight. Her voice, clear and excited, drifted in to Dirk. "Boats! Lots of boats and flags. What does it mean? There's no festival at this time of year."

Dirk cried out, "Inside! Get back inside quick!"

Something in the tone of his voice checked her protest and she glided swiftly into the cove's mouth. Dirk knelt just inside the entrance, one arm resting on his knee, the other on a low boulder. His broad hat was off and his eyes were strained.

108

Without shifting his gaze from the high frame of rock that looked out onto a strip of the channel, he said, "Boats. But no festival. Those are war drums." The booming and clashing swelled and swelled, filling the hidden cove. Then the blunt nose of a barge came into view. In the bow a group of men in flat helmets thudded at cylindrical drums, clashed gongs and cymbals, blew on conches. The bow passed beyond the rock frame and the waist of the craft appeared filled with more helmets. Spear points flashed, halberds caught the sun. Then they were lost to view and the high, platformed stern moved on, long, narrow, vertical banners flapping from high poles over the men in elaborate armor and deep, vizored helmets.

"Why, they look like the Daimyo's guards," said Trudi in a disappointed tone.

"Not like the Daimyo's," said Dirk, lowering his voice as though it might carry across the straits to the barge that was moving with tide and current close to the Kyushu shore. "Another barge!"

The second prow emerged, vanished, a third and a fourth, the sun strong on the helmeted men. Now the barges held well-groomed horses. Now the pikes and halberds were replaced by clumsy arquebuses, with banners of blue and red and white.

Dirk counted to himself. "Twenty — twenty-one. Is that all? No. Twenty-two. More coming. Say a hundred men to each barge."

Trudi tugged at his sleeve. "What is it? One Daimyo going to visit another?"

"No. Didn't you see Itakura's banner?"

"Itakura's?"

"The Shogun's chief of staff. The first barges held Kyushu men, but all from the north, around Karatsu. The arquebusmen were from Aki and Bingo on Honshu, the main island. This — this — yes, from Tosa, on Shikoku."

"Where are they going?"

"They're riding the current south as far as they can. After that — if I could only see how the leading barges are heading now."

"From the beach you could see easily."

"And be seen — a man in foreign clothes watching Imperial troops."

"What if they did see you?"

"They might send a boat ashore to make sure that I didn't spread any news. Besides — a boat putting in here might not object to us, but they'd see the cove. Now Mori may need it more than ever."

"Always danger! This isn't the Japan that I remember. Has it really always been like this?"

"Pretty much. Thirty-seven. Is there another coming?" Cautiously he got to his feet. To the south the narrow channel was gay with tossing banners while the sound of drums and gongs hung like a thinning cloud over the flotilla. North the waters were empty. Not even a fishing boat rocked against the green-brown shore.

Trudi spoke, close behind him. "Have they all gone, Dirk?"

"I think so. Now I've got to find out which way they head after they pass Hirado Bay. I've got to find Caron. I've got to find Mori. There's no time to lose." He held out a hand to Trudi, helped her up to the track that they had made coming down.

The climb was not difficult for him, but her feet, lacking the protection of her tabi, hindered her, and she kept stepping on the flowing skirt of her kimono. Dirk went ahead of her, stripped off his coat, telling her to hold tight to one sleeve. Catching up the hem of her kimono, she struggled upward. "He shouldn't have talked to me like that. Just the same — I wish those barges hadn't come. They've upset him. He's worried. I wish I could do something — " At the crest, she slid her feet into her wooden geta while Dirk stood looking south, shading his eyes. He nodded to her absently as she joined him, then led the way along the old trail, holding back each branch and bush for her. Then they were at the worn pillar and clear of the trees, looking south down the island-flecked channel. The rear barges were nearing the mouth of Hirado Bay, and were hoisting sail as the current of the narrow Specx Strait lost its force.

The van of the column, barely visible, was wavering like a loose rope end. The leading barge, a dot against the crisp blue of the sea, swung toward Kawachi, swung back toward Kyushu, and Dirk's heart sank. The flotilla was making for the Gulf of Omura and the roads that led on through Isahaya to Shimabara. The line of barges curved sharper. Then, as though flicked by some invisible hand, it nosed south and west. Dirk, his voice husky with relief, cried out, "Nagasaki! They're going on to Nagasaki! That means they won't go to Shimabara."

"Why are they going to Nagasaki — or anywhere, for that matter?" asked Trudi.

"Don't know," he answered, eyes still on the barges. It seemed to him far too early, and yet — could these troops be mustering for Manila and Macao? They might be stationed in the Goto group to form a nucleus for those who would be drawn from Kyushu, the men of Arima and the men of Shimabara, when the time came.

He turned abruptly and started inland along the trail. Trudi called, "Where are you going?"

"To find Caron. Come on!"

He slowed his pace and they went on together, Trudi's geta clacking along beside his silver-buckled shoes. Trying to match his gait, she said breathlessly, "But you may not find him at his house, Dirk. Petronella told me that someone came to the gate early this morning, and Heer Caron got dressed and went out with whoever it was. It was before sunrise. Petronella says her father is often called like that and then they don't see him for days or even weeks."

"Yes, I know the way he goes about," said Dirk. "That's what I'm afraid of now."

They found the Caron household busy with the day's routine. All the sliding wall sections had been pushed back, flooding the rooms with sunlight. On the second floor, plump-faced maids hung thick, quilted mattresses over the railings, beat at them with bamboo wands. In the half-seen interior, other servants waved dusters of trailing silk scraps, or rolled back the last of the heavy wooden shutters that sealed off the house each night. Heedless of all the activity behind him, the master of the house, in a suit of soft brown, lounged idly by the roofed gate, drawing contentedly at a tiny-bowled silver pipe.

Dirk was relieved to see Caron. "My apologies for rushing you so, Trudi. But if he had been gone, we'd have had to pick up his track somehow and go after him."

"There! Heer Caron's waving to us," she said. "Do you think he knows about those barges?"

"He usually knows almost everything."

"Then they can't mean anything bad. See how peaceful he looks."

III

Caron swept off his hat to Trudi. "Goeden morgen. Have you been to the cliffs to watch for a run of fish? And your tabi! Madame is out, but I'll have a maid bring you a fresh pair. Then we'll sit in the sun with a pot of tea."

A few minutes later, fresh white tabi on her feet, Trudi knelt by the platform-like edge of the Carons' main room, while her host and Dirk dangled their legs into the garden, European fashion. As she poured tea from a Satsuma pot whose pattern was gay with sprays of autumn leaves, Caron eyed her quizzically, asking, "And there were fish running down the straits?"

"None that you didn't see, I'm sure, Heer Caron," she replied, smiling at him.

Caron took the cup which she held out to him. "Yes. Of course. I expected them, but not so soon."

Dirk looked up in surprise. "You expected them? When did you have a chance to get word?"

"Don't you remember, Dirk?" cried Trudi. "Petronella told me that someone came to the house before sunrise."

"Oh," said Caron carelessly. "He just wanted to tell me that he wouldn't be able to bring me wild fowl from the Tomioka marshes in Amakusa, at least for some time. So when I heard that, I went to the high ground back of the factory to watch for what we all saw."

Dirk nodded with understanding. "So there'll be no Tomioka wild fowl because trouble's broken out there. They've had no Gentaro Mori to keep matters in hand. And because trouble's broken out, troops have been sent from the north, Imperial troops under Itakura." He shot a glance at Caron. "Will the trouble spread?"

All trace of easy negligence left Caron's face. "I don't know. The Amakusa people have risen, for unknown reasons. Local troops will be sent against them. If more are needed, Itakura's Imperials will move in — our friends from the barges." His face darkened. "They ought to have no trouble in crushing whatever has started there. It will be terrible for the rebels. But that very crushing ought to serve to keep the Shimabara and Arima folk quiet. So it will mean misery for hundreds, instead of for thousands and tens of thousands, as would be the case if the spark had started in Shimabara." He looked keenly at Dirk. "There are other considerations."

"I know," said Dirk. The Amakusa business would probably be local. But a flare-up in Shimabara could not only end all hope of the Manila venture, but could also engulf the Company as deeply and as finally as the islands where the Daimyo's tea caddy came from. "I'd give a lot to know just what lit the spark at Tomioka. I think that one or both of us ought to go over to Nagasaki and see what we can see."

"To Nagasaki?" exclaimed Trudi. "With all those soldiers there? Why, you were even afraid they'd see you on the beach by the cliffs!"

"This would be different. I'd just be blundering into port to see our agent, Verstegen," said Dirk.

"Peste!" said Caron with a wry smile. "I'm afraid it would be blundering. No, for the moment, no foreigner should be seen in Nagasaki. Besides — look down at the bay."

The waters, silvery in the sun, were calm and peaceful as ever. The junks and heavier craft rode at anchor. Light sampans were being sculled slowly shoreward. In and out among the vessels, moving or at anchor, a barge flying the colors of the Daimyo threaded its way. No prow headed for the straits.

"Embargo," said Caron tersely. "No one is to leave port and the lighter craft are being beached."

Dirk watched soberly. "I'm afraid you're right. I'd been hoping that there'd be a way of getting someone over to Shimabara."

Trudi spoke quickly. "Dirk! We've forgotten! Tell Heer Caron about our cove!"

"So you've got your own private harbor, Sayo-ko?" said Caron, using her Japanese name. "Are you going to compete with the Company?"

"It's your cove, Trudi. Tell him about it," urged Dirk.

Caron listened with polite interest. When Trudi had finished, he sighed. "You have described most accurately a cove which I said did not exist. Do you think that anyone else has been there recently?"

"Oh, no," cried Trudi. "The paths were all grown over and there wasn't a mark on the face of the cliff or on the beach."

"Of course, of course," said Caron, his eyes on a high-wheeling carrion bird. "A pretty place, no doubt, but inaccessible. So inaccessible that I fear you'll find no one on Hirado interested in your discovery except Dirk and myself. Just us — and one other man. So don't bother to tell anyone else about it."

Trudi compressed her lips. "I understand. And I know who the other man is. Dirk told me."

"Very well," said Caron. "Dirk, you had better go to the factory. For my part, I am so taken with Sayo-ko's description of that cove and its beauties that I feel bound to go and retail them, while they are fresh in my mind, to that other man. Madame Caron would be glad to find you here, Sayo-ko, when she returns, which should be soon. In the meantime, all the Caron maids, needles and thread are at your disposal." He bowed and sauntered across the garden toward a gate that opened onto a west-bound path.

Dirk lingered, hoping for another word with Trudi, but she, with a smile and a wave, vanished into the house, calling for the head amah. He went slowly down the path toward the factory, his mind full of conflicting thoughts. He tried to fasten onto the meaning of the flotilla, clung to the importance of the cove, of which Mori would soon learn from Caron. But he found himself regretting his words and actions by the hidden cove. He had behaved like a clumsy lout and was thankful that she had not rebuked him sharply. Of course he had meant what he said. She had been assuming, day by day, a larger place in his thoughts, without his having been quite aware of it. Could she be right? Would he feel the same growing absorption in her if there were other foreign girls on Hirado? There was no way of telling. In any event, be it spring or fall, Trudi would leave the island for good. Here was his life, his career. Would it not be wise to follow custom and find a wife, Japanese or Eurasian? It was a step that de Groot and Zell were contemplating, while Hofmeyr had entered into formal negotiations with the family of one of the head potters of Hirado. As Dirk opened the outer door of the office, he thought dully that, when the embargo was lifted, he would do well to induce the Portuguese, Remedios, to speak more definitely.

114

VIII

Reconnaissance

Two days later Trudi and her uncle were seated in their softly lighted dining room. She looked about her with quiet satisfaction. She had found the heavy silver candlesticks in a barrel out in the plaster-walled kura and the light from their thick tapers flowed down to a spotless white tablecloth. The table itself was set with porcelain and china from Seto, from Satsuma, from Hizen and Imari, intricate flower patterns alternating with pieces whose charm lay in their shape, their finish of soft gray or brown, or in the graceful characters that traced an ancient poem on side or face.

Opposite her, her uncle sighed happily as he finished the last of a pair of pigeons, the final pat of sweet potato. "Ah, it was so when mijne lieve Haru-ko was alive. When she died, I grew careless, but you have brought her pretty ways and notions to the house again."

"You've so much Company business, Uncle, that you've never had the leisure to go through your things. But I've plenty of time," said Trudi, beginning on the yokan, the smooth bean paste from Kyoto, that Nobu set before her.

Van Os's heavy face sagged in a mass of wrinkles. "Yes. Of course. I just hope you don't find too much time. Hirado must be dull after Batavia."

"No. Hirado isn't dull. And Batavia isn't at all the way you think it is. There were only a few Dutch girls there and most of them had Japanese or Javanese mothers, daughters of people who had been here or Batavia or Amboina."

"And the young men?" asked her uncle.

"The Hirado ones are much nicer, Uncle. In Batavia, they used to wait outside the house where Mevrouw Kuyter had her school and call at us when we came out. Mitsu-ko Vossler used to encourage them, but the rest of us didn't like it."

"Vossler — I remember her father. He was at Nagasaki for a

while. Yes, the jongens here are well enough, and they know their places."

Trudi looked at her plate. "Heer Jongh — he — well, he proposed to me two days ago."

Van Os stared at her. "Jongh? Proposed?"

Still looking down, Trudi said, "Yes. The day all those barges went by."

Her uncle made rumbling noises in his throat and he flushed. "Jongh? A mere clerk? I'll attend to *him!*"

"Oh, no!" she cried quickly. "I just told him that I was going home in the spring with you and that's all there was to it."

"Hrrmph," he snorted. "It better be. Proposing to a koopman's niece. Doesn't he know that a Van Os commanded one of the walls of Haarlem in the siege of 1574?"

"Please, you won't say anything to him? Or hold it against him? I wouldn't like that, really."

Van Os waved magnanimously. "If it pleases you, my niece, I won't. Yes, I can understand, perhaps, how he forgot himself — or how any of the others here might. You see, you're the only girl of their own sort they've seen in years."

Trudi sat up straighter in indignation. "Just because — " She fell silent. Hadn't she said the same thing to Dirk herself?

Her uncle talked on. "Yes, it's a change for them. They'll all marry into Japanese families like the rest of us. Hofmeyr's making arrangements with the Ichiki family up by the potteries. The others will do the same in their time. I did hear that Jongh was talking seriously with old Remedios over at Nagasaki." He pushed back from the table, rose heavily. "Be a good stroke of business, too. The girl's Eurasian, so there probably wouldn't be any children, and it'd give us a hold on a source of fine pottery."

Trudi went slowly out of the room as he stood aside for her. It was one thing to speak of her sailing away to Holland. It was quite another — though of course no concern of hers — to think of Dirk staying on Hirado and marrying a Portuguese-Japanese girl, who would bring him pottery interests and no children. Or was it really true that Eurasians never had children?

It was dim in the next room and she moved warily to avoid an armchair while her uncle called for candles. From the night outside, a vague, unreal pattern of light shimmered on the floor. Van Os stepped to the window that looked down to the bay. "Hello! Something's happening there. Lanterns and torches. I can make out a mast. Thought the harbor was closed."

She joined him, looking out into the night. Blobs of colored light moved along the sea wall. A single yellow point, high in air, swayed gently at the top of a mast. One window of the factory showed orange, another. Van Os reached for his cloak. "This is something out of the ordinary. Want to come along with me and see what it is?"

"I'll stay here, Uncle," she said.

From the window she watched him go, while Nobu brought in candles. Then on an impulse she went into the hall and caught up a flaring cape of the type the Japanese had copied from the Portuguese.

As she approached the factory she could look into the broad casements of the main office. Her uncle had just seated himself and seemed to be questioning Becker, who sat in the Director's chair, fussing and fidgeting. At the foot of the table, Dirk bent over a roll of fuzzy-looking paper that she could see was covered with Japanese characters. He seemed to be disturbed by what he was reading. "It must be something about the barges!" she thought as she hurried around to the front of the building.

The high-masted ship that lay by the sea wall was a type unfamiliar to her with its tightly covered deck and high bulwarks. An officer or two stood by the sea wall, lantern light falling on strange-looking uniforms and armor. Toward the point, where the stubby powder house showed dimly, a swarm of waiting coolies squatted, their paper lanterns resting a respectful distance from the magazine. She asked the nearest officer what was happening, but his eyes, hard and distant under the vizor of his crested helmet, gave no sign that he had heard her and his tight mouth gave no answer.

Trudi gave him a lofty glance, then turned to the open door of the main offices, her curiosity thoroughly aroused. A soldier stepped from the shadows and raised the butt of his pike mechanically. She firmly pushed the butt down, stepping past it into the office.

"Goeden avond, Heer Directeur. Uncle, I thought I'd come down here with you after all!"

Becker shifted uneasily in his carved chair. Van Os seemed to share his superior's discomfort, muttering, "Ah, yes, of course. Perhaps another time — "

Then all sense of embarrassment left Trudi as Dirk sprang up, moved forward a seat for her. For the moment, care had left his eyes and forehead. "Neem plaats, Trudi, sit down. I'm just translating these orders from the Daikwan at Nagasaki."

Becker snapped, "And you've been long enough about it! All idlers. What does Nagasaki want anyway? Whatever it is, they've got to pay for it."

Dirk spread out the roll of soft paper. "Heer Directeur, this is a requisition on the Company. There are only two items. The first calls for three hundred kegs of the best-grade powder, to be paid for at current rates."

Becker brightened. "Three hundred? You're sure? That will look well in your books, Van Os. And when the *de Rijp* and the *Petten* come in, they'll bring enough to replace it in the powder house. Go on, jongen. What next?"

"The other, sir, is five cannon of — well, the symbol here corresponds to what Trelawney calls Pattern C."

Becker, suddenly in high good humor, rubbed his hands and winked at Van Os. "This is good business. Five cannon! We don't give *them* away at a stiver apiece. Saint Nicolaes! I showed a long head when I insisted on Jongh's learning Japanese. We're sure of the right translation and we don't have to rout out the interpreters. Ha! They'd expect an extra present on New Year's Day if we did. Now Dirk, mijn jongen, how about shot?"

"No mention of shot, mijnheer!"

"What? No shot? But we've got plenty — and at a good price," expostulated Becker. "Look again. They must want some."

Trudi glanced at Dirk, who seemed unruffled by the Director's veering moods. He said evenly, "In June, I sent you a memorandum about shot, sir. The Japanese are using stone balls, not iron or lead. When the stone ones strike a hard surface, they scatter splinters around. The metal shot either go through or bounce off."

"Then why haven't we got stone shot to sell them? What have you been up to when I've let you go prancing about the country? What's Caron been doing? You're supposed to find business for the Company, not bring up a lot of objections about why there isn't any."

Van Os interposed, "We've a fine total without the shot. Anyhow, there's not much margin of profit in them. I've an idea this powder is for the New Year celebrations in Nagasaki. Isn't that likely, Jongh?"

"The celebrations are getting closer," said Dirk cautiously. "The Daikwan always makes a big display at Nagasaki."

Trudi edged her chair closer to Dirk's. "Or at Tomioka?" she said coolly.

Becker caught the word. "Eh? What's that? Tomi — Tomi? No, that's not the place, mijn lieve." He smiled indulgently. "Nagasaki. A big city to the south. *That's* where the Daikwan is. The more celebrations the better — for us. Nothing more in that paper, Jongh?"

"Nothing beyond the usual formalities, greetings and so on."

"Then get the powder on board. Get the receipts signed."

Dirk got to his feet quickly, slipping a hand under Trudi's elbow as though urging her to follow him. Surprised, she rose as Becker asked, "What are we waiting for?"

"This," said Dirk, bowing toward the door. Trudi turned with the others, then fell back a pace behind Dirk, as though sheltering herself. The Japanese in the doorway was fairly tall, with an odd, black, brimless hat perched on his head, like a stiff Phrygian cap. His eyes, under knotted brows, were hard and unwavering. A heavily embroidered coat hung loosely below the man's waist, and instead of a kimono he wore baggy silk breeches so long that the ends fell over his toes, forcing him to hitch up the garment at each step. She heard Dirk, bowing even more deeply, utter a highly formal phrase of welcome.

The newcomer's glance barely flicked toward Dirk. He said something that Trudi could not follow, in a harsh, grating voice. Dirk faced Becker and Van Os. "This is Kurita-san. As he represents the Daikwan, who represents the Shogun, he suggests that you rise. You would be well advised to follow the suggestion, Heer Directeur."

Trudi fell back another step unconsciously. She had missed the details of Kurita's speech, studded as it was with formal archaisms, but there was no mistaking his meaning, nor the fact that Dirk had considerably toned down the real import in his translation.

Becker and Van Os stood awkwardly by their chairs. Kurita motioned roughly to Dirk, who bowed and proffered four long sheets of paper that swam with twisting characters. The Daikwan's agent drew a brush case, a heavy seal and an ivory box from his sleeve and traced out his name on each of the sheets, stamped the Daikwan's seal in vermilion ink from the ivory box and motioned again to Dirk.

Dirk glanced at Becker. "He wants your signature now, Heer Directeur. These are the receipts."

Becker grunted, "I don't like putting my name to what I can't read. Sure these are the receipts?"

"All in order."

"Well, tell him not to look so damned surly about it," said Becker. He picked up Kurita's brush from the table, gripped the fine ivory handle and scrawled his name and title on the sheets.

Kurita glanced at the forms, stowed them into his sleeve. Then, without a change of expression, he snapped the brush in two pieces, tossed them onto the floor and stalked out, holding up the ends of his trousers.

"I'd like to use my boot on him," Becker said angrily.

Van Os looked up from some notes that he had made on Dirk's translation of the requisition. "Nu, nu, Heer Directeur. He took his scowl out the door with him, but the profits will stay on the Company's books," he observed placidly.

"Profits!" snorted Becker. "We ought to make a thousand per centum for putting up with all this. You stay here, Jongh, and be sure you get the keys to the powder house from the head coolie. Count every keg and see to it that they only take five cannon from Trelawney's sheds. Come along, Van Os. Nothing for us to do here, now that — " He wheeled toward the open door as a footstep sounded outside. "Now why the devil couldn't you have been here when I needed you? I've just closed a deal and had to leave the details to an inexperienced clerk."

François Caron, his broad hat atilt, silver pipe dangling negligently from his hand, bowed to the Director, then to Trudi. "If matters were arranged by you, Heer Directeur, I fear that I would only have been in the way. There's nothing that I could have done that was beyond Dirk's powers, I'm sure. Sayo-ko, ma chère, that deep red is most becoming. It's a pity that custom doesn't allow married women to wear shades like that, for it's just the tone for Madame Caron." He lounged into the room, seated himself on the edge of the table.

Becker put his fists on his hips. "And where *were* you all this time?"

Caron smothered a yawn. "I spent the afternoon drinking some excellent Amagasaki sake with the landlord of the inn between here and Kawachi."

Dirk leaned forward suddenly, asking, "With old Hyakutake?"

"Yes, a gentle soul and oddly learned for an innkeeper, Heer Directeur. He told me something that I find even more interesting than the presence of the Daikwan's officers here." Caron was addressing Becker, but Trudi saw that his eyes were on Dirk — yes, and on her. The Frenchman went on in his calm voice, "He told me that there is a heavy blight on the crops on Amakusa, especially around Tomioka."

"Crops?" Becker cut in. "What's all that got to do with us?"

"And more," Caron went on imperturbably, "it is the studied opinion of the best agricultural experts that the blight will *not* spread, as some feared, to the mainland and on to Arima and Shimabara. It's all most interesting. Sayo-ko, mijne Heeren, I bid you all good night." He sauntered out of the office, humming the chorus, "Yori-ya, aikori-yo," to himself.

Becker caught up his hat and went out.

Van Os glanced inquiringly at Trudi as he rose. She shook her head. "I'm going to stay a little while and watch the loading, Uncle. Dirk will look after me. It's so pretty, with all the lanterns and the reflections in the water."

Van Os frowned. "Jongh will be pretty busy — " he began. "Oh, stay if you like. Don't be too late, though." He left the room, calling to Becker to wait for him.

Dirk gathered up his papers resignedly. "I wish I didn't have all this to attend to, Trudi. I'll find a safe place for you to watch, out of the wind."

"What an awful expression Kurita had!" Trudi exclaimed. "I've never seen anyone like him. He's even worse than Toda."

"He's one of the antiforeign crowd," said Dirk. "There are a lot of them, and if they had their way, they'd drive every European from the Empire for good. You saw the way he snapped his brush in two after Becker'd used it, didn't you? They'd break us, just as gladly. All they want is an excuse."

"You mean — if the blight that Heer Caron spoke of had reached up to Arima and Shimabara, that *might* be an excuse?"

"It could be. But don't worry about it, Trudi. Even if worst came to worst, it would only mean that we'd all be given safe-conduct and allowed to sail for Batavia."

"You're sure of that? Don't be afraid to tell me the truth, Dirk."

"I was told so by the Daikwan himself, and he speaks for the Shogun."

They stepped out onto the promenade together where red and blue and green paper lanterns, marked with the Daikwan's seal, were set at a respectful distance from the line of men who trotted toward the ship, each carrying a keg.

Dirk spoke softly, "Mori knows about the cove now, Trudi, and your finding it. He's very grateful. He was able to work his sampan up there in spite of the embargo."

When Trudi reached her room that night, she found Nobu waiting in near panic. Her tic was more pronounced than ever and her hands shook as she gave Trudi a package wrapped in silk so darkly purple as to be almost black. In Nobu's opinion, there were strange doings on Hirado. She had been taking tea with the cook, right there in the kitchen by the charcoal brazier on which dinner had been cooked. One moment, there was the brazier sitting peacefully in its box of sand. The next moment, the parcel lay on the sand by her elbow. The maid shuddered and muttered about the tanuki and the tengu, the long-toothed mountain demon.

Trudi carefully unwrapped the silk, then gave an exclamation of pleasure. Out of the cloth slipped a box of pale olive-green lacquer. It was very old and beautifully made, the lid showing in high relief a conical mountain down which gushed a waterfall edged with feathery bamboos. Under the trees, miniature men sat in a golden tea house. Both box and wrapping were marked with the Mori crest.

"But I do not understand why he should do this!" she exclaimed in bewilderment. Nobu said nothing, but her expression clearly indicated that there were things one did well not to try to understand.

A few days later, Dirk stumbled sleepily down toward the sea wall, drawing his cape closer about him. Just ahead, Caron walked airily along, seemingly indifferent to the fact that sunrise was more than two hours away. Dirk caught up with him by the floating wharf. "I know that it's a good idea to go to Nagasaki and see what's happening, but why do we have to leave in the middle of the night?"

Caron clapped him on the shoulder. "Because we're going to break our journey at a small island a little more than halfway down. There's an old Buddhist priest there whose conversation may interest us both. We won't see Nagasaki before tomorrow morning. Now, in with you."

The next dawn, Dirk looked over the thwarts of the sampan which was skirting the walled, artificial island of Deshima, close to the Nagasaki waterfront. It had been built by the Japanese to house the Portuguese, with the view of keeping a closer eye on the comings and goings of the latter. Dirk nudged Caron, who was yawning and stretching beside him. "I wonder how Remedios likes being cooped up there. The houses are good enough, but it's like being a prisoner. Deshima! I don't know why, but there's a sort of menace in the sound. Come to think of it, it's the same with most names around here. I used to think they were musical — Isahaya, Deshima, Shimabara. But now there's a sort of thunder in them." He looked up at the sharp hills of the city, temple-crowned, then at the seemingly unbroken carpet of silver-tiled roofs that swept down close to the waterfront and the broad gate that led from the wharves into the city itself.

As the sampan swung in by a low dock Caron pointed to the swarms of soldiers, some with drawn swords and others with bared pikes, who patrolled the wharves or stood rigidly by all the entrances to the town. "You may be right," he said.

Dirk sprang ashore, Caron close behind him. A stocky guard lowered the butt of his pike, advanced the point. Caron coughed apologetically. "We don't seem to be welcome, Dirk. Can you see where he's from?"

Dirk assumed a look of innocent surprise and sauntered closer to the soldier, who snapped brusquely, "Back to your ship!"

"It is forbidden to land?" asked Dirk politely, his eyes taking in the painted crest on the man's flat helmet, the style of his lacquered cuirass, the pattern of his surcoat.

"Back to your ship," the guard repeated.

Dirk sighed. "It's a pity. I wanted to see a merchant or two in the town. But if those are your orders — Are you from the village of Hongo, in the province of Suwo?"

The man's masklike face suddenly showed pleasure and he raised his pike point. "From Hongo? Yes. How does a Komo like yourself know of that village?"

Caron stepped up beside Dirk. "Hongo? That place up in the hills with the temple under two big pines? I've stopped there. Most courteous people there."

"And isn't there a shrine to Amida on the right as you come into town from the Hiroshima road? You look south to the Inland Sea from it, I think," put in Dirk.

"The same, the very same," chuckled the guard.

"This is very pleasant, Dirk," smiled Caron. "Like meeting a friend unexpectedly." Then he sighed. "But your orders. At least, we thank you for calling them to our attention so courteously."

"Like a true Hongo man," put in Dirk. He turned as though to leave.

The guard leaned on his pike. "Wait a moment." He lowered his voice. "Look to your left while I talk. Go straight along the waterfront to your right, cross the first bridge and then bear toward the Chinese anchorage at the Yaku-en. There's a gate there and not many guards. Such as there are come from Aki province, a slack lot. Go past the Aki men, who won't think to challenge you, and enter the city at the far end. No one will halt you once you're inside, because they'll think you came in before the gates were closed."

"Men from Aki?" exclaimed Caron. "Isn't one-eyed Sado-san their commander?"

"Sado-san it is," the guard answered. "May Kompira, god of

124

travelers, go with you. And when you next pass Hongo, bow to the image of Amida in my name."

Dirk and Caron followed the guard's directions and soon walked into the east edge of Nagasaki. There seemed to be few people about and all the shops were shuttered. Down side streets they caught glimpses of troops in massed formation, heard the throb of drums and the blare of long trumpets and conches.

"So far, so good," said Caron. "I think we'll chance this next left turning and work toward the center of the city. I'm not quite sure what to say, though, if more guards halt us."

"Only one thing to do," said Dirk. "We'll merely tell them what the Suwo man suggested — that we were here before the gates were closed."

"H'm," said Caron. "That will do if we're not questioned too closely. In that case — ah! I have it!"

He led the way to an inn that seemed open for business. A wizened old man bowed and bowed to them as they entered. Caronsan was always welcome and it was an honor to be permitted to greet a friend of Caron-san's. In a room that looked out over a miniature garden of hillocks, rocks and water, Dirk and Caron drank tea and nibbled at sweetish, soggy cakes. When the endless compliments had been exchanged, Caron said casually, "By the way, Tani-san, when I left my room here this morning, I think that I forgot to bring with me a small package wrapped in green silk. Will you ask the maids if they found anything like it?"

The wrinkled old eyelids drooped for an instant, then lifted in an innocent stare. "Sa! Caron-san. I myself went to your room the instant you left. There was no parcel."

Caron dismissed the matter with a wave. "It's of no importance. No doubt I left it at the silversmith's when I called there. I had found some tea whose package was patently misbranded 'Uji,' and I wanted to show it to my friend Nasu-san, the tea merchant from Arima. This is the day he usually comes into town."

Dirk watched the old innkeeper closely. His expression did not change and his voice was courteous as ever, but something went out of him, like a lamp that is slowly turned down. "Nasu-san? I think you will not see him. Travel is difficult these days between here and the Gulf of Shimabara, Caron-san."

"I shall be sorry not to meet him," said Caron equably, as he rose. "My thanks to you for your diligence in seeing that I left nothing in my room."

Out in the street once more, Caron looked at Dirk. "What did you think of friend Tani?" he asked.

"I didn't think much about him," answered Dirk. "What I did think was that it is odd that he is quite willing to assure any officials that we spent the night in Nagasaki, and yet thinks it most unwise to talk even to you about a tea merchant from the Shimabara area."

"Very odd indeed," said Caron thoughtfully. "Let's try for a cross-bearing on that. Let me see. Whom else do I know in this part of the city?"

"We're on Fundaiku-machi, about — yes — the second block. There's a silversmith in the fourth block who's making some silver buttons for me," said Dirk. "It just occurs to me that I'm very anxious to have them."

He set out along the street, turned up a narrow, reeking alley, Caron sauntering indolently along behind him. There was no one behind the low counter of the open-fronted shop where Dirk stopped. He called out in Japanese.

Footsteps shuffled in the inner reaches of the shop, a curtain was pushed aside and a fat-cheeked man appeared, looked quickly at the two foreigners, then dropped his gaze to the floor. No, the buttons were not ready. The piercing of them was special work and he had sent the blanks to a smith at Obama. It was not far, of course, but he could set no date for their return. He asked pardon for the delay and withdrew.

Dirk joined Caron in the alley and they headed for the wider streets. "That man's been frightened," observed Dirk. "There's good profit in those buttons for him, but Obama is too far away, he thinks, to collect that profit just now. Obama — on the west coast of the Shimabara peninsula."

"Perhaps the Obama smith is doing work for my tea friend, Nasu-san, and hasn't had time for your buttons," said Caron. He stopped in the middle of the street and looked about him. "Dirk, I think we'd better separate. I'll take the west part of the city, you take the east. By sundown we'll meet at Tokitsu, up on the Gulf

126

of Omura. You know the head of the boatmen's guild there?"

"Oh, yes. You want to go home by way of the Gulf of Omura, then?"

"If we've learned enough to warrant going home. There won't be another Hirado sampan at Nagasaki for two days. We might not want to wait. Sundown at Tokitsu, then." With a wave of his hand, Caron strolled off toward the west.

Dirk reflected that he might just as well be walking blindfolded as he toiled up the steep streets that slanted toward the Dai-on temple. There was nothing of significance to be seen or heard, nothing but the painted torii, the great camphor trees, evergreens, magnolias and orange trees that crowded about the low houses, as though they were withholding priceless secrets from him. There were no shops where he could drop in casually in hope of picking up a word or two. The few Japanese whom he passed looked away from him and hurried on.

When he reached the outskirts of the city, he began to feel hungry. He headed for a shed where a group of laborers and carters squatted on a matted platform, chopsticks busy in blue and white bowls. They stared as Dirk seated himself on the edge of the platform and ordered the coarse fare of the house — boiled noodles with a bit of fish resting on the thick coils. The men began to comment audibly and frankly on Dirk's clothes, his height and his light skin. Then they burst out laughing as he joined in their conversation with a very fair approximation of their clipped idiom. He quoted a full-flavored proverb, parried a thrust about his costume and praised a fine pair of waiting oxen, judging their weight to a nicety. The talk ran on and Dirk heard of thatches that were wearing out, of the difficulty in finding proper wood for ox yokes and the prices offered parents with daughters to sell. It was all very intimate and interesting, but only academically. Dirk racked his brains for a topic that might produce fruitful comment. Then his eyes fell on the oxen and he asked the nearest teamster casually, "If I knew someone who wanted to charter six yoke of oxen in about a week's time, what should I advise him?"

The lean owner of the yoke laughed hoarsely. "Tell him he'd do better to find a team of dragons. By next week they'll be more plentiful than good Kyushu oxen." He broke off suddenly as one of his companions whispered warningly, "Abunai-yo!" A third man muttered that business was brisk for those who owned yokes. All were engaged far in advance, he said, concluding, "Tell your friend to wait on the head of the carters' guild. That's the best way to make arrangements."

Dirk paid his score and walked away, deep in thought. Before sundown, having talked with a pork butcher, a bold-eyed girl in a tea room and a blind masseur, Dirk sighted the waters of the Gulf of Omura and the straggling roofs of Tokitsu. He hurried on toward the house of the head of the boatmen's guild. As he neared the high board fence that surrounded it, he heard a familiar voice singing.

Dirk hailed, and Caron stepped out of the gate, holding a red-kimonoed baby in his arms. "Come in, Dirk!" Caron called. "Kodera-san has a craft for us. I'll give this young swordsman back to his mother and we'll sit on that bit of driftwood while we put together what we've both learned and see if the sum warrants our going back to Hirado tonight."

He carried the child into the house, then joined Dirk on a great balk of water-soaked timber. "You start, Dirk," said Caron.

Dirk told of the scraps that he had picked up here and there, hoping that they would somehow assume significance. From the teamsters he had learned of a sudden demand for draught teams in a normally slack season. From the pork butcher he had learned nothing. The bold-eyed girl at the tea house had spoken of a lover, a worker of sword blades, who had shown signs of unexpected prosperity. This the girl had applauded, although the sudden deluge of his work left him little time to see her. The blind masseur had gone to make his scheduled call on the son of a noble who lived in a great castle nearby. The son was gone and no one would tell him where, but in feeling his way through the entrance, he had noticed that the suit of armor that usually stood there was missing. "And that," said Dirk, "is about all that I learned."

"It may be more than I did, at that," said Caron. He then told of a shomyo, a petty noble of his acquaintance, who complained that his daughter's wedding had been postponed owing to the unexplained absence of the groom, who held a command in the local troops. Like Dirk, he had learned of unheard-of activity among the armorers, particularly among those who understood the mechanism of the arquebus. Rice in bulk, he found, was commanding an unusually high price and he thought the purchasers were largely Heizo's agents. Last of all, he had spent a half hour with the wrinkled manageress of a most luxurious joro-ya who had been very busy buying up daughters of impoverished families in the Shimabara peninsula. For some reason, the last two consignments had not yet arrived, which had vexed the old woman, who seemed to be counting on a great influx of free-spending guests for some time to come. "And that," said Caron, "is the sum of what my prodigious talents and wisdom have brought us."

Dirk stretched out his legs. "Let's start with our first samples. Your innkeeper and my silversmith did not like to talk about Shimabara and said that there had been little travel recently between here and there. I picked up hints of that in other quarters. That suggests to me that, in some way or other, that whole area has been officially sealed off."

"No doubt of it," said Caron. "Your blind man and my shomyo have told us, without knowing it, that local officers have been called to the colors. We've both found out that there's a big stir among the makers and repairers of arms. Now what else?"

"There are my oxen," said Dirk. "It's obvious that unusual numbers of animals are being requisitioned, and by the Daikwan. Why? Obviously to transport supplies for the men from the barges and from the local levies."

"Good," commented Caron. "Now my sprightly old beldame, with her complaints about nondelivery of her delicate merchandise from Shimabara, confirms the sealing off still more. And beyond that, *why* does she expect a great throng of men in a festive mood? There's no great fair or celebration in the offing. So she is relying on the well-known affinity between Mars and Venus."

Dirk nodded. "In other words, the men from the barges. They are still in Nagasaki. The local levies are not, or else your shomyo would have his wedding. Where are they? I'd say, in Amakusa, around Tomioka."

"They've got to be. But the others — the Imperial troops. Ah! I have it. They will stay in Nagasaki to see what happens. They can move to either Shimabara or Amakusa with equal ease. They'll reinforce the local troops if necessary. Or — " he paused — "they're waiting to see if the flame spreads to the old ruined castle over the gulf. If it does, they move there."

Dirk got up and began to pace about. "I think, knowing all this, we can go home. The one thing we haven't found out is just what spark lit on Tomioka."

"The point's academic," said Caron. "The local levies ought to be enough to stamp it out. And that stamping will be so hard that it will certainly discourage the Shimabara folk from welcoming a spark of their own. Unless — remember what you overheard the charming Toda say? Something about stamping out a rebellion before it starts? That, I think, is our only danger now."

Dirk stopped. "I think I'll let you go back to Hirado alone — with your permission, of course."

Caron looked up quickly. "What idea's struck you now?"

"Someone ought to take a look at Shimabara. That someone ought to be me. You're needed to keep an eye on things at Hirado and to get right in touch with Gentaro Mori. Here's what I'll do. I can hire a horse in Tokitsu. I'll go along the gulf and then hit up through Isahaya. At Kuremo I'll hire a boat and a safe crew. I'll cruise clear around the peninsula, keeping close to the shore. There's no telling what I might see or hear."

Caron got up abruptly. "It's worth the chance. I'll clear you with Becker. Cruise as far as you can and then hurry to the factory."

Down by the beach, where a light surf hissed and mumbled among piles of seaweed, Kodera, the boatmaster, was shouting orders to a group of thick-legged men who grunted and strained over the task of launching a sampan.

An excited stranger suddenly materialized from among the dunes, and headed for Kodera. His head wagged from side to side as he talked and he made quick, cutting motions with his hands. Then he glided away as mysteriously as he had come. Kodera stood irresolute while his men maneuvered the sampan toward a quiet pool. Caron hailed him and he came over reluctantly, eyes on the ground. "Are you ready, Kodera-san?" asked the Frenchman.

Kodera's eyes shifted right and left. He stepped closer, spoke in a low voice. "I have heard news. You and Yang-san will not say where you heard it — or if you heard it?" he muttered.

Caron said quickly, "If there is danger to you in the news, Kodera-san, it better remain untold."

"No," said the boatman uneasily. "It may concern you. I owe you a debt for sending me the balm that saved my son's life last year. The news is this. There has been trouble on Amakusa."

"I know that," said Caron.

"Do you know how deep the trouble is, Caron-san? Listen. Local troops were sent against the Tomioka rebels. Those troops were beaten. They took refuge in Tomioka Castle, those who lived, they and the governor. Two days ago, Imperial troops, the men of Karatsu, moved to Amakusa against those rebels. Since then there has been only silence."

"Can you guess what the silence means, Kodera-san?" Dirk asked.

Kodera shook his head. Caron laid a hand on Dirk's shoulder. "If nothing else, it means this — that your idea of not coming to Hirado with me was a good one. Yes. It's necessary now. Good luck, Dirk. Watch and listen. It ought to be quite easy to find out if the trouble is confined to Amakusa."

"Trust me," said Dirk, and walked away.

Caron embarked hurriedly and the sampan pushed out into the Gulf of Omura. He curled himself up in the stern, his cloak about him, and dozed. Hours later, he woke with a start. The sky was overcast, the night inky black, but he thought he could make out a white line of surf along the Kyushu cliffs, a sign that the craft had left the gulf and was heading north. He rubbed his eyes, got up, stamping his feet to shake off the early morning chill. His vision slowly became used to the darkness and he was able to verify the ship's position roughly.

Beyond the sharp prow of the sampan, something gleamed and rocked on the short, steep waves. Now it was on the port bow, a heavy bulk, moving and restless. He vaguely made out a sail, a rounded hull. The sampan overhauled the mysterious craft and Caron could make out men on the deck, men in white robes who did not answer their hail. Other forms in white, or splashed with white, were stretched on the shadowy deck.

Caron leaned out as far as he dared. Then he withdrew quickly to the stern. "White!" he thought. "The Japanese color of mourning. Those men lying on the deck — I have it! The Karatsu men! One barge and its thwarts are draped with white bunting. It means — it must mean that the Amakusa rebels have very nearly wiped out the Karatsu men. White for death and defeat. Those must be the bodies of the Karatsu leaders, tended by Shinto priests in white! Those poor devils of Amakusans, without knowing it, have drawn the sting that might have pierced right into Shimabara — and Hirado."

He watched the lumbering craft as it fell astern. "Of course the rest of the troops will move at once. It ought to be over very quickly — and horribly. But at least, it will not spread. Ventre de dieu! If this had happened in Arima and Shimabara!" He shuddered.

The air grew clearer and clearer. A band of crimson flamed over the Kyushu shore. Far astern, the great barge rocked and dipped, its white shroudings bright in the new morning.

IX

The Tower

IT was past midnight when Dirk's hired sampan rounded the north-east knuckle of fist-shaped Shimabara and headed south, hugging the shore. To his right he could just make out the coastline with the mass of Mount Unzen rising high into the shimmer of the stars. The night was heavy with an eerie hush that was accentuated by the slow hiss of the prow and the sullen slap of the waves. Twice on the north shore he had landed on fruitless questings. One house where he had counted on sure news stood gutted and roofless. Another was empty save for a torn fishnet. In dull disappointment he reflected that he would have done better to have gone back to Hirado with Caron. Then he saw a cliff standing out boldly in the night, made out a grim, tangled mass on the summit. Going forward, he called to the boatman to put him ashore. There might be people lurking about the ruins of Hara up there, people with whom it could be worth his while to talk.

As the prow grated on the sand, Dirk sprang out. He crossed the narrow beach and worked his way upward along a steep, slanting path that showed yellow against the face of the cliff. The going was hard and once or twice he thought he would have to turn back, but at the end of a half hour he stood, panting and triumphant, at the foot of the shattered outer walls of the old castle.

There was a blocked-up gate to his left, its mouth so debris-choked that entry was impossible, but beyond it he found an irregular gap in the wall itself, stretching from turf to top. With rocks rasping his hands and dirt crumbling under his feet, he wriggled and pushed his way through. The ground ahead of him stretched away, rough and broken, to the great mass of the castle keep in whose shadow he had heard Mori's plea to the people of Arima. In the mid-distance, whitish shadows wavered, formless and ghostly, where plumes of steam oozed from hot springs.

Dirk left the shelter of the wall and made his way cautiously over the open space toward the keep. If any of the malcontents were about, that would be the place to look for them. The white walls and towers of the castle grew plainer and plainer as he pushed on, planning to skirt the northeast corner and find the great mass of masonry where the meeting had taken place. There was a dark mass in the center of the eastern face and for a moment Dirk thought that it was a broad rent in the wall. Then he saw that it was the principal entrance to the castle, its beams and uprights in seemingly very fair condition. He stepped inside, listening, but could hear no sound beyond the scrape of his foot against a fallen block. As much for the reassurance of the sound of his own voice as in hope of an answer he shouted, "Anoné!" The echoes went rattling away in the fathomless darkness, faded, died, leaving him alone in the empty night.

He was about to leave the gate when an oddly familiar smell seeped to him, a smell that somehow recalled the old stone powder house of the Company in far-off Hirado. Frowning, he stood irresolute, then walked cautiously to his left where his eyes, growing accustomed to the gloom, showed him a small door in the thickness of the walls. Hands before him, he went on, the pungent smell stronger and stronger. Then an outflung palm rested on something curved and rough and his breath went in sharply. Powder kegs stored in the meeting place of the malcontents! How the devil could they have gotten there? His hand strayed on and he jumped back as though he had touched hot iron. Branded into the staves of the kegs was the mark of the Dutch East India Company.

Dirk's first impulse was to run, to get as far away as he could from those kegs with their damning brand. Then he recovered himself and began to reason. Under the rigid laws of the land, only the Imperial Government — that was to say, the Shogun — could own powder. These kegs, then, must have been diverted to Hara by rebel sympathizers, possibly members of the Daikwan's own suite. Dirk rubbed his knuckles across his chin as another possible angle struck him. If these kegs were found by the Daikwan's agents, the powerful antiforeign clique at Nagasaki and Tokyo could claim complicity on the part of the Company. There were the kegs, in

Hara, with the Company brand on them. Defense against such a charge would be difficult.

Another thought took slow shape in his mind. It was perfectly conceivable that they had been deliberately planted in Hara by the antiforeign element, to be discovered with convincing surprise and horror by Government agents. In any event, the news of his find must reach Caron at Hirado as soon as possible, and as accurately as possible. Sidling along in the dark, he began a careful count. When he had tallied thirty kegs, the staves gave way to sacks of rice, neatly piled, then boxes of dried fish, more powder kegs.

Light seeped in through the door and he crouched behind the kegs. Voices sounded under the main entrance. Torches flared and Dirk saw flickering shadows in the passageway. In the confused blur he made out crested helmets, the jut of sword hilts, and shrank farther back. If these were the Daikwan's men — Then a friar's cowl wavered black against the white wall and Dirk drew a breath of relief. He moved quickly toward the door of the magazine calling, "Fra Hilario!"

He saw the black shapes stop abruptly, heard a harsh voice call, "Who's there?"

"Yang-san of the Company," Dirk answered as he reached the door. His voice died away in his throat. The cowled man was not the gentle-faced friar who had addressed the crowd with Mori that night of the meeting. This friar was tall, bearded, with a keen face and eyes that glowed strangely in the torchlight. About him, tough-looking men in battered helmets gathered as though to protect him. The friar pointed a muscular hand at Dirk. "Who is that?" he asked in halting Japanese.

Again Dirk identified himself, his eyes searching under the helmet brims for a familiar face, searching in vain.

The friar spoke again. "This man has seen too much. He must not leave."

Dirk turned to the foremost Japanese. "You must know who I am. I have been here before. Mori-san is my friend. I know Tokisada-san, too."

One of the Japanese began, "If he knows Mori-san — "

The friar cut in. "That is nothing to us. Did Mori-san help us when we rose at Amakusa?"

"But he would have had he known," urged another Japanese. "I tell you, Fra Fidel — if he knows Tokisada-san too he must be safe."

Fra Fidel, hot eyes on Dirk, disregarded the interruption. "Take him to the archers' tower. Keep him under guard. Later we will make up our minds."

There was no use in protesting. Fra Fidel obviously commanded the complete obedience of the Japanese. Four of them closed about Dirk, pushed him not too roughly toward a gaping stairwell that showed in the wall. Resigned for the moment, Dirk started up the stairs, wondering what the presence of the friar and the armed men could mean. They had said little enough, but the mention of the Amakusa rising could only mean that they had participated in it. It was also quite possible that Fra Fidel, with his fanatic's eyes, had been the spark that had touched off the tinder down there.

The stairs bent twice, ended at a broad landing that was faced by a heavy, barred door. Apparently this part of the ruin was in a fair state of repair, had possibly been improved by the rebels. The door swung open and a guard motioned Dirk inside. As the door slammed behind him, the last flare of the torch showed that the room was empty and windowless. Then dark closed in about him.

He put his hands out before him and walked carefully on. At the end of twenty paces his hands found rough mortar that seemed to be reinforced by a thick transverse beam. Allowing five paces for his first entry, that made a depth of twenty-five. The next move would be to find the other dimensions. Hands high above his head, he sprang up as far as he could, but touched nothing. Then, dropping his coat on the floor as a marker, he worked step by step along the walls, counting slowly. He covered one wall, another, found the door, kept on his way until his feet caught up the folds of his coat to show that he had made a complete circuit.

He sat down, knees drawn up to his chin. The room was about twenty-five paces square, very high-ceiled and with a heavy plank floor. There were no openings in the wall, barring the door, a fact which puzzled him, since it appeared obvious to him that he was in a small tower, probably jutting slightly over the main wall. It should have been pierced for archery. He thought of other castles that he had seen — Hideyoshi's great mass at Osaka and the white walls of Karatsu. The outlines were clear in his mind. Each had slotted towers at the corners or protruding at scientifically calculated intervals.

Fatigue blurred his thoughts. He rolled up his coat for a pillow and stretched out on the floor. Even a short sleep would give him a fresher mind. He closed his eyes, his ears filled with the distant beat of the surf and the steady *pat-pat-pat* of bare feet doing sentry duty just outside the door.

Some time later he woke. The room about him was dark as ever, but vertical lines of light seemed to shimmer along the wall in front of him. He looked at the rear wall and found the same phenomenon — vertical lines all parallel and all beginning about four feet above the floor.

He felt his way toward the nearest set, ran his fingers carefully over the rough plaster surface. In some mysterious way, light was filtering through the masonry, yet he could detect no crack. In any event, random fissures could not have been set so regularly, in vertical parallels. With his fingernail he scratched back and forth on the nearest line, and plaster fell to the floor in a thin trickle. The mystery was solved. The archer's slits that he had looked for during the night had been plastered over at some time in the past, and through this thin skin light was sifting.

To verify his deduction, he moved to the next grouping, prodding and prying. In some slots the plaster was too solid to move. In others, it crumbled bit by bit. He went back to the face of what he judged to be the south wall, carefully worked out long chunks that would remain sufficiently intact to replace. Light flooded in like a thin wand and he looked eagerly through the little opening.

His tower was on the southeast corner of the castle. Below him, he could see a long tangle of matted grass that stretched away, dotted with chunks of masonry, to the outer walls. Over their jagged tops, the Gulf of Shimabara glittered in the morning sun, calm and peaceful. A few fishing boats rocked gently half a mile offshore and a single sampan scudded across toward the flat land that led on to Kumamoto and a surge of green hills. By securing a different angle through the slot, he managed to look south and west. The rolling countryside was empty. There was an oddly shaped hogback ridge just in sight and over it crept the brown stretch of road that led south to the extreme tip of the peninsula and the straits that separated it from Amakusa.

Suddenly his hands closed on the edges of the slot, wrenched at them as though to force them wider apart. Across an open field on the slopes of Mount Shichimen, a single figure ran. Higher up, more figures appeared, bursting from a stretch of pine. They were men, and even at that distance, Dirk could see that they were ragged and that they waved their arms as they ran. He leaned closer to the slot and imagined that he could hear shouts, thin and faraway. More men were running up a deep draw that joined the southbound road, more appearing to the east by the very edge of the cliff. In twos and tens and twenties they materialized, flowed together, broke up, joined again, all waving and running toward the south.

"What is it?" muttered Dirk, his eyes straining.

Now he could catch glints of steel. On the shoulder of a nearby hill, a man stood on a rock, waving a sword. Close by the outer walls of the castle, half a dozen men ran, two of them laboring on under the weight of clumsy arquebuses. There was a new surge of runners, a general drift to the north, and a living hedge formed along both sides of the road where it dipped out of sight over the hogback that he had noticed before. Shouts floated back to him, audible but maddeningly unintelligible. Then the shouts died, and the ragged men who lined the road stood motionless, looking south at something that Dirk couldn't see.

A hush of expectancy hung over the scene and the empty road, humping itself across the hogback, seemed to move before Dirk's eyes as though it were flowing toward him, carrying with it some nameless manifestation. He braced himself, knuckles white from his grip on the old masonry. The men in the fields dropped to their knees, lifted their arms high. The road was no longer empty.

Over the crest came a great procession, headed by a helmeted man who held up a huge cross. Color swam in the air and massed banners fluttered. On and on they came, held aloft by men in armor, men in kimonos, men bareheaded and men in bright helmets. The wind caught the banners, blew them taut to show embroidered crosses, bleeding hearts, crowns of thorns, royal crowns. The nearest banner swung close by the outer wall and Dirk mentally translated the inscription, "For Sant' Iago and Spain."

The banners passed out of sight but still the road spilled out its host. File on file of arquebusiers, marching with the swing of seasoned troops; rows of glittering pike heads and halberds; the bristle of arrow-filled quivers and strong bows slung over shoulders. The waves of armed men ceased and the road was choked with cattle, with women and children, with old men and women, more cattle. The dun coats of oxen and cows, ragged and dusty, threw into relief the reds and blues and greens and purples of the kimonos. More pikemen followed, led by an armored officer on horseback. A high, narrow standard fluttered behind him and Dirk, now beyond all surprise, made out its crest and read the whole story of the march.

There could be no question. Fra Fidel and the armed men who had surprised Dirk in the magazine had been an advance party for the people of Amakusa who, victorious over the Imperial forces, had crossed to the peninsula and now marched on Hara, to turn it into a mighty fort of rebellion. All that Gentaro Mori, all that Fra Hilario, had fought against had come to pass, and Caron's great venture against Macao and Manila was doomed. Penned up, helpless, Dirk saw the ragged army come on into the mile-wide enclosure of Hara's outer walls. Off on Hirado, Caron and Mori were surely unaware of this development, of its scope and menace. All that there was to know about it Dirk knew, and that knowledge was shut up with him in the archers' tower.

Two days after Dirk's capture by the Amakusans, Gentaro Mori, ceremonial swords thrust through his obi, his old cuirass and dragon-crowned helmet gleaming, walked slowly up to the gates of Matsura's palace. His mind was full of a tranquillity that was tinged with sadness. The last word from Tokisada seemed to settle matters, once and for all. Fresh troops had been sent against the Amakusa rebels, who were even now being hunted down and slain. Yet, reported Tokisada, the Shimabara area stayed quiet and would surely remain so with the last embers stamped out in Amakusa. Mori sighed. He felt deeply for the poor folk on that island. Yet their very tragedy prevented a greater one. It was as though a fire in a godown had been put out before the flames could reach the main house whose conflagration could easily wipe out the Empire of Japan. No longer would he be needed to control the frantic men along the Gulf of Shimabara. His old sampan could rot peacefully in the hidden cove that the Dutch girl had found for him.

More than that, the prospect of dearly bought peace had prompted him to make an important decision, a decision so grave that he refused to state his business even to Suzuki, the Daimyo's steward.

"This is most unusual, Mori-san," said Suzuki, turning his official wand in his hands.

"So is my mission, Suzuki-san," said Mori. "It is for the ears of our lord alone."

"Were it any but you —" Suzuki began, then led the way into the palace after Mori had deposited his long sword in the rack by the main door. The steward kept looking over his shoulder at the young samurai, trying to guess what could be so important as to exclude him. Then he knelt by the door of the great audience hall, gently slid back the cedar-wood panel and saw Mori enter, kneel, then place his short sword on the mats by his left hand. With a cavernous sigh the steward slid the door to, lingered an instant and then reluctantly shuffled back to his post.

In the hall that was paved with a full fifty mats, Matsura knelt tranquilly by a screen made of arrows. Before him, Gentaro Mori spoke, his forehead pressed to the matting. In a low steady voice he was asking pardon of his Daimyo for past obstinacy. "My ears have been deaf to you, my lord, and I know that I was wrong. I kneel before you, ready to perform any public ceremonies that law and custom demand to show that I renounce all Christian ties. I am prepared to make public denial of a faith that my father once held, but long since cast off."

Matsura's old eyes opened slowly. "I have little time before me in this land, Gentaro Mori. Into that little time you have brought me happiness. I have long hoped that you would take this step."

"The fault is mine, Matsura-san," said Mori.

"In my own heart, I honor you for it," murmured the old Daimyo. "You held to the old ways that would not allow you to seem to criticize a former act of your father. In that lies deep piety. Yet you are of the new world, Gentaro Mori. You are urged to examine each fresh thought that comes to you. You do not reject the new because

140

it is new, nor cling to the old because it is old. I am pleased with you."

"The last Mori is yours, Matsura-san."

The Daimyo rose. "We shall drink tea in the little room by the garden that looks to the hills. Give me your arm. We shall sit by a warm brazier and look out to the slopes of Mount Yasuman that I have loved so well." They walked slowly along a corridor, the old man speaking gently. "I have always wanted to make more use of you, which shows me a selfish man. But I could do little until you had publicly renounced a faith which you had never practiced. Tomorrow I shall write the Shogun and it might be well if you yourself took the letter to Tokyo. Then the whole capital will know that you obey the laws in all ways. Before you start, you and I will don the proper robes, observe the proper fast and walk together to the Shinto temple under the high pines."

A panel in the wall slid back and Mori followed the Daimyo into the little room where a complete tea apparatus waited. The old man savored the powdered tea, busied himself with water and glowing charcoal. "Ah, the good tea of Uji! The water wants cooling, if the brew is to be perfect. So. The infusion is perfect and I fill our cups."

They drank with ritual slowness while Mori knew a peace of unimaginable depth. The old man murmured on, "There are other things. I am ill pleased with my guard, which you shall command on your return from Tokyo. I have noted your way with men and they will benefit by your care. Then there is the matter of the Mori lands, which may now revert to you on your renunciation."

Mori started and set his cup down hastily. "You will not think that I—"

The stiff silk of Matsura's haori rustled as he held up a frail old hand. "It is by my order that you accept what is now yours by right. More than that, I have heard that the elder daughter of Sugiura is ripe for marriage. The match would be a good one, and I should be honored to act as go-between."

Mori bowed to the mats. "My poor name is not worthy of such intercession."

Matsura smiled. "Old heads are better judges of such matters than young. There is another point. Men have told me that you have traveled much of late. I do not ask why, nor where. But by this very coming and going, you must have learned means of traveling where you want, without waiting on time, on man or beast, and without proclaiming your presence. There may be matters now and then in Kyoto or Osaka or even in Tokyo where a true man, speaking softly under the seal of his lord, may do much good."

That afternoon, Trudi and Petronella walked through a light snowfall along the path that led past the foundry. Petronella, skipping ahead of Trudi, cried, "And next week we go to the Daimyo's palace!"

"Next Friday, Petronella," answered Trudi. "The Asano girls will be there — oh, ever so many people. And we're going to play the incense game."

"The incense game? Is it hard?"

"We won't play it the grown-up way. The Daimyo's steward will bring out five kinds of incense and call each by the name of some animal. Then he gives each name a number. When he lights a stick — and you won't know which one it is — you have to write down the number you think is right. Then you've got to remember the name and the number. Whoever guesses best, wins a prize."

Petronella looked thoughtful. "My father's played that with the Shogun in Tokyo and he won, too. It sounds hard. Anyway, it'll smell nice."

"Very nice," agreed Trudi. "And we'll see all the Daimyo's wonderful bronze incense burners and the eldest Sugiura girl is going to read a poem on a theme the Daimyo set for her. It's 'Moonlight on Ruined Castles.' Oh! Look at the flames coming out of the foundry! They must be very busy. We'll go in and I'll show you the model of the cottage that Martin Trelawney built."

Just then Trelawney, his white hair rippling in the wind, stepped out, wiping his hands on his leather apron. "Eh! Good day to you, Trudi. Come in from the weather. The sight of you two does me good."

Trudi lifted Petronella over the high sill and stepped into the warmth of the shed. "Martin, do show Petronella your cottage. I was telling her about it and she wants to see it."

Martin chuckled. "Of course. Right over here on my own work-bench."

Petronella slipped her hand into the old man's, announcing, "And we're going to an incense sniffing at the Daimyo's. Oh, what a little house! Where are the shoji and the amado? Do the walls push back?"

Trudi stood by Martin while he explained the house to Petronella. Something vaguely disturbing hung in the back of her mind, something to do with the incense party, but its exact nature eluded her. The old man talked on, while Petronella poked tiny doors with her finger. "Aye, that's what I'll build for myself, close by Chatham, where the king's ships do lie," said Martin, dropping the roof.

"Chatham? Where's that? Is it many miles from here?" asked Petronella.

Martin sighed. "A weary way, but you'd best measure it in years, not in miles."

The Master-at-Arms turned to Trudi. "The *de Rijp* and the *Petten* dropped anchor off Kawachi this morning, and the next anchor to splash off there will set bedded in the mud till you and I and your uncle go aboard in the spring. You'd do well to go down and see them. Such batteries! Enough to blow a galleon out of the water."

Trudi looked sidewise at him. "And I suppose that Claes and Dirk and the rest have gone down to see about the cargo?"

"Likely," said Martin. "Now take that port battery — "

"Oh, but Dirk hasn't gone down to Kawachi," said Trudi quickly. "There's plenty without him. No doubt he's at the offices."

"He — he isn't there, either. Martin — do you know *where* he is?"

Martin looked at her in surprise. "Dirk? Not I. I do hear that he goes about for Caron."

"And where would he be likely to have gone for Heer Caron?"

Martin rubbed his shaven jaw. "There's a thousand places in the Empire he could have gone, but which one, I wouldn't know. I was never one to morris about."

"He went away with Heer Caron," said Trudi. "Heer Caron came back, but Dirk didn't."

Martin picked up Petronella and seated her on his bench. Then he looked keenly at Trudi. "So you brought Petronella down here to see the cottage? You'd no other thought in mind?"

"Of course not. I — I just happened to think of him when you spoke of ships," said Trudi defiantly. "Then I remembered I hadn't seen him and — well, I just asked, that's all."

Martin laid his hand gently on her shoulder. "Look now, Trudi. You're not going to sail with an empty heart when the spring ships come in, are you? Dirk's a good man, but you're sailing home and he's staying here."

Trudi looked up at him. "Martin! How silly! Of course I like Dirk, but — "

"But you're a sensible girl, I hope," said Martin. He studied her carefully composed features.

"Of course I'm sensible, Martin. I'm just counting the days till spring. Tell me — when do you think Dirk'll be back?"

"You'd best ask the Frenchman."

"But he won't see anyone and Uncle Van Os wouldn't know and I don't like to ask Heer Becker, so — "

"So you thought of pleasuring Petronella with a sight of my cottage," chuckled Martin. "No matter. I only wish I could answer your question." He looked down the shed as someone shouted, "Daikwan-no daruma-sen! The Daikwan's barge!"

"About time," said Martin. "It was supposed to be here this morning. Well, my men can roll what's wanted to the water gate."

"The Daikwan's barge!" cried Trudi, remembering the night when a similar barge came for the powder in charge of an officer who glared cold hatred at the Company people.

"No less. Ha! Let me show you what they've come for. Over here!" He strode to a dark corner, picked up a lighted lamp. Its rays shone down on a squat body, a gaping muzzle. "No master-at-arms has ever dared do this before, but I've solved it. Up to now, if you put too much powder in, the breech'd burst. Now I've reinforced the outer breech and fashioned a wider hollow right at the base. It'll take double the powder charge and that means double the range. And see how the trunnions are set? Petronella could serve as master gunner with such a piece."

Trudi looked into the muzzle as Martin withdrew his arm. "My, what a big cannon!" she said in feigned awe.

144

Martin snorted. "Cannon? You call that a cannon after all the hours you've spent playing in the same shed? Mortar! No, no. Cannon are to shoot straight along the ground. But my mortars, they toss their shells high over the walls to crash down on the folk back of those walls. Hey! Here are the Daikwan's men now. You'll excuse me while I see to them."

The snow had stopped when Trudi and Petronella started back toward the factory. The child chattered on about the incense party and about the model cottage. Trudi smiled absently at her, her mind busy. Suddenly she stopped as she recalled her earlier vague uneasiness. Now it seemed to lie not only in the talk of the incense party, but also in something Martin Trelawney had said. Cannon? Mortars? The mortars were built to toss shells high over walls. Castle walls, perhaps. Then she understood. The subject of the Daimyo's poem — "Moonlight on Ruined Castles." The poor men over in Shimabara, Dirk had told her, met in a ruined castle. But it was stupid to feel uneasy over two utterly unconnected thoughts — Martin's mortars and the Daimyo's poem.

Petronella gave a squeak of delight as they reached the side path that led onto the Company street, and ran ahead, arms stretched wide and crying out in a weird mixture of Japanese, French and Dutch. Trudi quickened her pace as she saw the girl's father coming down toward the offices. He could tell her about Dirk. She waved, calling "Goeden dag, Heer Caron!" Then she stopped when she saw his expression. His mouth was tightly set, with the corners drawn down, and his eyes were hard and unseeing. Petronella ran toward him, little arms still outstretched. Caron halted at her cry and his face changed as though a mask had been lifted from it. He dropped to one knee and caught the girl up. "Well, ma petite! Tu t'es bien amusée, hein? Goeden dag, Sayo-ko. What have you two been up to?"

Petronella patted his cheek. "Sayo-ko's been telling about incense sniffing at the Daimyo's and I saw Heer Trelawney's cottage and cook-san's going to make real Tokyo-zushi for me tomorrow!"

Caron set her down gently. "Do you suppose cook-san will make enough so your father can have at least one roll? Run up the hill and ask her and then when I come back, I'll tell you the story of

Momo-taro, the boy who was found inside a peach. Thank you for staying with her, Sayo-ko. I'd be very glad if you'd go up with Petronella." He bowed and kept on toward the main building, cheerily whistling "Berg-op-Zoom."

Trudi stared after him. "What's happened? He didn't feel like whistling when I first saw him. And I forgot to ask him about Dirk."

When Caron reached the office, his face had set once more in the expression that had disturbed Trudi. He entered the Director's office where Becker sat talking with Van Os. With a curt nod he drew a small key from his pocket, opened the most secret strong box and drew out some carefully folded papers. Then he stepped to the porcelain stove, nearly useless in the Hirado climate, opened it, struck fire and began carefully to burn the first sheet of the packet. Becker stared at him, then jumped to his feet. "What are those papers?"

Caron, without looking up, answered briefly, "The Shogun's maps and the plans that went with them."

Van Os looked mildly startled. "But see here, Heer Caron. Aren't those pretty important?"

"Very," said Caron, lighting another sheet and carefully crumbling ashes.

Becker lunged across the room, snatching at the last sheet unburned, but Caron held him off with one hand, unhurried and effortless. "Heer Je!" spluttered Becker. "Those are *my* papers. I'm responsible for them. The Governor General shall hear about this."

Caron turned from the stove as the final sheet charred away to nothing. "To their ashes, you're welcome, Heer Directeur!" Becker resumed his seat, and Caron faced the two men. "It's happened. Forget about Macao and Manila. The project's dead as Caesar. Listen to me. A few minutes ago, a Japanese made his way into my house. This is what he told me. The Amakusa rebels scored a complete victory over the Karatsu men and over those sent to reinforce them. Then, urged on by a Spanish friar, a young, vigorous man who'd been smuggled ashore not long ago, the whole force, with their old people, women and children, with their cattle, waded across the little strait, the Hayasaki-kaikyo, at low tide and came up the Shimabara peninsula, into the one spot we'd hoped to see quiet."

Becker frowned in perplexity. "What's that got to do with us?"

Van Os raised a calming hand. "Gently, Heer Directeur. Heer Caron doesn't act on impulse."

Caron turned patiently to the Director. "I've explained this over and over to you. Many of the rebels are Christians. So are we. Ergo, we sympathize with the rebels. That's how it will be put out by the antiforeign pack all through Japan. But I haven't finished. The Amakusa people, led by this friar, came onto the peninsula. Most of the Shimabara folk have joined them and they've taken possession of the old Castle of Hara or Shimabara, call it what you like."

"But *we're* not with them. Well, let 'em stay in the castle. They've got my permission," Becker spoke impatiently.

"But not that of the Shogun. The Imperial troops will move against them. They'll take that old ruin if they have to use every last pikeman and archer in the Empire. Then — " he smiled bleakly — "it's my opinion that their eyes will look this way. Unless a miracle happens, this will tilt the balance against us."

Becker jumped to his feet, white-faced. "Again and again I've told you that. I did not wish *my* subordinates crawling to the damned Japanese. Now you've got us into a beautiful mess." He threw up his hands. "Very well. You'll have to get us out of it."

Van Os spoke quietly, "What do you suggest doing, Heer Caron?"

"First of all, Heer Van Os, I suggest — or rather I urge — that you anticipate your retirement. Take Juffrouw Sayo-ko and sail out of here on the *de Rijp*. Old Trelawney better go too. I'll write a letter to show van Diemen in Batavia."

Van Os shook his gray head. "Trudi will go, of course. But I can't conceivably surrender my accounts to anyone not authorized by Batavia to take them over. Besides — it's possible I could help you a little."

"He'll need help!" shouted Becker.

Van Os went on, as though the Director had not spoken. "Yes, Trudi and Trelawney must go in the *de Rijp*. How about your own family?"

"I've taken thought about them. Of course, they can't go on the *de Rijp,* but I've other steps to take," said Caron. "Really, though, you'd best sail with the others. I appreciate your concern, but there'll be nothing to do here — except wait and watch. Now, let's consider the immediate present. We know what's happened. That's one advantage. Another is that Dirk Jongh's still over there. That's a huge asset. He'll either come in himself or send word."

"That boy's developed amazingly," said Van Os. "I agree that it's good to have him there. Now what's your first move?"

"I have two in mind — very obvious ones," said Caron, addressing Van Os as though the Director were not present. "First, in honor I've got to take this news to Gentaro Mori. Secondly, I must see Matsura. I doubt very much if either has heard anything. Surely not the Daimyo. My informant — well, he's under old obligations to me and would not be apt to go to the others." He pushed back from the table. "I'll start at once. Of course I'll tell Matsura nothing. If Dirk comes in, or word from him, while I'm gone send Claes after me."

He picked up a light cape, cocked his hat over one eye and left the room where Van Os sat in grave silence while Becker was alternately paling and flushing, the noise of his heavy breathing filling the room.

Caron went quickly through Hirado village and on inland until he sighted the tottering Mori house. The gate was open and he stepped into the bare garden. Gentaro Mori, in full armor and ceremonial dress, was talking by the corner of the house with the local tree merchant, pointing here and there as though giving orders. Mori looked quietly content and rested as though some long strain had been relieved. "God help me," muttered Caron. "And I am the one who must disturb that deep pool of serenity." He advanced bowing, and Mori greeted him warmly.

Mori's face went impassive with Caron's first words. He listened without the least change of expression. Then he said gravely, "You are a good friend, Caron-san. I shall mention your name when I kneel before the graves of my ancestors."

Caron took his leave and started for the Daimyo's palace. At the last turn of the narrow road, he glanced back. Mori's gates were shut tightly, and the tree merchant, looking very crestfallen and disappointed, was heading for the village.

There was no difficulty in being admitted to the palace. Matsura received him with his usual gentle friendliness and with his own hands prepared tea, smiling with pleasure as Caron spoke easily about formal gardens, archery and the etiquette of the winding-water-banquet. Caron's mind was nervously alert under his casual manner, but he could detect no change in the old man. The only thing that disturbed him was that the room in which they drank tea looked out onto the execution grounds. Several headless bodies lay on the short turf and a few officers of the guard were testing the keenness of their swords on the corpses, shouting applause over strokes that neatly detached an arm or split a torso deftly. When the cricket, drowsy and sluggish with the winter weather, had been brought out and admired, Caron took his leave, the old man actually escorting him to the main door, a frail old arm through the Frenchman's.

He made his way home through Hirado, lost in unpleasant thought. "My wife must go at once to her father. Old Eguchi will see that she is all right. Maria and Petronella must go with her. That last will be easy. But — Madame Caron will surely refuse to leave. How can I persuade her? Perhaps she'd be willing to take the children to visit at Fort Zeelandia in Formosa. Van Os must go, of course. The rest of us will have to stay. But the two of us — Dirk and I — have got to save the Company, even if we have to crawl on our hands and knees over the Tokaido from Kyoto to Tokyo."

People began to hail him as he passed through the narrow streets and habit was strong enough to make his answers easy and cheerful. When he reached the sea wall, he stopped and leaned his elbows on the parapet, eyes seaward in hope of catching sight of some craft, Hirado-bound with news from Dirk.

X

The Storm Breaks

DIRK paced restlessly up and down his cell which was lit by pale shafts of sunlight through the archers' slots. Three days had passed since Fra Fidel and his Amakusa men had found him in the magazine, long hours broken only by fitful snatches of sleep and the grudging appearance of his guards who brought him scant rations of rice, fish and tea. He fretted endlessly over what might be happening in the world outside, especially about the chance of word of the sudden outbreak having reached Hirado. It was quite conceivable, in the upset state of the country, that no news had crossed to the island province. Mori, hearing nothing for a few days, would judge that his associates merely had nothing to report. As for Caron, the Frenchman could quite logically reason that Dirk was lingering in the Shimabara area to complete a final report. In the meantime, he could only wait until the leaders of the revolt saw fit to free him from the tower.

He wondered what element among the Amakusans considered him dangerous and hostile, and what they felt they gained by holding him so closely. He leaned his elbows on the sill below the westernmost slot in the masonry. To the south he could see the long road over which the people had poured on that first day. Now there were scattered groups of armed men striding on toward the castle gate. From time to time he saw them wave toward the hidden northwest as though in greeting, and Dirk judged that other parties were making for the old ruin and the rebels whom it sheltered. Axles screeched through the thin air and four low carts piled with pikes and arquebuses toiled on from the south. Old men, women and children struggled to keep up with the turning wheels or clung to dangling ropes as though to tow themselves along. There was no hurry among all those people. The Imperial defeat on Amakusa must have been complete, allowing the islanders to pillage Imperial stores and arsenals on the peninsula at their leisure.

Between him and the hogback, where the road crossed, alert and military-looking armed men stood guard along such stretches of wall as were unbroken. But directly below, in the enclosure itself, chaos reigned. The people who had swarmed in through the yawning gates in hundreds and thousands had settled themselves by whim and by chance. Rude huts were formed of fallen stone roofed with flimsy thatch. Lengths of rotting wood propped up thick straw mats set edgewise. The curved ribs of an old boat served as a cavelike dwelling, the gaps patched with bits of old canvas or bundles of dried grass.

The strip of ground which Dirk's slot commanded was rough and broken, probably the least desirable site in the whole mile-square enclosure. So it was certain that the scene repeated itself over and over beyond the limits of his vision. There was not the slightest trace of order or planning. People had apparently thrown up their shelters at random, blocking the approaches to the wall, pre-empting the ground about the bubbling springs, hot and cold. Through the door of a nearby hut, he could make out sacks of rice carefully stored. Farther on, smoke rose thin and blue into the air. Off by the walls, a mother and two children bobbed and bowed before each hut, a bowl held out as though begging. A blind man, marked by his loose-ringed iron staff, stumbled and wandered through the maze and Dirk could just make out his high, cracked voice, calling some name.

The whole place was an invitation to slaughter, to a vicious rushing attack. Dirk tried to reason out what the Imperial reinforcements were doing. It seemed likely to him that they had been sent to retrieve the previous disasters on Amakusa and then had found that their prey had gone. Then what would they do? Remembering the usual Japanese inability to improvise when a previously set plan proved useless, he told himself that there would be long councils of war at Nagasaki, followed by a slowly evolved plan, which would be meticulously adhered to. The delay might be long, but he doubted if there was sufficient leadership in the castle to take advantage of it.

151

Then, too, the Imperial forces, in addition to whatever plan they thought out, were probably counting on treason among the rebels. His knowledge of Japanese history told him that this was quite likely to occur. Most of the Japanese heroes were revered not so much for valor as for trickery. There had been at least two campaigns that had been settled by a canny lord hanging on the fringes of the fight until he saw which way the tide was turning, and then throwing his weight to the probable winner. It was possible, too, that an amnesty would be proclaimed, followed by the massacre of those who took advantage of it.

There was a stir below him and he saw heads looking toward the east. People dropped to their knees and Fra Fidel, his cowl thrown back, came into sight, flanked by two helmeted Japanese. The friar halted, faced his companions, and his right arm made brusque motions as though stressing a point. The helmets wagged in disapproval but the friar, with a curt nod, turned and walked on, the others following reluctantly.

Dirk watched them out of sight, wondering what the disagreement could be. Among the huts, people returned to their tasks. Some women unrolled a great white sheet and bent over it as though sewing. Dirk made out the shape of a huge purple cross. In the awful welter below, it seemed that those women, and all the others too, could be set to more profitable tasks.

The door scraped open and he wheeled about. On the threshold stood another friar, a little, elderly man who regarded him benevolently, thumbs hooked through the cord about his waist. On the landing, a lean man with a pike watched uneasily. The friar spoke in fair Japanese. "Permit me — I am Fra Hilario. I think, Señor Jongh, that this confinement is quite unnecessary."

"You're letting me out? I can go back to Hirado?" asked Dirk.

Fra Hilario raised a worn hand. "At least, you may leave this tower. Will you come with me?"

As Dirk followed the friar, he remembered a block of moon-soaked masonry and a mass of ragged desperate men. He said, "I've seen you before, Fra Hilario. You spoke to the men of Arima, after old Asakawa tried to get them to rise."

"No doubt. I have spoken often — and always in the same vein."

"It's a pity that this happened, in spite of your work," said Dirk.

"Who knows?" answered the friar. "The important thing is that it has happened. I must work according to events, not my wishes."

They were passing along the passage where the powder and rice had been stored. Men were breaking open the rice sacks, spilling the grains wastefully along the floor. Beyond them, others squabbled over an open powder keg, filling their flasks from it and leaving a deadly trail of black dust about it.

Dirk's sense of order was shocked. "Shouldn't someone see to all this? A few people are getting all the rice."

"There is much to be seen to. It is possible that there are one or two outside who may listen to you. I heard you well spoken of by the Arima folk and came at once to let you out. A fresh voice that is respected could accomplish much."

They were out in the sunshine, weaving an erratic course among the huts. Children swarmed everywhere. Two women quarreled over a cooking pot. Whole families were arguing loudly over possession of a site that held a hot spring. Close by the castle wall, bewildered by the weird setting and the clamor about them, an old man and an old woman sat side by side, their eyes moving fearfully right and left. At each new outburst they moved closer together.

"Much to be done. So much to be done," said Fra Hilario, shaking his head sadly.

"How many people have come in?" asked Dirk, more and more depressed by the tragic confusion about him.

"Some say ten thousand souls, Señor Jongh. I would not intrude my own views, but I believe that fifteen thousand is the closer number."

Dirk stepped wide to avoid a wan-faced woman who nursed a child by a pile of sodden mats. "There can't be that many, Fra Hilario."

"All things are possible in this land. You've only seen those inside the walls. They build huts on the outside and down into the western valley, all those others."

"I wish I could help. But I think I'll be of more use if I go back to Hirado."

"I'm afraid that may not be." Fra Hilario slackened his pace and Dirk fell into step with him. "I must tell you, Señor Jongh, that all this happened without thought or plan. There was, on

Amakusa, a young priest of my order, Fra Fidel. Fidel is an intensely devout man — most devout. Also, he has all the impetuosity of youth. His preaching led to the rising on Amakusa. Since it was successful, he brought all his people, who regarded him with something like worship, into this place to liberate the Shimabara Christians. Many more joined him on the way, along with countless non-Christian sufferers. From here, he plans a crusade that will plant the cross in Tokyo."

"What?" cried Dirk. "Against all the Imperial forces?"

Fra Hilario sighed. "I remarked that Fra Fidel is both devout and impetuous. He spends all his time here preaching his crusade, with whose aim I cannot quarrel. But he neglects his means. Further, rifts have sprung up already. He holds that he is the leader of all Christians and will hear no advice. Worse than that, he favors the Amakusans over the Shimabara people. Naturally, the Shimabarans resent this and the Amakusans are perhaps unduly exalted in their own minds." He sighed again. "Fra Fidel means so well. But he will not see that thought, added to faith, is a most valuable thing."

"How about the non-Christians?" asked Dirk. "There must be plenty of them."

"Hewers of wood and drawers of water, in his eyes," said Fra Hilario. "I warn you that he will have little use for you. But the two most important of the Christian Japanese will listen, and with some respect. I speak, of course, of Tokisada and Nirado."

"I still don't see what I can do," persisted Dirk. "I'll slip out somehow. I know where there's a sampan and I'll get back to Hirado."

"I fear you would find it difficult, my friend," said Fra Hilario. "As for what you can do, you know the respect the people have for the word of a Komo, of one from that outer world which they scarcely know. In addition to that, I have heard of you long before this. Tokisada and Nirado both speak very highly of you."

Dirk said stubbornly, "I'll talk to Tokisada and the others on condition that I have free passage from here afterward."

"I doubt if you are in a position to bargain, Señor Jongh, though I'll do what I can for you. Fra Fidel combines violence with piety to a rather alarming degree. To him, you are worse than a non-

154

Christian Japanese, since, in his eyes, you have deliberately strayed from the faith."

"And in yours?" asked Dirk.

"I could wish that your heart spoke differently to you, Señor Jongh. But I must respect its speech," said Hilario simply.

The tangle of huts and mats was thinning as they neared the outer wall. By a blocked-up gate Dirk saw Fra Fidel standing with folded arms while two Japanese, whom he recognized as Tokisada and Nirado, spoke earnestly to him. Young Tokisada, handsome and slim, caught sight of Dirk and Fra Hilario and turned to them with a bow. Nirado, squat and powerfully built, called out in recognition.

Dirk studied the young friar. In the daylight he looked a little like François Caron. His eyes were deep-set, black and piercing, lit up by a fanatical intensity, hotly intolerant, even arrogant. He spoke sharply to Tokisada in halting Japanese, then fell back on Portuguese. The two Japanese turned reluctantly to him and he led them out of earshot.

"Aren't you going to talk to him?" asked Dirk.

Fra Hilario shook his head. "It is better this way — for the moment."

"But you're of his faith and of his order."

"Unfortunately, he holds me weak in the faith because I preached against violence," said Fra Hilario sadly. "The most that he accords me is a sort of angry respect, since I am his superior. But authority is hard to enforce when its source is halfway around the world. And if he and I come to open dissent, these poor people here will suffer. To their present suffering I cannot add. Ah! Here he comes."

Dirk stepped aside as Fra Fidel strode up to the old friar and the two began a conversation in what Dirk judged to be Spanish. Their voices rose and fell in his ears, Fra Fidel harsh and violent, Fra Hilario calm and tolerant. At last the younger man marched off, his lips compressed under his beard. Fra Hilario turned to Dirk. "He claims possession of you, since Amakusans captured you, but he releases you into my temporary care. Now I in turn release you to Tokisada and Nirado. There may be something that you can do for these people. If so, do it in the name of God, whom we all follow, though along different paths." He made the sign of the cross and slipped away among the huts.

It was apparent at once that Fra Hilario had been right about the respect accorded by Japanese to the word of the Komo. As soon as the formal greetings were over, Tokisada and Nirado began to shower Dirk with questions that ranged from the placing of guards to the protection of the countless young women of the growing city within the walls. While the two talked, Dirk studied them. Tokisada was very young, scarcely into his twenties, but he seemed to think rapidly and with an unusually mature clarity. Dirk was surprised to find that he had had no military training at all. Nirado was well past thirty, a strong, stocky man with a hairline of mustache in imitation of bygone Shoguns and generals. His scarred, weather-beaten face told of past campaigns, but his grasp did not, in Dirk's lay mind, equal Tokisada's in military matters.

At last Dirk held up his hands in protest. "I'm not a soldier. I don't even know what a lot of your questions mean. As far as I can see there's not a thing I can advise you about. If you want my opinion, though — " He paused, trying to look at the whole scene from an orderly, trader's standpoint. "Here's the first thing I'd do. Clear away all these huts. Mark out streets. Don't let a few people monopolize the springs while the rest go thirsty and dirty. Appoint a headman for each street and group of streets. Appoint two or three bath masters. Confiscate all the food, all the powder, and put it into a common store and under guard. Find a reliable man to serve it out fairly to the people. Probably you've thought of all this."

Tokisada and Nirado exchanged glances. The younger man said diffidently, "You know how we live in our towns and villages, Yang-san. Each house is responsible to the head of the street. Each head of a street to the head of the chomé, the block, the chomé to the cho, the precinct, and so on. But here — " he threw out his hands helplessly — "here we have no streets, no chos and no chomés. The people don't know what to do."

"Then name someone with authority to get things started," said Dirk crisply. "It doesn't matter much whom."

Nirado frowned. "If it's an Amakusan, the rest of us won't like it. If it's a man from around here, the Amakusans will object."

"Then appoint one of the friars. Do *something!*"

"Most people listen to the young friar," said Tokisada dubiously. "Eh-to! Very difficult. We sent men to dig earthworks along the high ground to the west outside the walls and he objected. He wanted men to build shrines, to find cloth to make holy banners. At the moment, they dig, but when he has talked to them, they may drop their tools and follow him."

Dirk leaned back against a block of stone. "I'm sorry. That's all I can suggest. But remember this. You've still got a little time. It may take days to bring the Imperial forces from Amakusa to Shimabara. But those days will pass. If they pass before you've found a man who's both a governor and a soldier — " He looked at Nirado. "You're a military man. How long would it take a general like Itakura to capture this old ruin?"

"Ah!" said Nirado. "I wonder."

"Here's another thing I've just thought of," said Dirk, straightening up. "Have you sent word to Gentaro Mori?"

"Three men have been sent," said Tokisada gloomily. "All of them were caught at Isahaya, where there's a small garrison."

"What!" exclaimed Dirk. "Is that all you've tried? He'll hear, of course, in time. You ought — Look here! This is one thing that I *can* do for you. Get me out of here, and I'll reach Hirado. The Daikwan's men or Itakura's would never interfere with me. I've met the Daikwan several times. He'd vouch for me."

Tokisada avoided Dirk's eyes while Nirado shook his head. "The young friar would not allow it."

"But what could he do, once I had gone? Suppose he is angry. Wouldn't it be worth it to have Mori here?"

"We do not know that he would come. He's not from Shimabara or Amakusa. And if the young friar were angry, he might set the Amakusans against us," objected Nirado.

"Then send some man who knows these waters. I'll show you a way out. There's an old path that slants right up the face of the cliffs by the north wall." He pushed past a team of tethered oxen, stepped over a sleeping couple and headed for the north wall, Tokisada and Nirado following irresolutely.

As Dirk hopped over hastily scooped refuse pits, skirted little fires where tea water boiled, his eyes were busy. There were no guards on the east wall, where the cliffs fell sheer. On the north wall, there were only two or three, placed near its junction with the west.

He reached the gap in the walls, twisted past the fallen blocks and stood on the cliff's edge. Far below him, on a tiny crescent of beach, lay the sampan, and at the sight of it he drew a deep breath. The way was clear for him now, permission or no permission, if he kept his head. It would be hard to do alone, but he was sure that he could do it somehow. Before too long he would sight the old powder house, the deep horseshoe of Hirado Bay and the step-gabled Dutch houses. Then he and Caron would pool their knowledge and make a plan. There would be so much to think of. Suddenly his mind showed him Trudi, slim and pretty, swinging gracefully down the hill. He realized that she had constantly been in the back of his mind, overlaid a little by present emergencies, but still vivid. Would she be wondering about his absence?

By his elbow Tokisada cried out sharply, pointing out into the gulf. A broad-beamed barge was working slowly in toward the cliffs, a banner floating from the mast. Nirado shouted, "The Daikwan's colors!" in the same instant that Dirk recognized them.

Tokisada yelled to the men on the walls to join them on the cliff, to bring others with them, and Dirk caught his breath. It would be simple enough, given strong arms, to send heavy stones crashing down onto the barge's deck as it made the little beach, its obvious goal. Men swarmed out of the gaps in the walls, seized long beams and began to pry at the stones nearest the edge, while Nirado, leaning far over, raised a cautioning hand, calling to them to wait for his word.

In fascinated horror, Dirk leaned with him. The barge, its sail lowered, was coasting in easily. Fifty yards more and it would be in the path of a dozen boulders! Then he shouted a warning, snatched a lever from the nearest man. Far below, on the blue surface of the gulf, the barge crept in. Men moved swiftly on its deck, unrolling what looked to Dirk like strips of bright canvas. The men on the barge sprang to the thwarts and all eyes on the cliff looked down at the broad, colored strips that were laid out on the deck in the shape of two arcs, whose upper ends joined — the Mori crest! Dirk's breath went out in a great gust of relief.

He turned to Tokisada. "There's your governor and soldier. Did you have any doubt that he would come?"

High on the walls, others saw the rude crest far below on the deck and men began to shout, "Mori! Gentaro Mori!" Dirk stretched out on the turf, looking down. The barge had been beached and he thought that he could make out Mori, directing three other men, who seemed to be unloading something from the barge. Picks and axes! What did Mori want of them? Then the men began to swing them against the ribs of the barge and the dull *thud-thud-thud* of the tools echoed faintly. It seemed to Dirk that the men were knocking out plugs from holes previously drilled in the bottom. At a command from Mori, they heaved the craft into the water again, where the tide caught it and drew it out farther and farther into the gulf. It must have been in heavy ballast, for very soon the waves lapped over its thwarts and it sank in a sullen swirl. Then Mori made a gesture to his men and started up the path.

Hirado seemed a cheerless, alien place to Trudi as she walked slowly along the southern arm of Hirado Bay. The sun was strong, but a chill wind that held a hint of fog whistled through the tumbled walls of the old English factory, stirring up ghostly echoes as it riffled through the rubbish heaps. She drew her padded haori closer about her, keeping on toward the head of the bay and town.

The times were strange and everyone was strange with them. Becker, over there at the Dutch factory, kept himself sullenly soaked in brandy. Her uncle, though outwardly calm, was obviously worried. To her, he spoke cheerfully of their coming departure on the *de Rijp,* now anchored close to the old powder house on the point, where no Dutch sail had ever been seen before. But at night, as she lay sleepless, she heard him endlessly pacing up and down the little room that he used for a study just below. Heer Caron was always courtly and debonair when he spoke to her, but when she came upon him unexpectedly, his strong face was set in the same mask that she had seen when she and Petronella met him on their way home from the Company foundry. Most of the time he stood with a strong telescope, scanning the Kyushu shore, or running up to the cliffs above the factory whenever a sail or flash of oars was sighted.

Twice she had joined him in his watch, because she knew that he was watching for Dirk — or a message from Dirk. But his concentration was so intense that it frightened her. It was as though he had passed into a state of suspended animation that could only be broken by something from Dirk. When she had asked him for news, away from the sea wall, he had always evaded her by saying that Dirk could be trusted to take care of himself. Any day he would return, and the longer he stayed away, the more bountiful his cargo of news would be when he finally landed at the floating wharf.

Her geta clicking sharply on the stones of the beach, she tried to draw comfort from Caron's assurances. After all, he knew more than the Shogun himself about happenings in the Empire. If he were really worried about Dirk, he'd know a dozen ways of ending those worries. But she hoped the *de Rijp* would not sail before Dirk returned. She wanted to say good-by to him. She wanted to see the expression on his face when he saw the silken case that she had embroidered to hold his treasured tea caddy which had come from the bottom of the sea, Matsura's gift to him. She wanted to see — She gathered her haori tighter. She wanted to see Dirk.

As she kept on along the curve of the beach, movement inland caught her eyes and she stopped. Up on the slopes, perhaps half a mile away, men were standing about a shabby house, leaning on their pikes. Close by the roadside she could make out the black and gold glory of the Daimyo's norimono, and she wondered what could have brought old Matsura to such a poor house. There were more men in the fields beyond, men who hacked with long poles at the dikes of a small rice field. Smoke welled, black and oily, from under the tiled roof of the house and the pikemen withdrew, watching. The smoke rose higher and higher as though lifted by the bright flames below. The roof shivered, then slowly sank into the flames, whose hoarse crackling Trudi could hear faintly. In the fields, the men still hacked at the dikes, breaking them down. She thought mechanically, "But they're ruining the field. And the next one! They're plowing it with oxen. They're dumping loads of sand and plowing it into the loam!" She felt her cheeks grow

160

cold. She should have recognized the house before. Gentaro Mori's house. Mori, one of the Daimyo's favorites and Dirk's friend!

Blindly, she began to run, stumbling and tripping over the barnacled rocks of the beach. Twice she had to stop, hand to her side and breath coming sharp and hard. Then she was in Hirado village, running along a narrow alley that led past some fish shops and a bathhouse into the main street.

Back to her, a pikeman, Matsura's crest on his haori, stood blocking the way, his weapon held easily across his knees. She tried to sidle past him, but he merely swung his pike butt in front of her without so much as a glance. There were more soldiers in the street, heading on toward the road that led up to the palace. Then came a file of bearers, carrying high the old Daimyo's norimono. The shutters of the palanquin were open and Trudi caught a glimpse of Matsura's peaceful old face. He recognized her, raised his frail hand and smiled his weary smile. Then he was gone, the last pikeman trailing after him.

She stood, bewildered. Matsura had ordered Mori's house burned and Mori's fields plowed up and ruined. Mori was Dirk's friend. Yet Matsura's recognition, in public, of a young girl had been a rare favor and he seemed friendly as ever. She could not imagine what Mori could have done to bring down the Daimyo's wrath.

She hurried on, hoping to have a chance to speak with Martin Trelawney. Some word of Dirk might have come into port while she was across the bay. Only yesterday, Martin had spoken most reassuringly as he drove the last peg into the case that held his model cottage, now safely stowed in the hold of the *de Rijp*. The workshop doors were ajar, but Martin was at the far end that opened onto deep water, perched in the stern of a barge that held two long cannon. As she watched, the barge put out and headed for the *de Rijp*. Then she saw a second barge, richly carved and painted, alongside the Company ship and she recognized the Daikwan's colors at the stern.

She turned away, dispiritedly. There were too many uneasy questions in everything that she saw. She decided to go up the hill, taking Madame Caron some Kyoto bean paste, knowing that the older woman and her children loved the slick, smooth, tasteless yokan. As she took the side path that led upward, she saw several men in official robes along the promenade. Could there be more questioning in store for the Company people? Recently she had spent tedious hours answering questions about priests and churches and symbols, as she had on her arrival at Kawachi.

When she reached the Caron house, a strange hush hung over gate and roof. A timid maid finally answered her knocking, held the gate open a mere fraction of an inch. No, Caron-fujin had taken the children that noon and had gone south down the island with several bearers. There was no word of when she was expected home, but it would surely not be for several days.

Trudi turned away uneasily. She sat on a high, square stone set at the right of the hill trail, her eyes on the Kyushu shore, seemingly so close. The sun was sinking and there was a new chill in the air. Idly she watched the wind ruffle the spreading mouth of the bay as the sun touched the white walls of the Daimyo's forts on the south point.

Then she was on her feet, staring in unbelief. The *de Rijp* was standing out into the channel, all sails set, while the Daikwan's gilded barge glided ahead of it. The other barge, which she had seen at the foundry, was in tow of the Company ship. On the poop of the *de Rijp,* several Japanese, unmistakable in their kimonos and helmets, stood by the rail. A little apart from them stood a tall figure in European clothes. The *de Rijp* was putting to sea and François Caron sailed with it!

For an instant, Trudi felt an odd relief. Wherever the *de Rijp* was sailing, its final departure would be delayed. In the meantime, Dirk might return. But where was the *de Rijp* bound? Not for Kawachi and its anchorage, for in that case it would be merely towed by the ship's boats into the current and ride the stream down the shore.

A thin voice spoke behind her and she turned with a start. An old begging nun, shaven head bound in white, was leaning on a staff dotted with brands of the shrines she had visited. "Komo no uchi?" the nun quavered, pointing at Caron's house.

"Yes. A foreigner's home. There's no one there," answered Trudi. The nun drew closer. "Caron-san?" she asked.

Trudi indicated the *de Rijp,* now well into the current.

The nun's face was impassive. Then she held out a hand, whining.

162

Mechanically, Trudi fumbled in her obi, drew out two or three pierced copper coins and dropped them into the bony hand. The nun bowed, blessing Trudi in the name of Ebisu, god of prosperity, of Kompira, god of travelers, blessed her again in the name of the Komo held captive by the Amakusa men in the ruined castle by the Gulf of Shimabara.

In a daze Trudi watched the nun totter off down the hill. At last she knew where Dirk was, and the knowledge chilled her. And how did the old nun know, and who had sent her? Dirk, a prisoner at Hara! And Caron, the one man who could help him, was sailing south down the channel. As she walked slowly toward her uncle's house, she reasoned that Dirk's knowledge of Japan and of its people would soon set him free. He couldn't come to any harm. Of course he couldn't, and in a few days he would come back to Hirado.

Later, as she sat at dinner with her uncle, her carefully built assurance ebbed slowly away. Van Os, gloomily eying the packing cases that filled most of the house, was obviously depressed. "Our head interpreter talked with the Daimyo's steward," he said. "Bad doings yonder on Kyushu. They'll use the whole Imperial army to track down the rebels if they have to. Of course, there'll be torture and massacre at the end. I tell you, we ought to be on the *de Rijp* now."

"But there's the *Petten,* at Kawachi," she observed, forcing herself to nibble at the grilled reed birds that Nobu had set before her.

Van Os shook his head. "Caron gave orders for her to slip away."

Trudi's hands dropped to her lap. "Then we've nothing?"

Van Os shrugged. "Oh, the *de Rijp*'ll come back. It's cleared for Nagasaki, carrying a load of mortars and cannon and powder. But I can't say when it'll anchor off the sea wall again." He pushed back from the table. "I'm sorry to leave you, Trudi, but I'd best go down to the office. Caron's gone. Becker's useless with brandy and we may have other demands from the Daikwan. Why did Jongh pick this one time to go for a frolic to Kyushu? Oh, I nearly forgot! Will you do something for me? I showed you the secret drawer of my cabinet last week, didn't I? Well, in that drawer you'll find a roll of paper. It's a copy of a map of Kyushu that Caron gave me.

It ought to be burned. Will you see to it for me? I ought to have done it long ago. Good night, my niece. Don't sit up for me."

When he had gone, Trudi left the table and went into his study. The cabinet was a heavy carved piece and had not yet been crated for shipment. She opened an upper cupboard, felt along its smooth inner side, then pressed down on a bit of wood. A section of the interior dropped forward and Trudi's fingers closed around a roll of soft, thick paper. She drew it out, unrolled it and held it to the light, vaguely curious. There was all of western Kyushu, neatly drawn and with the place names marked in Japanese.

She bent over the map. Here was Hirado, and the south-running channel between it and Kyushu. Here was the chain of islets, then the Gulf of Omura, opening deeply, east on the Kyushu shore. Omura and its castle were well marked. Beyond Omura was the dreadful country where she had seen Nagato's bailiffs at work. East, beyond the far end of the Gulf of Omura, was Isahaya in the middle of a narrow neck of land that presently swelled into the great bulk of the Shimabara peninsula. Her finger traced the route, step by step. The end of the Gulf of Omura. Isahaya and then over the upper knuckles of the Shimabara fist, south over the jutting finger joints. There it was, carefully marked in Dirk's script: "Cliff very high here. Ruins of castle called Hara."

She pulled up a chair and sat studying the map. Then she rose with a sudden movement, burned the map in the flame of the lamp and crumbled away the ashes. Her mind was made up as surely as though she had pondered the matter for months. Dirk was held captive in Kyushu. Very well, she would go to him. She went up to her room and changed rapidly into heavier clothing, then made her way down to her uncle's study. She opened the strong box marked with her name, took out ten oval gold pieces and some silver, slipped the coins into her obi, and left the house without a backward glance.

Head down, she walked swiftly to the beach road and into the village, her geta crunching in the sand. The light surf drew a line of frothy white along the beach and cast up phosphorescent bits that glowed eerily. Near the end of the village she halted and rapped on a flimsy gate. Inside a door slid open and footsteps padded to the gate, which opened a crack. There was a low cry of surprise and Aoki, the lame boatman, exclaimed, "Eh, why didn't you send fat Nobu and spare yourself the trip, ojo-san? I would have come to you gladly. Please enter. The house is poor, but it holds only your friends."

Trudi shook her head, then spoke rapidly to him in low tones. Aoki exclaimed "Ara!" and stepped back a pace, instinctively. She spoke on and he listened, shaking his head violently from time to time. Finally Trudi threw back her head. "Then I go alone." She started away from the house.

Aoki limped after her. "I will lead you, ojo-san. I will lead you!" He vanished indoors, reappeared, his arms flapping as he struggled into a padded coat. Then he set out along the road that followed the south arm of the deep bay toward the white huddle of the Daimyo's forts on the point.

The night was still, save for the rustle of the easy surf. Far up in the hills a dog barked violently and from an isolated house a thin voice sang, quavering on the high notes. The wind rolled seaward and brought a tang of charred timbers that told of the end of the house of Mori. Trudi drew her coat about her and kept on, eyes on the bob and sway of Aoki's shoulders just ahead. Now they were moving along the lower stretches, past the old English factory and onto the flats that marked the end of the south arm.

A sliver of light showed among coarse sea grasses and Aoki, asking Trudi to wait, limped forward, then knocked on a tottering gate that swallowed him up. She leaned against a huge chunk of driftwood. With her geta she heaped up a mound of sand, flattened it, heaped it up again. The gate creaked and Aoki stood beside her, shaking his head. "It is no use, ojo-san. They will not listen."

Trudi drew herself up. "They must! You told them they would have gold?"

"I told them. They laughed."

She stood irresolute, as though her determination were ebbing. She looked across the bay where the lights of the Company shone along the old sea wall. Her throat tightened as she thought of her uncle, busy over there and expecting to find her at the breakfast table the next morning. She couldn't vanish into the night like this, leaving him deeply troubled about her. Maybe there would be other ways of reaching Dirk, of rescuing him. She could go back now and talk it all over with her uncle. But she knew that he could be of no help, that he would certainly prevent her going on her rash journey. There was no other way. She stepped past Aoki, pushed open the gate and slid back the door of the hut beyond it.

The three men who crouched over an hibachi stared up at her. Trudi surveyed them, her mind working mechanically. The thin man and the gap-toothed man she disregarded, speaking only to the third, with his heavily pockmarked face and the eyes that shrank to shiny points as his mouth stretched in a ceaseless grin. She spoke rapidly and in a low tone, and the pockmarked man grinned into the glow of the hibachi without looking at her. She felt as though she were talking to a lump of driftwood. With a sudden motion she reached into her obi and spread three gold coins on the torn matting. "When you come back to Hirado, go to Aoki-san, who will give you three more coins like these."

The pockmarked man still grinned into the hibachi, while his mates stared open-mouthed at the gold. There was a rustle behind Trudi and she knew that Aoki had slipped in to join her. The leader ran a calloused hand over his stubbly hair. The ragged sleeve of his coat fell back, showing a muscular arm along which a white scar spiraled up and up. Then he spoke, eyes still on the coals. "You see this arm?" He held it out, flexing the muscles, and the scar seemed to live, to writhe upward. "Once I offended the Daikwan and hung in the pit, like the Christians in the old days. I was tough. I lived. I was banished to Hirado. If I am caught in Kyushu, I will get more than scars and banishment."

Trudi looked hard at him, at the others. With a deliberate gesture she stacked the three gold ovals in a pile, and her fingers closed about them as she started to rise.

Still not looking up, the pockmarked man motioned to his fellows. "Iko! Let's go!"

X I

City of Huts

THE next morning, Dirk stood at the summit of the tower that
dominated the southwest corner of the outer walls. The outsloping
stone foundations stretched firm and tight, shutting in the mile-
square enclosure, and above them the white walls rose and dipped,
now reaching a solid thirty feet in the air, now falling away to the
gray masonry below. The castle itself had partially crumbled to the
ground, its original lines marked here and there by the stump of a
tower, like the one in which he had been confined, an unbroken
strip of wall, a half-gutted storehouse. North, east and south the
blue sea rolled and slapped against the high cliffs of the promontory.

Beyond the west wall of the castle, Dirk could see men crowding,
but the great meeting where Mori, Tokisada and Fra Fidel were
speaking was hidden from him.

He looked westward where the land fell away into a broad
valley, marshy and cut by a small stream, then rose in a sharp ridge
over which the road to Isahaya trailed. The ridge itself was joined
by the hogback that he had seen from his archer's slot, slanting
up from the southeast. There were working parties along the
ridge that was already scored by trenches and earthworks, but the
hogback, which covered the southern road to Amakusa, was bare
and unmarked. This puzzled Dirk, since it seemed to him that the
Imperial forces would mass on Amakusa and then follow the trail
of Fra Fidel's people north into Shimabara, a route which would
eventually bring them to the hogback. That a skilled soldier, as
Itakura was said to be, would transship his whole force and strike
from Isahaya and the west seemed preposterous.

Mori appeared around a mass of tumbled stone, talking earnestly
with Tokisada and Fra Fidel. The tall young friar was marking
each step by bringing his fists together as though chafing under

167

heavy restraint. Then Mori left the other two and started for the tower. Dirk heard him mount the inner stairs slowly and wearily as though discouraged. As the dragon-crested helmet emerged, Dirk asked quickly, "Have you taken command?"

Mori took off his helmet and joined Dirk by the parapet. His handsome face was drawn and haggard and his eyes looked dull. "In command?" said Mori. "Yes. But I've no really free hand. Compromise, dicker, compromise again. I command the castle, but the Amakusa men are answerable only to Tokisada, the Shimabara people to Nirado and the non-Christians to old Asakawa. Of course, all three leaders are responsible to me, but the arrangement is a loose one." He sighed. "Fra Fidel is the chief trouble. He claims command of everything, from rations to grand strategy. I wish I knew how to handle him. What would you do?"

"I?" echoed Dirk, surprised. "I haven't any idea. I've never had to deal with friars of any kind before."

"But he's a Komo, a European, like you," Mori insisted.

"Your ideas are as good as mine. I'd stress to him the fact that your father was Christian. You don't need to say that he's now a Buddhist priest. Was he the only one of your family who was Christian?"

"No. My paternal grandfather, who was converted by the great Saint Francis Xavier."

"By all means mention that. Then suggest to him that he's far too valuable to waste his strength in military matters. Tell him that the souls of his followers need him, that they're his first charge."

Mori was irritated. "His duty to those souls seems to justify everything that he wants to do."

"Then there's Fra Hilario," Dirk went on.

"Yes. He will be a help. There's so much to be done. I finally managed to get two hundred men together to fortify the hogback over there. It should have been done before, but Fra Fidel was told in a dream by Santa Barbara that the attack would come from Isahaya. That's why the Amakusa approaches were neglected. I must say that Fra Fidel has great power and a good mind. If we can only turn them into the right channels, it will be a great gain."

Suddenly the tragic futility of the whole enterprise struck Dirk. What good were gains to any of the people in Hara? The Imperial forces would keep on striking until the ghastly and inevitable end. Every soul swarming down there in the enclosure, every man, woman and child, was doomed hopelessly. And no one was more hopelessly doomed than Gentaro Mori, the leader, who had cast away everything to come to the aid of people who had relied on him in the past. He had offended against the Emperor, against the Shogun and against gentle old Matsura, who held him in high favor.

Dirk glanced at Mori, who must know all this as surely as he himself knew it. The young samurai's face showed only deep weariness and concern for the present. Dirk said diffidently, "I don't like to bring this up when you've so much to do, but was any ruling made about me?"

Mori looked graver than ever. "I had hoped to send you through the Imperial lines, when they form, with a letter to Itakura explaining how you came here. Fra Fidel and the Amakusans are afraid you'll tell about our dispositions, even though unwittingly."

"But I can't stay here," Dirk protested. "There's no sign of Itakura yet. Why don't I just walk out of the gate?"

"I spoke of that, but they said that sooner or later you'd be bound to meet Imperial troops. The best I can do is to arrange for you to go down to the beach tonight. A little skiff is hidden under a mass of seaweed there. It's your only chance."

Dirk nodded reluctantly. "I'd rather leave here with everyone's consent, but if this is the only way, I'll have to take it. I wish I could get out without involving you."

"What does it matter?" asked Mori. He turned, looked out to the gulf, and his face grew graver.

Dirk looked with him and what he saw struck him like a physical blow. A long line of barges and sampans was working up from the south, slowly growing more and more distinct. Along the bulwarks, steel glinted and at each masthead the Daikwan's banner flaunted.

The flotilla came on and formed in a great arc about the promontory where the ruined castle stood. The heavier ships anchored. Lighter craft circled about, took position and began to patrol as close inshore as they dared, manned by troops who would greet any fugitive from Hara with arrow or sword. The blockade of Hara had begun.

Mori laid a hand on Dirk's shoulder. "I am very sorry — " he began.

Dirk shook himself as though emerging from cold water. "I'm not giving up. We'll find some way. In the meantime — in God's name give me something to *do!* I can be useful, so long as I've got to stay here. There's nothing I can do out with the troops, but look at the confusion among the huts."

Mori fingered the brim of his helmet. "Yes — there is much to be done. But the Amakusans — "

"Exactly!" cried Dirk. "I can go among all the factions impartially. Fra Hilario can help me with the Christians. Just let me tell them all that I speak in your name and that Fra Hilario represents Fra Fidel."

"It might do," said Mori slowly. "You'll need helpers. I'll give you most of the men on guard on the south wall. All those ships of the Daikwan are for blockade only, I'm sure. They haven't got enough men to attack and besides, the cliffs are sheer most of the way around. So if you want me at any time, come to this tower. If I'm not here, there'll be someone who knows where I am."

Dirk went quickly down the tower. Not only would the task ahead give him something to keep his mind busy, but he could also be on the lookout for a chance to escape.

In the great enclosure, the din was terrific. Children ran everywhere, whooping and screeching. Cattle, unfed and unwatered, lowed heavily. Not far from the tower entrance, men struck at each other with long sticks as they disputed the ownership of a sack of millet. Dirk climbed on a stone block and looked about him. He caught sight of Fra Hilario, deftly bandaging the knee of a child. Then he caught hold of the nearest urchin. "Are you from Amakusa?"

The boy nodded as he tried to wriggle away. "Then I give you the rank of gocho — of corporal," said Dirk, still holding the ragged collar of the kimono. "It is by the order of Gentaro Mori, the great soldier."

The boy stopped wriggling. "I — a gocho, by Mori-san's order?"

"As I tell you. Go among your people. Tell everyone you see that it is by Mori-san's wish that all who were heads of wards, precincts and streets assemble here."

The boy scampered off importantly. Fra Hilario joined Dirk just as the latter, after several failures, caught a Shimabara boy, solemnly gave him rank and sent him off like his fellow.

"How may I serve you, Señor?" asked Fra Hilario quietly.

Dirk explained what he had done and the friar looked inquiringly at him. "You think they will come?"

"Most of them. Just now, they are lost in all this mess. Mori's summons will set them apart, give them some of their old importance."

Fra Hilario nodded. "Yes, they will come. But how may I help in all this?"

"You've seen more of the world than I have, Fra Hilario. You'll think of a dozen things that would escape me. Of course, it puts you in the position, being here with me, of vouching for a Protestant."

"There is no difficulty there, so long as what you wish does not go against the faith."

"In that case, it would be unconscious on my part and you could warn me. Something's got to be done for these people. They won't do it themselves."

Fra Hilario looked at Dirk for an instant. Then he said, "Your whole concern is for them. I'm sure that the question of faith will not arise. Ah, here come your people."

By twos and threes, men began drifting toward the foot of the tower where Dirk and the friar stood. They were middle-aged or elderly men, accustomed to authority which came to them from still higher officials, but helpless when superior hierarchy failed to send them orders and instructions.

Dirk bowed courteously to each as he came up, begged them to be seated on a stretch of turf by the foot of the wall. Then, using semi-formal language as befitted their rank without honoring it too much, he began, "Gentaro Mori has accepted the command of Hara and its forces. He knows of your wish, as officials in your own towns and villages, to bring order to the people here. He would speak to you himself, but being busy with matters of war has asked me to take his place. First of all, there is your wish to set out here a true

171

town or towns, so that you may take up your former important duties as headmen. He agrees that huts should be torn down, rearranged neatly and with an experienced official at the head of each street. He is glad that you wish to do this at once."

Heads with short queues, shaven heads, spiky heads, stirred as Dirk paused. Then from the back row a man spoke, "But Fra Fidel—" Someone else cut in, "The matter of building chapels and shrines—" "Yes, and the sacred banners to hang on the walls—" "Maaa! It is all useless, since he says that we march on Tokyo and Kyoto soon."

Dirk glanced at Fra Hilario, who stepped forward, a veined hand raised. "It is known to you, surely, that Fra Fidel and Mori-san consult on all matters. Fra Fidel and I will look to your souls. It is you who must look to your bodies, to your health, or we may bring a plague on ourselves."

The murmuring died away and Dirk went on: "I merely say what is in your own minds to let you know that it is approved by your commander. This castle was once inhabited, and there must have been truck gardens about it. Let each headman appoint two of his most skillful farmers and gardeners to find the old sites and see if anything edible grows in them. Send out your best coopers and bath men to examine the hot springs. Sink as many barrels as possible into the earth for baths and cover them with a shed."

A wizened man close to Dirk quavered, "That has been done in two springs, both of which are in the area where my townsfolk now live. They are ours."

Another man shouted, "Yes. And he won't let my people use those baths. And why should I send men to work on more baths that others will use while my folk go dirty?"

Dirk raised his voice. "We are going to lay out our towns with good straight streets, which will mean moving a lot of people. When we're through, you may be a hundred yards from where you are now. As for baths, gardens, food, cold water—they must be shared in common."

The first man cried obstinately, "My people settled around that spring!"

Dirk asked patiently, "What was your town?"

"Saizu, on Amakusa."

"And when the head of the district told you that a road would be built through Saizu, did you tell him that the land belonged to your town and that he couldn't have it?" Someone nudged the Saizu man in the ribs and a few mildly jeering remarks came from the back of the crowd. Dirk pressed his advantage. "So, here in Hara, Gentaro Mori is your district head, who urges you to bring about the order that you want. Your people look to you for guidance. Give it to them. Appoint a committee to take over the rice stores, the barley and the millet. Appoint another to divide up the land equally. Then a third, to see that each household digs a benjo in the proper place. Men must wait on Fra Hilario for the proper siting of your chapels and shrines. This is what you wanted. Gentaro Mori gives you a free hand to carry it out."

Dirk stepped back, watching the group closely. For a moment they sat irresolute, then as drawn by a magnet they all clustered about an old, bent man, bowing and murmuring formal phrases. The wheel had begun to turn as he had hoped. By instinct, they were putting authority into the hands of the senior official of the largest town represented within the walls of Hara.

Fra Hilario touched Dirk's arm. "There is another matter, Señor. I have had complaints from the families of young, unmarried girls. In all this confusion —" he sighed — "youth is impulsive and parental authority breaks down. I suggest that we build a house for the young unmarried women with a discreet duenna in charge of each group."

"Of course," Dirk agreed. "And an outer guard drawn from the fathers of families."

"An excellent idea," said Fra Hilario. He glanced at Dirk and went on, as though changing the subject, "There are many people here, Señor."

"Close to fifteen thousand, Mori says."

"They have come from many towns and villages and farms. Can we answer for every man here? Spies could be among us without our knowing it."

"Of course," said Dirk. "But that's something for Mori and Tokisada and the others to worry about."

"Yes," said the friar softly. "The others. Many others. It occurred to me, while you were speaking — may I say most skillfully? — that a spy bringing word of your talk would be heard with much interest in Nagasaki or even Tokyo."

"What would they care? They know about me through the Company. I've got nothing to do with the rebellion."

"No doubt. But how would your words appear to the antiforeign clique? They could say that you gave aid and comfort to rebels against the Emperor himself. And is it nonmilitary to show people how to survive better, when they survive only to fight?"

"It could be made to seem like that. But the old Hirado Daimyo would vouch for me, and so would the Daikwan, I think."

"Let us hope so," said Fra Hilario. "Ah, here come the headmen. My friend, I believe that you are going to be begged to offer a little more nonmilitary advice."

The group, headed by the bent old man, edged toward Dirk almost shyly, bowing and hissing as they came. Then the leader spoke. Would Yang-san, known to many in Hara and an impartial man, decide where the street lines were to be drawn? It was a very small matter and beneath his notice, of course, but the group would be honored by his thought on the subject.

For the rest of the day, Dirk and Fra Hilario wandered about the mile-wide confines of Hara, extended their survey to the huddle of huts that clung to the outer wall. In their wake, dust clouds rose, huts tumbled to the ground, dirt flew and, beginning from the south wall, regular streets took shape. By sundown, as Dirk and the friar hurriedly ate a thin gruel of millet, they looked out onto the baths of the northeast corner. A mass of naked men and women sluiced themselves with buckets of scalding water, scrubbed themselves with oatmeal bags, sluiced again while waiting for the heads that showed just above the rims of the brimming barrels to climb out reluctantly. Later, when he mounted wearily to his tower room, lit only by pale moonlight through the archers' slot, he realized that he had done nothing about his escape. After a few hours' sleep he'd walk about the enclosure again, looking for badly guarded spots.

He awoke with a start, shivering under the ragged quilt that the old woman by the eastern baths had given him. He looked about him for an instant, then rolled to his feet. It was still dark outside

174

and as he looked through the archers' slot, he could only make out a confused mass below in that portion of the enclosure that his tower commanded. He drew in the crisp air with relief as he realized that he had not slept too long. There was still time to try to escape. Settling his clothes, he went down the stairs, now unguarded, and out into the ebbing night. All about him, he could hear snores and stirrings as the exhausted inhabitants of Hara slept after their heavy labor. Already, even in the gloom, the lines of huts showed in even alignment and as Dirk's eyes adjusted themselves, he could make out a broad fire lane, the long roof that sheltered the central baths.

He turned the southern corner of the old ruin, and then began to move more cautiously, realizing that he would soon leave the civilian zone and enter the area allotted to the real combatants, who would keep stricter guard. Then he passed the last of the huts and walked among men sleeping in the open, arms by their sides. It was not hard to move among them, each unit seemingly lying in formation, almost as though at attention. The outer walls of Hara loomed ahead of him and he made for their shelter, slipping along the stone foundations toward a partially blocked gate that he had noticed earlier. To his surprise, there was no guard on the inner side and he scrambled through the tangle of fallen stone, making as little noise as possible. The walls of Hara were thick and his passage was slow. At last he stood by the outer masonry, braced for a sudden sprint.

Something heavy swung across his chest and a voice challenged: "Daré da? Who's there?"

Dirk pushed away the pike butt that the unseen guard had raised, and identified himself, explaining that he was engaged on work for Mori. The guard was polite but firm. His orders were that no one was to leave the enclosure. Dirk tried to argue, but the only result was to lessen the man's politeness. Exasperated, he made his way back through the gap, sought out another and lesser gate, where a guard threw up the blade of his pike so sharply that Dirk's sleeve was slashed. Here there was no trace of politeness, the man merely uttering a harsh "Ikan!" as though to a coolie or a beggar. Dirk kept on around the inside of the wall, only to be turned back at every possible exit. Once he thought that he saw a chance at a spot where the wall had crumbled very low, but two alert men sat in the gap, inflexible.

He dropped to the ground, rubbing his rasped hands. There was no chance of escaping now according to his original plan. He stood lost in thought, as the people of Hara began to stir about him. How could he leave the old confines, fully sanctioned by all authorities? Then he thought about the roofing needed for the central baths. The Japanese had agreed that very heavy uprights were needed if the structure was to be solid. A quarter of a mile west of the walls lay the ruins of a solid old house whose beams, as he had seen them from the tower, would be ample for his needs. He would explain the matter to Mori, take a working party out to select the best timbers and then, while the men were busy, make a break for the west. The more he considered the plan, the better he liked it. He would avoid Isahaya, where he knew that there was a small outpost of Imperial troops, and make for the north coast, following it west along the thin wrist and thence to the Gulf of Omura. Once there, he had no doubt of his ability to reach Hirado safely.

Night was fading faster and he guessed that Mori, whose consent was essential to his plan, would be at the headquarters tower. He walked on through a maze of troops who marched and countermarched, filing away toward one of the main gates and heading for the lands that lay beyond the walls. The guard at the foot of Mori's tower lowered the butt of his arquebus with a cheery "O-haiyo gozaimas'" and stood back to let Dirk enter. When Dirk reached the crumbling summit, he found no one there save a stocky young man clad in a white tabard embroidered with a great purple cross. No, Mori-san had not yet arrived, but was expected soon.

Dirk thanked the man and went to the parapet, leaning his arms on it. Mists were lifting as a land breeze sprang up. The earthworks on the sharp ridge that looked toward Isahaya were astir with men, long columns marching away from them toward Hara, while other columns took their places in trench and redoubt. To the southwest by the hogback, the scene had utterly changed since his last sight of it. No longer empty, it was seamed and crisscrossed with trenches. He could make out men still toiling with pick and shovel. A long line of women trotted up the slope, carrying great baskets of woven wicker which were quickly filled with earth and incorporated into the defense line. Near the center of the works, men were struggling with what looked to Dirk like a portable bridge, fitting it across the trench, then dragging it back. Among the workers, pikes and arquebuses were neatly stacked.

Dirk was amazed. The appointment of Mori as commander, even hampered as he was by Fra Fidel and by the various factions, had worked wonders in a few hours. No longer purposeless, the forces of Hara took on an appearance of formidable solidity. Absorbed by the whole picture, he turned, to look at that part of the impromptu city that was his.

The disorderly tangle of huts within the enclosure had largely vanished. He looked down on regular streets, laid out at severe right angles, the whole pattern cut at intervals by wider fire lanes where no building was permitted. Off by the north wall dust stirred, and he knew that the last and most difficult bit of straightening that he had suggested the night before was being carried out. But the south baths looked flimsy. When the main task of bringing order was finished, he would ask for skilled masons to lay a stonework foundation, to install well-paved drains to carry off the bath water. It was too soon to think of diverting labor to such a task, but tomorrow or the day after — Yes, he would recommend such a step to the head of the stoneworkers' guild.

The tabarded man by the head of the tower steps suddenly shouted, "Ki wo tsuké," as though calling an invisible command to attention. Dirk turned to see Mori, haggard but keen-eyed and alert, come onto the summit of the tower. After him, hands thrust into his sleeves, stalked Fra Fidel with young Tokisada at his heels.

Mori greeted Dirk with a brief compliment on the progress made within the walls, then stepped to the parapet, Fra Fidel moving up beside him. The friar's voice was harsh in Dirk's ear. "Those women — I ordered them to make banners to hang from the walls. You have taken my men to waste their time there, when they could have been building the main chapel for the south wall."

Mori answered with patient courtesy, "To all your wishes I have agreed. I have assigned our best carpenters for your chapel. But first the hogback must be secured. If Itakura attacks there, it will not help us if the men and women are busy building a chapel inside the walls. Once we are secure from the south, you have a free hand."

Fra Fidel's beard bristled. "But it will not come from the south. I told you about my dream, my vision. Do you set yourself above Santa Barbara, patron saint of artillerists, who says that the attack will come from Isahaya and the west?"

Still patiently, Mori said, "Who am I to debate with a saint who now doubtless holds converse with the great Saint Xavier? There will be an attack from the west — but also one from the south. Did your vision tell you it would be from the west only?"

Fra Fidel shuffled his sandaled feet uncertainly. "The south was not mentioned, but — "

"Then we may rely on her faith in our wisdom to foresee the attack from the south, while she warns us of one from the west, which we might have failed to prepare for," observed Mori.

Fra Fidel fell silent. Mori beckoned to Tokisada. "Look at the hogback. I'm sure that it will hold against any attack. The west looks solid, too. I only wish that there were more room. We have plenty of arquebuses, too many in fact. There just isn't space for them. I wish I could think of a way to employ them all. As it is, the men in the trenches will fire, doing much damage to Itakura. But then — it takes so long to reload."

Dirk, following Mori's gaze, could see that the problem was a difficult one. Suddenly he remembered stories of the siege of Alkmaar by the Spanish more than half a century ago. He said diffidently, "I have heard that the Dutch once did this — " Mori looked at him a little impatiently, then listened with growing respect to Dirk's plan. Mori could throw every arquebus available into the front line, where the men would be divided into groups of four, one man firing, the second taking the discharged weapon and handing him a fresh one. The empty arquebus he would then pass on to a third man, who would give him one ready-loaded. Thus the third and fourth men would be continually receiving empty weapons, reloading them and passing them to the front again, making an endless chain between numbers one and numbers four.

When Dirk had finished, Mori merely glanced at Tokisada, saying, "Go to the hogback, call all unit commanders and tell them how to arrange matters. I'll be there soon to make sure that every-one understands."

Fra Fidel watched suspiciously as Tokisada clattered off. Dirk followed up his advantage, calling Mori's attention to the timbers that lay beyond the works on the western ridge. "You want them all for construction? Ah, sa! That is difficult."

"Just enough to make uprights for the south baths. I can take the men out there, pick out the timbers I want and be back in half an hour," Dirk explained.

Mori hesitated, then said, "All right. You can do something for me at the same time. I'll send other men to help you. I want long, flat timbers brought over to the hogback."

"I'd know better what to choose if I knew what you wanted them for," observed Dirk.

"It is simple," replied Mori. "The hogback is well fortified. We can beat off anything sent against us, especially with your plan for continuous fire. But that isn't enough. We must counterattack. Look. Can you see those men massing along the edge of the south wall? There are twenty-five hundred of them. Once the attack is smashed, they will move out and hit Itakura's men before they have time to recover. I have two portable bridges so my attackers can cross the trenches quickly and in good order. I need two more. Send me timbers for them and take anything else for your baths that you need."

"Suppose Itakura's strength comes, as Fra Fidel believes, from Isahaya?" queried Dirk. "Could you move your men down below here to meet it in time?"

"I have taken other steps for that. There are two ways to estimate an enemy. One is to throw your whole strength against what you hope he'll do. The other is to sum up everything that he can do, and adjust yourself to meet every possibility. That is the science of war, Yang-san."

"But when your knowledge is sure — as mine is," began Fra Fidel. Then he lunged toward the parapet, eyes fixed on the west. He flung both arms in the air. "The sign! The sign! Santa Barbara has not forsaken me!"

Dirk and Mori turned quickly. The inner slopes of the western redoubt suddenly crawled with men, sprung from nowhere, all heading toward the earthworks. Silhouetted against the sky, a lone figure blasted on a long trumpet. Drums and gongs picked up its last note, throbbed and rumbled through the marshy valley, pounded against the walls of Hara.

There was a heavy shuffling below the tower and Dirk saw old Asakawa, the Korean veteran, leading out a dense column of men, helmeted and sworded in the fashion of an earlier day. Dirk strained his eyes to the west. The redoubt and valley were stiff with troops. Then in the hidden lands of the west a horrible din of conches, trumpets, drums and gongs burst out, distant but heavy in volume.

Fra Fidel's eyes shone. "I knew it! My vision was true." Along the distant lip of the redoubt, smoke gushed from arquebuses, mixed with more smoke that rolled from the west. Once Dirk thought he caught the flight of an arrow, arching high toward the valley. Then he was sure of it. A dark shadow like the flight of immeasurably swift birds, Itakura's arrows began to swoop into the redoubt, to fall into the valley.

Fra Fidel gathered his robes. "I leave you," he said to Mori. "I must take my people into battle."

"Wait," said Mori. Dirk noticed that he was paying little attention to the din from the Isahaya redoubt, but kept looking to the southern road, to the beaches that ran down beyond the last fall of the cliffs. There was still a good deal of mist hanging low in that quarter, but so far as he could see, the countryside and the shore were empty. Could Itakura have outguessed Mori? Dirk's eyes went to the redoubt again. The smoke was thicker and more arrows whizzed out of the sky from the unseen attackers. The smoke thinned and a long pole, gay with silk streamers, appeared on the far edge of the redoubt and soldiers, minute at this distance, struggled about it. Dirk tugged at Mori's elbow, pointed to Itakura's banner. Mori nodded impatiently, laid a restraining hand on Fra Fidel and resumed his watch of the south.

The bright banner vanished. A brisk gust blew the smoke away and Dirk saw that the redoubt was still held by the Hara forces. Mori exclaimed "Ara!" and Dirk turned quickly.

The mist was lifting in the south and the sun struck on faint patches of color, far away. There was movement on the most distant reaches of the north-south road, movement and more color and flashes of bright steel. Offshore, vague hulks loomed, drew in toward the beaches. On the hogback, a man left the works, stood in a grassy patch, waving a banner in quick circles. Dirk glanced west and saw that the redoubt there was quiet, save for random shots from the defenders.

Mori cried, "I was sure. There was too much noise and too little firing from the west. They hoped to make me commit my reserves there. Now the real attack comes."

Fra Fidel said again, "I leave you. I must lead my people into battle."

Mori shook his head. "You are needed here." He raised his hand as Fra Fidel started to protest. "I know you do not fear arrow or sword. But if you were killed, there would be no one to see to your flock except Fra Hilario."

"But I—" began Fra Fidel, as Dirk nodded covert approval to Mori. Then the friar said, "So be it. But this much I can do." He leaned from the inner face of the parapet and shouted to the non-combatants below. Women and old men began scaling the south wall, following the course of broken ramps, dragging heavy bundles after them. Dirk stared as the south wall blazed with color. The bundles unfurled in long strips of sheer white with crowned crosses, bleeding hearts embroidered on them. Outside the wall, armored men knelt and crossed themselves. Others looked on indifferently. Fra Fidel left the tower and Dirk saw him reappear among the reserves.

"What now?" asked Dirk.

"Watch," said Mori.

From the high tower, Dirk looked far along the ground that rolled south from the redoubt. Close to the lines, the field was clear, but beyond it was dotted with wind-twisted trees and decaying buildings. In the middle distance, tall red uprights and crossbeams marked the approach to a deserted temple set among thick pines. Overhead, broad-winged birds rocked and dipped.

Dirk cried "Ah!" as the masses of color far down the road, the thick clumps of men who had landed from the barges along the beach, began to move. The two bodies flowed together, shook, halted, came on again, and Dirk could make out blues and greens and reds against the dull brown of the road. The light wind brought him the hollow rumble of drums, throbbing and swelling. Plainer and plainer the attacking force showed, the great column headed by a dense cluster of bamboo poles from which fluttered the colors of the various commanders. Then came a small body of arquebusiers followed by hundreds of archers, and after them the pikemen. The color bearers broke formation, each man trotting back to his own unit. From the rear, a group of horsemen galloped up, gained the head of the column, where they all dismounted, handing their horses over to their grooms — all save one man who rode on alone, his silver helmet flashing and the banner that followed behind him bright in the sun. Mori muttered, "That's Itakura himself."

Itakura's sword licked out, flashed above his head, and the column broke into a sharp trot, the arquebus men fanning out right and left, pieces over their shoulders and their forked rests in their free hands.

In the hogback works, Dirk could see men crouching, as though careful to keep hidden. The Imperial column came on, heavy and menacing, and still no sound or movement showed along the hogback. Itakura's men, in their unbroken progress, seemed machinelike, overwhelming. Dirk wondered uneasily if something had gone wrong, if treachery explained that awful silence from the hogback. They were close now.

Mori sprang suddenly to the parapet, stood motionless, then snatched off his helmet, waving it in circles about his head. From a fold in the ground between the castle and the redoubt, a man appeared, stood clear and repeated Mori's signal.

A ripping crash cut the still air and the whole line was masked by a rising blanket of white smoke. The blanket thinned, sank away, thickened again, rolling higher and higher. The arquebus teams worked smoothly. Then the smoke ebbed, settled, drifted seaward. The long slope south of the hogback was covered with flying men. Close by the parapet, Dirk saw a man in a shining helmet, freeing himself from a dead horse. It must be Itakura, the only rider in the attack. The Shogun's commander unhurriedly got to his feet, then without a backward glance walked steadily away, stepping in utter unconcern over the tangle of bodies that littered the approach.

Dirk, dizzy with horror at the slaughter, and with relief at what that slaughter meant to Hara, called unsteadily to Mori, "You've smashed them! They're wrecked."

Mori shook his head impatiently. "Not smashed, only checked. They'll come on again."

Off by the beaches, around the old deserted temple, men were rallying about Itakura's banner. Conches and trumpets blared, drums pounded, and the Imperial columns, solid and thick as ever to Dirk's untrained eye, resumed their ominous march.

It was like watching a second presentation of a pageant, with no details changing. The Imperial forces drove steadily on, almost to the lip of the earthworks. Once again Mori raised his helmet and once more smoke gushed from the hogback, blotting out the world beyond it. Suddenly the earlier pattern altered. Mori made a sign to the waiting men below and rank by rank they started for the hogback at a double. Fra Fidel ran beside them, holding up a cross. Men from Shimabara, from Amakusa, began to shout, "For Sant' Iago and Spain! For Sant' Iago and King Philip!" Probably not one of the shouting thousands knew what he was crying out. To each it must have been a mere war cry, taught him by Fra Fidel and his daring predecessors. Banners with Christian symbols appeared. By the head of the column, a great Spanish flag rolled its colors to the wind.

From the right, old Asakawa brought on his veterans of the Korean wars. The two columns strained up the slope. Dirk saw frantic men heaving the portable bridges into place. The counterattack crossed easily, lunged into the wreck of Itakura's men. The fight rolled on and on and men stabbed and slashed on the beaches, about the old temple and its high red gates. By the hogback, there was a renewed burst of firing as a handful of Imperial troops, swords high, charged screeching against arquebuses. The firing ceased and the men who had charged in hopeless desperation lay motionless on the slope.

There was no rallying of Itakura's men this time. The pursuit drifted out of sight to the south. Dirk leaned shakily against the parapet as Mori said under his breath, "It is all over." He left the tower, Dirk following on unsteady legs. He had seen men die violently before, but never like this.

When he reached the enclosure, men were cheering and shouting and Dirk found himself cheering with them. His voice died away in his throat. What was there for him to exult over? One attack had been utterly wrecked, but more would come until one day the frantic charges would sweep over the broken walls of Hara.

He stood by, stunned and not listening as the unit commanders came in to report to Mori. Up to now, he had taken his own escape for granted, even viewed the passing time with a little complacency as he thought of the countless added details he would bring to Caron. And where was Trudi? He could see the stone houses at the north tip of the horseshoe bay, and a slim dark girl walking in her bright kimono along the old sea wall. He recalled her smile of pleasure when he found the ivory Dutch trumpeter for her, the look in her clear eyes when she had seemed to yield to him for an instant in the cave the day when Itakura's troops had first come down the narrow Specx Strait.

Hara had no ties on him. By his exertions, he had earned the right to some thought from them. Mori, Tokisada, Fra Hilario must help him find a way to return safely to Hirado. He waited impatiently, trying to catch Mori's eye as the commander listened to tales of the action. Tokisada was saying over and over that while the Imperial forces had lost more than half their men, not a single Hara soldier had been killed or wounded, save for the few struck down at the west redoubt. Nirado at Mori's side repeated over and over, "It is a miracle." Only grim old Asakawa seemed cast down and Dirk heard him grumble, "We won, but unfairly. The sword is the only true weapon of the samurai. It was unfitting to shoot down Imperial troops like game."

Two blood-smeared peasants made their way timidly through the crowd, knelt before Mori. One of them held out a helmet, richly worked, from which rose two horns of silver, with the Itakura crest at their base. The other slowly unrolled a strip of matting from which the head of the Shogun's commander stared at his unbeaten foes through sightless eyes.

Dirk turned away, sickened, and found himself facing Fra Hilario, who looked sadly at him. "I keep telling myself, Señor Jongh, that these poor folk fought for their faith. Perhaps that justifies all this slaughter. I wish that I knew. I would give much to be as sure as Fra Fidel."

Dirk was touched by the old friar's obvious distress. "Faith in what you preach to them must justify everything," he said. Privately he thought that faith had little if anything to do with the fighting about Hara. Thousands of people, oppressed beyond the limit of human endurance, had risen in violent protest. Many of those people happened to be Christians. That was all. He wondered if that same thought was in Fra Hilario's mind.

The friar went on, "I talked with men from the western redoubt. They told me a thing which I held might be useful to you, who did not come here of your own free will." He lowered his voice. "There is a new commander of Imperial troops about Isahaya. His name is Nomura. Perhaps you have heard of him."

"Genzan Nomura? Of course I know him." For years Nomura had been a leader of the pro-foreign group in Kyushu, a man who had always held out for trade, for greater freedom for traders and especially for the spread of the knowledge and skills that could come to the Empire from Europe. There was more to Nomura's story. Two years before, his fortunes were at a low ebb and he seemed likely to lose all his lands. Dirk had called his attention to iron deposits on his estates which Nomura, an agriculturalist at heart, had overlooked, and the Nomura properties were saved.

Fra Hilario looked gratified. "I am glad if my news may suggest action to you. I do not think much risk would be involved. His men might not be too polite, but they would be sure to take you to him or his officers, for questioning."

"It's a chance I'll have to take," Dirk answered. "I'll manage somehow to go out with the relief at midnight and then keep on across the lines. Asakawa says they've withdrawn nearly a mile from our redoubt there."

"My prayers will go with you," said Fra Hilario. "I shall miss your clear thought and unceasing action, as will my people. You have done much for them, Señor."

Later, Dirk found Mori by the main gate, watching the string of carts that came in from the fields laden with captured arms and armor, with sheaves of arrows and pikes, with the few arquebuses that Itakura, who seemed to agree with Asakawa about the sword being the samurai's weapon, had allowed himself. Dirk spoke of his plan to Mori, who nodded. "You will be missed, but it is not right that we hold you here in a fight that is not yours. Yes, the midnight relief would do very well. I'll go with you as far as the redoubt."

Dirk left the gate. All about him men shouted in triumph. In an angle, Fra Fidel knelt with a group of Christians who raised their voices in a chant of thanksgiving. A few paces away, bloodstained men bowed low before a shrine to Hachiman, god of war. On a sudden impulse, Dirk knelt by Fra Fidel.

XII

To Shimabara

BEFORE dawn of the same day, Trudi stood on the beach at the east end of the Gulf of Omura, her geta sinking into the wet sand. As she looked out into the gulf she could just make out the sampan that had brought her on from Hirado. She felt a wild impulse to call the unsavory crew, to beg them to take her back. As on the previous evening, a deep pang struck her as she thought of her uncle to whom she owed so much and who, at that very moment, might be a prey to intense anxiety on her account. She faced inland. It couldn't be helped. The most important thing in the world was to find Dirk. She knew now that she had been in love with him, but it had taken the nun's story of his danger to make her realize it.

She struck resolutely along a path that led away from the beach, the start of her fifteen-mile journey to Hara. If the rebels wanted to keep her there, at least she would be with Dirk and sooner or later release would come. She told herself that she had only to face a walk through desolated country, keeping away from towns. At any peasant hut, her silver would buy her food, might even hire a horse or a litter. The path was smooth. Over such ground she could walk all day without tiring.

Suddenly from the dimly seen fields to the left, a conch blared. Drums began to boom and were echoed from the right. The ground itself seemed to stir and shake. In the growing light Trudi saw the fringes of an awakening army. On all sides, men staggered to their feet, rubbing their eyes and yawning. Close to the road, a little man in a helmet sprang to a barrel-shaped drum resting on a sawhorse and pounded vigorously at it, adding its din to the swelling rumble.

The road began to fill about her. From a lumbering cart, live fowl in deep wicker baskets squawked and flapped. A file of men with shouldered pikes set out east at a brisk pace, pushing aside coolies who trotted on, buckets of water dangling from both ends of their long carrying poles. Carters shouted, "Do-do! Do-do!" to their oxen Two horsemen cantered past eying Trudi curiously from under their vizored helmets. Then from the opposite direction, more riders came on, herding a line of ragged, bloody men, their arms bound tightly behind them. Two soldiers, close by the roadside, stared at her and one of them shouted something, leering and beckoning. She went pale as she caught his words, then flushed angrily as the man's companion said, "Look at her clothes. She's from some Daimyo's tent. You'll get into trouble!"

She hurried on, head bent, furtively looking for some path that would take her out of this world of armed men. Then she realized that, for the moment at least, she was safest in the midst of this jumbled traffic. She kept to the middle of the road, on one hand a line of creaking carts heavy with rice bags, on the other loads of dried fish, of daikon, bundles of long, wicked-looking pikes. But sooner or later the road would lead her into Isahaya where she would be sure to be questioned about what she did among the troops of the Shogun. Her uneasiness increased as she saw in the fields to the left a long roofless tent of striped canvas marked with a crest that was strange to her. By the edge of the road, a picket of mounted men leaned forward in their saddles, closely watching the flow of men and animals. She slackened her pace, realizing that the tent and the horsemen must mark the post of some Daimyo. If she could only stop, gather her thoughts and plan before the guards saw her!

Then on a low ridge to the right, rising from a field empty of troups, she saw the red frame of a torii that marked the approach to a Buddhist temple. She wove past the tail of a cart loaded with sake kegs and hurried off toward the torii. The path that ran under the great beams led up the ridge and into a pine grove, and she saw broad steps flanked by stone lanterns and a low-curving roof beyond. She was out of breath when she reached the temple and sank down onto the base of a pedestal that supported a grinning monster, half dog, half lion. The path over which she had come was empty. Now she could collect her thoughts and reason out her next step. She closed her eyes as her mind refused to work, filling itself with useless questions.

Geta clacked on the stone pavement and she opened her eyes to see

188

a shaven-headed old man in gray silk, a crimson ceremonial scarf about his neck. He seemed to find nothing strange in her presence so close to an armed camp as he courteously asked what service he could be to her.

Trudi thanked him, asking if she might have tea. The priest seemed delighted and clacked off, saying that if she would wait in the little building by the low bell tower, he would bring her food as well as tea.

Soon she was kneeling on a clean matted floor, suddenly aware of the hours that had passed since she had been given a bowl of coarse noodles on her boat. The low lacquered table that the priest set before her held fine tea, a bowl of clear soup with seaweed floating in it, a grilled fish and plenty of good white rice.

When she had finished, the priest waved away her thanks, saying that the temple had prospered with the coming of the armies, since many of the officers had brought their families with them, and rich offerings had been sent by them already. He looked curiously at her. "No doubt your father commands many troops," he ventured.

Trudi hesitated. The old man, probably nearsighted, obviously took her for a Japanese. She thought for an instant of claiming to be the daughter of some noble, but instead she found herself telling who she was and exactly where she was going and why. "It is not as though he were a rebel," she ended. "He has done nothing against the Shogun. I must go to him."

The priest nodded with the calm acceptance of old age. "I will help you as much as I can, but you have set yourself a difficult task. For days, troops have been massing between here and the Gulf of Omura. Last night, many moved down the road toward Hara." He rose. "Come with me."

He led the way across the stone-paved court, where shaven accolytes were busy sweeping up pine needles. Trudi paused to drop some silver into the red, slat-topped box by the door. Following the old man, she skirted a stone-lipped pool whose surface was broken by the fins of big carp, and stopped by a gate set in the outer wall. He threw open the gate, pointing to a faint path that strayed on through more pines. "Keep to this path," he said. "Not far, you will come to a ruined stone wall. Turn left there and you will go up a sheltered valley well past Isahaya. The end of the valley comes out far beyond the last camps. This I know, since I went down it just yesterday. You will come out close by the Gulf of Shimabara."

With a last bow, Trudi stepped through the gate and followed the path through the pines and cypresses that hemmed it in. The world about her was silent and she could hear only the muted clacking of her geta among the pine needles. The path climbed, dipped and climbed. She heard the booming of more drums off to her left. Cautiously she edged around a tree, looked down through thick branches into a deep valley where men with curved bows slung over their shoulders filed off toward the Isahaya road which she could just make out half a mile away.

When she had recovered her breath, she went on swiftly, eyes and ears alert. She made out a crumbling stone wall ahead of her, the remains of some ancient building, moss-grown and dripping with water. A frog plunged into a hidden pool and a ratlike animal, furry and gray, scurried across the path. A rabbit started from a clump of bushes, stopped, then shot off along the path with long-legged, springy bounds. Few people used this old trail, evidently. Trudi leaned against the dank stones. For a long moment she looked toward the temple which could be her first stage on her return to the west and Hirado. Then she chose the left fork that led on to the lost valley and the Gulf of Shimabara.

The sun had crept up the sky, but an unseen shadow hung over the narrow world that Trudi could see. Somewhere, far off to the east, a faint snapping and poping broke out, like the steady crackle of burning brush. The trees drew away from both sides of the trail. On the left four houses gaped to the sky, their heaped timbers charred and blackened. Ash-gray circles marked spots where ricks of rice straw had been burned. Off by itself, a heavy farm wagon sagged, wantonly smashed. She stared at the wreckage and hurried on, wondering when this tiny community had felt the anger of Nagato's bailiffs. What had happened to the people who had lived here?

The path led on down and she knew that she had actually entered the valley of which the priest had spoken. There was no sign of life about her and the day was still, save for that odd crackling that still whispered in the east.

The left wall of the valley suddenly fell away and she crouched quickly behind some azalea bushes as she saw, through the saddle-shaped depression in the ridge, the Isahaya road. The few yards that she could see were empty, but the very nearness of the highway frightened her. She sprang up and scurried toward the line of low trees to the right that edged a swift brook. Sword-edged bamboo grass slashed at her ankles and sharp thorns snagged her trailing sleeves. Ducking under branches, stumbling from hummock to moss-grown rock, she made her way along the brook, while willow fronds brushed her face and caught in her hair.

The road again, and closer this time, just ahead of her. She shrank back among the willows, heart beating fast. Somewhere behind her, unseen as she made her way along, path and brook must have crossed, the latter leaving the valley and the former following it. Her ears caught the shuffle of tired horses, coming from the east. Then on the skyline was silhouetted a stumbling man who led a riderless horse, stirrups crossed over the saddle. Another followed and another, so close that Trudi could have hit them with a pebble. As they came on, she saw that the leader wore a crested haori and that the trappings of the horse were rich, the black lacquer stirrups heavy with silver inlay. The man was weeping as he lurched along the road, his face blind with misery. So they filed before her, the long line of weeping grooms who would never again saddle up for their masters, now dead on the slopes of the north redoubt that sheltered the Castle of Hara.

The last grief-stunned man stumbled out of sight and the road was empty once more. Trudi turned quickly and retraced her steps along the brook, eyes searching for the steppingstones that must mark the crossing that she had missed before. At last she saw it, the flat slabs awash with clear brown water, and made her way to the other bank and the trail which she never should have left.

For a slow hour she kept on under the climbing sun. The crackling noises from the east had died away and there was no sound in the valley save the crunch of her geta and the occasional rusty croak of some high-sailing carrion bird winging east. Her back and legs ached and her ankles smarted from the cuts of the bamboo grass. Stubbornly she fought against weakness and dizziness. A hidden hollow tripped her and she fell to her knees, rose painfully on un-steady legs, her breath coming unevenly.

Not far ahead she saw another gutted house with most of its walls and part of its thatched roof intact. There she could stretch out in safety, shielded from the eyes of any chance passer-by in the deserted valley.

The smell of charred wood about her, Trudi sat on a flat stone slab, her legs stretched out and her back against the blackened wall. Slowly at first, then with increasing speed, the house and world outside spun before her eyes. Perhaps she should lie down just for a moment.

She slipped off the padded haori and spread it on the floor. Floor and haori were amazingly soft, as she lay at full length, hands behind her head. Some of the dizziness went out of her and she closed her aching eyes. She would not waste her time of resting. Coolly and methodically she would take stock while her body relaxed. In an instant, she was asleep.

When she woke, the sun was low and a brisk wind rustled through the willows by a little pond. Panic seized her. What was she, Trudi Van Os, doing alone in that shattered house in the heart of the Shimabara peninsula? At once her fears were overlaid with vivid mental images of Dirk. She saw him gay and laughing, saw him seized with quick concern for her, saw him urgent yet tender, as he had been that day in the cave. The road ahead was the only road for her.

She got to her feet and a wisp of hair fell across her face. She saw the pool with its swaying willows, its surface smooth in the clarity of the dying light. Kneeling on the bank, she combed her hair, gravely studying her reflection. Her rest and the renewed faith in her course had taken some of the tenseness from her face. The water mirrored her smooth forehead, the line of her brows, and she could even guess at fresh color in her cheeks and in the reflected lips that smiled back at her.

With a final touch to her hair and to the set of her collar, she took the path that led on east. The sun dropped behind the western ridges and the stars came out. The evening was silent save for the occasional distant boom of a drum. A faint moon dusted the land with silvery light. Her Japanese name — Sayo-ko — meant night and here was the very spirit of the night shining down at her. The ground sloped in front of her and she mounted easily, fatigue and hunger forgotten. In the gloom she thought she saw a man sitting by the road and hurried on, calling softly, "Are you from Hara?" Another step and she saw that the supposed man was a lump of stone, crudely carved as the god Jizo, guardian of children. Another good omen. She ran her fingers over the stone head, felt the little red flannel bib tied about its neck. The path swung toward the left and she thought she could make out a lighter line on the near horizon, as though the sea lay not far beyond.

A dog barked harshly, rushed toward her with a crisp patter of feet. It was a huge dog that raced on, circled her, and she saw it clearly, a big, short-haired animal with a ropelike tail. She whistled to it, recognizing one of the great Tosa dogs, bred especially for fighting with their own breed, but gentle as kittens with humans. She called, "Chibi-san! Kochi kitte! Come here!"

The Tosa rounded on her, wagging his tail. Then his head moved forward, catching the trailing sleeve of her haori. She shook her finger at it. "Let go, Chibi-san!" The tail kept on wagging, but the grip of the jaws was firm. Trudi called again, "Let go!"

There was a clank of metal to the left, and footsteps. Two helmeted men appeared close by. Armor gleamed in the moonlight and Trudi, with a sinking heart, made out a Daimyo's crest on the nearer man. The Tosa released his hold and sat beside her, heavy tail swishing the ground in self-approbation. The nearer man grounded his pike. "Naruhodo! A woman!" he panted.

With an effort Trudi rallied herself, clinging desperately to the fact that the old priest had at first taken her for not only a Japanese, but the daughter of an officer. She patted the Tosa's head, calling out, "Oh, please tell me where I am. I'm looking for my father's camp."

The two short-legged men leaned on their pikes and stared at her. "Where are you going?"

She managed to answer lightly, "But I just told you. To my father's camp. I walked to a little temple and then I must have taken the wrong turn."

The pair whispered together and she listened anxiously, hoping that their accent would tell something about them. Then the taller of the two spoke to her suddenly. "You were going to Hara!"

"Yes!" she cried. "To Hara, when my father's men have stormed it."

The men whispered again, but all she could gather was that they were not from Kyushu. She broke in on them before they could resume their questioning. "And you are Bizen men?" she asked, naming a mainland province.

The shorter man grunted. "Bizen? Do you take us for ninsoku, for coolies? We're from Settsu."

"Your pardon. I should have known," said Trudi quickly. "Settsu folk are always courteous and brave soldiers. That I have read."

One of the men looked more closely at her. "You are ai-no-ko, half-caste?"

A bit of lore, told her by her mother long ago and half forgotten, crept into her mind. She made an angry gesture and the Tosa sprang to its feet beside her as though in protection. "Ai-no-ko? Are those Settsu manners? I am from Sanuki, on the island of Shikoku!" The men stared at her and she met their gaze with what she hoped was haughty disdain. She dropped her hand to the Tosa's head as though seeking comfort.

The soldiers conferred again. "Eh-to! Sanuki?" . . . "Of course. None but a baka, a fool like you, would miss it. Sanuki people say that they're a race apart, not like the rest of us. They grow big." . . . There was a snicker. "I'll bet she's like anyone else under that kimono." . . . "Baka, again! Look at that kimono, even in this light. Remember what happened to Mito for trying to fool with a bugyo's niece, and this girl's father must be a shomyo at least." The taller raised his voice. "And where is your father's camp?"

"Over by the Isahaya road," said Trudi.

"There are many camps there. Near what other camp is he?"

As a random shot, Trudi chose the name of another Shikoku province. "I am not sure, but there were Awa men all about us."

The man nodded to his fellow. "She's all right." He bowed to her. "It's lucky our dog stopped you. We are a long way from the camps and if you'd gone on, you'd have walked into the rebel lines. We're the last outpost on the right. Go back the way you came, then strike north till you reach the Isahaya road. I haven't seen the

Sanuki camp, but the Awa men are a couple of miles this side of Isahaya. Your father's name is —"

"Kuroki, commander of a thousand men," answered Trudi, quite sure that a man from so distant a province as Settsu would not know the names of many officers in this hastily assembled army.

Both soldiers nodded vaguely, repeating, "Ah — Kuroki-san!"

Trudi struggled with her voice that was unsteady with relief. "I shall be glad to speak to him of the kindness of the Settsu men."

The shorter soldier shifted his pike. "It would be an honor if I could escort Kuroki-san's daughter to his tent."

"Oh, no!" she cried hurriedly. "I can find my way back. I even remember the place where I made a wrong turn. I just go back there and take the north path."

"But I might be blamed for allowing — " began the man.

His companion broke in. "And be blamed more by the lieutenant for deserting your post — blamed with the cutting edge of a sword." He turned to Trudi. "Your father will understand why we can't come with you."

"I know that Settsu men are above reward," she said, slipping a hand into her obi. "But in my name please give these silver pieces to whatever shrine you choose." Metal chinked, the two men bowed low and Trudi retraced her steps down the trail, with a farewell pat to the Tosa. The dog looked after her wistfully, then broke into a lolloping gallop to catch up with his masters, who were outlined for an instant against the sky and then vanished.

A hundred yards down the trail, she stopped to think over what she had heard. This outpost was the extreme right or southern end of the line of the Isahaya army. If there were other troops moving on Hara from the south, then there must be a gap between the two forces. She would wait while she counted to one hundred and then take the path again. She was quite sure that the Tosa, having scented her once, would pay no attention to her passage this time. She began to count. When she had reached one hundred, she paused, then repeated the tally.

The path sloped on down, bush-shrouded. So far as she could see, nothing stirred to the right or the left, and the deep hollow which she entered seemed equally deserted. She stopped by a thick laurel clump, puzzled by the heavy sweetish smell that made breathing difficult. She moved forward hesitantly, her feet stumbling over heaps of unclean cloth, broken poles. She moved off the path and the debris was thicker and the smell came more strongly. The hollow was ending in an upward slope, long and gradual. At her far left, a lighter band climbed the slope, marking the eastward course of the Isahaya road.

Trudi stumbled, moved sidewise with a cry of "Ara!", staring down at the first corpse that she had ever seen, a squat, powerfully built man whose teeth gleamed in a perpetual snarl to the moon. She gathered the skirts of her kimono and fled up the slope over which the feigned attack had broken earlier that day. There were other bodies, discarded helmets, a rigid arm that seemed to reach up for her. A tiny, flying figure in that landscape of death, she ran on, crying brokenly, "Dirk! Dirk!"

Out of the ground two dark shapes rose, gigantic against the sky. Heavy arms closed about her, a thick cloth muffled her eyes and mouth and she felt the sudden bite of cords lashing about her wrists and elbows while a hoarse voice shouted, "We've got a spy — another spy!"

XIII

Fra Hilario

THE night relief for the western redoubt was forming just inside the main gateway of Hara, arquebusiers and archers on the flanks, pikemen and swordsmen in the center. Even in the dark Dirk could tell that the men moved with more assurance, bolstered as they were by their shattering defeat of the Imperial troops during the day. Off by the east wall, he could hear the creak of a windlass as some belated householder drew water from a communal well. Close by the crumbling keep, the harsh notes of a koto twanged out, accompanying a nasal, high-pitched song that told of great deeds in the old, old days.

In another half hour he figured that he would be hailing the pro-foreign Nomura's pickets, who would pass him on to their commander. From Nomura's headquarters he could push on to the Gulf of Omura and thence to Hirado. He saw himself running up the hill from the sea wall to Van Os's house. Trudi would be standing at the big window of her uncle's study, or leaning over the half-opened Dutch door. She would —

He heard firm footsteps off to the right and dimly made out Mori's dragon-crested helmet looming half a head above the men who accompanied him. Mori called, "Are you ready?"

"One thing before we start," Dirk said. "Remember the new line of huts we were going to build by the north wall? Well, be sure that the men use those timbers we brought in from the outside. Better put Oish'ta-san in charge."

Mori touched his arm. "Don't think about anything except getting out of Hara. We're deeply grateful to you for what you've done." He raised his voice. "Haya-ashi! Quick march!"

The men swung into column and filed out through the old gate. Dirk looked back for a final glimpse of Hara, whose walls and outworks were touched by a climbing moon. What would be the fate of all those people with whom he had planned and worked? How long would those lines of huts stand within the great enclosure? He fell into step with Mori. His own responsibilities lay far away on the other side of narrow Specx Strait, not on the Shimabara peninsula.

Dirk marched on, the clank and rustle of equipment in his ears, a steady sound that was underscored now by a hollow drumming as hundreds of feet padded over a flimsy bridge, now by a squelching that told of marshy ground underfoot. He glanced at Mori, who stepped out briskly, as though concerned with nothing beyond the supervision of the relief. Dirk felt the silence oppressive, yet what was there to say to a man whose life was surely limited in space to the peninsula and in time to a few days or weeks?

As they took the slope that led to the western redoubt, Mori remarked casually, "Matsudaira himself is commanding against us now, since Itakura's dead. That'll give us a respite of a few days. It will take time to rearrange matters."

A few days! By then he would be safe in Hirado. If the danger to the Company passed away, it was likely that he would learn, by degrees probably, of the grim end of the rebel force. If an antiforeign wave swept over the factory on the point —

Mori touched his arm, pointed to a shaft of light off to the left. "See that hut? That's headquarters for this part of the line. I'll take you on beyond it to the last outposts and you can go straight west from there. I'll look in at the hut on my way back."

Beyond the outposts, Dirk would walk to probable safety, while Mori would return to the doomed garrison. Mori talked on easily. There was no danger of an arquebus shot in the dark. Like Itakura before him, Matsudaira looked on firearms as beneath a samurai's dignity. Dirk felt uncomfortable. He had every right to leave Hara, whose troubles were no concern of his, and yet — somehow he felt bound to these people, especially to Fra Hilario and Mori.

They were passing quite close to the headquarters hut and Dirk glanced in. A dim lamp flickered against the rough walls and in one corner coals glowed in a big hibachi, about which a few men crouched. Looming over them was the tall, hooded figure of Fra Fidel. The friar moved to one side and Dirk could just make out a woman, her face lost in the gloom. Her arms were bound behind her and faint light shimmered on her clothes, which seemed torn and draggled. He called Mori's attention to the group. The latter nodded. "No doubt a woman spy."

"A spy? What will they do with her?"

Mori was indifferent. "They might cut off her head and throw her body out between the lines. Or they might nail her to a cross where the enemy can see her while she dies."

Dirk stopped. "Will you let them?" he cried.

"What can I do? It is customary."

Inside there was a sudden stir. The woman gave a wrench and a twist, butted past one of the men and burst from the hut. Mori took a step toward her, then stopped short as she brushed past him crying, "Dirk! Dirk!"

Dirk gave a shout of amazement. Then he swept Trudi to him while his free hand jarred against the first man who rushed from the hut in pursuit. As Dirk's arm fell about her, Trudi gave a cry of relief. All the danger left her and she felt utterly free as though the cords about her had been cut. She had reached her goal. She whispered unevenly, "I knew you'd come, Dirk."

Dirk was deaf to the shouts that rose on all sides. He could only look down at Trudi in unbelief that slowly changed to assurance. He tried to speak, but could only stammer incoherently. A hard hand fell on his shoulder and Fra Fidel loomed before him. "Let her go!" he said harshly. "She's a spy and a heretic."

Holding Trudi closer, Dirk turned angrily on Fra Fidel, but Mori strode up calling sharply, "I command at Hara. She's to go free. Does anyone challenge my authority?" He laid a hand on his sword hilt and the other Japanese fell back.

The friar said hoarsely, "I challenge it!"

Dirk looked down at Trudi, who, still bound, leaned against him. He said gently, "Don't worry!"

She answered simply, "But there's nothing to worry about — now. I heard you were here and came to find you. I'll tell you later — oh, please cut these cords."

Dirk cut the bonds and she stretched her arms, then slipped a hand under his. "You — you came all the way from Hirado alone through a whole army?" he asked.

"It wasn't very hard, Dirk. You see, I was afraid the *de Rijp* would take me away while you were still here. So I came to find you."

"I just can't grasp it yet. You came to find me?" Dirk shot a glance toward Mori, who, back toward him and Trudi, was speaking sternly to Fra Fidel. Then he lifted Trudi clear off the ground. Her arms slipped about his neck. He said, "I'm only just beginning to believe it." Her hair brushed across his cheek as her face turned toward him. Her muffled voice came softly to him, "Believe it now?"

Dirk set her down gently, knowing that the Japanese would be profoundly shocked by the sight of a European embrace. He was relieved to see that they were completely absorbed by what Mori was saying. Trudi slipped her arm through his, leaning against him. She rubbed her cheek against his sleeve. "I'm terribly tired, Dirk, but happy, too. Where do we go?"

Dirk drew in his breath quickly. The shock and then the joy of finding her had driven his own plans from his mind. He drew her closer to him. "We're going to Hirado. Right now. Do you think you can walk a little more?"

"Of course," she answered confidently. "How are we going?"

"Just the way you came here. But I think it will be easier for you this time."

"Of course I can do it. We can — Dirk! I forgot! We can't go the way I came. I could never find the path in the dark and there are men there, men with Tosa dogs."

"Don't worry about the men," said Dirk firmly. "They are Buzen men under Nomura, an old friend of mine."

"Buzen men?" echoed Trudi. "No, not Buzen. They're from Settsu. I talked to some of them."

"You're sure about Settsu?"

"Of course. Is it important?"

The Buzen men had been relieved! Dirk answered, his voice thick with disappointment, "I'm afraid so." He called to Mori, standing nearby, and told him the news.

"The Settsu men would cut you down without a question. I am very sorry for you," Mori said wearily.

"Then we have to stay here?"

"I am very sorry for you," repeated Mori.

Dirk's arm tightened about Trudi. "But can't we pass her through the lines?"

She cried out, "No, Dirk, no!"

"You'd send her out to be crucified?" asked Mori grimly. "The Settsu men would never believe that she wasn't a spy."

"But she can't stay here!" protested Dirk.

"Dirk, of course I'm staying here!" said Trudi.

"There is no other way," Mori put in.

"For the moment, then," agreed Dirk reluctantly. "But somehow or other we'll manage it."

Fra Fidel stepped closer. "You have set aside my protest against admitting her at all. But I say that if she enters, she must go to the women's barracks. No exceptions have been made. None can be."

"It would be a dangerous precedent," said Mori slowly.

"Very well," said Dirk. "For tonight she can go there, but tomorrow — we'll be married." He bent toward Trudi. "Am I right?"

She answered gently, "But why else did I come, Dirk?"

In a joyous sweep of triumph, Dirk faced Fra Fidel. With all its perils, Hara seemed suddenly a most desirable place, since Trudi had spoken.

"Who will perform the ceremony?" asked Fra Fidel ominously. "Neither Fra Hilario nor I would bless a union of heretics."

"Then we'll have a Japanese marriage," said Dirk. "Do you think we'd defer to you — why, think what she's done — all the way from Hirado? You agree, Trudi?"

She said uncertainly, "Oh, but Dirk — a Japanese marriage — that's only an exchange of sake cups. It's not like being really married."

"And it is not for Europeans," said Fra Fidel sharply. He turned to Mori. "You've barred me from temporal matters here, but you gave me a free hand on the spiritual side. A Japanese marriage would only be evading the rules that you yourself laid down. If you permit this, I'll call a meeting of all the headmen. I'll let them see how you shape your laws to suit your own pleasure."

Trudi's arm tightened in Dirk's. "At any rate, we're together. That's something that he can't stop."

Dirk bent, whispered in her ear, "Wait till I've had a talk with Fra Hilario. Now it's time that I took you to Hara and turned you

201

over to the widow Saito. She'll see that you're well looked after in the barracks. Don't worry — it won't be for long."

The troops that had marched out of Hara with Dirk and Mori had long since filed away to their posts. Now the night was astir with the passage of weary men whom they had relieved. Mori, with a last glance at the troops, set out for Hara, Dirk and Trudi following. A few paces behind them, Fra Fidel stalked, alert and watchful.

Two days later Trudi woke in the shed that had been built against the north wall of Hara. She could hear the stir of wakening women all about her, ready to begin a new day in the besieged castle. To her left a stocky peasant girl was yawning and scratching herself, her open kimono showing her thick, dumpy body and short legs. On her right, a slim woman with worn, fine features was knotting her obi with care, her slender hands, hard with unaccustomed calluses, rippling through the silk.

Trudi threw off the tattered quilt that covered her, got to her feet and dressed quickly, wondering what the next few hours would bring. She had only caught distant glimpses of Dirk since he had left her outside the women's stockade on that first night, but women who had been outside the quarters on working parties had brought her word from him. If only she could arrange to be sent out to cut grass for bedding or gather scrap wood for the communal kitchen.

As she went out of the building she could make out the clumsy cross-topped tower of the church that the Christians had erected close to the stockade. Someone was chanting in Latin within its flimsy walls. Nearer, a flat gong boomed at regular intervals as a Shinto priest intoned, "As the many-piled clouds of heaven are scattered at the breath of the Wind-Gods. As the morning breezes and the evening breezes scatter the morning mists and the evening mists . . . There let the goddess who dwells in the myriad meeting places of the myriad sea paths . . ." The age-old words of the Purification Ritual echoed in Trudi's ears. "Ara-shio no shio no yaoji no —" as she made her way under the slanting roof where the communal kitchen had been built against the north wall.

Coals glowed in the fat hibachi and water steamed and bubbled.

She bowed to the sharp-eyed old woman in charge and picked up a chipped bowl, a fine lacquer cup which had somehow found its way into Hara, filled one with pale tea, the other with a thin rice gruel, and left the kitchen, heading for a little group of huts where tottery old men stood shaking by the low doors.

At the hut closest to the stockade gates, she called softly as she crossed the threshold. On a heap of dried grass in the corner, faintly lit by the growing dawn, Fra Hilario opened his veined lids and smiled at her. His voice was thin but steady as he said, "This is kind of you, but you shouldn't have troubled."

She knelt by the bed and handed him the cup of tea. "It's still early, Fra Hilario. I had nothing to do."

He sat up with difficulty, trying to steady the cup. "Nothing to do except to take thought for an old man who wishes you well?" He sipped the tea with an effort, then set the cup down.

"Now the rice," said Trudi, handing him the bowl. "Really, it's good this morning, much thicker than yesterday's. Oh, you must eat more than that. How are you going to get well if you don't eat?"

Fra Hilario lay back in his bed and folded his veined hands on the thin covers. "These fevers," he said. "I've had them before and the lighter the diet the quicker I mend." He turned his worn old eyes toward her. "But your thought for me gives me strength, too. I wish I could help you."

She laid her hand on his. "I understand, Fra Hilario."

"Fra Fidel was right," he said gently. "It would be against the rules of the Church."

"I told you yesterday not to worry about it," she said. "And I'm sure that Dirk feels the same way." She picked up the bowl. "Now do try to eat some more rice."

He shook his head. "Take it to the Saga woman. She looked very thin when she came here last night. And be sure that you eat, too." His eyelids fluttered, closed. "I'm feeling sleepy again. I shall pray that your work today takes you where you can see Señor Dirk, at least. He is a good man."

Trudi reluctantly picked up the cup and bowl, rose from the floor. "Sleep, then. But I'll bring you more rice this noon and perhaps I can find a bit of fish to go with it." She saw that Fra Hilario was dozing, and left the hut on tiptoe.

At the kitchen she ate her scant ration, then helped fill the jars and buckets to be carried out to the men in the lines. The crone in charge of the barracks banged on a copper pot and began shouting orders. Trudi set down her ladle and listened. So many women to cut grass by the south wall; so many more to tend the sick; one group to go through a heap of garments stripped from Itakura's dead; another to stitch rice bags at the storehouse in the old castle. Only a few women were left about the kitchen. The old woman began pointing. "You — you — you — " her shriveled finger indicated Trudi — "you and those two others over there — will prepare tea leaves. At once, now."

Dully Trudi trooped away with the others to an extension of the kitchen roof where old men and very small boys were piling wild-tea plants and other growths that bore some vague resemblance to tea from a bed outside the north wall. A tall, sharp-faced woman in a gray kimono stood by a line of earthen ovens that were topped by rusty iron plates and began to give instructions in a high metallic voice. Resignedly, Trudi reached for a branch and began stripping off the leaves as directed, dropping them into a deep basket. At first the twigs scored her hands but she managed to turn her palms so that the least tender parts were affected. Machinelike, she fell into a rhythm of work.

The sun topped the east wall, poured down into the packed enclosure of Hara, and Trudi bent and pulled with the others. She began to sort out her companions by their speech. One or two were obviously of samurai rank, like the delicate-faced woman who had the bed at her right in the barracks. These women worked on with the rest, but spoke seldom and then only when needing fresh branches. There were wives of fishermen and teamsters, daughters of petty tradesmen or makers of tatami, girls from little sheds where soba was sold and women who, in better times, had supervised fashionable Nagasaki restaurants or tearooms on the great road that ran north to Kokura and the Inland Sea. The girl across from Trudi had been converted by one of her clients in an Isahaya brothel and spoke at length and with dispassionate details of her life therein. From time to time, as the baskets were filled, the sharp-faced woman emptied their contents onto the hot iron plates that formed the roofs of the ovens. The two old women, palms toughened by years

204

of such work, spread the leaves carefully over the plates, keeping a careful eye on the curling green edges.

At noon, there was more work in the kitchen and Trudi listened hopefully to the talk of those women who had been out beyond the stockade. Two groups were arguing heatedly about the diminishing rations. A red-faced woman shouted that if Fra Fidel had his way, they all would eat to their hearts' content, taking care to pray for divine action to replace what was used up. "It's the fault of that Gentaro Mori," the woman stormed. "He listens to that heathen Komo from Hirado, Yang-san. You wait and see. Mori's selling our surplus to the Dutch Company."

Another woman, bending over a rice kettle, snapped, "Who saw to it we shared wells and baths equally? Who made each street provide decent benjos so your babies wouldn't be crawling through filth? Yang-san saw to all that. He had our food rationed, too. Do you remember the first night here when thousands went hungry and a few dozens stuffed themselves? That hasn't happened since. Why? Because of Yang-san. And who found the lumber for Fra Fidel's church out there? Yang-san again!"

Trudi edged closer to the woman by the kettle. "You have seen Yang-san today?"

The other nodded. "And every day. He's outside the walls now, making the people clear away those huts by the big gate." She straightened up. "Eh-to! It's a pity that Matsudaira's men know about him!"

Trudi started. "What? They know about Dirk being here? I mean, Yang-san?"

"And why not? Some people have lost heart and tried to make their way to the Imperial lines. They all died, of course, but not so quickly that they didn't have time to talk. It's even said among our troops that the siege will be lifted if we deliver Yang-san to Matsudaira."

"Deliver him?" echoed Trudi faintly. "But why?"

"He is a Komo. The Imperial troops have lost heavily against us and their leaders fear to lose more. If they have a Komo in their hands, they can throw the whole blame on him, raise the siege and pardon all the Japanese. Of course, they'd make a spectacular torture of the Komo, probably in Tokyo."

Trudi went white. "But surely no one would betray him!" she said.

"Not I," said the woman. "But there might be weak heads who believe that we others would be pardoned." She filled a bowl and walked wearily off.

Dirk in the hands of Matsudaira! But Dirk had many powerful Japanese friends. Caron had many more, and far more powerful. If Dirk was taken prisoner, he and Caron between them would have a very good chance of bringing enough influence to bear to release him. Only — where was Caron? Then she comforted herself with the thought that wherever he was, he would hear about things. He would save Dirk somehow.

She filled cup and bowl and made her way to Fra Hilario's hut. The old friar was still stretched on his grass bed, his robes stripped down to his waist. A Japanese doctor knelt by him, skillfully hammering long, wooden-headed needles of gold and silver through the skin of his abdomen, while a buck-toothed assistant held out a crude anatomical chart. From the doorway, Trudi looked on dubiously. She had little faith in the Japanese science of acupuncture, but she had heard Caron himself say that the insertion of the needles often produced surprising cures. She set the bowl and cup down just inside the door and went back to the shed where the tea rollers were assembling.

The afternoon work was more trying than the morning's. The old women cried out shrilly when the tea leaves were roasted enough. Then Trudi and the others had to roll the hot leaves between their palms, which smarted painfully as sharp juices oozed onto skin already raw from stripping the tough branches.

Trudi straightened up with an effort, pushing her hair back from her forehead with a gesture of dismay as more baskets of leaves were brought up. It was all very well for the peasant women with their tough hands, she thought. The juices seemed no more than hot water to them. She caught sight of the samurai wives, working silently and uncomplainingly across from her. If they could keep on, then certainly she could.

Work stopped abruptly. Off to the south a sudden banging and clattering broke out and a dozen heads turned toward the sound. Far across the tangle of roofs, Trudi could make out the south wall with a thick haze rising beyond it. A woman behind her cried out, "Ara! There are no men along the parapet!"

"What is it?" asked Trudi, staring with others.

"The south lines, by the hogback," someone answered. "There is an attack. Where are the guards on the south wall? Why hasn't the alarm drum sounded?"

Then a great booming thundered out from some unseen drumhead. The overseer of the tea shed clapped her hands sharply. "To the wall! Everyone!" She caught Trudi by the elbow, hoisted her roughly to her feet. "You too! Everyone is needed. Run!"

Jostled and elbowed in a stream of racing women, Trudi was carried on past the kitchens, past Fra Hilario's hut and through the stockade gate into the streets of the refugee village proper. She saw low huts with feeble old men peering from doorways, a frantic mother catching up a pair of docile, solemn-eyed babies, a stupid-faced man who squatted open-mouthed while his hands fumbled mechanically in the act of fixing a new pike head to a shaft. The crowd grew denser as other streams of women joined Trudi and her fellows, pouring out of narrow alleys, swirling in wide streets like the fire breaks in Hirado village, so far away.

She caught the arm of a pretty, white-faced girl. "What are we going to do?"

The girl quavered, "They'll tell us," and ran on faster.

Trudi stopped short while people butted and shoved against her. Somewhere up ahead by the shattered walls of the old keep she heard a voice shouting, a voice that she knew. She plunged forward, thrusting past those who had elbowed her. She could see open ground over a mass of black heads in front of her, a great curtain of white wall at its base, a tall man in brown jacket and baggy breeches who gestured to the oncoming mass with a broad-brimmed hat.

She cried "Dirk!" and broke blindly from the mass.

She heard an answering cry of "Trudi!" and his arm fell about her shoulders. Then he began shouting to the women. She saw that his eyes were hard and his mouth set in a tight line that snapped open only to give terse orders. "To the wells, the first group! The next, bring up the barrows with the matting!"

Something bright and hissing arched high over the bare south wall, fell in a shower of sparks and flame among the huts. Three more followed it. "Ah, I knew it! Fire arrows!" Dirk's arm tightened for an instant about her. "Go help the women over there with the mats — see? Where they're bringing up the water buckets."

She raced off toward a low barrow heaped with matting that women were soaking with well water. Catching up a dripping sheet, she threw it about an old man, smothering the flames of his haori. Tottering with fear, the old man whimpered out his thanks, then snatched the matting from her and bravely heaved it onto a flimsy burning roof nearby.

Trudi went from hut to hut as the arrows sang over, now snatching up a bucket to wet down smoldering timbers, now running with three other women to throw a soaking strip of mat across a dry roof. From time to time she looked over her shoulder at Dirk. Japanese were running to him, then racing away, so that she saw him in a whirlpool of helmets or shaven heads. Twice he caught her eye and waved encouragingly to her.

Outside, the rip and crackle of musketry went on. Inside the enclosure, with a rattle of pikes and clank of sheathed swords, a thick column of infantry headed for the main gate at a double and Trudi thought she caught sight of Gentaro Mori urging them on.

There was a new sound in the afternoon air and hundreds of eyes looked skyward, questioning. A sleek-haired girl near Trudi cried, "Thunder! The old gods are angry with us!"

The sound roared out again and a high-pitched voice yelled, "Cannon fire! The Shogun's cannon!"

The guns stunned and rumbled somewhere off beyond the south wall, but no shot sailed across the sky to crash among the huts and the huddle of helpless people about them. Then all at once the guns were silent. Somewhere a child cried, an old man coughed with a hollow, rending sound. Trudi drew a deep breath, half relieved, half fearful.

Hands dropped lightly on her shoulders and she turned with a start. The next instant she was sobbing with relief against Dirk's chest while he stroked her hair with an unsteady hand. His voice was gentle. "It's all right — for now. The attack's beaten off. It's all right."

"How long do I have to stay in the barracks, Dirk?" she whispered.

"I hope not long. But you see, it's hard for people who are fighting for their lives to give much thought to us." His arms tightened about her.

"But we've got to get out, Dirk!"

"I've been thinking about that, too. Mori would help us if he could. Fra Fidel keeps the others stirred up by saying that we'd tell Matsudaira all about Hara if we reached him. There are others who say I've been too useful." He smiled wryly. "They'll say that about you, too, if they watched you working on the fires." He took her arm. "Come up to the top of the wall. We'll be able to talk for a little while, anyway."

Arm in arm they climbed the ramp to the vacant south wall. "Just what did happen, Dirk?" she asked.

"I don't know, yet. Some of the outposts on the hogback were withdrawn without Mori's orders. Someone — no one knows who — cleared the watch from this wall. Then the Imperials rushed the hogback and took it. They got through our second lines, right up to the foot of the walls. Mori had his counterattack organized, but before he was ready, Fra Fidel led a lot of people against the Imperials. It was the wrong time and they were cut to pieces."

They had reached the summit and Trudi looked curiously south and west. She could see what Dirk had called the hogback, and earthworks running along it, bright with pike heads. Five hundred yards closer to the castle, a second line ran, jammed with troops. She was puzzled. "It all looks so quiet. There are even men sleeping between the lines."

Dirk said dryly, "They're not sleeping. They are dead."

In the hush that followed the attack, men were moving in twos and threes from both sets of entrenchments, walking slowly among the piled bodies. Dirk turned her quickly so she faced the sea. There would be enough horrors about her without her seeing the soldiers of each side coolly disposing of enemy wounded with sword or pike. "There's the Imperial blockade," he said, pointing to the anchored ships, to the smallest craft that plied endlessly between the stationary line and the shore. "They've got little patrols on the beach, too, watching for people who might try to slip out of Hara."

Then she remembered the words of the woman at the kitchen. She faced about, her hands clutching the front of his coat. "Dirk — you've got to be very careful. Listen — " Quickly she told him of the rumors that he was to be given over to the Imperials as a price for the immunity of the others.

"I've heard something of the sort," Dirk said quietly. "But I doubt it. Mori would have to be in on any negotiation as important as that. It's nothing that he or Tokisada or Nirado would have anything to do with. Besides, they know how much any promise of immunity would be worth. No, my dear, we're safe so long as the castle holds out, and that will be for a long time."

"But the cannon!" she cried.

"They've got four guns mounted behind grass screens beyond the hogback. The balls can't even reach our second line, and if they were brought closer, they're too light to do any damage against the stonework. Odd, isn't it, to think that those are Martin Trelawney's guns."

"But how about treachery?" she persisted. "Or spies?"

"We can forget about spies. As for treachery, the people have got too much confidence in Mori. And another thing, this affair is not limited to the Shimabara peninsula. People are talking about it from Kagoshima to Tokyo and beyond. Caron must have heard that I'm here by now, though probably not that you are. He'll be moving in the right quarters. We'll be hearing from him."

"I'd forgotten that." Her lips contracted. "I do wish that Uncle Van Os could know I'm all right." She fell silent for a moment, then said slowly, "How are you so sure about spies, Dirk? There are so many people here."

"Mori has a plan," answered Dirk.

Suddenly a trumpet blasted and the air was thick with the shuffle of feet as the Hara garrison, barring those actually in the lines, assembled on the parade ground. Dirk pointed to the level space, partly hidden by the old keep. At one moment it was black with moving men. The next, neatly aligned ranks covered it. They saw Mori leap to a block of stone and a hush fell over the ranks. His voice came faint but clear.

"There have been spies among us," Mori blared. "They are still among us. Let every man look at his right-hand neighbor. If he is not known to you, seize him!"

The files stood, swaying a little. Then Trudi saw a scuffle at the extreme left, another in the center, more disturbance in the rear. Struggling men were dragged forward, forced to their knees. Before she could cover her eyes, swords flashed, roundish objects bumped to the ground and the swordsmen stepped aside from headless bodies that spouted blood. She shut her eyes tightly, swaying. Then she passed a hand over her forehead. "Dirk, I want to go down."

He led her slowly down the ramp and into the hut-lined streets. People were settling themselves into their routine in the wake of the attack. Two men, one old and in a kimono, the other in armor and wide blue breeches, were arguing. The soldier, smacking a pike butt on the ground, said sharply, "I don't care what you did in the Korean wars. Fra Fidel's attack was right. It was God's will. He said so himself. Would *you* question God's will?"

"That's what's bad for us," Dirk said soberly. "Whatever Fra Fidel wants to do is God's will and most of the Christians follow him blindly. He lost us over a thousand men today, as well as the hogback. I'll take you as far as the women's stockade, then tonight I'll see what I can do to have you assigned to work outside. We'll at least have a chance to see each other during the day."

Trudi tried to look confidently at him. "You'll find a way, I know you will." She held out her arms at the gate and Dirk caught her up quickly, heedless of the shocked expression of a mother who muttered, "Ara! Rubbing their mouths together!" as she scurried away.

Through the gathering dusk Dirk walked on through the village, stopping once to pat a sleek-faced cat that arched its back, purring loudly as it thought of the paradise of mice and rats in which it found itself. Dirk wondered, as the cat walked away, what Caron's first move would be. There might be an appeal to the Shogun himself, that would result in his safe-conduct from Hara — with Trudi, of course. Or Caron might find friends among the officers commanding the besieging units and arrange something with them. The Frenchman might even offer himself as hostage, as he had done years before in the affair of Pieter Nuyts, a near-tragedy that had sprung from Nuyts's deliberate affront of the Shogun. At any rate, Caron would not be idle.

Dirk left the east wall and headed on toward the keep where he hoped to find Mori. Close by the powder magazine he found the young Christian, Tokisada, wearily tightening a bandage about his knee. Tokisada looked up. "Komban-wa, Yang-san. Good evening. Things went well today."

Dirk thought of the thousand casualties, the loss of the hogback. "Well? I don't understand, Tokisada-san."

"Splendidly! God spoke directly to Fra Fidel and our action today will lead us soon to victory."

"We can hope so," said Dirk noncommittally.

"And the cannon! They make a big noise, but they can't hurt us." He lowered his voice. "Some were afraid that the Shogun would bring the big Dutch ship with all its guns against us — the one that was anchored at Hirado."

"The *de Rijp?*" asked Dirk quickly.

"The name sounds something like that. But there is no fear of that ship. This we learned from a spy before he died. The Daikwan had the ship bring cannon to Nagasaki, little guns like those beyond the hogback, useless things. Then he ordered that ship and all the Dutch on it to cruise far to the south. We shall not see it in the Gulf of Shimabara."

Dirk went cold from head to foot. The *de Rijp* at sea, probably well beyond Kagoshima, perhaps as far as Okinawa. And Caron on board, probably sure that Dirk was safe at the factory! He sat down slowly on a block of stone, running his fingers absently through his hair, his heart sick within him.

The Mortar

THE loss of the hogback seemed to bring the fall of Hara no closer. The people within the outer walls went through their daily routine of living without noticing much change, save that the reports of arquebus fire were louder and Mori's reserves were mustered more frequently to beat off attacks on the re-sited lines that in some cases were within a couple of hundred yards of the ragged walls. The Shogun's cannon boomed and roared at odd intervals, but the gunners were unskilled and the heavy balls bounced harmlessly off the foundations of Hara. From the towers, no less than six of the ugly pieces could be seen, roughly masked with grass screens, but only four of them were in action, the others having been blown up through careless loading.

In a noon hush, some days after the retreat from the hogback, Dirk and Trudi sat in the sun at the foot of the old keep, each busy with a bowl of watery rice in which a bit of dried fish floated. "Wasn't it lucky I was put to cutting grass today?" she said, and laid a hand over his. "Just the same, this is only the second time we've been able to meet since that day on the walls. Dirk — are they always going to keep us apart?"

He set down his bowl with a helpless gesture. "You're sure that Fra Hilario won't ever consent to marry us?"

"I asked him again yesterday. I hated to, because he's so feeble now," she said, eyes on the brownish-gray mass of Hara village. "I know that he would, if his rules let him. He admires you, Dirk."

"He's a good man, as good as I've ever met. I can't help respecting Fra Fidel, too, even if he is a fanatic. No, I'm afraid that even if Fra Hilario were willing, Fra Fidel would stop him. And Fra Fidel would start a revolt, I think, if we were married Japanese-fashion. He says that that would be nothing but an evasion and you've no idea how many of the people here rely utterly on what he says."

"I hear enough, there in the women's quarters." She looked troubled. "Anyway — does it truly seem to you that a Japanese wedding would be a real one — for us? Isn't Fra Fidel right?"

Dirk pushed back his high-crowned hat. "Real? I don't know. People in the Company service marry that way. They've married at Hirado often enough — like your uncle and Caron. It goes something like this. Members of the Company should marry under Dutch law when they can, *but* if there's no predikant available, then a marriage according to the laws of the country where it's performed is perfectly legal and binding."

"You're sure of that?"

"Perfectly."

She was silent for an instant. Then she said in a low tone, "If — if that is the only way, I'm willing, Dirk."

"But Fra Fidel isn't," said Dirk grimly.

"Fra Hilario thinks he's wrong. He says it's a matter for us to decide, not for his church."

Dirk glanced up at the sun that was beating directly down into the great enclosure. "If you're sure you're willing — " he began.

Trudi, eyes on the ground, nodded. Dirk went on, "I'll talk to Mori again. Then I'll see some of the headmen. If they don't object, then I don't see what Fra Fidel can do about it. But they follow him so." He got to his feet and Trudi rose with him. Hand in hand they walked toward the entrance to the keep.

"More grass cutting this afternoon?" asked Dirk.

She held out a reddened palm. "Thank goodness, yes. I simply couldn't roll tea leaves again today." She leaned her head for an instant against his arm. "I wish that the Japanese wedding weren't the only way — "

"Even that is not going to be easy," said Dirk. "But I'll do my best." He inclined his head as they passed a door that led into the keep. "Konnichiwa, good day, Takai-san."

The Japanese squatting outside the door stared at him and Trudi, then rose quickly, finger to his lips, and motioned toward the door. "What is it, Takai-san?" asked Dirk.

Trudi whispered, "He's telling us to go in. Do you know him?"

"Yes. He's from Saga, across the gulf. Come on."

The Saga man, finger still at his lips, kept beckoning with his free hand. Dirk handed Trudi across the threshold, ducked in after her. Then they both came to an abrupt stop.

Fra Fidel stood, arms folded and defiant, in the middle of the room. Against one wall, Mori squatted, his face impassive. From a rude stretcher on the floor, Fra Hilario, his back toward Dirk and Trudi, lifted a frail hand. "I have made my plea, Fra Fidel. Again I say, you have no right to interfere in this highly secular matter."

"I have every right," said Fra Fidel shortly.

Fra Hilario's voice grew stronger. "There is no superior to whom we may appeal. I may only bargain with you. Do not interfere in this marriage and I relinquish to you full power in all matters spiritual in Hara, despite the fact that I am your senior if not your superior. I will follow your counsels, I will bow to your rulings."

Fra Fidel's black beard sank against his chest. Then he raised his head and stared at Dirk and Trudi as though seeing them for the first time. His hot eyes moved toward the stretcher. "You grant me full powers? You will not oppose me in matters such as — "

Fra Hilario said firmly, "In no matters, so long as they do not offend our church and our order."

Fra Fidel hesitated, then said, "I accept," and strode out through the door.

Trudi dropped on her knees beside the stretcher and caught up Fra Hilario's thin hand. "You shouldn't have left your bed! You promised me this morning that you wouldn't do anything except baptize the Kodera baby!"

Fra Hilario's eyes closed. "This has done me more good than all the gold and silver needles in the Empire. It is a very small way of thanking you for the care you have given an old man. Now please call my bearers. I must bless a new banner that the women of Shimabara have made. No — don't come with me. You two have much to talk about with Señor Mori."

The bearers slipped into the room and trotted off with their light burden. Dirk turned to Mori, who still squatted by the wall, one hand absently stroking the crest of his helmet. "You see no objection to that?"

Mori rose, held out a hand to Dirk and Trudi. "There is no objection. I am very happy, Yang-san, Sayo-ko-san."

Trudi clung to Dirk's arm. "Married! We can really be married!"

"Yes," said Dirk gravely. "Thanks to Fra Hilario." He looked at Mori. "You can arrange things for us?"

"Of course," answered Mori. "Eh-to! The formalities. They must be carefully observed. I wish that I knew more — ah! I'll send for Kudo-san. He was a high court official before he lost all his lands in the days of Iyeyasu."

In a few moments, an ascetic-looking old man in a mended gray kimono came into the room, bowing and hissing. His Japanese was so formal and archaic that Dirk had trouble following what he said, until he changed from court language to common speech.

"Ah! Muzukashii! Very difficult," said Kudo when matters had been explained to him. "First, there must be the parents of the young people. There must be the go-between to arrange matters with the parents. Presents must be exchanged."

Dirk bit back his impatience. "Do we really need all that, Kudo-san?"

"Most important," Kudo said firmly.

"I think so too," Mori interposed. "All Hara will be watching."

"But we have no families here," said Trudi.

Mori bowed to her. "If you will permit it, I will represent your family. You agree, Kudo-san?"

Kudo agreed volubly, concluding, "And I will represent the family of Yang-san, if he will do me the honor."

Dirk expressed his thanks in the most elaborate Japanese at his command. "Then that's all we need, isn't it?"

Mori and Kudo both looked shocked. "By no means!" cried Kudo. "Next we must find the go-between, who will approach Mori-san on my behalf."

"But we're all agreed!" protested Trudi.

"There must be a go-between," said Kudo flatly.

"It is better," said Mori. The two Japanese plunged into a long discussion of the most suitable man in Hara to request from Mori, on behalf of Kudo, the hand of Trudi for Dirk. When that matter was settled, Kudo laid down the law on the wedding ceremony itself. There must be proper cups for the exchange of the nuptial sake. Two butterflies or young girl attendants must be found, properly trained and costumed. Kudo and Mori must exchange gifts and Dirk must see to it that a present of some kind be made

216

to the go-between. A palanquin must be built to carry Trudi on the wedding day from the women's barracks to Dirk's quarters. As to Mori's quarters, they must be draped in mourning white, to show that the bride was dead to her family, as represented by him.

As each point was checked off, Dirk fidgeted inwardly. When Kudo had finished, he said, "I suppose that's all necessary, but — "

"Highly necessary," said Mori.

"But that will take at least until tomorrow," cried Trudi.

Kudo held up his hand. "Time must elapse between the visit of the go-between and Mori-san's acceptance on your behalf. Then I must take time to consider if the match is suitable for Yang-san. There must be purification ceremonies. Tomorrow? Four days, five days." He gathered his gray robes and got to his feet. "Now I go to speak to the go-between. Then he — "

The little room was filled with a violent throbbing. Somewhere out in the sunlight, strong arms were pounding the great alarm drum that stood on its wooden horse by the main gate. Mori bounded up, eyes questioning. "An attack? It can't be. There is no firing."

He ran out of the room, followed by Kudo. Dirk caught Trudi by the arm. "Come on. We'd better see what's happening. We'll go up the south wall."

Trudi clinging to his sleeve, Dirk raced up the battered ramp to the summit, where people were looking south, pointing and shouting. He paused to hand her over the last rough bit, then drew her beside him at the parapet. "What can it be?" she panted.

"Verdomd!" cried Dirk in a strained voice as he pointed.

Out in the gulf a big ship was standing in toward the shore. There was no mistaking its rigging, its hull, nor the ugly bristle of guns along its sides. "The *de Rijp!*" Trudi gasped. "Dirk! Dirk! We're saved! They've come to get us!"

"Saved? How can we get to the ship? How can anyone on it get to us? We can't — "

Someone touched his elbow and he turned to see a young officer of Mori's staff. The officer bowed. "It is Mori-san's advice that you do not stand where you can see the Komo's ship. There are some who will think that you signal to her." He pointed at the masthead of the *de Rijp*. Above the colors of the Company flew the crest of Matsudaira, commanding the besieging forces. "Ill-disposed people in Hara would misunderstand."

With a last look at the Company's ship, Dirk put his arm about Trudi's shoulders and helped her slowly down the ramp.

Unshaven, his jacket rumpled and his breeches flapping untied about his knees, Nicolas Becker stood at the head of the narrow companionway and looked forward where Caron and Van Os stood talking by the port rail of the *de Rijp*. The Frenchman was freshly shaven and his clothes were neat, even to the bright silver buckles on his shoes, while Van Os looked as though he were about to begin a new day among his ledgers.

Becker muttered, "Pah!" as though their apparent unconcern irritated him. His own world had been turned upside down ever since that evening, a few hours after the *de Rijp's* departure from Hirado, when he and Van Os had been bundled, virtually prisoners, onto a wallowing barge and brought to Nagasaki. Then had come the transfer to the *de Rijp,* and days of endless, aimless cruising among the islands to the south, a Japanese pilot setting the course and a guard of Japanese soldiers on deck. There had been unexplained anchorings in strange harbors, equally mysterious departures. Official barges and larger ships had hailed them, delivering papers to the commander of the troops.

Then the cruising had come to an end. The *de Rijp* had held to a steady course and two days before had dropped anchor under some very high cliffs, topped by a ruined castle. There seemed to be some kind of fighting ashore, but Becker had taken little interest in it until Japanese arrived with lighters to remove the ship's guns and to demand the services of the old Englishman, Martin Trelawney. He was sure that Caron had mistranslated his protests, as well as his demands for payment for Trelawney's time.

He glanced up the deck again. Caron! What had he done, with all his boasted knowledge of the language and the country? Here he was, Nicolas Becker, a prisoner on his own ship, out of touch for weeks with his own factory at Hirado. Who was there now to look after things? Probably that useless Dirk Jongh, and the other clerks. And what use was Van Os to the Director? The man of figures had done nothing except to fret about his niece, back in

Hirado, to whom he had been unable to get word the night the barge took them to Nagasaki. What if she did worry? She'd be all right. Let Van Os give a little thought to his Director and forget about the niece.

He started along the deck toward the others. Caron greeted him affably, Van Os with a grave nod. Becker said, "Well, Heer Caron, no doubt you have already arranged with your powerful Japanese friends for us to go back to Hirado."

Caron answered easily, "My powerful Japanese friends, as well as those of less power, seem rather reluctant to talk to me, Heer Directeur. I might as well have been blind and deaf since we left Hirado. In all frankness, I know as little as you do."

Becker looked sharply at his subordinate, but the latter's face showed only polite regret at his own ignorance. "Hmph!" said Becker. "Perhaps I know one thing that you don't, and that is that your growlings and cringings have brought us just where we are today. If you'd been man enough to speak up when they first took the *de Rijp,* we'd all be safe on Hirado now."

Caron inclined his head. "No doubt, Heer Directeur, I have made mistakes."

"Mistakes! How will I report to the Company on all this? What will the Board in Amsterdam say when they read that you let the Japanese use our ships and our guns against Christians?"

"What indeed?" murmured Caron.

Van Os's lined face looked even more troubled. "May I remind you, Heer Directeur, that the articles under which we operate caution us to do everything possible to maintain friendly relations in all countries where we are stationed? The exact words are 'at all costs.' "

Becker turned on him. "When I wish advice from subordinates, I shall request it. And here's another thing for you to think over, Heer Van Os — how did all this start? With the arrival of your niece. Jongh went crawling to the Daimyo, begging permission for her to stay, and all the time *I* knew that he wouldn't dare act against us."

Caron looked shoreward. "I can hardly agree, Heer Directeur, that pretty little Sayo-ko is responsible for all this." He waved toward the beaches. On the skyline, grass mats flapped in the wind,

219

marking the positions of the Company guns. As Caron watched, the nearest puffed out smoke and flames. Presently the flat shock of the discharge made the air about the *de Rijp* shiver slightly. There was more smoke and flame from the piece beyond, an unhealthy flare followed by a still flatter explosion.

Caron raised his eyebrows. "I should say that the Japanese have managed to blow up another gun. Yes — there are people running toward it."

Becker stamped on the deck. "Another Company gun! What's the use of your letting them send Trelawney and the best of the ship's gunners ashore if they can't do better than that?" He started toward the companionway, shouting over his shoulder, "All I know is that *I'm* responsible for none of this!"

Caron yawned back of his hand. "Our Director is not in his sunniest mood today. This business — c'est une vraie galère."

Van Os sighed. "For myself, I'm not worried, as long as you're with us. Sooner or later the Japanese will want to talk to you and you'll manage to end our troubles somehow. I've seen you do it before. Verdomd! It's Trudi who worries me. What is happening to her back there at Hirado?"

"She's a very courageous and level-headed young lady," said Caron. "She has probably heard enough from our people along the waterfront to know what has happened and she'll wait calmly on developments. Besides, Dirk must be back there by now."

"Ye-es," said Van Os slowly. "I suppose so. You're sure you can't find some way of getting word back to the factory though? It'd be a great comfort to me."

Caron's firm mouth tightened. "And to me."

Van Os laid a hand on his shoulder. "I'm not forgetting about Madame Caron and your children. But at least they're of the country."

"And, by marriage, of the Company," observed Caron. He struck his hand on the rail. "I tell you, I don't understand all this — and yet I've got to, somehow. In the Nuyts affair, when I was a hostage, all the Japanese officials talked with me, usually very frankly. But now — " he dropped his voice as though to steady it — "now it's almost as though they'd decreed that the Company no longer existed. Ventre de dieu! Why did this have to happen *now?* Another fortnight, another month, and we'd have been off on the Manila venture, high in the Shogun's favor!" He bit his lip as he eyed the tall cliffs. At some points he could just make out the ragged crest of the outer works of the castle. At others, the land fell away enough to show the worn white walls clear down to the gray foundation stones.

Van Os turned from the rail. "What would have happened if we'd refused — so far as we could — to help in this business?"

Caron shrugged. "The Company would have ended in Japan. We, who serve it, would undoubtedly have furnished sport for the executioners of Nagasaki — all of us. Then the young samurai would have used our bodies to test the temper of their blades." He swore in a mixture of French and Dutch. "Do you think *I* like to see the Company's power turned against those poor devils up there in the castle? A lot of them are Christians — and all of them are there because they were treated worse than animals. No! I'd gladly mount our guns on the walls of the castle if there were any way of doing it. I'd use our ships to bring them supplies. But I've no choice. The Company has got to live."

"I wasn't doubting your motives, Heer Caron," said Van Os quickly. "I must say I hadn't thought much about the people up there. Until you stop to consider, it all seems so impersonal. But I suppose you must know a good many of the men in Hara."

"There are thousands of them, I judge, so I could hardly help knowing some. It's more than likely that young Gentaro Mori is with them. I hate to think of him up there. He'll never leave Shimabara peninsula alive, due in part, possibly, to our presence here."

"You think we add that much weight?" asked Van Os.

"We could." Caron pointed forward, where a short, wide-mouthed mortar crouched in a sinister huddle under a tarpaulin. "The guns up there on that ridge are too light to do much damage to Hara. But Trelawney's mortars could easily toss shells from here right over the walls among those poor devils who must be crowded in there like a school of tai-fish."

Van Os stared. "The mortars? Are the Japanese going to use them?"

"They are impressed by the roar and flash of the cannon. Likewise they can actually see the balls bounce off the walls of Hara. But

I have made disparaging remarks about mortars in the hearing of Matsudaira's officers. I have every hope that the mortars will not be used. There's only one thing that could bring them into play. If the Japanese made the life of the Company depend on their success here —" He paused.

"Well, what?" asked Van Os.

"I'd turn the mortars on Hara if I had to lay them with my own hands."

"But those conditions could never come about!"

"They could!" snapped Caron. "An alternative could be that the Imperials, afraid of the slaughter they've suffered up there, would rig up a truce and throw the whole blame for the uprising on us. Or it could be—" He pushed away from the rail. "My head's splitting trying to foresee what could happen."

He crossed the deck to the starboard side, looking out into the gulf. In the bright morning, fishing boats rocked and dipped on the calm waters, the crews going about their affairs as though a deep peace reigned over the Empire and the Orient. Van Os joined the Frenchman. "At least, Heer Caron, we can turn our backs on Hara for a few minutes," he said.

"But not our minds," muttered Caron.

There was a shout from below and they looked down to see one of the ship's boats rounding the stern of the *de Rijp*. In the bow Martin Trelawney, white head bright in the sun, reached for the gangway. Caron hailed, "Ah, Trelawney! What's happening over there?"

The old Master-at-Arms to the Company touched his forehead to Caron and Van Os. "Happening?" His lined, weather-beaten face was grim. "Those Japanese! They blew up another gun, the No. 2 piece of the east battery and I'd left Wolfgang Gylak, the German from Ulm, to see to matters. While he was sighting between rounds, the Japanese rammed home a treble charge, slapped the portfire on the breech. The gun crew's dead, of course."

"I see," said Caron, face impassive.

"And the Japanese are claiming indemnity for the men who were killed — their own men, that is," Trelawney went on.

Van Os flushed. "No! That's no proper charge against the Company."

Caron said, "We pay."

"Pay?" echoed Van Os. "Do you think Becker'd ever authorize it?"

"I've the keys to the strong box," said Caron tersely.

"But, God verdomd! What will Batavia say to a payment like that?" sputtered Van Os.

"We're in no position to argue." Caron turned to Trelawney. "What impression are our guns making on Hara?"

Trelawney spoke bitterly. "About as much as the reed arrows the Hirado brats play with. We're firing at too long a range for one thing. For another, the Japanese commander insists on hitting the stone foundations. If he'd let me aim higher up, I could make a breach quick enough." His face lit up with professional pride. "I showed them something about gunnery, though. There's a path that runs along a little ridge from the rebel lines to the castle gates. By the great Harry, I never laid a piece better when I was gunner to Will Adams. The first shot was a few yards over, the next a little short." He rubbed his hands, chuckling. "That third shot! Right in the center of the path. I tell you, a lot of slant eyes grew round when they saw that."

"What effect will that have on the siege?" asked Caron.

"Effect? Why, if the Japanese have got the sense to leave that piece sighted as I left it, they can deny that path to the rebels."

"H'm," said Caron. "You remember one of the Daimyo's officers at Hirado — a man called Gentaro Mori?"

"Mori? Yes, I mind him. A proud man, but civil. Poor as an owlet, he was, for all his rank. I liked him."

"I'm quite sure he's in command over there in Hara," said Caron.

Trelawney stared at Caron. "Young Mori? In command of the rebels? If anyone but you had said that I'd laugh at him. The devil! But I tell you, Heer Caron, my guns won't bother Mori much. It would be different if the Japanese would use mortars. I'd guarantee to bring about a rebel surrender in twenty-four hours."

Caron and Van Os exchanged glances. Van Os asked, "Do you think there's any chance of that?"

Trelawney made a gesture of disgust. "They're too thick-headed to listen to a gunner."

"You suggested our mortars?" said Caron sharply.

"It did no good. And now that I know that Mori's over there,

223

I'll forget that I ever laid a mortar. I wouldn't want to drop a ball on his head."

"Good," said Van Os. "Have you been able to learn anything ashore?"

Trelawney shook his head. "Only that the commanders are in a sour mood. God knows how many men they've lost, and they're no nearer to taking Hara than they were before we landed our guns. I heard one of them say that the rebels have found out a way of keeping up a very heavy volume of arquebus fire. It's unheard of, and they're having trouble in getting their men to face it. I know of at least three commanders who have committed seppuku because of failure to advance."

"Commanders of what rank?" asked Caron.

"Taisa — colonel, I heard." Trelawney examined his powder-blackened hands. "I'm going below to get this grime off me. And I'll take your hint, Heer Caron, and forget I ever saw a mortar."

"Thank you," said Caron gravely. "Just the same, the time may come when —" He moved quickly to the starboard rail as a booming of drums sounded under the *de Rijp's* stern. Caron called over his shoulder to the others, "En garde! It's Matsudaira himself!"

"The commander-in-chief?" cried Van Os.

"Look for yourself," said Caron, pointing to the carved and painted barge that swung under the stern of the *de Rijp,* a canopy of crimson silk ruffling in the wind. After it came three other plainer barges filled with officers and a guard of honor.

The troops scrambled up the gangway and formed a double line on the deck, rapping their pike butts on the teak planking. Their uniforms were rich and under their armor red and black silk glowed. Their vizored helmets shone and deep color showed on the neckpieces that flared about the backs of their necks.

"We must be careful, Van Os," warned Caron. "Nothing but the most perfect kenson will do."

At the head of the gangway, a brimless skullcap appeared, topped by a stiff streamer that curled forward like a squirrel's tail, then a handsome, almost aquiline face, rich purple robes and wide blue silk trousers as Matsudaira, Daimyo of Izu in central Japan, stepped onto the deck of the Dutch ship.

Caron bowed deeply to him, Van Os and Trelawney copying him

224

as best they could. Caron's voice flowed out smoothly in fluent Japanese, expressing his deep appreciation of the honor done the Company, inquiring anxiously concerning Matsudaira's health, the health of his father, of his eldest son.

The Daimyo answered with easy courtesy and Caron felt relieved.

"Our ship's tea is a poor substitute for Uji tea," said the Frenchman, "but we should be even more honored if —"

Matsudaira raised his hand. "Arigato, thank you. But I am pressed for time. I wished a few words with the oji-san, the old man who sees to your cannon."

Masking his surprise, Caron motioned Trelawney forward. Matsudaira looked at him with both curiosity and respect. "I have watched you ashore," said the Daimyo. "You are wise as well as skillful."

Trelawney bowed silently.

Matsudaira went on, "It is always well to listen when skill and wisdom are joined. When you first landed your guns, I heard you say they would not do against Hara, that mortars ought to be used. I confess that we were all too much impressed by the great noise and flash of the cannon. We didn't listen to you. In what way are mortars better?"

Caron and Van Os turned pale, while Trelawney shifted his feet uneasily. In halting Japanese, he said, "I — I spoke too soon. It was before I realized what had to be done. I should have known at the start that skilled soldiers like your officers were right. Cannon are best, Matsudaira-san."

"I have been told," the Daimyo said, "that you served as gunner to Anjin Miura, the man whom you called Will Adams. A skilled gunner could have told at the first glimpse of Hara which of his tools were suited. And none but a skilled man could have been gunner to Adams." He looked keenly at the old Englishman. "Why have you changed your views?"

Trelawney glanced hastily at Caron, but could read nothing from the Frenchman's expression. He stammered, "I've done nothing but make guns for many years, Matsudaira-san. I've lost my old skills. It's a long time since I sighted a piece or canted a mortar. No, the long guns will do better. I admit they've not accomplished much so far, but the crews are raw. They'll get better each day."

225

Matsudaira inclined his head. "You are modest, as well as wise, Trelawney-san. I saw you fire this morning. You have lost no skill."

"That was luck," muttered the old gunner.

The Daimyo went on relentlessly, "Even so, I must report to the Shogun that we have tried all means here at Hara. I have seen you fire the cannon. Now I wish to see you handle a mortar." His long-nailed finger pointed to the mortar crouching under its canvas cover up forward.

Trelawney hesitated and Caron stepped quickly forward. "Our Master-at-Arms is overcome by the honor you do him, Matsudaira-san. Yes, Trelawney, get the cover off the mortar. I know that your gunners are all ashore, but you can draw on the crew."

A few sailors were summoned and Trelawney watched miserably as they stripped the tarpaulin from the mortar, brought up a keg of powder, a tin measure, disks of tow, round shot in a net.

Caron nodded encouragingly. "Allons-y, Trelawney. Matsudaira-san is waiting."

The gunner knelt by the mortar and a look of absorption crept over his lined face. He took two of the disks and dropped them into the mouth of the mortar and tamped them down with a short rammer. Then he squinted up at the walls of Hara and his absorption deepened. Eye and hand were steady as he measured out the powder muttering, "Twenty-eight — thirty pounds." The powder was poured into the mortar, two more disks dropped on the load and a thirty-pound shot thudded down after them. Trelawney sprinkled loose powder about the vent, sprang to his feet waving a slow match and shouting, "Stand clear, all hands."

The loose powder fizzed. There was a shattering roar, a vivid flash half lost in clouds of smoke, and the shot screamed away in a high arc, plainly visible from the deck. An instant later, whitish dust gushed from the south wall of Hara, the ball bounced away, soared into the air, lost momentum and plunged into the sea at the base of the cliffs, a white plume of water marking its disappearance.

Matsudaira looked questioningly at Caron. "The long guns do as well. Besides, they make far more noise."

Trelawney rubbed his chin as he studied his target. "Too light a charge," he said, as the sailors swabbed out the mortar, ready for the next loading. Once again the planks of the *de Rijp* shivered and

Trelawney squinted through the smoke. His shot had cleared the wall easily, but no telltale cloud of dust arose to show where it had landed. Matsudaira sighed. "At least I can report to Tokyo that we've tried everything. Cannon, mortars — what difference does it make? The sword is still the true samurai's weapon."

By the mortar, Trelawney muttered, "Thirty pounds and the shot fell short. Thirty-five pounds, it went too far. We'll give this one thirty-two and a half." A few moments later, he was nodding in professional approval. Just back of the walls, a thin but unmistakable plume of dust rose, wavered high in the air, was swept away with the breeze. Then his satisfaction vanished like the plume of dust. He had shown the commander-in-chief exactly how Hara could be taken. He flushed a dull red and cursed himself. Why hadn't he kept to the lighter charge and assured Matsudaira that the weapon could do no more? Now shot after shot would crack down on the helpless people behind the castle walls and —

He started as Matsudaira spoke close beside him. "You were right, Trelawney-san. These guns are useless. We'll keep on with the regular cannon ashore. I thank you for your courtesy in showing me the truth."

When the Daimyo and his retinue had gone, Trelawney mopped his forehead and stared at Caron, who was clapping him on the shoulder. "Did you hear that, Heer Caron? Doesn't he realize that we can drop shot right on those people, like dropping stones on a frog in a well?"

Caron laughed. "If no one was hurt in Hara, no harm is done. You see, if you could have shown Matsudaira a few stones tumbling about from the walls, he would have ordered up all the mortars in the Empire. As it is, he'll just keep on with the cannon, which, you say, can't do very much damage. Come down to my cabin and we'll drink brandy to the health of a man who thinks the sword is mightier than the mortar and hence can't judge what powder and shot may do."

Trudi didn't like the hut that had been assigned her for the days that must elapse before her wedding. It was small and drafty and, standing by itself, was a focus for frankly curious eyes. For long hours, older women lectured her on her approaching change of status, often speaking with a candor that left her hot-cheeked and uneasy. Then, too, she had an uncomfortable feeling that in the dead of night there were stealthy movements outside. By daylight she examined the area where the sounds seemed to originate, but as her hut was built against a pile of rubble close to the outer wall, a dead end to any paths, her investigations left her more puzzled.

At the end of one fruitless search among the tumbled stones, she stood by the doorway of her hut, looking out on the bustle and stir of Hara. She had an odd feeling of timelessness. The ramshackle town inside the walls would always be there, and she would always be in it. The slow wheel of the seasons would turn, people would be born, grow old and die to the accompaniment of the sullen crackle of fire outside the walls and the occasional boom of the Shogun's cannon. An apprehensive, depressed mood was strong on her and even the thought that in two more days she and Dirk would be married did little to cheer her.

Outside, the guns were booming again. One explosion seemed louder than usual. She heard a thin whine high in air, saw the guard on the south wall crouch against the parapet. Something thudded against the masonry from the outside and the guard cautiously straightened up and looked south.

The south? That was where the *de Rijp* lay, unless it had sailed away again. She and Dirk had both been forbidden to mount that wall and for all she knew the Company ship might be lying off the Papenberg in Nagasaki harbor by now. Even if the ship were still there, its berth was far below the cliff level, so that last shot could not have come from it.

She walked toward the great stretch of the keep, hoping to wheedle from the guards a little fish for Fra Hilario. The old friar's fever had left him, but his strength ebbed. That explosion again, louder this time, the same thin whine curved across the sky, to sweep down on her, and she hurried to the shelter of an old strip of wall. The whine raced on, ended in a crash far off by the north wall, just short of the women's quarters.

Heavy timbers flew in the air, showing like whirling black birds through a thick haze of dust. People in the streets stopped, frozen in their tracks. Then one by one they ran shouting toward the spot where the second shot had lit. Trudi saw Dirk racing around the far corner of the keep, a swarm of men at his heels. She called, "Dirk! Dirk! Wait for me!" but her words were swallowed up in a fresh whining shriek that swept down out of the sky, hammering and crashing into a line of huts.

All Hara whirled about her. Hard ground knocked at her knees and swirling dust filled her eyes and mouth. Dizzily she wove to her feet, stumbling forward. "Dirk!" she called shakily. "Where are you?"

When the dust settled, Trudi rubbed her eyes. Then she gave a low cry and plunged into the knot of men who had gathered in the street around Dirk, who lay motionless, face down, a thick beam across his bleeding head.

X V

The Tunnel

In his cabin at the stern of the *de Rijp,* Caron hummed to himself as he pulled on a pair of long boots. For no ascertainable reason, the Japanese had suddenly ended the semi-imprisonment in which the Company officials had been living, and the Frenchman was eager to go ashore to see what news he could pick up. From the deck he had been able to make out the trademark of an old acquaintance on the canvas walls of a sake booth close by the beach. Higher up the slope, he knew, he would find the quarters of a young noble with whom he had once traveled down the Nagara River, and beyond him the tent of an Osaka horse dealer who was in his debt for past favors. With entree to these three, he felt sure that his evening ashore would yield a vast and fascinating store of knowledge. As he buckled on his dress sword, he wondered why this freedom had been granted. Perhaps as a reward for the shots that Trelawney had fired at Hara that morning?

As he reached for his hat, someone rapped at his door. He called, "Come in." The door opened and Trelawney's white head appeared in the gloom of the passage. "You're going ashore, Heer Caron?" he asked.

"Unless I can do something for you, my friend."

The old gunner closed the door carefully and lowered his voice. "It may be I who can do something for you. You heard that talk among the Daimyo's guards this morning about Imperial agents slipping in and out of Hara?"

The Frenchman's expression became of intense interest. "Agents in Hara? Yes."

"You'd like to talk to one?"

"I'd give enough gold kobans to roof Osaka Castle for that privilege."

Trelawney smiled. "No need of that, Heer Caron. Not ten minutes ago a man tried to come up our cable hand over hand. I helped him. He'd been swimming and the currents carried him dangerously far. He's just come from Hara and he's in my cabin, drinking hot tea while his clothes are drying in the galley."

Caron threw off his sword, scaled his hat onto a stool. "Trelawney, the Company owes you a lot for your work over the years. But tonight's work is the best you ever did for it. Bring him here." Caron set out a brandy bottle and glasses, dragged forward a thick strip of matting, then he paced impatiently up and down until Trelawney rapped on the door again.

The man who followed the gunner into the room was a giant by Japanese standards, nearly as tall as Caron and topping the Englishman by half a head. Swathed in a long boat cape, he looked even taller. Caron greeted him in swift Japanese, making him welcome and offering him the choice of a stool or the strip of matting. Wrapping his cape about him like a kimono, the man knelt on the matting, bowing and hissing.

"So des," said Caron, handing him a glass of brandy with a ceremonious gesture. "We are honored to have you on board." He eyed his guest keenly. "It's not often that I have a chance to talk to a man from the north. You are from Rikuzen? Perhaps from the city of Sendai itself?"

The man looked bewildered. "What sort of a Komo are you to place my province and city?"

Caron waved airily. "Where else do men of your height and strength come from? Then there is your speech. You clip your words and yet you speak slowly, not like the gabble that we hear in Kyushu."

The man stretched out his muscle-heavy arms complacently. "Oh, these southern people are well enough, but only in Rikuzen do we breed true men." He sipped his brandy. "Maa! This is good, like a cool fire."

Trelawney, seated by the door, watched with growing impatience as Caron chatted on. The man from the north noticed a beautifully carved Takarabune, the legendary Treasure Ship, which with its cargo of the Seven Happy Gods stood on a shelf above the Frenchman's berth. The Japanese studied the workmanship. "That came from Nikko?" he asked. "I thought so. Nikko is far from Sendai, but it is still the north country, a good land. Here in the south I grow homesick."

Caron nodded in sympathy, spoke at length of the coastline as it curves up by Ishinomaki Bay, of the island-dotted waters about Matsushima, recalled old hill trails and pine ridges where sheets of white water pitched steeply on their way to the sea. The Sendai man listened, breathing heavily through his mouth, a wistful expression on his face.

"It is so. It is as you tell it," he said sadly. "Why did I, youngest of the Ido family, ever come south, where the air is soft and rotten?" His prominent mouth puckered in disgust. "My father fought in a true war against the Koreans. He fought again for the House of Tokugawa, the Shogun's house, later. And I? I have to fight against people so debased that they rebel against the law of the Empire."

Trelawney spoke quickly from the door. "Yes, Ido-san. And these rebels —"

Caron raised his hand. "These rebels are no concern of ours, except that they interfere with our lawful trade. Tell me, Ido-san, do you know the priest of that Shinto temple that stands by the north road as you leave Sendai?" He filled the man's glass again.

Ido drank gratefully. "The temple on the north road? I know it, but not its priest. Ara! I'd give a gold koban to be striding up that hill road, with my belly full of eels and rice, crisp brown eels, split and fried." He drank again. "There are no eels and little rice up there in Hara."

"The Hara people have only themselves to blame," said Caron, carelessly. "Ah, this talk of the north. It makes me think of the ebi fried in batter at the place in Sendai they call Gin Sui. It is a pity, Ido-san, that the siege drags on this way. It may be a long time before you see Sendai again."

Ido's right eye, reddened from the unaccustomed brandy, winked at Caron. "Long? There are ways, many ways, of capturing a castle. Some take much time, others only a little." He winked again. "A few of us have made our way into Hara, have mingled with the people there. Our reports have gone back to Matsudaira-san. I think that I shall see Sendai before too long."

Caron filled the glasses once more. "I should have guessed that a soldier of Matsudaira-san's skill would find a way to end things. I'll

232

be glad when the times are peaceful again and we can resume our trade in the old way. I have a plan for shipping out —"

Ido waved his glass as though brushing aside such trivial matters as trade. "Yes. It's all ready now or nearly ready," he cried, his voice thickening and his words blurring a little. "First we tell that mad friar, Fidel-san, that most of the Imperial army is with him. He is to open the gates and then lead us all against Tokyo and the Shogun."

Caron nodded judicially. "That's a good plan, if you can convince the friar."

"He's convinced," chuckled Ido. "But there are things to be done first. That Hara army is held together by a man named Mori. But he couldn't do much — and this is the strangest part of the story — if he didn't have a sort of quartermaster helping him."

Caron asked politely, "A quartermaster?"

Ido leaned forward. "This quartermaster, he's a Komo, like you."

Caron glanced in warning at Trelawney. Then he said idly, "A Portuguese, I suppose, who came with the friar. They're sharp, very sharp. I remember once when I traded with them —"

The Japanese, intent on his story, broke in, "There are probably many kinds of Komo. This one, whatever he is, has seen to the issue of rations. He has arranged the life of the whole town up there. He showed them how to store their powder." He dropped his voice. "And more than that, he's the one who told them how to keep their arquebuses firing in such volume that the troops are afraid to face them."

Caron smiled indulgently at Ido. "You could earn a fine living as a professional storyteller, Ido-san."

"You don't believe that I've been in Hara?" said Ido in a surly tone.

"To be sure you have," said Caron soothingly. "In imagination, and I'm sure that things up there must be as you've described them. Don't take offense, but consider how this must sound to two merchants. You've been in Hara? Then others can go there. So why not send a hundred, a thousand, to attack from the inside as well as from the outside?"

"That's a merchant's question," said Ido sulkily. He pointed a muscular finger at Caron. "If you were a soldier, you'd know one man or ten men can go where a hundred or a thousand couldn't."

"No doubt. No doubt," said Caron amiably, with a broad wink at Trelawney.

Ido set down his glass with a slam. "Baka! Nonsense!" he sputtered. "You still don't believe me? I can tell you what Gentaro Mori looks like. I can draw you the dragon crest of his helmet. I can make you a map showing where the depots and storehouses are. I was there when your shots came over the wall and I can tell you just where they fell."

"I'm sure you can," said Caron, stifling a yawn.

"Yes! And I can tell you what damage they did. I can tell you that a beam knocked down the Komo quartermaster. I know where he is, and I know that he's still unconscious. Do you want to know his name? They called him something that sounded like Yang-san. And he's in a hut by the main gate."

Caron strolled negligently to the cabin door, upsetting a stool as he did so. Under cover of the clatter he turned the key in the lock, saying quickly to Trelawney, "Careful! There's more coming."

Ido seemed intent on his glass as Caron resumed his seat. The latter poured brandy again, saying, "Yang-san? That doesn't sound like a Portuguese name."

"I told you I didn't know what kind of a Komo he was," said Ido irritably. "Yes, he's there by the gate, unconscious. Ara! You'll end by believing me. And there's a girl tending him. I didn't see her close to, but she's tall enough to come from Sendai or Sanuki." He began to chuckle. "Jodan des'. This is funny. They were to be married in a few days' time. But before then, that other business I spoke of will be attended to. We're going to slip a strong party right through the gates. It's all arranged for tomorrow night. They'll kill Mori and one or two others. The Komo they'll take alive." He chuckled again. "The tall girl will have to look for another man. They say she's pretty, so she won't have much trouble. Her name's Sayo-ko. I didn't hear her family name."

Caron looked toward the door, where Trelawney stood braced, his face deadly white. The old man stammered, "My shot! It was my shot that struck Dirk!" His eyes blazed. "Did you hear that, Heer Caron? Trudi's there! The girl I tended like my own daughter." Ido looked suspiciously at Caron, puzzled and displeased by the flood of unfamiliar Dutch. Then he gathered the boat cape about

234

him and rose. "My clothes must be dry. I thank the Komo for their care and for their new drink."

Caron rose with a bow. "We have been honored by Ido-san's company. May we hope that he will be kind enough to do one thing for us in return?" Ido looked inquiringly at him. Caron went on, "We wish to know the way you get in and out of Hara.".

Ido laughed hoarsely. "So would many others. I'll tell you this much. Our officers found plans of the castle in Nagasaki. In the old days, the lords of Hara dug a tunnel that comes out not far above the beach where the cliff slope is gentle. Pretty ladies, willing and unwilling, were often brought in that way, I hear." He moved toward the door.

Caron looked at him with amiable interest. "Ido-san, where is that tunnel and where does it come out inside the castle?" He waited for the answer, smiling pleasantly.

"I've told enough to satisfy the curiosity of a merchant," Ido said contemptuously. "Where are my clothes?"

Caron said calmly, "You'll get them as soon as you answer my question — fully. Until then you stay as you are, and in this cabin."

Ido's eyes met Caron's and read their expression. He glided backward two steps. With a quick motion, he shook off his cape and stood naked, save for a loincloth. A sheathed knife dangled from a cord about his neck. There was a flash of steel and the blade glittered in Ido's muscular hand. Trelawney cried out a warning as the Japanese crouched in the low cabin, then sprang at Caron, his knife describing an arc.

Caron's feet shifted quickly, his body bent sideways and his hand shot out. Trelawney saw Ido's body pitch to the left, saw his heels swing in air to crash against the cabin roof. Then the Frenchman stood over Ido, his grip firm on the knife hand. Caron spoke quickly between clenched teeth. "Bear a hand, Trelawney. There are cords in that chest by the berth." He went on in Japanese, his eyes never leaving Ido. "You know this judo hold? If I push an inch more, your arm snaps. Or if *you* push, it will snap. You will do well to lie still. I don't want to hurt you, but you're going to answer my questions."

Trelawney, his hands trembling, brought thin, hard cords and under Caron's direction bound Ido tightly. Caron stepped back, threw the cloak over the trussed man. Trelawney panted, "I'll make him tell. By God, I'll make him tell. If Trudi's harmed — he was laughing about her — "

Caron held him back. "Gently, Trelawney. He won't be affected by threats. Go get that brazier that stands outside Becker's cabin. Bring it in here."

Resentful and puzzled, Trelawney went out, returning with an earthenware brazier in which charcoal glowed. Caron picked up Ido's knife, turned it in his hands and then plunged the blade into the brazier. He looked meditatively at Ido, who, with closed eyes, was straining at his cords. Caron spoke as though to himself. "The blade will heat quickly. Then what shall we do with it? The skin on the inside of the thighs is tender. Yes, a burn there would be painful. Under the arm? That might be even better. Or the palm of the hand." He bent over Ido. "There are many things I can do with this knife when it's white-hot. I don't want to do any of them. But I'll have to unless you tell me how to get into Hara, and where I can find Yang-san and Sayo-ko-san. The choice is yours."

Ido snarled in defiance. Trelawney, his eyes hot and pitiless, growled, "How about the soles of the feet, Heer Caron?"

"I'd thought of that," answered Caron. "Come, Ido-san. We're wasting time. Where is that tunnel and where are Yang-san and Sayo-ko-san?"

Ido lay silent on the floor. Caron stepped to the brazier and drew out the knife, its blade nearly white-hot. Trelawney muttered, "How are you going to use it?"

Caron shrugged. "The way he forces me to. Look at this blade, Ido-san. I could burn your thighs, your hands or feet with it. I could lay it across your eyes. I'm not going to. I'm merely going to touch your forehead with it, quite lightly."

"That will do no good!" cried Trelawney hoarsely.

Caron rested the knife on the coals again. "I'll brand him with the sign of the cross, the way the more fanatical Japanese Christians used to mark themselves. Ido-san, what will Matsudaira's officers think of a man whom they send among the Hara Christians and who comes out branded? How long will such a man live? Or, more important perhaps, *how* will he die? And even if your explanation

236

is believed, you'll be marked for life as a Christian. The cross will not be popular anywhere in the Empire."

Ido remained silent. Caron sighed, picked up the knife and knelt beside him. Suddenly the Japanese began to talk in a shaky voice, while Caron listened carefully. When Ido stopped, Caron tossed the knife into the brazier. "Trelawney, please send word to the galley for Ido-san's clothes. Then tell the boatswain that I want a boat and two of his hardest men."

Trelawney stared at him. "You — you're going to put him ashore?"

"What else? I'd be glad if you'd hurry."

Trelawney burst out, "And what about Trudi and Dirk? That man knows how to save them — and you're letting him go. Give me that knife. *I'll* make him talk."

Caron said pleasantly, "The galley first, then the boatswain, Trelawney."

The old gunner started to protest, but years of discipline sent him out of the cabin, cursing under his breath.

When he had carried out Caron's orders, he hurried to the cabin, crying out, "I've done what you said. Now it's *my* turn with Ido. I'll — " He stopped on the threshold, mouth agape. Caron had slipped out of his European clothes and was struggling into Ido's shirt, haori and baggy breeches. His shoulder-length hair was gathered up in a fairly presentable topknot and drawn up over his scalp. The Japanese, still bound, lay silent and motionless on the floor.

Caron knotted his black obi. "How is this, Trelawney? I could scarcely pass in Tokyo, but here in the dark — yes, I think it may do. I'm too tall, but Ido is almost the same height."

"Splendor of God!" said Trelawney. "What tanuki tricks are you up to?"

Caron smoothed down the breeches, still damp from sea water. "I'm going to carry out my original plan and take a walk on shore. Where are the boat's crew?" Sea boots clumped outside and Caron saw two scarred, bearded faces peering curiously over Trelawney's shoulder. "Ah, Barentz, van Hel," observed Caron. "Now, lads, just loosen our guest's bonds enough so he can walk. Then we'll march him to the gangway. He'll be quiet. My knife's at his back. Ready, Trelawney. Better pick a cutlass out of the rack as we pass the armorer's."

The deck was empty and silent as the strange group went down to the gangway and into the boat that rocked below. When the party was settled, with Trelawney still protesting in the stern, Caron called, "Row out about a hundred yards from the ship, then halt."

The boat pulled silently out over the black waters of the Gulf of Shimabara. The sailors rested on their oars at a command from Caron. Then the Frenchman leaned forward and spoke earnestly, "There are two gold pieces for each of you in tonight's work. You're going to take us to the southern face of the cliffs below the castle, where I'll get out. You and Heer Trelawney will stand guard over this Japanese. He is not to struggle or shout. Is that clear? Very well. If I am not back in two hours, you'll know that our bound friend here has betrayed me. You can go back to the *de Rijp*."

One of the sailors asked in a rough voice, "And what do we do with the prisoner if you don't come back?"

"In that case," Caron answered, "it won't matter to me what anyone does. I leave his fate to you and to Heer Trelawney. Now, pull for the shore."

In the darkness, Trelawney caught Caron's arm in a tight grip. "What are you going to do ashore?"

"As I said, I'm going to take a stroll. It's quite possible that I'll meet Dirk and Sayo-ko and bring them with me. Then we'll all go to the *de Rijp,* thanking Ido-san for his help. That's all."

Trelawney's voice broke with excitement. "You're going into *Hara?*"

"I expect so."

"But the shore guards! They'll stop you."

Caron shook his head. "If Ido isn't lying, they were removed two days ago."

"You're going blind into that tunnel I heard Ido tell about? You're trusting him?"

"It's the only way," said Caron. "Sayo-ko's hut is just by the upper exit, he says, and they make her stay there at night while she's waiting for her wedding. I'll find her, and she'll take me to Dirk and we'll come down to the boat."

The old gunner reflected for a moment. "Very well. I'll go with you."

Caron touched his shoulder. "This work needs two heads, one at the castle, one at the beach."

"Then I'll go to the castle. Look, Heer Caron! Think of Trudi. You appear suddenly out of the night, dressed as a Japanese. It will be a shock to her. She might call for help and you'd have all Hara on you. But if she saw me — well, she'd run to me as she has all her life."

"No. I'd like to have you with me," said Caron. "But you're in European dress. You speak Japanese, but with a strong accent. Also, while I'm sure that you're still skilled with a cutlass, it would be like a stick against Japanese swords."

"But you — you're not even armed!"

Caron reached into the bottom of the boat and picked up a heavy Japanese broadsword. "You didn't see me take this from my cabin when we left? It was the last thing that I did. As to your cutlass, I wanted you to have that in case Ido tried to argue while I was gone. You and the sailors with their boarding axes can easily take care of him."

The bow of the boat cut into the sand and Caron stood up, ready to leap out. Trelawney tugged at his sleeve. "Then give me the broadsword. I tell you, I'm the one who ought to go."

Caron looked down at the white head. "You know the cutlass, I'm sure. But I've spent a great deal of time in the dojo, the fencing schools here. There is a big difference between the two weapons. Steady now!" He poised, then sprang ashore.

Without a backward glance, he strode across the beach, past tumbled rocks draped with wreaths of dry, crackling seaweed. When he was above the high water mark, he stopped, crouched and looked upward, trying to pick out the landmarks that Ido had described against the black sky. At last he made out a lone, twisted pine, lined it up with a white rock lower down, and plunged forward into waist-deep bushes with long, kicking strides. The undergrowth grew thicker on the slope that rose steeper and steeper.

He paused, looking for the old path through the bushes. Then he hunched his shoulders and pushed on. All at once the undergrowth gave way before him and he felt a hollow path under his straw zori.

The going was easier now, despite the steepening slope. He climbed steadily, heaving himself up now and then by a jutting root or an overhanging branch. At a level spot he stopped to breathe, looking down at the gulf that lay black below him. He could just make out the dark blur of the boat lying against the lighter sands of the beach. Far out on the water were the riding lamps of the *de Rijp* and along the western shore the strung-out stars and pools of light that marked Matsudaira's camp. With a last look he tightened his obi, made sure that his sheathed broadsword was secure and resumed his climb. The way was even steeper now and his feet slipped and slithered. Twice he fell flat, his hands clutching at grass and sod, yet he felt a growing assurance as his difficulties increased. So far, every step of the way was as described by Ido. Panting, but coldly exultant, he fought on until he saw the branches of the twisted pine, the marker that he had used on the beach, stretching clawlike just above him.

Twenty paces beyond the pine he stopped, picked up a stick from the ground and cautiously prodded about in a dense curtain of vines ahead of him. Twice his stick rapped against earth and rock. Then it ripped through the vines, met nothing as far as he could reach. With a long breath he parted the vines and ducked inside.

It was like going suddenly blind. Unfathomable blackness closed in on all sides of him, a blackness that had no limit and yet wrapped itself about him. His right foot moved forward, felt smooth ground slightly sloping. His left foot followed. He swung his stick in slow arcs, heard it strike against stone on each side. He said to himself, "So far Ido has told the truth. I found the path, the pine and the tunnel. I'm lucky. Where are we now? He spoke of a flight of stone steps. I ought to have reached them by now."

The tunnel bent and twisted twice to avoid buried boulders. Beyond the second bend, his stick rapped against stone directly in front of him. "The stairs!" Carefully he mounted the steps whose old masonry reached upward and upward, broken by deep platforms at irregular intervals. The walls were closer on each side now and once his outstretched hand touched an iron bracket set into the stonework.

Somehow the very touch of the rusty iron gave him a little comfort in the black world of the tunnel. "A bracket for a torch," he reasoned. "Peste! What a pretty sight in the old days when the young samurai in rich robes came down here by torchlight on their way to their barges below."

He went on more cautiously now, making as little noise as possible and using his stick very gently on the ground ahead. By a ragged platform he stopped abruptly, sniffing. There could be no doubt about it: cool night air was sifting down toward him, scattering the close, dead atmosphere of the tunnel. He was nearing the upper end of the tunnel. "Now," he said to himself, "the hard part is over. I've only to find Sayo-ko and Dirk."

He began to tremble as black possibilities raced through his mind. What if Ido had lied about the shore guards? They could have disposed of Trelawney and the crew with little trouble. And then? At that very moment a furious Ido might be leading a party up the tunnel, looking for him.

Slowly and carefully he told himself, "You should have thought of all that before, Heer Caron. Also, you should not be thinking of it now. There's an old Japanese proverb, 'Hell is always just an inch ahead.'" He laid down his stick quietly, made sure that his sword hilt was clear, and went on.

The steps ended and he moved on over smooth ground where the slope was barely perceptible. His gait slowed even more and he put his hands out in front of him, his eyes staring uselessly into the darkness. Suddenly there was rough stone and mortar against his palms and he halted, then began to shuffle sideways to the left, his hands running up and down the wall that seemed to block him in completely. Step by step he went, his heart beating faster, and his teeth clenched as the thought of a possible cul-de-sac gripped him. The night air was fresher in his nostrils and it must enter somewhere.

His arms stretched wider and still found nothing but stone. Then he gave a low cry of relief. A steady breeze was blowing directly into his face, despite the evidence of the rock under each hand. Cautiously he slid his left hand toward his right, then dropped both of them. "See, friend Caron," he observed to himself. "It's all been very simple. You merely reached out too far to the left and missed the most obvious gap in front of you. Your journey's over."

The gap was narrow and he had to make himself flat to get through at all. It twisted, rose over piled rubble, masked itself in vines. Once it widened so he thought that he was in the open, then closed in again as tightly as ever. The end of a beam grated across his chest. He gave a turn and a wrench, then stepped quickly back.

He was within the great mile-wide enclosure of Hara. Clouds had spread over the sky since his entry into the tunnel and thin rain fell, yet his eyes had become so accustomed to the almost palpable blackness of the underground passage that he blinked as though in a strong light. The rebel city, shining faintly under the rain, spread before him from wall to far wall. Here and there fires glowed. High in air, a single light burned in a shattered tower that showed against the sky.

Crouching low by a heap of rocks, he drew a deep breath and studied all visible landmarks in order to orient himself. The tower off to the left at what must be the southwest corner of outer walls; a vague bulk a quarter of a mile in front of him that he took to be the castle proper; while far beyond the roofs of the huts a blacker line showed against the black sky, marking the north wall.

Then he became aware that life moved in this weird city. Not far away, someone was pounding rice in a clear-toned mortar. A man laughed, deep in his throat, crying, "Hazukashii, anata. You're bashful." A girl's soft voice seemed to deny the charge. In some unseen street, the tramp of a body of weary men drummed slowly out. By a shrine, a thin voice intoned, "Namu amida Butsu. Homage to Buddha!" Far away, a faint chant rose, as the Christians knelt about their church.

Caron felt a strong urge to go deep among the streets of Hara, to sit under a roughly cobbled roof and talk with the people. He shook off the impulse, for this city was but a city of the soon-dead. He turned to look at his point of exit from all angles, so he would be sure to recognize it on his return from his mission. The tunnel mouth was well concealed, issuing as it did from a mass of rubble. Even a man reasonably familiar with it could miss it in the dark.

He felt along the ground, found a few sticks and arranged them in a seemingly meaningless pattern a carefully measured five paces from the tunnel mouth. As he straightened up, he saw a helmeted man, bent with fatigue, looming close by. The man called, "Who's got the second relief tonight?"

Pitching his voice cautiously, Caron answered, "I'm trying to find out. There's been a change." The man stumbled on wearily through the rain. Caron was satisfied with the encounter. In the dark, at least, he had passed for a Japanese. So long as he could keep out of a strong light, his costume and accent would frank him anywhere in Hara. Then he started off.

Kneeling in her hut, Trudi laid down the bit of silk on which she was sewing and trimmed the wick that floated in a saucer of rancid oil. An hour ago she had left Dirk, being escorted to her pre-bridal quarters by a delegation of women. Dirk still lay in a coma, but the doctors had told her that it was passing, slowly but surely. She had sat by while they pierced his skin with the silver and gold needles. She had helped in rolling the little cones of dried grass for the moxa, the burning of parts of the body chosen with care under the guidance of anatomical charts and horoscopes. If he were conscious the next day, the ceremony of the exchange of sake cups would be held and she would be formally recognized as one of the married community.

She clung to that thought. She and Dirk would be married — and beyond that one fact her mind would not go. She tried to reason out a future from the many things that she knew as a citizen of Hara. Rations were running low. There were more and more empty huts as the siege brought its slow wastage. There was dissension and she heard furtive mutterings that Mori must be deposed and the defense turned over to Fra Fidel, through whom the wisdom of God spoke. That very day, at the baths, she had caught quick exchanges of glances between some of the women, hints of a great and beneficial change that was to take place. All this she knew, but when she tried to weigh her knowledge, her mind stopped.

If the wedding did take place the next day, she'd find time beforehand to go to Fra Hilario, who had surprisingly and despite shrinking rations begun to regain his strength. That very day he had walked all by himself from the church by the north wall to the storehouse in the castle keep.

Someone out in the night called softly, "Anoné! Sayo-ko-san!"

Puzzled, she answered, "Who is it?"

Something stirred outside, the flimsy door was pushed back and she stared in the dim light at a tall Japanese with a rather ragged topknot and a sword in his obi, who bowed to her.

"Goeden avond, Juffrouw Sayo-ko," he said.

Trudi drew back in sudden fear. She stammered, "You speak Dutch! Did Yang-san send you?" Her voice rose. "Don't come in! Stay where you are!"

The man entered, then straightened up. Trudi gave a gasp of unbelief. "Heer Caron!"

Caron said quickly, "No time for questions, Sayo-ko! We're going to the *de Rijp*. Where's Dirk?"

Trudi hesitated as though still not convinced of his identity. "He's —he's yonder in the keep."

"Guarded?"

Trudi nodded. "Yes. All the time."

"Can we trust the guards?"

"I—I think so. They're all Mori's men."

"They won't try to interfere?"

"I don't think so. Mori's always been willing for us—for Dirk to leave, if there'd only been a way. But there are others who—"

"Leave them to me," said Caron firmly. He touched her elbow gently, urging her toward the door. "Don't worry. Hara's very quiet just now."

With a last backward glance, Trudi stepped out into the rainy night, Caron throwing a haori from a peg over her shoulders. "Take me there by the shortest way, Sayo-ko," he whispered as he ducked through the door. "We can—Verdomd! What's this?"

A thin, frail voice answered, "A friend. I hope, Señor, that you can identify yourself by the same title."

Trudi turned quickly. "Fra Hilario! You shouldn't be out in all this rain!"

The friar inclined his head. "Thanks to you, I am a well man. I came to give you my blessing on your wedding eve. And this

244

gentleman? It is safe to speak. We're out of earshot of the nearest huts."

"This is Heer Caron, of the Company," said Trudi. "He just came — I mean, I don't know how he came." She caught the friar's worn old hands. "Fra Hilario, he's going to take Dirk and me away."

Again the friar bowed. "I have often heard of Señor Caron, as far away as Macao. How, Señor, do you propose to carry this out?"

"By luck, someone told me of an old tunnel that leads to an unguarded beach. As simple as that. We'll go back the same way."

"Ah," said Fra Hilario softly. "There are some in Hara who might not agree to your plan."

Caron laughed shortly. "I'm a merchant. I'll trade news for them. First, the existence of this tunnel. Second, of an attempt to make off with Mori, Dirk and a few others. That is for tomorrow night. Third, a plot to capture the castle by treason, through playing on the — you will pardon me, I trust — on the credulity of a colleague of yours."

"Ah!" said Fra Hilario again. "I think that you will succeed, Señor. With your permission, I shall accompany you."

"Of course!" cried Trudi. "Did you think I'd leave you in Hara?"

Fra Hilario shook his head. "I meant that I should go with you for the bargaining, if bargaining there is to be. It is just possible I may be of assistance."

"And *then* you come with us," urged Trudi.

Again he shook his head. "My place is here with my people." He bowed to Caron. "With your permission, I shall lead the way. None question my gown and hood in Hara."

"You *must* come with us!" Trudi cried. "And do keep your hood pulled up! You'll be sick again." She adjusted his hood, giving it a final pat as Fra Hilario moved toward the alley.

"Can't you persuade him?" Trudi implored Caron, catching his arm.

"No one could persuade him. And consider this. How could we explain to the Japanese the presence of a friar on a Company ship? He's happy in his choice. You just think of Dirk and of getting him to the *de Rijp*. If he's still unconscious, I can carry him. It's not hard if you know how."

The three went on through the alley, crossed a sleeping street,

245

entered another alley that rose steeply. On the crest, Fra Hilario paused, pointing. "There's the keep, fifty yards ahead of us. You see the door left of the center? It shows very black against the white walls. Our friend is in there. I show you this, because our path slants away from it for a while and you might wonder. Now we — " He stopped suddenly, hand raised.

Behind the keep a dull glow rose, shimmering in weird reflections on the huts to right and left, shining red through the gaps and broken windows of the old keep. Someone far away shouted, "Fire! Fire!"

Fra Hilario shook his head. "My people are so careless with lamps and hibachi. Two nights ago there was another fire close to the church."

He took a step forward, but Caron laid a hand on his shoulder. "We'd do well to wait a little," he said.

Trudi looked up at him, startled by the sudden hard tone of his voice. "But why, Heer Caron?"

Caron pointed to the space visible in front of the keep. There was new light there, as a fire arrow arched blazing to strike among the huts. From beyond the growing, leaping light, a man ran yelling, "The gates! Who gave orders to open the main gates?"

The nearby huts began to burst into flame, lighting up the space between the three and the keep. The running man gave a quick leap into the air, spun and rolled over, a long arrow jutting from his breast plate.

Trudi, still clinging to Caron's arm, felt the Frenchman draw himself up, heard him growl, "Ido lied, or the coup is twenty-four hours early."

Trembling, Trudi asked, "What does it mean?"

Caron drew a deep breath. "Just this. Fra Hilario, will you wait here with Sayo-ko?"

The friar stared at him. "Wait for what?"

"Why, it's obvious that we must get Dirk before they do. I can cross that fifty yards easily and bring him out in the confusion. Their main attack hasn't developed yet. They're still fighting — you can hear them — on the other side of the keep." Without another word, he ran forward, crouching.

Trudi and Fra Hilario stood watching him as though paralyzed.

246

The alley bent and twisted and in the growing light they caught glimpses of his head bobbing along, only to lose sight of it again. Then they saw him pause for an instant at the edge of the open space as though taking a last quick glance before crossing to the keep.

Trudi gave a sudden cry. "No! No!"

Men in polished armor suddenly poured from the keep, fanned out in an arc. Others joined them from the right and the left, swordsmen and pikemen. The armed pattern froze for an instant, then a little knot of men ran heavily through the door into the open, carrying a stretcher between them. The flames from the burning huts leaped higher, showed a tall form, a gleam of white bandage at the head of the stretcher, the flash of bright shoe buckles. As though at a signal, the arc melted away, re-formed in a quick-stepping double file shutting in the stretcher, flowed back through the keep.

Trudi gave a low cry, swayed, then darted forward. Fra Hilario threw his arms about her, holding her tightly. She screamed, "That's Dirk! They've got him! Let me go!"

"They'd shoot you down," panted Fra Hilario.

"I don't care! I've got to get to Dirk!" She turned, drumming her fists against the friar's thin shoulders.

"He'd still be alive, and you would die, my daughter."

She staggered back against the wall of the nearest hut, sobbing. Over and over in her mind she saw the flaring light, the armed men and the stretcher that carried Dirk away. She did not even look up at Fra Hilario's low cry of warning, or at his gasp of "Señor Caron!" as the Frenchman slipped up through the dark.

Caron said quickly, "We better hurry."

She only shook her head, sobbing. "They've got Dirk!"

Caron looked back of his shoulder toward the keep. The troops that had come out from the right and left to mask the capture of Dirk were still in position. Then a drum boomed off to the right, beyond the reach of the flames. Pike points glinted dully, an arquebus squibbed. The sounds came nearer and Caron made out the head of a heavy column of men led by an officer in a dragon-crested helmet. The Imperial raiders turned to face this new attack, then began to fall back sullenly in the direction of the main gate in the outer wall. Caron reasoned that the gates must originally have been thrown open through treachery, while a small, compact body of troops passed through them with the object of seizing or killing the marked men and then withdrawing quickly. At least they missed Mori, who was leading this counterattack from the right. He watched for a few seconds longer. Mori was striking quickly, and seemed to have cut off a part of the covering force, driving them away from the main gate and deeper into Hara.

He spun about quickly, caught Trudi by the arm. "There's no time to lose. Better keep with us, Fra Hilario."

Trudi tried to shake out of his grasp. He swung her off her feet, started in the direction of her hut and the masked mouth of the tunnel. As he made his way along he said in her ear, "Dirk's really safer with the Imperials than in Hara. I've friends among them and they're beginning to trust us better." As he spoke, he wished that he felt as confident as he sounded.

"But I could go with him. Put me down," moaned Trudi.

"In all that fighting? We'll get caught up in it yet, if we don't hurry."

"That is wise," said Fra Hilario at his elbow. "Here is the big street that we must cross. Sancta Maria! It's swarming."

Caron halted at the mouth of the alley. The street that had been so quiet on their passage toward the keep now boiled with men who came out of their huts, balancing pikes or buckling on shabby armor, joining other men who were marching away toward the north. "The devil!" muttered Caron. "We can't afford this delay. And they'll stop me if I try to cross."

Fra Hilario touched his arm and stepped out among the hurrying men, beckoning to Caron and Trudi. At the sight of the cowled gown, people fell back, leaving a clear path for the three, who plunged into the alley opposite. Fra Hilario glanced back at Trudi and Caron. "To the hut?" he asked.

Caron nodded. "As fast as we can. God verdomd. Run! Listen to that!"

Off to the right steel clashed, a bowstring twanged and an unseen man screamed. "Run!" cried Caron again, catching Trudi's arm. "Some of the raiders have been driven off this way. We've got to get to the wall before they do!"

Dazed by the successive shocks of the last few hours, Trudi looked wildly off in the direction of the new sounds, then stumbled along, Caron guiding her by one elbow, Fra Hilario panting bravely at the other. She was brought to a quick halt as Caron's grip on her arm tightened. The three were standing just inside the alley that faced her hut and the south wall. She looked inquiringly at Caron, who stood with one hand raised, as though listening. "What is it?" asked Fra Hilario huskily.

"Those men who were assembling in that street back there. Hear them? They've turned to join in the nearest fight. Or some of them have." Caron leaned cautiously beyond the corner of the alley. "Two —four knots of men, fighting off there. Here come some more."

"What have they got to do with us?" asked the friar.

"Nothing—I hope," answered Caron. "If they'd only head the other way—away from us. I've got to look for a landmark in the dark and I can't afford to be seen in my looking."

"Then we can only wait," said Fra Hilario.

Caron shook his head impatiently. "I can't afford that either. A Japanese down there on the beach will be killed if I don't get back there soon. He's not a very agreeable person, but he doesn't deserve to die."

The friar shook his head sadly. "You take a good deal into your hands, my friend. Where is the landmark you've got to find?"

"Not far from Sayo-ko's hut," answered Caron. "It's the mouth of the tunnel, but it's so well masked by rubbish and brambles that I couldn't be sure of finding it in the dark without the markers I put there." He peered around the corner again. The fighting had stopped for a moment and he could make out a small compact body of men in regulation armor backed up against the south wall, a hundred yards to the west of the tunnel. A hesitant ring of ill-armed men hedged them in, but seemed disinclined to make any move against them.

He stepped back into the shelter of the alley, where Trudi knelt. Beside her, Fra Hilario gently patted her hand and whispered words of encouragement. Caron bent toward them. "As far as I can make it, this is just a little body of Imperials, cut off from the rest. They're loosely hemmed in by some of the Hara people, who seem badly led."

249

"What will happen then?" asked the friar.

Caron shrugged. "If I know the Japanese, the Imperials will make a rush to cut their way out — or be cut down. In any event, our way ought to be clear. If they're successful, they'll make for the main gate. If they're not — " He shrugged again.

Off to the west, a single, high-pitched voice yelped a command. Again Caron risked a look. His hand fell unconsciously to Trudi's shoulder, his fingers gripping hard. She winced and he muttered an apology as he whipped back into the alley.

Then he said, "Fra Hilario, will you step to the mouth of the alley with me?" Bending over the friar's shoulder, he whispered, "The Imperials just threatened a charge and the Hara people broke. Now the raiders are standing there, talking. I'm afraid I was wrong in thinking that they were cut off. They came this way on a definite mission."

"Ah," said Fra Hilario, in the same low tone. "Perhaps I can guess what it is."

Caron nodded. "They keep pointing to Sayo-ko's hut. It looks to me as though they were after more than just Dirk and Mori. I should have thought of that."

"Then why are they waiting?"

"For a dozen reasons. For one thing, they feel pretty sure of themselves, just one compact body in this mile-square maze. For another, I'd judge that they were waiting for some higher officer to join them, either alone or with reinforcements. You know how the Japanese like to work to a plan."

Fra Hilario folded his hands across the knotted cord about his waist. "And if you move toward the hut, you'll be seen by them?"

"Exactly. And there don't seem to be any Hara people about here," said Caron.

The friar bowed his head for an instant. "Yes, yes. I see. How useful it would be if someone could distract their attention away from this area." He squared his thin shoulders, drew a deep breath, then slipped past Caron and ran with surprising speed toward the knot of armored men. Caron shouted, "No! No! Come back here!" But Fra Hilario only waved his hand as he ran on, then darted up a broad street that opened to the west, parallel to the alley. There was a sudden shout from the group of raiders, "A priest! A priest!"

250

Swords glinted and the troops raced off after Fra Hilario. Right and left, the ground at the foot of the south wall was empty. Open-mouthed, Caron clutched the edge of the hut. "Dieu de dieu! He did that so we — "

He braced himself, turned quickly into the alley and touched Trudi's shoulder gently. "It's safe now. But we'll have to hurry." He helped her to her feet, hand under an elbow.

"We can go?" asked Trudi. "But where's Fra Hilario?"

Caron bit his lip. "He's — he's gone on an errand of mercy. Keep tight hold of my hand and follow me."

Hurrying after him, Trudi panted, "Shan't I see him again?"

"He's sure you will — sometime. This way."

"He was so good to me and Dirk."

"He was a saint," said Caron as they reached the deep shadow at the foot of the south wall. "Now where are my markers?" He dropped Trudi's hand and moved with quick steps, feeling along the ground. "Is this it? No. Where was it that I came out? Don't move, Sayo-ko. I'll turn my back to the wall. What was it that I saw when I came out of the tunnel?" He dropped to his hands and knees, fingers searching right and left. All at once he gave a cry of triumph. "My sticks. Now I know where we are. Sayo-ko! Right over here. Can you see me?" His voice ebbed in his throat. Trudi was nowhere in sight and he stood alone by the foot of the wall.

Cold sweat trickled down his back. What could have happened to her? The raiders might be back any moment, for he had no illusions about how long Fra Hilario could keep ahead of them — nor of his fate when they caught up with him. "Verdomd, this is bad," he groaned. "Have I failed in everything?" Raising his voice as much as he dared, he called, "Sayo-ko! Where are you?"

Quite close by, she answered him, "Here, Heer Caron!"

He bit back a reproach and caught her outstretched hand. "This way, then. See? Where I'm holding the vines back. You can slip through easily. I'll be right behind you. You've smooth footing for about twenty yards. Watch that turn to the left. It's very dark and it will get darker as we go along, but don't be frightened."

Trudi's voice was quite steady. "I'm not frightened, Heer Caron. Not very much. Did you mind my leaving you? I wanted to get the haori I was going to wear at my wedding, so I just slipped back to the hut for it. Dirk bought the cloth here. I — I couldn't leave it behind, could I? Heer Caron, why did Fra Hilario go away so quickly?"

"He felt that he had to. Go carefully now. We'll come to some old steps very soon."

"You mean someone needed him? He was always doing things for others."

"Never more than this time."

"It was about the Hara people?"

"Yes — about people in Hara."

"I ought to have known," said Trudi. "He was more than a saint, Heer Caron."

"Much more," said Caron tersely. His throat tightened as he thought of the old friar coolly and deliberately exposing himself so the girl who had saved his life by her nursing might have a chance to live.

Suddenly she stopped. "Listen!" she whispered. "Voices!" Caron slipped ahead of her in the dark, loosening the hilt of his sword. Then he drew a breath of relief and pushed her gently past him.

"It's all right. They're outside," he said, ear to the dank stone at his left. He reasoned that he had not yet entered the tunnel proper and that the way still ran parallel to the outer wall. Over the beating of his heart, he could hear the shouts faint but clear. The raiders had found Trudi's hut empty and were cursing their luck, blaming one another for their slowness.

Trudi plucked at Caron's sleeve. "What is it? What are they saying?"

"Nothing. Nothing." The Frenchman raised his voice and urged her on, hoping that his words had drowned out the last bitter cry from the outside — "Anyway, I got the old priest!" It was evident that Trudi had not heard, for she stepped out bravely through the dark. Caron kept working his shoulders as though he had received a heavy blow. Of course, Fra Hilario's dash into the open had been a doomed one, but the Frenchman had kept alive the hope that the friar's knowledge of the twisting alleys of Hara might have saved him. With an effort he forced his mind from the past to the present, and to the immediate task of getting Trudi to the beach safely.

Step by step Trudi moved on through the dark, feeling her way carefully. There were rough, broken platforms of stone that gave way to uneven steps, another platform and more steps. The dead air of the tunnel lay heavy on her face and it was difficult to breathe. Yet as she went on through the dark, her spirits rose a little. Dirk was in the hands of the Shogun's men, but at least he was out of Hara, and Heer Caron, who had so miraculously found this way into the castle, would be able to secure his release.

She stopped suddenly as her ears caught a vague stirring somewhere ahead of her in the tunnel.

Without a word, Caron stepped past her and she heard the dry hiss of his sword as he unsheathed it. Close as he was to her, she couldn't see him but sensed that he was standing in a half-crouch, his blade advanced. The stirrings and rustlings came nearer, a stone rattled away down the unseen slope. She could hear someone panting as he labored up through the dark and she knew that Caron had moved a step or two in advance. Then a voice muttered in English, "God damn it, if a Frenchman could do it, then a Kentishman can."

Caution forgotten, Trudi cried, "Martin!" and tried to run forward.

She felt Caron's hand close on her arm, heard him call, "Trelawney! You were supposed to stay on the beach!"

Trudi thought she could make out a dim figure moving in the darkness as the old gunner quavered, "You've got them? They're safe?"

"Sayo-ko's right behind me," answered Caron. "Why didn't you wait?"

Trelawney panted, "You're there, Trudi? You're all right?"

Caron broke in, "What have you done with the Japanese, with Ido?"

His voice still closer, Trelawney answered, "Time was getting short. I told the crew to do nothing till I came back. You were gone a long time and I thought you might need an extra arm. So I came."

"Then Ido's not hurt?"

"No. Where's Dirk?"

"He has been taken out. Give Sayo-ko your arm. I'll bring up the rear, though I think we're out of danger." Caron handed Trudi forward and she gave a little gasp of relief as Trelawney took her arm and faced her toward the lower end of the tunnel. "Easy, now, Trudi. There's nothing to this. You and I have scrambled over rougher ground than this in the old days, when we looked for jushimatsu nests along the Hirado cliffs. Is Dirk right behind?"

Trudi shook her head and fear swept over her again. "They captured him, Martin. They carried him off. I saw it. He was hurt."

"God help me," thought Trelawney. "And it was my shot that did it. The Japanese said so."

Trudi went on, "But Heer Caron will tell them to send him out to the *de Rijp*. He said he would. It was awful, seeing him carried away, but then Heer Caron said that any place was better for him than Hara."

Trelawney clutched at the hope. "That's it. You trust to Heer Caron. Steady now. The going's rougher here."

Leaning on Martin's arm, Trudi felt the fresh breath of the night on her face. A dozen steps more and she saw a rough oval, lighter than the black of the tunnel just ahead of her. Then she stood in the open. Below her was a stretch of beach where a boat lay. Far out on the water were the lights of the *de Rijp*, lights that were repeated again and again along the curving shore in Matsudaira's camps. And somewhere among those shore lights, men were carrying a stretcher. She turned to look up at Caron. "You'll see about Dirk right away, won't you?" she asked.

"Of course," said Caron, reassuringly.

"You've done so much for us already. But if I just could know tonight . . ."

Trelawney took her arm again. "You leave it to Heer Caron. The first thing's to get you on board and into a berth. It won't take long, because the path's easy now."

The rain had stopped and the moon showed through a scattering of thin clouds, lighting up the distant *de Rijp*, the beach and the waiting boat. High above the slope the broken walls of Hara showed harsh against the sky, brooding with a sullen menace at the edge of the cliffs.

XVI

Deep Peril

THE voyage seemed endless to Dirk. Perhaps it was because he was tired, very tired, and was not able to collect his thoughts. He could feel the sampan pitching gently under him, but he couldn't tell how long he'd been aboard it, or when he'd fallen into so deep a sleep. The last time, and the time before, that he had wakened, he had felt the easy sway and lurch of the ship, but whether minutes or hours had elapsed between the awakenings, he couldn't tell. Gunst, but he was too spent to raise himself enough to see if he was still on the Gulf of Omura, or if he was already in the narrow channel that led up the Kyushu shore to the stone powder house on the north arm of Hirado Bay. He began to fret feebly. Would Trudi be offended by his long absence? Of course he must find Caron at once. He had so much to tell him, but he'd at least have a chance to see Trudi.

His head throbbed and he tried to raise his hand to his forehead. An interminable time passed and he was startled to feel his palm just over his eyes. "When did I do that?" he wondered. "Ja. I remember. My head began to ache." There was so much to tell Caron. What was it? His thoughts scurried, frightened. What had he to tell Caron? But he had left the Frenchman only the night before, at the fisherman's hut by the Gulf of Omura. Or had it been two nights ago? Two nights at least, or even more.

The past escaped him, leaving him only the present. His head throbbed more violently and his neck and shoulders seemed to shake with it. Then for a miraculous instant, the throbbing and shaking stopped. Past and present merged. He saw Trudi standing by his side in the room in the shattered keep of Hara, with Fra Hilario smiling at them from a stretcher. He cried out in sudden terror and tried to raise himself. The throbbing returned with redoubled force and the past slipped away from him. Someone held a little porcelain cup to his lips and he felt bitter, thick liquid on his tongue. The

255

motion of the sampan, the hiss and slap of the waves, faded with the pain. "Dank je, Trudi," he muttered.

Minutes, hours or days later, his consciousness rose from vague depths into a world where there was no pain and where the roll of the sampan had given way to a slow, steady motion, where the sound of the waves was replaced by the pad of feet and the smell of the sea by the crisp scent of evergreens. He opened his eyes and light striking them brought no ache to them. He was being carried somewhere in a palanquin whose curtains were closely drawn. That he was heavily guarded — or escorted — was plain from the rustle of feet outside and from the muted clop of horses' hoofs.

Memory suddenly came clear to him. The guns of the *de Rijp* had begun booming down in the gulf. He had set out at a run to see where one of them had hit. There had been a yelling rush high in air and he had seemed to walk slowly and easily up a long slope of dazzling light that had ended in sudden and utter darkness.

He had been struck down in Hara. That much was certain. In Hara — Trudi! Where was she — and where was he? Could the castle have fallen while he lay unconscious? Or could a sudden sortie have cleared a path to the outer world? That might account for the tightly laced curtains, hiding him from hostile eyes. In that case, Trudi might be in another palanquin close by. The two might have been spirited away to the east shore of the gulf, which would account for his confused memories of being at sea. He moved his arms, his legs, and sudden hope filled him. He was not bound. He tried to sit up, then sank back realizing that the bone-deep weakness that filled him was as effective as the strongest ropes.

He lay quietly for a moment, wondering what was best to do. Coming to a decision, he slapped feebly at the curtains, crying "Anoné!" The sound of feet outside ceased and the sense of movement ended. The lacings of the right-hand curtains rustled, daylight flooded in through a narrow slit that was instantly blocked by a head, a shaven head whose eyes looked down at him in benevolent inquiry. "Where am I?" asked Dirk. The man outside was a stranger to him, but the kindly expression was reassuring.

"Ah, so!" said the man and vanished, carefully retying the curtains.

Dirk cried "Anoné!" again, and once more the curtains parted enough to admit a hand holding a small cup of brownish liquid. "More kusuri, more medicine," the stranger's voice announced.

"I don't need medicine," protested Dirk. "Just tell me where I am."

"Yes," agreed the stranger. "You take medicine. Otherwise, pains come back."

Mechanically Dirk reached for the cup. He could remember enough of the sharp ache in head and limbs to realize that their return would incapacitate him for thought or action. He tossed off the bitter draught that tasted vaguely familiar to him, and at once regretted it. His eye-lids sagged, his tongue thickened and his hands dropped helplessly by his sides. He tried to call out "Trudi!" before the curtain of unconsciousness dropped over him.

There was no longer any motion and he was lying on something soft into which shoulders and hips sank gratefully. The smell of aromatic wood was strong in his nostrils, mingled with the fragrance of fine matting. He forced his eyes open and saw that he was lying in a good-sized room, close by the tokonoma, the tall niche which held a long Chinese painting and an ancient bronze incense burner. The tinting of the plaster walls, the quality of woodwork and matting, told him that he was in a great house, if not actually a palace.

He moved a little on the thick green mattress. Silvery light streamed through the high paper panels at the end of the room. Against the soft glow a man stood silhouetted sharply. He wore a vizored helmet and his haori bore the crest of Matsura, Lord of Hirado, between the shoulders. Matsura, friend of the foreigners, must somehow have arranged this strange exit from the castle of Hara, and in that case two could have been smuggled out as well as one. Dirk cried weakly, "Where is Sayo-ko-san?"

The man stood motionless for an instant, then turned deliberately toward the mattress. Dirk started in alarm as he recognized the face under the vizor, saw the cold, unblinking eyes of Toda, the officer of Matsura's who by no means followed his Daimyo in his attitude toward foreigners. Dirk remembered his call at Matsura's palace the day Trudi arrived from Batavia. He could still see Toda coldly slashing the chest of the Korean to see if blood would show on the new clothing for the executioner. But after all, however Toda might feel, he still wore the crest of Matsura. "Where's Sayo-ko?" asked Dirk again.

Toda clapped his hands and six men came into the room. Dirk glanced quickly at them. They too, wore Matsura's crest and at least two of them he knew by name. Toda made a brief gesture and the men lifted Dirk's mattress, carried it toward the paper panels. He looked closely at his bearers, but they showed no recognition or interest. Without a word, Toda slid back two of the panels and Dirk caught a hint of a grim smile as he pointed outward.

With an effort, Dirk raised himself on his elbow, struggling to choke back an exclamation of surprise. He was not looking down on the horseshoe of Hirado Bay. There in front of him, almost at his feet, lay Nagasaki harbor, with the kidney-shaped islet of Deshima a few yards offshore. There were Japanese soldiers by the gate that shut off the bridge connecting Deshima and the mainland, more and more guards along the waterfront, their pike points glinting in the afternoon light.

Every movement down there in the harbor spelled out the meaning of the scene with harsh clarity. Not far off the sea front of Deshima, four Chinese junks lay at anchor, and barges shuttled between them and the islet. Broad Deshima-machi, the street that crossed the width of the island, was filled with Portuguese in skullcaps and full capes, with women in vivid kimonos, with children in a medley of costumes. They walked slowly and heavily toward the water gate where the barges were heading in and helmeted soldiers urged them on with the butts of their pikes. The door of Japan was closing on the Portuguese, as Caron had predicted.

The room was very still. From the islet of Deshima, harsh orders drifted up, the pleading voice of a woman, the sudden, startled crying of a child. Toda drew the panels together with a sharp snap and jerked his head toward the floor. Silently, Dirk's bearers set him down by the tokonoma and left the room. Toda stalked after them. As he closed the inner panels with their pattern of snow-laden pine boughs, he said harshly without looking at Dirk, "There were no Portuguese merchants at Hara." Then he was gone.

Dirk lay back on his mattress, fighting off the waves of weakness

258

that swept over him. There was no question that he was in the hands of the Imperial forces, seized at some time and in some manner which he couldn't guess. But Trudi! Had Hara fallen? Had they seized her, too? Or was the castle still holding out? In that case, treachery inside the walls must have led to his capture. God verdomd! What would happen to Trudi, still penned up there with the Hara forces and no one to turn to save the frail old Fra Hilario? As for himself, there was no doubt that he would soon be examined. Then some of his questions would be answered. Until they were, he could lay no course for his own actions. In replying, he would have to keep in mind Trudi first, then the Company and lastly himself.

Smothered sounds from the harbor and the islet came into the room. The Portuguese were being driven from Japan. That would be a serious blow to them, but at least they were going unharmed so far as he could see. Suddenly Toda's cold words came into his mind again, "There were no Portuguese merchants at Hara." But there had been a Dutch trader.

He was still so weak physically that it was an effort to raise himself to his elbow. This he attributed to whatever blow had knocked him unconscious inside Hara and to the drugs that had been given him on his journey to Nagasaki. There was a tender area at the left side of his head but he was hardly aware of it except when his hand touched it. Sleep and food would cure his weakness and time would kill the smarting.

It was less easy to reason out his position in the hands of the Japanese. By rights he should be in one of the dark prisons up by the Dai-on temples. Instead, he was in a room that was luxurious by Japanese standards. From his knowledge of Nagasaki, he guessed that the room was in one of the houses in the compound of the Governor. As to his guards, the presence of Toda and the Matsura crest showed that Hirado had been called upon for troops to put down the rising against the Emperor. The assignment of Hirado troops to guard him was another puzzling angle. Matsura was well known in Tokyo as pro-foreign and a good friend of the Dutch, and it would have been much more logical to have drawn the guard from Bizen or Settsu, where far different views were held. The appearance of the antiforeign Toda was accidental, he thought, for the cold-eyed man was too insignificant officially to change the basic tone of Matsura's men.

He turned his head as someone rapped lightly on the painted panels through which Toda had withdrawn. "O hairi nasai! Come in!" he called. The panels slid back with a soft hiss and Dirk's eyes widened as four men servants, decorous in gray kimonos, came in, bowing and apologizing profusely for the intrusion. Each man carried a foot-high table littered with covered lacquer bowls and china dishes. Kneeling, they set their tables in a neat arc about the mattress, bowed again and backed from the room. "Chotto!" said Dirk. "Wait a minute!" But the panels slid into place and he was alone again.

Dirk looked carefully at the tables, which were quite in keeping with the room. Only from Kyoto did lacquer of that quality come, only Kyoto craftsmen could have turned out the fine gold incrustation of the bowls and their round snug-fitting covers. A pair of deer-horn chopsticks lay by the first bowl and a running inscription, half verse, half motto, told him that they had come from the sacred deer herd at ancient Nara. He shook his head. "This is all very well," he thought, "but I'd be more comfortable if I could only reason out *why* this room and *why* this service."

The food matched the containers. There was a clear soup in which that delicacy, the single eye of a tai, looked mournfully and fishily at him. One flat Imari platter held great shrimp fried in brown crisp batter, with a rich sauce; beside it, strips of raw fish like rare roast beef and kamaboko or baked fishballs. The tea, if not from Uji, was of excellent quality and the pale green jars on the last table held sake, gold-flecked like Danzig brandy, that must have come from Amagasaki, near Osaka.

Dirk ate ravenously, down to the last crumb of rice, and with each mouthful felt strength flowing through his body. When he had covered the last empty bowl, he pushed himself erect and padded about the room in his stocking feet. Carefully he crossed to the front of the room where Toda had slid back the paper screens to show him the deportation of the Portuguese. His fingers pushed gently at the light wood frames, but they held firm. Someone must have passed along the narrow gallery that spanned the façade and fastened the screens from the outside. He clapped his hands and the servants returned, picked up his tables and left as silently as they had come.

Soon after, there was a rattling out beyond the paper screens that shut off the front of the room, and the silvery light dimmed. Dirk sat up. Someone out on the gallery had slid home the heavy wooden shutters that closed off the façade in bad weather. Then the paper screens slid back and he quickly knelt, trying to copy Matsura's position when the old Daimyo received guests.

In the opening of the screens, two elderly Japanese knelt, each with a stiff black Phrygian hat perched on his head and the shoulders of his haori extended several inches to the right and to the left. Dirk's eye took in every detail of their costume at a glance, noting particularly that while each obi held a short dagger, the long sword had been left somewhere outside. In perfect unison, the two bowed, drew their daggers from their obis and laid them on the matting by their left hands.

Dirk tried to mask a start. His captor-callers were observing kenson. The pattern of the call played itself out. He urged his guests to take up a more honorable position in the room. They declined. He urged, until they finally knelt by the tokonoma. The officials begged his pardon for their intolerable remissness in not calling sooner, and Dirk replied in kind, watching the two impassive faces for a clue to his treatment. When the last formalities were over, the senior official bowed, smiling and drawing his lips down over his buckteeth. "Yang-san knows much about the ways of our country," he said and his companion nodded emphatically.

"It has been generous in teaching so poor a student as myself," answered Dirk.

"Ah, so. Yes," observed the junior. "Yang-san has traveled much in our Empire?"

"We at Hirado are all grateful for the permission to travel that was granted us by the great Shogun, Iyemitsu," replied Dirk, inclining his head respectfully at the mention of the name.

"You have traveled in the Shimabara peninsula?" asked the first.

"Yes, as in all Kyushu and even up into Honshu."

The two Japanese exchanged glances and the elder went on, still courteously, but speaking directly. "Yang-san, we know that you were in Hara. Our troops brought you out of there."

Dirk bowed until his forehead nearly touched his knees. "It is proof of the mercy of the present Shogun that he risked his men to bring me out of danger. It is proof of his great knowledge that he was aware of the presence of a foreign clerk there."

The junior spoke quickly. "Yang-san may show his gratitude by increasing the knowledge of the Shogun's servants. How much powder have the rebels?"

Dirk answered evenly, "I regret that I am a clerk and not a soldier, who could state the matter exactly."

There was another exchange of glances and the questioning went on. How did the rebels get their powder? How many arquebuses did they have? Who was really in command? How was the supply of food? Were there many old soldiers, were there many ronin among the Hara people? Did he hear talk about a plot against the House of Tokugawa, the Shogun's house?

Dirk fenced carefully. He owed nothing to the Hara people, but the thought of betraying what he knew of them and their resources never entered his head. "I am a trader, a merchant," he said again and again. "I could tell you the price per picul of Cambodian nuts or of Leyden grogram, but these matters—"

The Japanese were silent for a moment. Then the elder said, "One thing you can tell us, Yang-san. You were not the only person from the Oranda Yashiki, the Holland Company, there. There was another. Yang-san, where is the girl known as Sayo-ko Van Os?"

As though a spring within him had been touched, Dirk's fists clenched and he pressed them against his knees to control them. The implications of the question were startling. It was obvious that Imperial spies had been in Hara. They had known exactly where to look for him. It would have been equally simple for them to have carried Trudi off along with him. But, unless the question were a trap, they had somehow missed her. With a great effort to appear natural, Dirk answered, "I do not know."

The junior bobbed, hissed and giggled. "Yes. Many people in Hara, too many to see all of them."

"I do not know," said Dirk again.

"Ah, so des'," said the elder. "Of course. Now I ask one more question."

"I hope that I can answer it."

262

"Chigai nai! To be sure. Ah — where is the young lady?"

Over and over the question was put, and Dirk reflected with exasperation that his one entirely truthful answer was the only one which the officials would not accept.

It was dusk when they took their leave and Dirk paced up and down the room after the shoji had closed behind them. A growing feeling of thankfulness filled him as he thought back over the interrogation. There must have been plenty of spies in Hara. The officials did not know where Trudi was. Therefore, she was not at the castle. Nor was she in enemy hands, else the Imperials would have known. He could not imagine where she had gone, or how, but the probability was that she was safe — or as safe as a foreigner could be in the Japan of 1638.

He began to feel hungry again and wondered when the servants would appear with more tables and trays. Another meal like the first would end the last traces of injuries and drugs. The panels at the back of the room swished open and Dirk turned expectantly. Toda stood in the doorway, grim and stony-eyed, while the rattle of arms sounded beyond him in the corridor. Toda made a curt gesture with his hand. "What do you want?" asked Dirk.

Two pikemen stepped past him into the room. Dirk picked up his buckled shoes that stood by the head of his mattress. "More questioning, I suppose," he said resignedly.

The pikemen produced lengths of thin, hard cord which they knotted expertly to each of Dirk's arms, the guards holding the loose ends. Toda turned on his heel and walked on down the corridor. The guards pushed Dirk out of the room and he found himself going through silent passages with pikemen massed ahead and behind.

Out in the night that was lit only by the pale gold and silver glow of the windows of Nagasaki, he tried in vain to fathom this sudden change in the Japanese attitude. The little column turned and filed through a heavy-roofed gate and out into the streets. Dirk watched carefully, seeking some hint from the people who stood staring by lamplit fish stalls and sake shops. He heard familiar murmurs of "Maaa! Takai des', ne! Isn't he tall!" One young mother held her brightly dressed child above the heads of the crowd. There was nothing to be gleaned from gesture or comment. Such exclamations always followed him when he walked, towering, through a Japanese town.

The street began to climb steeply and he sensed the general direction of the march and stopped wondering. The street could only lead up to the Dai-on temples and close by was the stone-and-plaster-walled prison. He should have been able to see behind the reason for his earlier treatment. The Japanese had hoped that, disarmed by such leniency, he would answer what they wished. They had failed and would probably try more drastic measures. At least, he would now have only the Company and himself to think about. Wherever Trudi was, she was safe.

The walls of the prison, that stood like a miniature castle beyond the temples, loomed above him. Lights flashed in the shelter of a deep gate and heavy doors swung back to admit the party. A grinning, toothless jailer led the way, swinging his paper lantern jauntily. High into a tower Dirk climbed, was pushed into an unlighted cell whose iron-bound door slammed behind him.

Dirk advanced carefully, noticed an oblong of light gray on the far wall and walked toward it. The little barred window looked down on the roofs of Nagasaki. Beyond them he could make out the glimmer of the harbor. Not far offshore were the riding lights of the Chinese junks that were evacuating the Portuguese, and he could see red-gold dots moving slowly from Deshima islet out to the anchored ships.

He looked around quickly as a feeble voice somewhere in the cell quavered, "Donata? Who are you?"

"From the Dutch Company. And you?" said Dirk.

The unseen man drew an unsteady breath and Dirk felt his way toward him. "Are you hurt?" he asked.

The man bleated, "Mizu! Water!"

"Is there any?"

"Yes. In the bucket by the door."

Dirk felt in the darkness until he found the bucket and carried it over in the direction of the voice, made out a figure lying by the wall. "You want to drink?" he asked.

"No. My hands. Pour water over my hands. I can't lift the bucket."

Dirk reached out, caught hold of a bony wrist and scooped up some water in his palm, dribbling it out where he guessed the man's hand to be. There was a yelp of pain, then Dirk could hear the grinding of teeth, followed by a feeble, "Arigato. Thank you."

"Why didn't you just crawl over there and dip your hands in yourself?" asked Dirk.

The man's voice was horrified. "Iye! The guards told me not to." Dirk knew the Japanese fear of authority too well to press the point. To have disobeyed would have been to disobey the sergeant of the guard who represented the officer of the day, who represented the head of the prison, who represented the Governor of Nagasaki, and so on through the whole chain of command until disobedience would have been to the Emperor and to the gods.

"What happened to you?" asked Dirk.

The man groaned and stretched out his hands. Bits of wood had been shoved deep under his fingernails and then ignited. Resignedly he said that he expected the same process would be repeated with his toes.

Dirk winced, although he knew this punishment was common enough. "What had you done?"

There had been a mistake in identity. A census had been taken not long ago and the official who set down the man's name had used a character with the same sound but a different sense from that of the victim. A man with a name corresponding to the mistaken transcription had been known to be with the rebels at Hara, and hence Dirk's cellmate had been arrested and questioned under torture.

Dirk swore under his breath. "But why don't you tell them about the mistake? Your name will show correctly on your koseki tohon, your family record, at the palace."

"Dekinai! Impossible!" cried the prisoner. Could he, a simple maker of matting, accuse an official of a mistake? Naruhodo!

"Then they'll just keep on questioning you," said Dirk.

"It can't be helped," the man groaned with utter fatalism.

Dirk poured more water for him and then, tearing a strip from his own shirt, bandaged the burned fingers as well as he could in the dark. The man thanked him and Dirk stretched out on the hard matting just under the window and soon fell asleep. He was awakened once during the night by a lantern glow in the cell and sat up to see a guard dragging his cellmate to his feet. The prisoner

265

whimpered and scuttled toward the door, his hands held above his head to ease their throbbing. An officer in the corridor snapped him across the fingers with a thin switch and the door slammed.

Dirk slept again, not waking until the gray of the window spread into the cell. He got up, thinking longingly of the banquet that had been served him in the Governor's compound, as he splashed water from the bucket over his hands and face. Then he settled his clothes as best he could and sat down to wait for what the day might bring.

The door opened and Toda entered the cell. Dirk greeted him politely and was surprised to have his good-morning returned almost amiably. "You were moved here," said Toda, "because it was feared that the noise from Deshima might disturb you."

"I appreciate the courtesy," replied Dirk. "My appreciation would be doubled if I had some food."

"It will be sent you," said Toda, strolling to the window. "Yes. The Portuguese have all gone."

Dirk looked keenly at Toda's face as the gray morning light struck it, but there was nothing to show why the usually grim man was suddenly so talkative.

"Did the Portuguese have any warning of this move?" asked Dirk.

"Warning?" said Toda, eyes on the harbor. "Of course. Weeks ago, word was sent to the Portuguese chief at Macao."

"And the people on Deshima knew at the same time?"

Toda looked surprised. "They? Of course not. It didn't concern them. Only their headmen in Macao."

"Did Macao try to protest?"

Toda turned quickly. "Didn't you understand me? I said that it was by order of the Shogun, who speaks for the Emperor. Do you suggest that such an order can be disputed?"

Dirk tried to cover his error by saying hastily, "I understood, Toda-san. But the Portuguese have been arrogant in the past, as you know. The Governor at Macao might have repeated past mistakes."

Toda looked a little mollified. "I see. As a matter of fact, he did. He sent an embassy up here to treat with the Shogun. The ship that brought it is off the Papenberg now. He sent —" Toda drew a slip

266

of paper from his sleeve — "he sent Pacheo-san, commander of all the Portuguese troops in the Orient. With him were Paredos-san, Cavallo-san and Pavia-san and some thirteen soldiers."

Dirk feigned surprise. "To *treat?* After an order of the Shogun, Iyemitsu-san?"

Toda nodded as though approving Dirk's amazement. "They have come, as I said."

"The ship will be sent back to Macao, of course," observed Dirk.

Toda permitted himself a smile. "The ship will be sent back to Macao." He looked out of the window again. "A fine view. Do you know the name of that bare hill off to the left, Yang-san?"

Dirk joined him by the window. "That hill beyond the temples? Oh, I see the one you mean. Close by, with no trees." He felt sudden cold along his spine as the name suddenly flashed into his mind. Hundreds of Japanese Christians, scores of friars — Augustin, Dominican, Franciscan, Jesuit — had climbed that bare slope and given it its name. He forced himself to say casually, "I've heard it called the Mount of the Martyrs."

Toda inclined his head. "Ah, so. Very interesting." He rose on tiptoe, looking into the streets below. There was no need for him to point out to Dirk what had drawn his attention.

Drums were booming and brasses clanging as a column of troops, pikes glittering above flat helmets, marched winding up the slope. Dirk counted four companies. In their midst walked four unmistakable Europeans, obviously high officials from their clothes. They were bareheaded and marched along with their carefully trimmed beards pointing defiantly ahead, as though denying the ropes that bound their arms behind them. As the column wound up the Mount, Dirk exclaimed, "But that's an embassy! They have official status!" Toda said sharply, "People who disobey the Shogun have no status."

Dirk turned quickly away, but Toda snapped, "It is ordered that you watch this."

Eyes closed, Dirk stood by the window while Toda stared out, giving an occasional low mumble of satisfaction. When Dirk opened his eyes again, the troops were filing away from the Mount of the Martyrs. Four headless bodies lay on the summit in their rich clothes. A few officers lingered near them, drawing their swords, balancing the blades carefully before testing their temper on the corpses of men who had disregarded an order of the Shogun.

Toda left the window abruptly. "Food will be sent you," he said tersely and left the cell, the door banging behind him. Apparently he had thought it superfluous to remind Dirk again that there had been no Portuguese at Hara.

XVII

Escape

Though the siege still rumbled on, curt orders from the Japanese reached the *de Rijp* and again the ship moved to Hirado Bay. There, the gentle March wind from the west stirred the new bamboo leaves that showed bright green among the somber pines, rustled through the little valleys and ravines that were ablaze with the deep pink of azaleas. It raised dust clouds as the ship's crew labored with gangs of coolies at the demolition of the great stone warehouse, the pride of the Dutch East India Company.

From the bow of the *de Rijp,* François Caron, carefully dressed and shaven as ever, watched the work, his face impassive. Beside him, Becker slumped against the rail. The Director had lost weight in the last few weeks and the skin hung loosely on his face and neck. As tiles cascaded from the roof in a deafening clatter, he looked uneasily at Caron. "There was no other way?" he asked.

Eyes on the workmen, Caron answered, "None."

"And what happens next?"

"There's no telling."

"No. No. I—I suppose not. Verdomd! I tell you, Heer Caron, I—I'm frightened."

"No blame to you, Heer Director. These are mischancy times."

Becker laid a shaky hand on Caron's arm. "I should have listened to you in the past."

Caron shrugged. "When a ship's in a typhoon, it doesn't matter who's at the helm."

"You're there now. I've given you full powers. I should have done it before. Only—only—" he drew himself up as though fighting back his fears—"only, I'm still the Director. If what you do displeases the Japanese, I'll answer for it. Heer Caron, we've got to save the Company. Look here—you know these people. Would it help if

269

I went to the Daikwan and gave myself up to him as hostage for the rest — for the Company?" He shut his eyes and shivered as though sentence were already pronounced.

Caron glanced at his superior. He had noticed the change in him since the expulsion of the Portuguese and the execution of their embassy, but this sudden offer was beyond his expectations. There was respect in his voice as he answered, "It would do no good, Heer Directeur."

Becker said huskily, "I'm not a brave man, Heer Caron. I won't pretend that I am. But if that would ever do the least good, I'm ready." He walked heavily off to his cabin.

Caron looked after him, eyebrows raised. "He means it," he said to himself. "Dieu de dieu. If I could only see the next step. What will the Daikwan order?"

A door under the poop opened and Caron saw a figure in bright blue silk covered with a cherry blossom pattern as Trudi stepped onto the deck and came toward him. "That's a firm little spirit," he thought. Then he called, "Good morning, Sayo-ko."

"You've no more news, Heer Caron?" she asked.

"None. We know that Dirk's alive and well. So far as I've been able to find out, he's not badly treated. Don't worry, Sayo-ko. I'm in touch more and more with the Japanese. I've found some old friends close to the Daikwan and in time they'll move for me. After all, they know how Dirk came to be at Hara."

Trudi looked up at him, steady-eyed. "Heer Caron, I'm not worrying. I can't afford to. I know this. I *know* that one day Dirk will come to me. That's all there is to it. It might have been this morning. It may be tomorrow or next week. That's why I've un-packed the boxes of clothes that were sent to the *de Rijp* before all this happened. I want to look my best for Dirk when he does come."

Caron nodded approval. "But we've got to think a little about you. The Japanese don't know where you are. I'm not even sure that they *know* you were at Hara."

Trudi shrank back from the rail. "But those men ashore — they can see me!"

"I doubt if they take notice," said Caron. "In any event, you could easily have come on board after we anchored last night. But we want to make sure." He thought a moment, then asked, "You've called on the Daimyo in the past, haven't you?"

"Oh, yes. He said such nice things about my father and my mother."

"I thought so. Then you and I had better go ashore. It's not the most appropriate hour, but we'll pay Matsura a visit."

They found the old Daimyo sitting on the mats in the little room that looked out over the western gardens with their stone lanterns and miniature lakes and rivers and mountain ranges. Waiving all formality, Matsura exclaimed, "Caron-san! My old friend. There are not many these days who can find the time to call on me." He shook his head sadly. "These are bad events, very bad. All my soldiers are either in front of Hara or doing duty at Nagasaki, and the Company people have been away, too. Eh-to! Sayo-ko-san and I have had to stand guard alone over this part of Hirado, I for the Daimyate and she for the Dutch." He smiled at Trudi. "But I think we kept good watch, you and I."

Trudi bowed in acknowledgment of his inclusion of her, though she couldn't guess why he spoke as he did. She glanced at Caron, who was sitting back on his heels, obviously relieved by something in the Daimyo's speech.

Over the first cup of tea, Caron, with apparent casualness, referred back to the Daimyo's speech of greeting. "Yes, Matsura-san, we of the Company have traveled far since the *de Rijp* sailed out of Hirado with us. But there is one of us who traveled even farther, though perhaps not in miles."

Matsura smiled politely as he sipped his tea. "Of that, I have heard something. I wondered when I heard the news. Of course, it was no concern of mine, but that young wanderer always showed me a courtesy that is lacking even in our own people these days."

Trudi set down her cup and started to speak, but a slight motion of Caron's hand warned her. Caron made a few remarks about the technique of playing the koto, adding a story about its inventor, Yatsuhashi, that set the Daimyo chuckling. "Yes," Caron went on, "the tone of the koto is exactly suited to the songs and stories of your old heroes, like Masahige and Yoritomo. It is that some tales are told best in a man's voice and others in a woman's. I think of one tale to which a woman's voice is best suited. You spoke of the far wanderings of one of our Company. Perhaps it would divert you to hear of them from Sayo-ko."

Matsura smiled at her. "It would be most agreeable."

Trudi related what had happened to Dirk up to his capture by the Imperial raiders. Matsura listened carefully, murmuring "Ah, so des'," or "Naruhodo," from time to time. When Trudi finished he calmly refilled the cups. "Eh-to! It is strange, Sayo-ko-san, that that story should have reached you, while passing me by. Yet, as I think of it, it is not so strange, since the matter concerned your Company rather than my Daimyate. The story interests me very much. I shall take pains to learn more of it from the Japanese side. Of course, the young man had no choice."

"Can you help him?" asked Trudi eagerly.

"He has my good wishes," answered Matsura as Trudi caught once more a warning motion from Caron. Matsura went on, "I could speak more confidently if these happenings had been in my own Daimyate, since the Shogun allows a free hand in most matters so long as we don't go counter to Imperial policy. But I shall think much on what you've told me." He turned to Caron. "It grieves me to see your great warehouse being pulled down. How did the orders come to you?"

"By messenger from the Daikwan. I received them, as Heer Becker has delegated his powers to me."

"Ah, so! And how did you reply?"

"Reply?" answered Caron. "I wrote at length, expressing my appreciation of the Daikwan's permission to tear the building down, as it was far too big for us and far too pretentious for foreign traders. What else could I say?"

Matsura clapped his hands softly. "Erai! Well done! I can assure you that if you had expressed resentment or protested or tried to delay, the messenger's escort would have cut you down."

"So I supposed," said Caron calmly. "Matsura-san, can you guess what the next move of the Daikwan will be?"

The old Daimyo shook his head. "I am sure that he is under strict orders from the Shogun in Tokyo. That is, if you act in this or that manner, this or that course is to be followed. But I can't guess, any more than you can, what those this's and that's may be."

Caron's jaw set. "Matsura-san, we're going to save the Company."

Matsura leaned forward with unusual animation. "You must! I don't speak merely as one who has benefited by the Company trade, nor as an old friend of yours and your predecessors. I speak as a Japanese. For hundreds of years, the only outside world that we Japanese knew consisted of China and Korea. From them, we took much of our life and our thought. But those countries are living in the past. Then when you and the Portuguese and the English and the Spanish came, we learned of another world that lay far beyond China and Korea, a world that was moving into the future. From my friends among the friars in the old days, I learned of the great discoveries that Europe has been making, discoveries that touched the mind and the spirit. I heard of Galileo, Copernicus and Harvey. We were just beginning to absorb some of that new learning when the persecutions came."

He paused, sipped at his tea and then went on, "Little by little, our door onto the outer world, the new, live world, began to close. If it closes entirely, then my country will go on living as though this were the year 600, not 1638, for I confess to you, my friend, that we have changed very little in a thousand years. In time, the new world of which I speak will engulf us, and we shall not be ready for it. We shall have to meet the eighteenth or the nineteenth century with seventh-century minds. But if there is the least chance of keeping our door onto the modern world the slightest bit ajar, seize it — and at all costs."

Caron nodded. "That is my intention, Matsura-san. Now you have given me an added reason. I shall be fighting for your country, which has been good to me, as well as for my own."

As Trudi and Caron walked down past the great gates of the palace, she asked almost timidly, "What do you think, Heer Caron?"

He started, as though lost in thought. "Eh? What? Oh, I think the Daimyo's quite right about what would happen to Japan if we all left. I must visit my friends in the Daikwan's court and see if I can set their minds working the same way."

"Yes. Of course. I see," said Trudi. "But I meant about Dirk."

Caron slipped her arm through his. "My apologies, Sayo-ko. I was thinking about the Company and forgetting that the Company was made up of people. Matsura will do what he can for Dirk. What that will be, I don't know. He's kept out of Tokyo doings

273

for years and a new generation has grown up at Court. As for yourself, of course you saw what he was driving at at the start of our talk."

"About me? I think so. But I don't dare be sure."

"Of course you're all right. Didn't you hear him say that you and he had kept watch here in Hirado? Officially, you've been here all the time. That's established. So you and I can work for the Company and Dirk with a free mind."

She stopped, looking up at him. "Tell me honestly, Heer Caron, what are our chances?"

"He's alive and well. Other Company people have been in greater danger in the past and have won out. Much greater danger."

"Like yourself in the Nuyts case?"

"Oh, that," said Caron. "There wasn't much to that."

"You were under sentence of death," said Trudi.

"But they didn't mean it. There've been a good many others who were much worse off than I was then or Dirk is now."

"Don't just try to cheer me up, please. I want to know."

Caron frowned. "Honestly, Sayo-ko, I don't know enough yet to judge. No Japanese would talk to me about the case when we lay over in Nagasaki. But remember this. Dirk knows the country and the people as well as any foreigner who's ever been here. Most Japanese like him personally. There are a lot of Japanese who feel as Matsura does. To them — and many of them are very powerful — Dirk will be a symbol and they'll guard him as carefully as they would their own families. I think you'd do well to go right to your uncle's house. He went ashore quite early this morning and you'll find him and the servants there."

As the two went on through Hirado village, Trudi turned over and over in her mind what Caron had said about Dirk. Then she gave a little cry of dismay. "Heer Caron! I've been talking all the time about Dirk and me. What about Madame Caron and Petronella and Maria?"

Caron looked touched. "They're down in the Goto Islands, quite safe. I'm sending a letter to Madame Caron today and she'll be pleased to know that she and the girls were on your mind. Now you'd better take this path around the bay and remember that Matsura says you were here all the time. I'm going back to the *de Rijp,* but I'll come ashore later in the day to see you. And I'll send your boxes to your house."

As he watched the bright cherry pattern of the kimono sway off along the path, a shadow fell over his face. "It's true that he'll be a symbol to the Japanese who want us to stay," he thought. "But he'll also be one to those who want to shut out the world." He walked slowly down the beach to the waiting boat. "Matsura was right. We've got to keep the door open, even if only a little — and at all costs. At all costs." He sighed. "God verdomd, but those costs may be heavy."

As he got into the boat he looked up the bay to the factory. The roof of the great warehouse was ragged and bare. Holes showed in the walls where coolies were heaving out great blocks of stone.

The doors of Dirk's prison opened unexpectedly and without explanation that same night and he was taken, in a guarded litter, to a big country house which, so far as he could judge, lay a little to the south of Nagasaki. Here, in quarters comparable to those which he had occupied in the Governor's compound, he was comfortable physically but tormented mentally. Hour after hour he was courteously examined by high officials who asked leading questions over and over, either bowing politely at his answers or giggling. While all these questions were vague, it seemed to Dirk that the officials were genuinely trying to get replies that were favorable to him. He realized that it was hopeless to try to take advantage of the leads given him, for other examiners could have tripped him a dozen times.

Added to the strain of the examinations and of his captivity was the gnawing worry about Trudi. Her name had not been mentioned again, but Dirk was sure that the Japanese were still ignorant of her whereabouts. He was equally in the dark about the fate of the Company and its staff. Even while he was being subjected to incessant questioning at the country house, Becker, Caron and the rest might have followed the Portuguese embassy up the slope of the Mount of the Martyrs. Becker, of course, was of no importance to the Japanese, save as Director of the factory, but there were many who bitterly resented the place that Caron had made for himself in

275

the eyes of the Shogun and of the latter's Nagasaki representative, the Daikwan.

He slept little and while ample food was brought to him, he had to force himself to eat. As his strength ebbed and his nervous tension increased, the sense of acute and pressing danger preyed on him more and more. He knew very well that even the most benevolent Japanese had an ingrained indifference to human life and suffering. The gentlest questioner might lose patience at not receiving the answer that he expected and wanted and resort to measures that did not bear thinking about.

It was growing clear that he was being tossed about by political tides that could easily reach to Tokyo. Those who wished to keep Japan open to foreigners were battling against the exclusionists, the struggle being complicated by the varying degrees of intensity with which powerful people held to those opposing views. Some ruling at the Daikwan's court had been responsible for the lenient treatment given him at first. A counter order had sent him to the jail in charge of exclusionists as personified by Toda. Now he was in the hands of the pro-foreigners again, still a prisoner. And these people wished to strengthen their case by presenting him to the highest authorities either as a foreigner who had had no part in the Hara business or — and this seemed to be their preference — as a foreigner who had faithfully served the Empire during the siege at the risk of his life. Once they had made their point, no matter how transparently, they would have no further interest in or use for him. As for the exclusionists, their aim so far as he was concerned was obvious. Here is a Komo, taken in arms against the Empire. No further comment was necessary.

The fourth day of confinement in the country house dragged on endlessly. No officials knelt bowing across the room from him to afford a distraction, even though an irritating one. The heavy wooden amado that shut off the front of his room were drawn, denying him any glimpse of the outer world which, when visible, was limited to a strip of garden, a white, thick-walled storehouse and the shoulder of a hill beyond. There was no sound in the house, no sound outside save the steady drill of rain on the roof tiles.

At noon, soup, fish, tea and rice were brought him by a servant who only bowed and smiled in reply to Dirk's questions. He managed to finish most of the rice by mixing it with his tea. The rest he set aside in the hope that his appetite might return later. "I've got to eat," he muttered as he slid the bowls into a low cupboard. "I'll wait till midafternoon and then try again. God verdomd! If there was only something I could *do!*" By an odd quirk of memory, he recalled how he and other boys, when swimming in the little pond by the Green Gate at Leyden, had tested the steadiness of their nerves by wrapping their heads in thick cloth and then diving into deep water. The sensation had been deliciously terrifying. All sense of direction was lost and they were apt to flounder deeper and deeper, arms and legs tangling in growing panic, until they stripped off the cloth and rose puffing and red-faced to the surface again. Now, on the other side of the world, he was in deep water once more, his bearings gone and his mind blindfolded.

Yet if his mind were blindfolded, it would be his own fault. Somewhere above him was the surface, and as long as he kept a cool head, he would reach it. He wandered idly up and down the room, then, opening a cupboard, found a lacquer writing case complete with paper, brush and ink block. There was no one to whom he could write, but to occupy his mind, he moistened the brush and began to set down the most complicated characters that he could remember. The necessity for keeping his hand steady and his eye true gradually absorbed him and he covered several sheets, pleased to see the ideographs stand out sharply against the white of the paper.

He looked up, brush poised, as someone rapped at the far panels of the room. "More questions," he grumbled, then called, "Come in!"

The Japanese who entered was short and fat and his eyes narrowed to mere glistening slits when he smiled. After him came two servants each carrying a small table of smooth unpainted pine. Dirk could not place the crest on the first man's haori, but judged him to be a functionary attached to some government office. The Japanese introduced himself, but the name meant nothing to Dirk.

Dirk set aside his writing case, saying, "Be seated, please," taking care to use a very deferential form of speech.

The man knelt, then motioned to the servants to set the little tables before Dirk. Puzzled, Dirk looked at the nearer one which held a curved-top box of the sort generally used to hold letters. He was about to stretch a hand toward it when his eye fell on the second table. He withdrew his hand with an apology for his haste while he tried to keep his features impassive. There was no mistaking the box that lay on the other table. It was the lacquer box that held the tea jar from the bottom of the sea that Matsura had given him.

His guest edged the second table toward Dirk, smiling and suggesting that he might find the contents of the box interesting. With forced casualness, Dirk took it, opened it slowly and stared at the jar that lay safely bedded in the lining. He had a sudden gleam of hope. Had the old Daimyo sent the jar to him from Hirado as a sign that forces were moving in his behalf?

Then the Japanese began to speak, and Dirk, bracing himself, continued his feigned admiration. Yes, the jar had been found in Yang-san's house at Hirado, when the factory was being demolished . . .

Dirk's hands tightened on the case as he repeated, "Ah, so. When the factory was being demolished."

The bland voice went on, "It was thought that a Komo who had the knowledge to purchase such a piece would be glad to have it in his hands again."

Dirk carefully set the case on the little table, taking pains to align it in the exact center. Purchased! So there was no connection between the presence of the jar in his room and Matsura. He bowed. "It was a courteous act to send this to me. But Caron-san had many finer pieces. Have they been given to him?"

The man's face went blank. "I wonder," he said, and Dirk knew that there was no hope of further information about the Company and its people.

In an instant, his guest was smiling again and pushing forward the table with its curved letter box. "Many letters came from Batavia on the *de Rijp*," he announced. "Those for the Company, the Daikwan has impounded. Our interpreters say that this letter is addressed to you and as it does not touch on Company business, it was ordered delivered." He deftly flipped open the curved lid as he held the box out to Dirk.

Dirk's hopes rose once more, then ebbed quickly as he saw the

278

folded papers inside. It might have been from Caron. It might even have been from Trudi. Instead, it bore the angular printlike script of his cousin, Japhet Place, resident of Plymouth on Massachusetts Bay.

When the official had gone, Dirk sat by the writing set, hands clenched tightly and his lips set. It was quite possible that the news of the demolition of the Hirado factory had been invented by the Japanese for their own unfathomable purposes. Assuming that it was true, what was the meaning of such an act? The last time that he had seen Nagasaki harbor, the houses of Deshima Islet were still standing, but the Portuguese had been evicted and their embassy had been wiped out. If the Dutch buildings were razed, it would seem to follow that the Company staff would have met the same fate as Pacheo. Yet that could not be, for in that case he himself would have been the first to suffer.

The only sensible thing for him to do was to wait for the next visit and keep his wits as sharp as he could. He opened the cupboard where he had stored his food and began to eat. As his chopsticks clicked, his eye fell on Japhet Place's letter. Idly, he picked it up and began to read. He had used English so little in the past few years that deciphering the pages would at least give his mind something to work on.

The letter had, of course, been opened, and he wondered what the Japanese interpreters, who had trouble reading the bastard Portuguese of the Far East, had made of it. "Deer Frend & Cousin," he read. "Yr. last leter I have not receivd." Good old conscientious Japhet, Dirk thought. The Plymouth cousin would keep on writing as a matter of course and take it for granted that those to whom he wrote would be equally dutiful. As a matter of fact, he himself had hardly thought of Plymouth and the New World since that earlier letter which he had received the night of the formal opening of Becker's new house, back there on Hirado.

He pushed the memory from him and turned to the letter again. It would be interesting to see how life had passed, off there on the coast of North America. For a long time Japhet's letters had spoken of a struggle for bare existence, but the last two or three had been more optimistic. What was life like now, in late 1635, the date of this letter?

He read on: "It has pleasd God so to blesse ye country with such access and confluence of people into it, as it was thereby much inrichd. . . . Cattle were grown to high rates, viz: — a good cow, £25, a pr. of oxen £40 and corn 5s. ye bushel . . . carpenters @ 3s. ye day and other workers according." Unconsciously Dirk began working out these rates in guilders and then turned the guilders into koku of rice. A careful man could grow rich quickly under such conditions. If only the Spanish allowed such trade, it might be possible to ship silk to the English settlements via Panama, receiving valuable furs in exchange. There would be a fine market among the wealthy Japanese and it ought to be possible to cut in on the one existing fur source, the Chinese merchants over there by the Yaku-en. He pulled himself up sharply. Threaten the Chinese fur monopoly, when the Hirado factory had been demolished?

He tried to project his mind out of Japan and far to the other side of the world. "A new church has been lately gathered at Ipswich (which was lately Agawam), another at Dorchester and a third at Lynn." Japhet wrote solemnly, "And surely God's face is turnd toward this land and His servants therin. . . . In Boston, three Dutch ships have arrivd, bearing Flanders mares, heifers and sheep. These I have seen as the mares are as lusty as those ownd by Master Vrooman, who livd beyond you in Leyden. Also two ships for Southampton in Engl. have touchd here and many from near-by plantations. The Dutch vessels came in 5 wks and 3 days! As for our own barques, they range where they please, trading even with the French and the Dutch."

It was incredible! The colony was thriving, ships of many nations touched at its harbors and its own craft went freely. Dirk remembered how he had pitied, half scornfully, half tolerantly, those who had gone from Leyden to the bleak New World. Now, firmly rooted, living under their own laws, those settlers seemed to have entered on an existence that was little short of idyllic. It was almost impossible to visualize a life where a man could live without giving a thought to the inexplicable whims that ran along the channel from Shogun to Daikwan to Daimyo to Headman.

Dirk glanced at the final paragraph. "Deal tenderlie with yourself, my cousin, and continue to hold in mind that many of your kin and frends are here who would welcome you. A man who might land here, unencumberd and with £30, could rise swiftly, were he diligent."

Thirty pounds! At the least favorable rate of exchange, there stood to his personal credit in the books of the Company more than a hundred English pounds. Passage for himself and Trudi could be paid out of that, leaving considerably more than the minimum sum mentioned by Cousin Japhet.

He laughed at himself. Thinking in terms of passage to the New World when he was not even free to step out onto the engawa of the room! At least, the letter from Plymouth had freed his mind for the moment from the endless, dizzying process of trying to reason out his position from day to day and from hour to hour.

A servant crept respectfully into the room and began gathering up Dirk's bowls and dishes. He seemed to be fumbling needlessly with them and keeping up an irritating humming to himself under his breath. Dirk was about to tell him impatiently to stop his noise and pay attention to his arranging of the things when he noticed that the man was a stranger and did not wear the same crest as the other servants whom he had seen. He looked more closely at him and realized that the man was not humming. He was talking in a low monotone between clenched teeth. On guard at once, Dirk turned his back, but kept his head tilted toward the servant. Sounds began to shape themselves into words. "You are to be taken from here. You will be confined in the kura, in the storehouse in the garden. Yudan suru na! Be on your guard! When you are in the kura, look in the small cupboard to the left of the door, and under the tatami, the mat below it!"

Dirk turned on the man angrily. "Baka! Clumsy lout! Do you have to rattle those dishes so much? Who sent you here anyway?"

The man apologized profusely, ending, "Ah, danna-san! I am stupid. I do not know. One tells me to do this and one tells me to do that. I obey as best I can. Ara! I have spilled sauce on the tatami under the cupboard." Hissing and bowing, he backed out of the room, leaving Dirk to mask his thoughts against eyes that might be watching him beyond the sliding panels.

He was deeply puzzled. A transfer out to the white-walled storehouse in the garden, if it were carried out, suggested a resumption of harsh treatment. These oblong houses with their heavy, hinged door and barred windows were built to house family treasures not at the moment in use, and would serve as admirable places of confinement, from the jailer's standpoint. But the servant had spoken of cupboards and a mat on the floor that Dirk must be sure to notice. Could there be a plot among the pro-foreigners to keep him in their custody or perhaps to free him?

Less than half an hour after the servant had gone, the panels of his room slid back and a helmeted officer appeared and told him curtly to follow him. Catching up the Daimyo's tea caddy and Japhet's letter, Dirk stepped out into the narrow corridor where pikemen flattened themselves against the wall to let him pass, then closed in behind him. At the bottom of the steep stairs there were more soldiers who tramped out through a side door and into the garden. The officer marched sternly beside him.

Dirk asked, "Where are you taking me?"

"Anata-no sh'tta koto ja nai," was the surly answer. "None of your business."

The officer's rudeness put him on his guard. Up to now, even at the jail under Toda's care, no one had snapped at him as though he had been a coolie or a Korean. Whatever the servant's words might indicate, he was not in friendly hands now. Under a clearing sky, he was led along a twisting garden path that led to the kura. The officer stepped ahead and threw open the door and Dirk entered. The door banged behind him and he was alone.

Dirk looked about him. In the past, the kura had been finished off as a room, with a ceiling of painted canvas and more canvas covering the walls to hide their stark white bareness. Cupboards, a tokonoma niche, staggered, polished shelves had been built in the conventional places and the floor was tightly paved with thick straw mats. There were even a few bronzes and lacquer pieces on the shelves and the tops of the low cupboards. The place had probably been fitted up to house a new concubine until her predecessor or predecessors in the main building had become used to the idea of a rival.

Dirk set the Daimyo's tea caddy and the letter box on one of the shelves and tiptoed to the thick door to listen. He could hear nothing beyond the dying drip from the eaves and the faint crunch-

crunch as his escort went back through the garden. So far the servant's story was proved true.

The next step was to find out what was meant by the cupboard and the tatami. There was a chance that he was being watched through some hidden peephole in the white walls, but it was a risk that had to be taken. There was no mistaking the correct cupboard, standing there by itself on the left of the door. He opened the top compartment and found it empty. Kneeling, he thrust his hand into the lower section, fingers scraping on polished wood. Something long, hard and rounded was under his palm. He drew it out and his breath whistled between his teeth as he looked down at the hilt of a Japanese broadsword. Further search in the cupboard produced a flat, oval guard worked with heavy gold figures.

"Mijn God!" he muttered. "A sword hilt and guard. That leaves only the tatami to be searched." Laying the two pieces on the cupboard, he ran his fingers along the mat below it, trying to pry it up from its right-hand neighbor. Slowly it gave and he turned it up on its side. The flooring under it was bare, although Dirk examined every inch of the six by three foot space.

His wariness returned. This was the sort of thing that some Japanese would consider extremely amusing — to give a prisoner all but the vital part of a weapon. He pried up the next mat, but the stonework under it was empty. He was about to tilt the first mat back into the place when it seemed to him that it was heavier than it ought to be. Turning it on edge, he ran his hand over one short side, then down a long. His hands shook when he saw the neat hold scooped out of the mat, caught the gleam of steel deep inside it. With clumsy fingers he caught hold of the bare haft and pulled. It was like drawing a silk scarf through a ring, the blade was so keen. He stood, hardly daring to believe his eyes as he looked at the sword, sharp and unspotted, with its flaming clearly marked. The servant had spoken the truth throughout.

He slid the guard down over the haft, capped it with the hilt and secured it. Feet crunched outside and with a bound Dirk crossed to the tokonoma and stood the weapon in the farthest corner. The sound died away, returned, died away and Dirk relaxed. A sentry had been placed in front of the kura and was methodically walking his post. In all probability other sides of the building were being similarly patrolled. The precaution seemed useless to Dirk, since the immensely thick door was securely locked and the only windows were high up under the eaves, showing as spots of light through the hangings, spots that faded as the day ebbed.

It was difficult for him to come to any satisfactory conclusion concerning his present status. Tentatively he decided that, while unknown forces were moving in his behalf, his present custodians were hostile.

The spots of light faded slowly behind the hangings and Dirk sat on the edge of the tokonoma, trying to assume inwardly and outwardly an Oriental patience. Twice he reached behind him in the dark to make sure that the sword was easily available, though he had no idea what use it could be to him. Still, it had been put there for a purpose and he would be wise not to neglect it. The last faint light died away and he sat in complete darkness.

He raised his head. There must be some kind of ventilator under the eaves, for now and then a trace of outer air drifted down to him. He heard a faint rustling in the wall. Instantly, he was on his feet, the sword in his hands. A spot of light appeared, became clearer, and a long bamboo pole pushed aside the canvas that covered the high window. Then a bare, muscular arm was thrust in, holding a bright lantern.

As though by instinct, Dirk turned away from the window and faced the door, blade advanced. The outer bolts were drawn stealthily and he heard a low scraping sound as the wedge-shaped piece was pushed slowly inward. Torchlight flared into the building as Dirk sidestepped to take advantage of the in-swinging door. Someone outside shouted, "Ready!" and a man, wide sleeves tucked back, sprang over the high threshold and stood crouching, his head turning in the uncertain light that glinted on his two-handed sword.

Dirk set his teeth and lunged. The man fell, although Dirk could barely feel the blade touch flesh. There was a cry outside of "Abunaiyo! Look out for that threshold!"

In a flash Dirk realized two things. First, the men outside thought that their fellow had merely tripped and, second, they were not aware that the prisoner was armed. Also, it seemed certain that they had not seen him, half hidden as he was by the door. A second man, his sword sheathed, glided in and stooped to pick up Dirk's victim.

With a twist and a lunge, Dirk dove through the door, sending the second man rolling with a kick as he did so. He cannoned into a soldier who held a torch, saw an officer tugging at the hilt of his sword. Dirk slashed at him, using the downward stroke that he had learned at Matsura's fencing school, and the officer reeled away, clutching at an arm that spouted blood. The torchbearer stood gaping and motionless. Then he dropped his torch that flared and sizzled on the ground and snatched up a pike that leaned against the wall. Behind him a voice roared, "Hitori de! I'll take him alone!" and Dirk whirled to see Toda emerging from the darkness beyond, his eyes cold and fixed and his sword out.

For an instant Dirk stood paralyzed. His few lessons at the school would be of little use against a swordsman of Toda's reputation. He measured the distance between himself and Toda, who had taken the squat, formal stance of the old school, then threw himself on the ground. One leg lashed out and his booted foot caught the pikeman in the groin. In the same motion, he rolled to his feet, snatched up the sword that he had dropped and darted away down a path that led off to his left. As he ran, he glanced over his shoulder. Toda was just starting in pursuit and the soldier lay on the ground, doubled up in agony. Dirk reckoned that he had only Toda to deal with, since whoever had held the lantern at the window must have been on a high ladder and probably had not been able to see into the room.

Gravel spurted under his feet as he raced along, running blindly with no notion of where he was going. His one thought was to put as much distance as possible between himself and Toda. He dodged past a stone lantern, took a narrow stream in one leap, looking back once more. He struggled to increase his speed for Toda seemed to be gaining on him. The pace began to tell on Dirk. Confinement, worry and irregular meals had weakened him; his lungs labored and he felt his knees growing weak.

He made a sharp right turn, sprinted desperately past a stretch of azaleas and then brought up short as a high white wall with a slanting tiled coping loomed ahead of him. He turned to face Toda, who tripped, stumbled, then came on again, the faint light glinting on his blade. With an effort that was wholly unconscious, Dirk hurled his sword at Toda, who was less than ten yards away. The bright blade spun through the air, turning like the sail of a wind-mill. It stopped and for a fraction of a second Dirk saw a bar of silver that reached from Toda's right shoulder across his chest. Then Toda was on the ground and the silver bar was hidden. Toda's own sword shot along the ground, turned over once and lay still.

Paralyzed, Dirk could only stare, and he crouched panting. Toda stirred, tried to raise himself, then collapsed. Dirk recovered himself, ran forward and bent over the fallen man, who was breathing hoarsely between clenched teeth. His own sword lay under Toda, its blade no longer bright. Dirk knelt by Toda, forgetting for an instant his own extreme danger. "Toda-san," he whispered. "Where are you hurt? I'll fix a bandage for you. The others will find you soon enough."

Toda writhed, turned and Dirk felt a retching in his throat. The thrown sword had slashed deep across the shoulder and from what he could see he gathered that the right arm hung by a mere shred of flesh. He said again, "Toda-san. Let me — " He sprang back as a dagger flashed in Toda's left hand.

There was nothing to do. He should have remembered that a Japanese of Toda's type would look on his own quixotic impulse merely as something to be taken advantage of, that chivalry in the European sense was despised by his kind. Out of reach of the dagger, Dirk paused for an instant, listening. He could hear voices far off by the kura, voices that shouted angrily, but there seemed to be no pursuit. Probably the wretched guard whom he had kicked was being blamed for the failure of the coup. Dirk turned, studied the wall for an instant, then ran forward and sprang. The tiles on the coping rasped his palms, but he clung on, wriggling and strug-gling. His chin was on a level with the tile, then his chest. He kicked out, felt his left knee catch on the crest, drew himself astride the wall and dropped to the other side.

He was in a steep narrow lane that led up into the hills, with the walls of smaller gardens on the other side. He had escaped, but into one of the worst places in the world that he could have chosen. All Nagasaki would be thrown into the search for him, which should be an easy one. His height, his foreign dress and features, would mark him down to the stupidest citizen.

He pulled himself together. "At any rate, I can't stay here," he thought and started off up the hill at as good a pace as he could maintain. As he made his way upward, he tried to reason out what had just happened. It was likely that the antiforeign clique had learned of an attempt to free him and had taken drastic steps to settle matters once for all. They had not known of the hidden sword and hence Toda had brought only three men with him. One Dirk had caught down in the kura. Another he had disabled with a kick. The third, standing on a ladder outside, had held a lantern at the high window. This, with the serious wounding of Toda, accounted for the lack of pursuit.

The alley was dark and quiet and the gates of the smaller houses on his left seemed tight shut for the night. He passed two gates, three, a fourth. Then from the shadow of the fifth gate came a gasp of surprise. "Maaa! Yang-san! Shimpai arimasen. Don't worry. This is a friend!"

XVIII

The Daikwan Speaks

DIRK jumped aside with his back against the wall. A Japanese, barely visible in a dark kimono, moved out from the shelter of the gate. "Shimpai arimasen," he said again. "We have been watching that house ever since you were brought there. Many of us. Naruhodo! I nearly swallowed my teeth when I saw you in the alley. You are most unwise. We had plans for you."

"So did some others," said Dirk grimly.

"Yes. We had plans," said the Japanese, clinging firmly to his original statement. "Now you better come with me." He led him past a modest one-story house, then through a back garden where a still smaller house stood.

"You will be safe here," said the guide, sliding back the front door. "This four-mat room to the right. Yes. Now tell me why you walked out of the garden, please."

Dirk told of his transfer to the kura and his finding the sword there, although for safety's sake he did not speak of the servant's warning. "So des'ka!" the host exclaimed when Dirk had finished. "But you should have let us know."

"Let you know!" echoed Dirk. "How could I have done that when I didn't know about you?"

The other nodded. "Yes. You should have let us know. Ah, sa! You see, Yang-san, there are many people who want to save your Company. And if they save the Company, then they save you. But there are others who hate foreigners. They do not want to save the Company or you. Then there are still others who want only peace here. They think if you are out of the way, then the other two parties will have nothing to fight about."

"I see," said Dirk. "One party wants to save me. Two want to dispose of me, but for different reasons. Which do you belong to?"

"The first party I think perhaps."

Dirk stared at him. "You think perhaps!"

His host nodded. "It is possible. Now listen to me, Yang-san. Many of us of the first party have been scattered through Nagasaki watching for you."

"It's lucky for me that you had just stepped out of your gate when I came by," remarked Dirk.

"There are many of us in this area and someone would have seen you."

"Would they have known me?" asked Dirk.

"As I knew you. I was only told that you were tall, even for a Komo. So, I see a tall Komo and know that it must be you. I did myself the honor of speaking to you. And my name is Arai."

"I'm in your debt, Arai-san," said Dirk. "But who is the leader of your party?"

"I wonder," said Arai.

Dirk gave a sigh of resignation, knowing that his host would say nothing more. It was quite possible, too, that he did not know himself, but had merely taken orders, Japanese fashion, from his immediate superior. There was information, however, that Arai might give, if he knew. "What has happened to the Oranda Yashiki, the Dutch Company?" asked Dirk.

"Ah! Very difficult," said Arai. "The big stone warehouse has been torn down. That is all I know."

"And the people?" Dirk tried to keep eagerness out of his voice.

"They were all at Hirado, when I last heard."

"Everyone?"

"I was told so."

"And the niece of Van Os, the accountant? Can you tell me anything about her?"

Arai frowned. "A niece? Eh to! Difficult. Sa! I remember. I hold a very small office at the shiyakusho, the city hall. I see a report from Matsura-san to the Daikwan. That niece was left at Hirado when the *de Rijp* came here. She has been there all the time."

"What?" Dirk's question was louder than he intended and he noticed that Arai's eyes went dull and that he seemed to withdraw a little. "I mean, she's at Hirado?"

"Do you doubt the word of Matsura-san?" asked the other stiffly.

"Not at all. It was — it was — oh, I've got to get out of here.

I've got to get back to Hirado. Your party wants me and the Company saved. Can you get me there?"

"I wonder."

"There's *something* that can be done," urged Dirk. "Now if I — " He checked himself suddenly, remembering the questions that he had been asked about Trudi by various examiners. "How many people know that the girl is at Hirado?"

"A girl is not important. But I do not think that many know. The report was marked shinten, confidential. I gave it to my superior."

"Do you think the Daikwan has seen that report?"

"I do not think so. I do not think that he would be troubled about a girl."

Dirk let deep relief spread over him. While the future was murky as ever, for the present at least, Trudi was among friends. Caron was near her and old Matsura had moved in her behalf, officially denying any connection between her and Hara. No one, save a superior, would dare contradict Matsura. "Now what do you think I'd better do?" he asked.

"I shall go now and report to my superior in the party," said Arai. "Then I come to talk to you again. I will send rice and tea to you. After that you better sleep. There is no danger. You are safe here."

Dirk took his rice and tea with a better appetite than he had known in days. The greatest spur to his mind and body was the news about Trudi. He could keep his mind completely clear of everything except the Company and himself. She was as safe as any Komo could be in Japan and if he used his wits he ought to have a fairly good chance of joining her once more. He was not worried about any stories that might come from Hara. A dozen spies, a hundred refugees from the castle swearing that they had seen her there would have no weight against Matsura's canny, matter-of-fact statement that she had been at Hirado all the time.

He stretched out on the mats and soon fell asleep, to wander through weird dreams in which boats sailed into Hirado from Massachusetts Bay and Connecticut, while he and Trudi studied the churches recently gathered at Ipswich and Hiroshima, advised by Cousin Japhet.

290

It was still dark when he was awakened by voices outside the thin paper panels of his room. He raised himself on one elbow. One of the speakers was Arai, the other an unknown, whose tone carried decision and authority. "Are they hostages?" Arai asked.

The unknown answered sharply, "Didn't I tell you so? If Yang-san is not returned, then all the Komo go to the executioner, beginning with Caron-san."

"Do they know where Yang-san is?"

"No. And they must not. You see, it was explained to me, if the other Komo cease to live, then we may make great use of Yang-san. He will be a rallying point. All who feel as we do will be able to say to the Shogun, these haters of foreigners are trying to strangle the Empire. Trade has dried up. People will starve. We will be blind to what happens in the outer world and will have no warning if foreigners come to us for war instead of trade. We can produce Yang-san and say to the Shogun, 'Through this man we may begin again, and he will call in the Dutch once more and perhaps the English.'"

"Saa!" Arai murmured. "But would they come back after their people had been killed?"

"To them, trade is more important than a few deaths," answered the unknown. "Tonight we shall move him to another house. Sayonara."

"Sayonara," echoed Arai as the unknown hurried off through the darkness.

Dirk lay back on the mats, trembling. Trudi, Caron and the rest would be handed over to the executioners if he could not be found. Or would they be, he wondered. In many ways such a decision sounded like a tentative move in the game of *go*. No. There was no consolation in that thought. The ruling must have been made several days ago while various factions quarreled about him. The decision was probably made by the Daikwan to secure peace by removing a source of friction. "Now," thought Dirk, "what the devil's to be done?"

It would be foolish to suppose that by giving himself up he would obtain lenient treatment from the Japanese. Also, it was quite possible that, having him in their hands, they would still carry out their program of utmost vengeance against the others of the Company. He turned the situation over and over in his mind, but each possible course of action seemed to have the same end. The dice were loaded against him and the Company. There was nothing to do except wait in Arai's care and follow the familiar pattern of watching developments. He tried to sleep again, but his mind prodded and nagged at him until he dismissed the thought.

He rose and slid open the rear panels of the room, which opened onto another of the same size. Crossing the matting he looked out onto a patch of bare ground and a white, tile-topped wall behind which a hill rose almost sheer. To his surprise he found that day was breaking. Somehow encouraged by the growing light he explored the rest of the house, but found no traces of occupancy. Returning to the open rear room he leaned against a post and watched the sun come over the steep hill. Before long, Arai would send him food and he could take the opportunity to find out if he could speak with the little man's superiors. Yet what would they know and what could they do? Plots and counterplots seemed to be afoot in his behalf, and it was very likely that these people moved independently and unknown to each other.

He stepped down onto the bare ground and strolled across toward the wall. Driven by a sudden impulse, he caught the coping, drew himself to the summit and dropped to the other side.

He could feel himself growing pale as he followed the worn track that slanted up the hill. Prickles ran up and down his spine but he set his teeth and kept on at a brisk pace. There was a little shrine to Kwannon, goddess of mercy, at the top of the hill and he leaned against it as he looked south, trying to find out where he was. For a moment he could not orient himself, then, one by one, remembered landmarks stood out. The roof of a temple, high and curving. A bit of distant waterfront, a glimpse of the harbor mouth with the miter-shaped Papenberg looming hard and sinister, and far to his right the roofs of the buildings that huddled in the compound of the Governor's palace.

Allowing for the intervening hills and ravines with their crowded houses, he estimated that it would take him a good hour to reach the compound. He drew himself up, shivering a little, and then chose a path that led west toward the city and away from the area where Arai's friends might be found.

Walking mechanically, his head down, he began weaving through narrow alleys where bath water gurgled in the drains and the clean aromatic smell of charcoal fires was strong. People stared at him from doorways and children set up the familiar chorus of "Maa! Takai des' né! Isn't he tall!" but no one interfered with him. He saw a patrol of city police moving along a wide firebreak at a trot and shrank back into an alley until they had passed, then darted across the broad thoroughfare and into another alley. He began to recognize signs and buildings in the wide streets that he crossed. A sake shop where he had drunk late with some Kyoto silk merchants, a stall where they sold excellent rolls of seaweed, rice and fish, a money-changer's where government-set rates might be avoided.

Life was stirring all about him, but barely touched his consciousness, save as its manifestations helped guide him on his way. On all sides, heavy wooden shutters were being rolled back for the day, but he did not hear them. In a doorway a very pretty girl, dressed only in a red kirtle about her hips, smiled at him and called "Ohayo!" as she plaited her black hair, but the greeting was wasted on him.

At the mouth of the narrow lane where awnings were being spread over fish stalls, he stopped short. Fifty yards ahead of him rose the walls of the Governor's compound, with a heavy guard assembling about the main gate. For an instant he leaned against the nearest house, heart beating fast and eyes closed. Then he opened his eyes, threw back his head and forced himself on. He walked stiffly and his legs seemed to kick out mechanically instead of bending naturally at the knee.

By the gate someone called shrilly and two men stepped in front of him, barring his passage with their pikestaffs. Some of the numbness left Dirk. He said hoarsely, "I am Yang-san of the Dutch Company. I want to give myself up to an officer of the Daikwan."

A bowlegged man with two superb sword hilts showing above his obi stepped forward, eying Dirk with cold dislike. From the crest on his haori Dirk judged that he came from the island of Awaji, off the fishing village of Kobe. "Donata?" snapped the officer. "Who are you?"

The certainty that the officer knew who he was nettled Dirk. He said shortly, "Are you an officer of the Daikwan?"

"On temporary duty with him. What do you want?" The officer used word forms usually addressed only to beggars and lepers. The soldiers snickered openly.

"You know who I am. I want to give myself up to the Daikwan."

"He isn't here," said the Awaji man gruffly.

Dirk was bewildered. The officer of the guard had made no attempt to hide his dislike and scorn of him, and yet he seemed to be reluctant to put him under arrest. Forcing an edge to his voice, Dirk said, "The Daikwan Heizo wouldn't go far without leaving a deputy. I demand that you take me to him."

The officer hitched at his obi, then growled, "Gunso!" A hard-faced sergeant grounded his pike and stepped forward. The Awaji man made a curt gesture with his head. "Take this Komo inside. I can't be bothered." He turned his back on Dirk and the sergeant pointed through the gate with his pike.

Dirk went into the compound, the sergeant trotting morosely behind him. Troops were drilling in front of the main building and Dirk thought that the officer in charge looked curiously at him. Other officials, hurrying about with legal-looking papers in their hands, stared frankly and once Dirk caught an exclamation of "Mezurashii! Astounding!"

The sergeant barked, "Kondo hidari no uchi! Next house on the left."

Dirk turned obediently. All weariness, all speculation, had left him. He was nearing the end of his wanderings that had begun months ago when he had left Caron on the shore of the Gulf of Omura to start his journey that took him to the cliffs of Shimabara and the ruined castle. He kicked off his shoes and stepped up into the corridor as the sergeant pointed. The building was quiet. Once or twice he heard the gentle rubbing of a panel sliding in its grooves and somewhere a man coughed rackingly. Near the end of the corridor, the panels of a room on the left stood open and the sergeant halted, gesturing roughly toward the open door with his pike butt.

Dirk wondered what sort of frozen-eyed official he would confront. The doorway was blocked against drafts by a single screen that stood just inside, some four feet high. Painted on its silk covering was a hideous crouching tiger, vicious-eyed.

Suddenly, from the hidden mats beyond the screen, a voice said, "Yes, I think he really sings better than the cricket I had last year. I shall order a fine cage for him."

Dirk's hands dropped to his sides and he felt his jaw grow lax. Then with a wild surge of hope he cried, "Matsura-san!"

A second voice cut in on the echoes of his own. "Dirk!" He kicked the screen aside, held out his arms as Trudi rose from the mats and ran blindly toward him. Once more she cried "Dirk!" as he caught her up, swung her clear of the floor. Her face was close to his and her arms were tight about his neck. He could only whisper her name over and over. Her voice was gentle in his ears. "Oh, where have you been, Dirk? I knew you'd come."

Reality forced its way into Dirk's mind. He set Trudi down. "You're going to be all right, dearest. I—I've just got to find the Daikwan's deputy. I'll be right back."

Still in his arms, she shook her head. "Never mind him, Dirk. Matsura-san's responsible for you now. He thought you'd come to him last night. He was worried when you didn't, but I knew everything would be all right."

"Matsura?" repeated Dirk, looking around. He had completely forgotten the old Daimyo.

A panel in the rear of the room slid discreetly back and the Daimyo's wise old head peered cautiously into the room. Trudi stepped quickly away from Dirk and Matsura came in, hand held out in European fashion, smiling as amiably as though Dirk had come to call on him at his palace above the horseshoe bay of Hirado. "Ah, Yang-san! It is good of you to take the trouble to come to me. A beautiful day! Sa! Please sit down, both of you, and I shall make tea for you." He clapped his hands and a servant brought in a table with the tea equipment.

Dirk bowed and unabashedly drew Trudi closer to him. "I hope that you will pardon my rudeness in not calling on you earlier, Matsura-san," he said.

Hands busy with caddies and hot water, the Daimyo murmured, "I had hoped that you would call on me last night, but this morning I heard rumors that you were unavoidably busy."

"Unavoidably so," said Dirk, smiling as Trudi, her cheek against his shoulder, slipped her hand into his.

"Thus it was told me," the Daimyo sighed. "And there was a grievous accident reported to me, doubtless as unavoidable as your absence. Yes, one Toda-san of my guard injured himself so badly that he died soon after. You remember Toda-san, perhaps?"

Dirk said gravely, "I was not intimate with him, but I often saw him at your palace." He began to understand the events of the day before. Matsura must have brought Trudi from Hirado within the last day or so. Orders had gone out to turn him over into Matsura's keeping. Toda and other radicals must have learned of this and had decided to take matters into their own hands rather than see him pass, even temporarily, into more lenient custody.

"And now what is my status, Matsura-san?" he asked.

The Daimyo handed Dirk and Trudi their cups in graceful ceremony. As he sipped his, he answered, "For the moment, I am responsible for you."

"And what am I to do?"

The Daimyo set down his cup. "You and Sayo-ko-san and I are going over into Shimabara."

Trudi started and Dirk quickly put his arm about her shoulders. "Where?" she asked, her voice breaking.

Matsura raised a veined, delicate hand. "There is no worry. We go there to present ourselves to the Daikwan, who confers with the commander, Matsudaira-san."

"And after that?" asked Dirk quickly.

"The Daikwan will inform us, Yang-san." He inclined his head politely to Trudi. "We should start as soon as possible. Perhaps you would like to get your things from your room."

For an instant Trudi clung to Dirk while the Daimyo became suddenly absorbed in studying the glaze of the little fat teapot. Then she rose gracefully. "I'll only be a minute," she called as she left.

When the panels had closed behind her, Dirk looked at the Daimyo. "There were rumors that all the Company people were being held as hostages for me."

Matsura's keen old eyes studied Dirk. Then he said, "Ah, so. I see. Such a measure was discussed, the day I came here to Nagasaki. Some spoke against it, and it was not adopted."

"Then what is the status of the Company?"

"I wish I could answer, Yang-san. The great warehouse at Hirado has been torn down. All of the people are there, except Sayo-ko-san and Caron-san. I expect that we shall see him when we get to Shimabara."

"And again — now that Trudi is out of the room — is my status like the others of the Company?"

"Again — I wish I could answer, Yang-san. You and I will appear before the Daikwan. I shall do what I can."

"I know you will," said Dirk. "However it turns out, I can never thank you enough for — for having looked after Trudi so well at Hirado while I was away."

"That was my privilege," answered Matsura. "She is a very brave young lady. I think that she would be quite capable of appreciating what someone I know of did at the rumor of the hostages."

"Gunst! You mustn't tell her!"

"I shall be silent as the great Buddha at Kamakura. And for as long as possible, she will think that we go to Shimabara merely to pay our respects to the Daikwan."

"H'm," said Dirk dubiously.

"I know," said Matsura. "She is a very observant young lady, so I shall be careful about what she observes."

The Daimyo's procession moved out of Nagasaki toward the Gulf of Tachibana, Matsura leading in a black and gold sedan chair while Trudi followed close behind in a curtained litter. From the stubby horse that Dirk rode after Trudi, he could see the officials and pikemen of the advance party well ahead of the sedan chair. More pikemen, officers from the Hirado palace and important-looking functionaries from Nagasaki formed a double column on either side. There was little chance for more than an occasional word with Trudi, so Dirk settled himself in his high, clumsy saddle and tried to keep his mind alert to notice all those small things that, in Japan, could rise to important totals.

The future was still cloudy, but at least he could relax a little in this fleeting present. There was Trudi, pulling back the curtains a little, smiling at him or waving a slim hand. There were the troops and the officials, not standing guard over him this time, but forming an escort of honor for Matsura and his guest. As the procession left Nagasaki and wound down through hill villages, he could see people pour out of their houses at the first sight of the advance party and begin sweeping the road over which the Daimyo would pass. Offerings of rice and fish and flowers were handed by bowing headmen into the sedan chair and, in the second village, an old woman timidly offered Trudi a great armful of azaleas, a cloud of rose.

The hills sloped more steeply and Dirk looked down across tier on tier of terraced rice fields, their flooded surfaces catching the deep blue of the sky that curved down to meet the Gulf of Tachibana, far below. There were more bowing officials at the waterfront village. Drums pounded and conches blared at the short wharf and the troops lined up in rigid ceremony as the Daimyo and his guests entered the carved, painted barge with its canopies and cushions.

Dirk dismounted and ran to Trudi's litter to help her out. It was good to have her hand in his again, good to look down into her clear dark eyes once more and to see her lips curve in a smile, happy and confident. "We'll be side by side in the barge all the way across the gulf!" whispered Dirk and her fingers tightened about his in quick answer. The Daimyo beckoned to them and Dirk's heart sank. Apparently, it was all very well for Matsura to make tea for Trudi in the privacy of the room at Nagasaki, but here, with dozens of eyes watching, convention demanded that she sit a little apart from the men under the canopy and at a slightly lower level.

It was cool and comfortable on the mats under the canopy. Matsura knelt facing the bow with Dirk at his right and Trudi separated from Dirk by a low, narrow table that was covered by the inevitable tea paraphernalia. Drums boomed again as the barge pushed off, the escort following in two other, plainer craft and at a respectful distance. Oar and sail set the little flotilla moving eastward at a fair speed over the blue dance of the gulf. The old Daimyo, in excellent spirits, spoke of bygone wars between the Matsura clan and men of Omura. "Those were brave days," he sighed, "but it is better now. Then, each Daimyate was a little nation in itself, allying now here and now there, hoping to gain enough strength to seize the Shogunal powers and rule in the Emperor's name until some stronger alliance drove it into oblivion again. Yes, I suppose it is better today. But sometimes I am frightened by the thought that we shall have so strong a central power that the rest of us will live at the whim of the man who holds that power, ruling solely through soldiers and police. Now in the wars between the Taira and the Minamoto—" He plunged into a long, involved narrative. Presently in the middle of a sentence, he began to nod, then drifted off into a peaceful, childlike sleep.

Dirk glanced at him, then leaned across the table to Trudi. "I want to know two things while we can talk. How did you get out, and what happened to me?"

In low quick words, Trudi told him about the appearance of Caron and of the double rescue that was balked by the Imperial raiders. "I can't tell you how I felt, Dirk," she concluded. "But there was nothing that any of us could do."

"Nothing," agreed Dirk. "Caron was absolutely right. The one thing to do was to see that you got to the *de Rijp*. I was beyond reach." He frowned. "That tunnel! Gunst! If I'd only known it was there! I could have gotten out the first night that Fra Fidel and the Amakusa people came. Then—"

"Hush, Dirk. Even if you had, it would have taken you so long to get to Hirado that I'd have reached Hara and found you gone. Then what would have happened to me? It's much better the way it is. We're together again. Matsura-san will present us to the Daikwan and then we'll all go back to Hirado."

Dirk smiled at her. "And we'll still exchange sake cups."

"Still?" Trudi's voice rose in surprise. "Why, Dirk Jongh, why do you think I've clung to my wedding clothes all this time? I *knew* I'd wear them for you. I just didn't know when, that's all."

Dirk managed to meet her eyes steadily, but he shivered as he looked east. The light haze that had masked the far horizon had begun to lift and little by little a dark line showed between the sea and the sky as the west coast of Shimabara revealed itself in sullen menace.

It was nearly dark when the barges reached Obama, and Dirk looked out from under the canopy at the rising mass of Mount Unzen, its thick ridges catching the last rays of the sun. It would be quite dark on the eastern slope now where the sharp spurs ran out toward the camps of the Imperialists and, beyond them, the white walls of Hara. He caught Trudi's eye and knew that she was wondering, with him, if the shadows would ever lift for the people behind those walls — for Gentaro Mori, for Tokisada.

As the barge was made fast, Dirk helped Trudi onto the wharf, having first been careful to give precedence to the old Daimyo, who looked benignly on them, like a thoughtful host who has found just the right spot for a picnic. Trudi clung to Dirk's hand for a moment. "Do you think we'll see the Daikwan now?" she whispered.

He shook his head. "He'll be farther inland."

She stepped closer. "Dirk — when you see him — try to say something for Fra Hilario. He was so good to us."

"Why, I couldn't forget him. Don't worry, we'll do what we can," said Dirk.

The procession was forming at the head of the wharf, much as it had left Nagasaki — a sedan chair for the Daimyo, a litter for Trudi and a horse for Dirk. As Dirk turned his mount, he bent from the saddle to call down to Trudi, "I just heard one of the stewards say that we'll stop here for the night and go on across the peninsula tomorrow. So wherever we stay, we'll be together, at least through dinner." The procession moved off through the streets of Obama. He fixed his mind on the fact that he'd been with Trudi all through that day, that he'd have a few more hours with her. Every instant must be stamped on his mind. The procession halted before a gate where slashed green curtains fluttered in the evening breeze. A group of women, headed by a gray-robed matron, stepped out of the gate and beckoned to the bearers of Trudi's litter. Dirk started to dismount, but the matron waved him along, crying, "Iyé! Iyé! No! No!" and the march began again.

Dirk sadly watched the litter vanish through the great gate. He should have known that separate quarters would have been provided for a mere woman, traveling under the protection of the Hirado Daimyo.

It was both eerie and sinister to ride through the still air of the next noon along the southern fringes of the Imperial camp. From his high saddle, Dirk recognized many landmarks that up to now he had only seen from the Hara towers. There on the left were the grove of trees and the old temple where Itakura's first onslaught had been shattered by Mori's counterattack. There was the lone pine under which the first days of the siege, a sake booth had been set up, easily distinguishable by the huge characters on its canvas walls. Through that ravine, off to the right, he had seen lines of pikemen filing away to mass for some futile attacks against the rebel arquebuses. For the first time he saw the reverse slope of that hogback which had been held so long and tenaciously, to be lost through treachery. Somewhere beyond it, cannon were slamming with sullen persistence, but the ugly black guns and the white walls at which they were battering were still hidden by the rising ground in front of him. It seemed to him that the Imperial lines must have been moved much closer to Hara. Otherwise he would have seen formations of Imperial troops on the crest of the hogback. His feeling of uneasiness increased as the Daimyo's column moved on.

The tents of the unit commanders, scattered right and left on either side of the road, were showing more and more elaborate designs on their walls, the banners that floated over them were richer, mounted on staffs of gleaming lacquer instead of plain bamboo. Then, in a hollow to the left, Dirk caught sight of the crest of the Daikwan and, beyond it, the banner of the military commander, Matsudaira.

Dirk watched the procession trail off along a road that slanted up a ridge, then curved down toward the Imperial headquarters. There were the officials, there was Matsura's sedan chair, followed by Trudi's litter and, after the litter, the file of pikemen who had taken up their stations behind it that morning outside Obama. The column halted and Dirk saw Matsura's senior officer approach the Daikwan's guard tent, bowing with each slow step. Then sedan chair and litter were set on the ground and the pikemen stood at ease. Dirk knew better than to dismount until the old Daimyo had left his chair and entered the Daikwan's quarters.

He leaned his elbow on the pommel of his saddle and looked impatiently about him. Without realizing it, he had ridden along the south slope of the hogback, whose high shoulder still hid the sweep of land to the north. Then life began to stir along the old works. Helmeted officers stood in groups, pointing or staring with folded arms toward the sound of the guns. In twos and threes, knots of foot soldiers joined them, taking care not to crowd too closely.

Dirk's horse began to graze, sidling aimlessly up the slope. He caught at the reins to urge the animal back into formation, but his mount made a quick lunge and carried him to the very crest, jostling against an archer who glared at Dirk. Dirk straightened in the saddle, then froze, the color draining from his face and his joints weak. There stood the old castle, white and ragged on its high promontory, with the blue of the Gulf of Shimabara asparkle beyond it. But no banners hung from the walls, no sentinels showed their heads above the solid stretches of the parapet, over which ugly whitish-yellow smoke rolled slowly. The great gates were open and heavy formations of Imperial troops were drawn up along the very stretch from which Dirk had cleared the hut that had been built against the outside of the castle. The cannon under their grass screens on the lower slope of the hogback roared and flamed but no balls crashed against the curving walls of Hara. The guns that had been cast by Trelawney were booming a salute to victory. The siege was over.

Trumpets blared by the main gate, drums thundered and the troops outside formed a living corridor that was lined with sharp pike points. Dust rose high, swirled out through the gate, and Dirk stared in horror. Driven on by light-armed troops, a long column of misery was forced out into the open, men and women, old and young. Some of them were bound together by a long rope, others, running and stumbling alone, were prodded on by the escort. Out of Hara the last of the rebels poured, on along the corridor of pikes and onto the narrow stretch of grass, bright with the spring, that lay between the south wall and the cliff.

Dirk tried to turn away, but found himself staring, hypnotized. The corridor of pikes ended and a dark confused mass rolled into the open, broke, halted. There was a flurry among the pikemen and a lone man struggled clear, a tall man in friar's robes.

Fra Fidel faced the terrified rebels, held a cross high above his head and began to walk slowly backwards, his gait sure and unhurried. For an instant, he was outlined against the sky. Then his brown robes fluttered against the face of the cliff, swirling down and down. The prisoners began to move, were forced on by pike point and butt. Like a hideous rope, linked bodies pitched over the lip, turning and turning as they fell to the sharp rocks and the beaches below. They fell in chains. They fell singly or were shoved over by the guards. Ghastly vignettes were stamped on Dirk's mind — a linked group that lurched and staggered, dragged nearer and nearer to the edge by the weight of those who had been pushed over ahead of them — an unbound man who broke from the guards, ran to the lip of the cliff, drew himself up and dove headlong — a mass of color falling, falling past the brown of the rocks, then a smaller blur that detached itself, turning over and over as a mother lost her grip on the baby that she had carried in her arms.

"S'teki da! Excellent!" a soldier near Dirk grunted with professional approval.

Dirk managed to turn his mount down the slope. Dimly, he heard his name called and tried to pull himself together as Trudi ran toward him along the lip of an old trench, waving. "Where did you go to, Dirk?" she called. "The Daimyo's gone in to see the Daikwan and he wants us to wait in that little tent. Dirk! What's the matter?" He dropped to the ground and she put an arm about him to steady him. "Are you sick?"

Through dry lips he said unsteadily, "I'm all right. Just been in the saddle too long."

"Dirk! Look at me! You *are* sick. Never mind your horse. Let's go up there where those men are. The air will be better and I know Matsura-san won't mind."

He shook his head blindly. "No. Not up there. You stay right here. I—I don't know why I didn't expect it, but Hara's fallen. I—I didn't know it would hit me so hard. After all, we knew so many of the people."

Trudi's eyes filled. "Oh, those poor people, those poor, brave people. Now they'll be prisoners!"

"Yes," said Dirk shortly. "Prisoners. Where's that tent where we're supposed to wait? I'm all right now." He staggered a little and Trudi guided him, arm through his. Then he cried out, "No! No! Not that tent!"

"I know, we're going two beyond it, where the sedan chair is."

Dirk managed to walk faster, hoping that she had not looked into the tent. Its wide front was open and seemed to have been set aside as a sort of trophy room. Close by the entrance on a little lacquered table lay a dragon-crested helmet that he had first seen on Hirado, long ago. On a frame beside it hung a carefully mended cassock.

303

He lowered his head and hurried on, shaken by the sight of the last relics of two men whom he had known and admired, men differing utterly in upbringing and training, yet strangely alike. One had been strong in selfless purpose as he had been in mind and body. The other, frail but enduring, had fully matched the samurai in his devotion to an alien people who needed him. Dirk glanced back at the tent. A gust of wind had caught the hem of the cassock and draped it over one of the dragon horns, giving a final unity to the relics of Mori and Fra Hilario.

By the sedan chair, Dirk felt Trudi's arm tighten on his. A buck-toothed officer motioned Dirk into the purple-walled tent, but when Trudi started to follow him, the officer shook his head at her. "Kochira, dozo. This way, please," he said, curtly but not rudely. Trudi entered the plainer tent where a woman with an expressionless face bowed to her and pointed to a strip of matting. Trudi knelt on it. Hands in her lap, she sat as erect as possible, trying to match her companion's impassivity. Her mind raced on. "I won't let her see I'm scared. I know Dirk hasn't seen that I am. People dropped dreadful hints at Nagasaki. What will the Daikwan do?" Her hands tightened. "He must be before the Daikwan now."

In the next tent, Dirk found Matsura standing placidly before a heavy purple curtain that masked the entrance to a bigger structure. The Daimyo smiled. "There will be a few moments before we kneel in front of the Daikwan. I do not need to warn you about kenson, but remember that the Daikwan Heizo represents the Shogun who represents the Emperor." He drew a roll of paper from his wide sleeve. "I have ventured to draw up a statement for him to read. It concerns you."

Dirk took the paper and spread it out. At first he found the highly stylized characters hard to read, but gradually they stood out clear, setting forth in detail how Dirk had come to be at Hara and how many factors had combined to prevent his escape. Naturally, there was no mention of Trudi. He bowed to the old man. "I am grateful to you. You have stated events exactly as they happened. Will you give this to the Daikwan when we go in?"

"Ah. Not necessary," said Matsura, looking almost boyishly pleased with himself. "He has a copy. After we have observed ceremony, I shall hand you this, and you wait to see what he says."

The curtain rustled back and Dirk and the Daimyo knelt at once in the opening.

When the endless bowings and expressions of homage had been completed, Dirk, forehead still pressed close to the grassy floor, watched Matsura out of the corner of his eye. When he saw the old man straighten up, he counted five and rose to his knees, the interval expressing deference to Matsura's revered age and rank. He caught a murmur of "Erai! Well done!" from the lord of Hirado.

Dirk looked at the Daikwan curiously. He was a little, wiry man with almost European features, who surveyed Dirk noncommittally but with no great hostility. He seemed worn and tired as though the rebellion, with possible blame accruing to him, had taxed him heavily.

Matsura was speaking in a low, even tone, with much formality. This, if the Daikwan would deign to notice, was the young Komo of whom the Daimyo of Hirado had spoken. Heizo's tired eyes rested on Dirk. "Give me the letter about him," he said and a bowing clerk handed him a roll of paper. At the same moment, Matsura slipped the other roll into Dirk's hand.

Heizo motioned to Dirk. "You have been given a copy of this letter, I am told." He held up the sheet for Dirk to see. It appeared to be identical with the one which Matsura had shown him in the anteroom, save that the salutation and subscription, which had been abbreviated in his copy, were set forth more fully.

Dirk bowed. "I have seen it, Heizo-san."

"You find it true in all respects?"

"In all respects."

The Daikwan, eyes running over the flowing characters, called sharply to a clerk, "Write what I tell you." Heizo began in clipped, rapid words to summarize the letter. Dirk listened carefully, even with admiration. Heizo was dictating a terse, skillful résumé of the contents. Still, what was the Daikwan making of it all? The fact that seemed to stand out in Dirk's mind, as he listened, was that he *had* been at Hara. The reasons for his not leaving were given secondary importance. The final paragraph did nothing to change the whole effect and Dirk wondered if Matsura would make any verbal embellishments of his own.

To his amazement, the dictation did not end with what Dirk had thought was the last paragraph. Heizo intoned, "It is to be noted that Yang-san undertook to go to Hara in the first place at the request of the Daimyo of Hirado, to keep him informed of activities on the Shimabara peninsula that might bring dangerous repercussions not only in said Daimyate, but throughout the Empire. There is no doubt but that in the first days he might have made his escape had he not been so concerned with fulfilling the request of the Daimyo of Hirado to the utmost."

The Daikwan's thin, high voice died away and Dirk stared at him, wondering if he had heard correctly. He managed to glance at Matsura, but the Daimyo's worn, ivory face expressed only respect for his superior. It was hard to believe that that quiet, guileless old man had given Dirk an incomplete copy of what he had written for the Daikwan, so that Dirk could answer that what he himself had read was true in all details.

The Daikwan was speaking again. "Yang-san has rendered a service to the peace of the Empire which will not be forgotten. He is free to rejoin the members of the Oranda Yashiki without let or hindrance. Let it be so ordered and let it be so written." He inclined his head in dismissal.

Dirk and Matsura backed out, bowing. When they reached the anteroom and rose to their feet, Dirk tried to stammer out his thanks and his amazement. "I am free now. Matsura-san, except for you, things could have gone very differently for me."

Matsura nodded. "Very different."

"And Trudi and I can rejoin the Company? At Hirado?"

The Daimyo's expression grew grave. "Where I cannot say. All we know is that you are free to rejoin the Company — wherever it may be."

"And when shall we know that?"

"In due course."

"Then let's find Trudi. Thank God she didn't suspect how all this might have turned out."

"May the wide sleeve of Kwannon continue to protect her," observed Matsura. "As to waiting, it may not be long. I know that several messengers have come in from Tokyo quite recently and the Daikwan will probably announce the Shogun's pleasure."

As they stepped out of the tent, a junior steward bowed to them and asked Matsura's permission to speak to Dirk. Then he beckoned to a servant who appeared with a tray on which were two boxes. Dirk gasped in surprise. One was the case that held the Daimyo's tea caddy. The other, the curve-topped letter box in which Cousin Japhet's letter had been placed. Matsura smiled and nodded. "I had the kura where you were attacked searched, and these were found. I thought they might give you a little pleasure."

As Dirk bowed his thanks, a cold wave crept over him. The boxes must have traveled with the cortege all the way from Nagasaki to the camp before Hara. They could have been given him before, but obviously the Daimyo had not been sure that Dirk would have any use for tea caddies or letters from the New World after his interview with the Daikwan. He had been very close to the edge of a cliff, nearly as close as those — He forced the memory to the back of his mind.

There was a commotion in the next tent and a moment later Trudi stood in the doorway. Half seen, behind her, the official's wife fluttered about in a storm of protesting little clucks and exclamations of "Ara!" Dirk moved quickly forward and caught Trudi in his arms, still clutching the tea caddy case and letter box. "It's all right, dearest! It's all right! We're free to go where we want. We — "

Then he stepped back, flushing. Whenever they met, there were always Japanese about, tacitly or openly disapproving of any public display of emotion or affection!

"I knew it would be all right, Dirk," she said. "Why, you didn't think I was worried, did you? That's absurd. When can we go back to Hirado?"

"We shall be told," said Matsura. "While we wait, let us sit in this tent. My servants will bring us food."

Trudi stepped aside to allow the old Daimyo to enter. "I don't mind waiting, Matsura-san. Do you think it will be long?"

The Daimyo paused at the entrance. "I wonder," he said.

"An hour or so? Or might it be longer?" Trudi persisted.

Again, the Daimyo said, "I wonder." Then he added quickly, "Saa! It may not be long."

Dirk turned, following the direction of Matsura's eyes. From a bright cluster of tents off to the left, a group of men moved toward the Daikwan's quarters. Matsura muttered, "Naruhodo! And he walks with Matsudaira-san, the commander-in-chief. No. I do not think that we wait long."

Beside Matsudaira, François Caron strode easily along, his hands moving in negligent gestures as he talked. His head was back and even at that distance Dirk thought that he could make out a confident smile on the Frenchman's face, a smile as assured as the red plume that circled his wide hatbrim. Yet there was something odd in his appearance, some minor detail that Dirk could not quite place.

Matsura rubbed his hands nervously and Dirk heard him mutter, "The door. It must not close. Somehow he must keep the door of our old world open to the new!" The Daimyo shook his head. "Now he goes to listen to the Shogun's orders. Come. We three shall wait, and dine while waiting." He went into the tent, Dirk and Trudi following. She laid her hand on his arm for an instant. "Now Heer Caron will settle everything, and we'll go back to Hirado."

"Of course." Dirk tried to sound in hearty agreement, but he had just realized what had been wrong with Caron's appearance: The gold-worked baldrick that usually held the Frenchman's best sword had hung empty by his side. The point seemed small, but Dirk knew that it might assume great significance. Caron had been denied the privilege of appearing before the Daikwan armed.

XIX

West to the New World

It grew warm in the slant-roofed tent and the smell of the food that the Daimyo's servants had brought hung heavy on the air. Trudi could not make out why Dirk was still so uneasy. He was safe, she was safe, and any other cares must be minor. The old Daimyo, too, seemed restless and did not take the nap in which she was hoping that he would indulge himself, giving her and Dirk a chance to talk. In spite of all uncertainties, she felt confident. There was nothing to do but wait, as the Daimyo had said. He had said, too, that he didn't think the wait would be long. François Caron could do anything. She mused on. Becker would soon be transferred, and of course Caron would become Director at Hirado. But Caron had caught the eye not only of Batavia, but even of Amsterdam, she had heard, and might be moved to much higher spheres of activity, and in that case she would be the wife of the youngest Director in the history of the Company. She and Dirk would live in the 1637 house and he would start at once to rebuild the great stone warehouse that Japanese temper had demolished. Matsura would come along the sea wall in the late afternoons to tea with them while more and more Dutch ships lay off Kawachi. Happy in her thoughts, she smiled across at Dirk.

Dirk thought of the three problems that he formed in his mind after his capture — the safety of Trudi, of the Company and of himself. Points one and three settled. The second, while almost abstract, was the most important of all from any standpoint but that of the individual. He wondered what was happening in the Daikwan's tent. Caron's whole manner and bearing had been reassuring, but the absence of the dress sword nagged at him. In his imagination, he saw the red lifeline of the Company reaching from Holland and on through the East to Batavia, running thence north to Japan. That lifeline was strong, but tight-strung, like the hawser of an anchored ship. If that part of the lifeline that ran up to Japan should break — or be slashed — would the backlash wipe out the other points to which that line was made fast?

Suddenly Matsura cried "Ah!" and sprang to his feet as steps sounded outside and a long shadow fell across the doorway. Then Caron ducked through the entrance, plumed hat under his arm. His clothes were glossy and unwrinkled, his stockings drawn smoothly up and his silver shoe buckles gleaming. He bowed to Matsura, murmuring a complimentary phrase that was nicely deferential. Then he dropped an arm about Dirk's shoulders. "I heard — at the Daikwan's tent. I — " He hesitated and Dirk saw that he was deeply moved, at a loss, for once, for the easy, graceful mot juste. Then he recovered himself. "But in any case, I should have had only to look at Sayo-ko to know what had been said there. Matsura-san, I am hopelessly in your debt."

In a low, tense voice Matsura said, "The door, Caron-san? What about the door?"

Caron dropped to the ground opposite and the full light from outside struck across his aquiline face. Dirk was shocked by the utter weariness that he saw in those usually composed features. "Ah," said Caron dully. "Yes. The door."

Matsura leaned eagerly forward. "It is still open?"

Caron held his thumb and forefinger slightly apart. "About that much, Matsura-san."

The old Daimyo seemed to shrink, to grow smaller and more frail. In a hushed voice he asked, "You were able to do no more?"

Caron threw back his head. "I was able to do that much."

The Daimyo drew himself up. "I spoke hastily. The door is open, even if only a little. That it is open at all is what matters."

"The Company stays?" Dirk broke in quickly.

Caron nodded. "It stays. But I'm afraid I have bad news for you, Matsura-san. You lose the Hirado trade. Our factory there is at an end."

Matsura's eyes closed but he said firmly, "What difference, so long as the door is open? Where does the Yashiki go?"

"I think you can guess. We take over the Portuguese settlement on Deshima."

"Deshima," murmured the old Daimyo. "Yes. I see. I can guess the orders that came down from Tokyo. Caron-san, how did you manage it?"

Dirk thought Caron looked even more worn and pale as though the Daimyo's question had recalled grim memories. "I, too, guessed what those orders *might* be. I also guessed that they allowed the Daikwan some small amount of latitude. He decreed that we might stay so long as we were housed in two old Chinese hulks in the harbor, with guard boats anchored around us. I told Heizo that those terms were not acceptable and — "

The Daimyo gasped and Dirk said quickly, "Terms? The Shogun doesn't give terms, he orders."

"Of course. Those orders, then, I defied. I stated that although we were only traders, we too had our dignity, which would not permit us to remain under those conditions. I risked the Company's life, but I reasoned that part of the Shogun's instructions stated that we should be allowed to stay. I might have been wrong."

"Wrong?" whispered Matsura. "If you had been, you would have climbed the Mount of the Martyrs."

Caron shrugged. "As I say, it was a risk I had to take."

Dirk thought back over what Caron had said. "Do you mean that we merely move our base from Hirado to Deshima in Nagasaki harbor?"

"I wish that I did. We shall live there under certain specified rules. No member of the Company can be armed or will ever be allowed to leave the island unless the Company transfers him to another part of the world."

"Not leave Deshima? But the whole island isn't two hundred yards wide and it's less than a hundred deep! I've been past it enough times to know. There must be *some* exceptions."

"Just one," said Caron gravely. "Each year, a selected number of Company people will have to make a pilgrimage under heavy guard to the Emperor at Kyoto and the Shogun at Tokyo. How our trade will pay for the presents that we're supposed to bring, I don't know. I assure you that that trip will be nothing to look forward to."

"I've always wanted to live on an island," said Trudi.

"What are the orders about trade?" asked Matsura.

"I couldn't possibly summarize the regulations," said Caron wearily. "There's a tremendous list of what can't be sent out and what can't be brought in. We can export nothing that even suggests things military. That does away with our plan for shipping out sword blades, Matsura-san. It even bans our exporting those ningyo, those dolls dressed like samurai that we used to sell to the native chiefs in the Moluccas. I merely cite those items to show the nature of the ban."

"And import?" asked the Daimyo anxiously.

"The list is longer and stricter. Nothing even hinting at the Christian faith can be brought in. This even extends to the boxes that we used to mark with a cross for identification purposes. We shall have to change our brand marks. Another section of the new law forbids foreign books of any sort."

Matsura blinked. "No books!" he murmured as though to himself. "The new knowledge, the new skills are to be shut away from us." Then he raised his head bravely. "It is doubtless wise of the Shogun, who wishes us to acquire new learning slowly so that we may assimilate it properly. I am sure it is wise." But his old eyes looked hurt and discouraged.

"Does that mean that we can't have our own books?" asked Trudi.

"I don't think so," answered Caron. "The orders only say that we can't distribute them or sell them."

Trudi turned to Matsura. "Then you can always come to us for them."

The Daimyo sighed. "So you, too, Sayo-ko-san, will help keep that inch of door open? That is the sort of thing your mother would have said. But all Japan can't come to Deshima." His thin fingers drummed on the matting. "It's wise. Of course it's wise. But not only our ports are closed; our minds are shut with them." He looked up with new animation. "Then, Caron-san, since the New World may not come to us, we must go to it. It may be that that is the Shogun's wish. Our habits must change. Our young people must travel. Perhaps chosen ones might enter your service and go to Batavia or even on to your Tokyo — Amsterdam, I think you call it."

Caron shook his head. "I'd be glad to encourage that, Matsura-san. But there are orders that affect all of your countrymen. No Japanese may leave the Empire, under pain of death."

"There will be ways to meet that. A ship could, quite by accident of course, be blown off its course," ventured Matsura. "Could our people be blamed if winds carried them to Formosa or Macao? Or across the straits to Fusan in Korea?"

"I'm afraid so," said Caron gravely. "There are no excuses. A shipwrecked sailor, trying to return to Japan, would be executed at once. But there will be few of them. All seagoing Japanese craft are ordered destroyed. From now on, all ships will be built very small and with the sterns open so they can cruise only slowly and only by day between Japanese ports."

"It is the will of the Emperor, which only the Shogun may know," said Matsura, as though in self-discipline.

"It's all very hard to understand," said Dirk slowly. "Still there are ways around. There must be. We can begin training a real corps of interpreters, with each man serving, say, two years. It will take time, but it will mean that there will be more and more Dutch-speaking Japanese in the Empire. We'll recruit them in Hiroshima and Osaka and Tokyo."

"You and Dirk will find a way, Heer Caron," said Trudi, nodding in approval.

The corners of Caron's mouth turned down. Then he smiled. "With you to encourage us, I'm sure we could."

"You mean will, not could," smiled Trudi.

The mask of weariness settled deeper over Caron's face. "We've been going at this piecemeal. I had better sum up as best I can once and for all. First, only a very few carefully chosen and carefully watched Japanese will be allowed on Deshima. As to the interpreters, they will be set up as a guild, limited to a few families. They will speak Portuguese with us, not Dutch." He was silent for a moment, then went on quickly, "I have arranged for Madame Caron to take Maria and Petronella to Formosa. No Company people may have their families in the Empire."

Trudi stared at him for an instant, eyes wide with sympathy. "You mean that you would not be able to see them? Heer Caron, how could you have agreed to that?"

"I cannot see them unless permission is given me to travel to Formosa. As to the agreeing—" Caron shrugged—"I did not agree. I was told."

Matsura said quietly, "Perhaps I could arrange an exception. After all, your wife's family, the Eguchis, is old and loyal."

"I am grateful to you, Matsura-san," said Caron. "But here I'm afraid even you would be powerless."

"Look here!" cried Dirk suddenly. "Does this mean present families only, or does it cover the future?"

Caron met his eyes. "Present — and future, Dirk."

"Then I can't stay with Dirk?" cried Trudi. "But I — how can I leave Dirk?"

"That brings up another matter," said Caron. "Dirk, there are no charges against you. But both Matsudaira and the Daikwan insist that you can't stay in Japan."

"The devil I can't," said Dirk. "You've trained me in the language and the ways here. They can't toss all that overboard."

"There's no argument," said Caron firmly. "They claim that you became such a bone of contention between various factions during the siege that you'd be a dangerous rallying point, even though against your will." He held up his hand. "Wait a minute. Don't think that I want to lose you, especially in the times that lie ahead. There's just no choice. Here's what I'll do, though. You can sail south with the *de Rijp* and I'll give you a letter to van Diemen in Batavia. Becker will endorse it."

"But all my training and experience have been up here. What can I do down there? I'd be lost in the Moluccas or Amboina. And I don't want to sit and scratch with a quill in van Diemen's offices, either."

"You'll have lost nothing, Dirk," said Trudi. "You've mastered one country. You'd master another just as easily. Probably much more so."

The bleak, defeated look that hung over the old Daimyo's eyes lifted and he looked benevolently at Dirk. "May an old friend suggest too, Yang-san, that you'd have a very wise little head beside you while you learn? That is an advantage you did not enjoy while you became familiar with Japan."

Dirk stared at him, then burst out, "Of course, it isn't that I'd forgotten. But who'll be here to work with — "

"I know, Dirk," said Trudi. "You were thinking about the Company and I'm glad you were. But you can't serve it here."

314

"No," answered Dirk quickly. "I couldn't anyway, even if they lifted the ban on me. Trudi, do you think I'd let you sail off alone? There's a berth for us somewhere and it's not our fault if it isn't here."

"I'd love Amboina," said Trudi.

"Amboina or Bangkok," agreed Dirk. "Of course, it may not be easy, at first." He glanced at Caron. "Wait a minute. Doesn't this mean that I start at the bottom again? That I'll be an apprentice again?"

"I'm afraid so, Dirk. It would be different if you were being transferred by the Company but you know the rules."

"At the bottom of the ladder again," said Dirk. "And my superiors would be my juniors in point of service." He sat back on his heels, his hands resting on the ground behind his back. "Eight years and more in the Company service erased. By the time I retired, I'd only be — " His hand brushed against something hard and he picked it up absently, set it across his knees. It was the curved-top letter box. "Yes, I'd be much farther down the ladder than I'd hoped to be." His fingers drummed on the box top.

"That doesn't matter, Dirk," said Trudi.

"True enough," observed Caron. "If anyone had told you a few days ago that you and Sayo-ko might be setting up housekeeping in Formosa or Batavia soon, how would you have felt?"

"Ye-e-s," said Dirk slowly. "But — " He looked down at the box, then turned quickly to Trudi. "You said you wouldn't mind Bangkok or Amboina?"

"Of course not."

"Then — then — " He snapped open the box and whipped out Cousin Japhet's letter. "Then what do you say to Plymouth on Massachusetts Bay? Cousin Japhet writes that there's plenty of room for us — or he would have said 'us' if he'd known about you. The colony's really flourishing and we'd be able to have all the land we wanted. It's peaceful there and the people are like us. I've enough on the Company books to see to our passage and set us up at least decently, according to Cousin Japhet. What do you think of that?"

"I'd love Plymouth," said Trudi.

Caron looked keenly at Dirk. "You mean, then, that you would desert the Company and go blundering off to the New World?"

315

"I don't see why I didn't think of it before," said Dirk firmly. "In any event, I wouldn't have stayed here without Trudi. And as far as other posts are concerned, it seems to me that my usefulness to the Company's at an end. I'd be no good to it as a junior apprentice."

"Good!" exclaimed Caron. "You'd be wasted and you'd rot. I don't like to think of you and Sayo-ko on the other side of the globe, but — " he shrugged — "There's nothing to be done about that. Yes. By all means, Plymouth, in Massachusetts."

Matsura leaned forward. "Where is that?"

Dirk told him briefly of the people who had left Holland for the New World, nearly eighteen years ago, of the growth of the settlements there, of the urge for freedom that had been the seed of that growth. The old Daimyo nodded. "Yes. I remember you spoke of them once before, at my palace. I — I am not sure that I approve of their having left their Daimyos in the first place. The name is ah, yes — Massa — chyu — settsu," he said slowly, adding a final vowel, Japanese fashion. "That is not so difficult. Perhaps my own people were there in the old, old days, for we still have a province of Settsu."

"Perhaps there are some of them still there," said Dirk, smiling. "If there are, may we be lucky enough to find among them as good a friend as we found in the Daimyo of Hirado."

"And I congratulate the Daimyo of that Settsu on the new subjects whom he will acquire. But there are other things which we must think about, Caron-san and I. We shall return to Nagasaki, where I shall see to everything — the sake cups for the exchange, the proper kimonos for the little girls who shall act as wedding butterflies, a suitable sedan chair to convey Sayo-ko-san to the house of the groom."

He looked at Dirk and Trudi and a wistful expression came into his eyes. "Let us have brandy and drink it to these young people who are going out to a world that is opening, leaving us, Caron-san my old friend, in a world that is closing. Yang-san and Sayo-ko-san, when you are in that far-off Settsu, think sometimes of an old Japanese who wishes you well."

Under a leaden morning sky, the Nagasaki waterfront was crowded and clamorous as ever, save for a wide arc that was kept

316

clear by pikemen wearing the Matsura crest. Dirk helped Trudi, still wearing her wedding haori, into the barge that would take them to the *de Rijp,* anchored far down the narrow harbor by the Papenberg, where they would join Van Os and Trelawney, Batavia-bound, like themselves. Caron and the Daimyo leaned their elbows on the coping of the sea wall as the barge pushed out into the harbor. Matsura sighed. "Now I really feel that the door is closing on us. People like those two could bring so much to my country."

Caron, answering Trudi's wave, shook his head. "Not quite closed. There is always hope so long as you and I and those who follow us keep it open at least this much. In time, it may slide wider and wider and that will be our reward."

"I'm afraid," muttered the Daimyo. "I'm afraid we shall be thrown back on ourselves, as I observed before. Of course, it is unthinkable that the Shogun is wrong, and yet — and yet — what will my country be like when the door does slide back fully to admit the world that will have moved so far while we have stood still? Eh-to! Those young people! I envy them. Just think what they will see and learn and come to know!"

The barge crept on down the harbor. Dirk and Trudi sat hand in hand in the stern and watched the shoreline slowly fade. The Nagasaki hills rose sullen under the lowering clouds that rolled on from the great fist of the Shimabara peninsula off in the hidden northeast. Dirk pressed Trudi's hand reassuringly. Then he gave a cry and pointed upward. Overhead, the clouds were breaking and a shaft of bright sunlight made a path south to the Papenberg, a gleaming path that reached on and on, past the ship, past the island, on and on like a beacon to a new world. Astern, the waterfront was still cloaked in gloom. Dirk and Trudi, looking back for the last time, could barely make out the two figures, one tall, the other frail and gray, who watched the barge work into the brightening morning.

Port of Hirado
Imari
Kawachi
Sasebo
KYU
Gulf of Omura
Sea of Japan
Tokyo
HONSHU
Kyoto
JAPAN
SHIKOKU
Pacific Ocean
KYUSHU
Nagasaki
N
Setting of the Venture in the East
JAPAN 1637-1638
SCALE OF MILES
0
5
10
15